THE PIANO
FACTORY

THE PIANO FACTORY

Jonathan Davies

LITTLE, BROWN

A *Little, Brown* Book

First published in Great Britain in 2004 by Little, Brown

Copyright © 2004 by Jonathan Davies

visit the author's website at www.jonathandavies.net

The moral right of the author has been asserted.

A CIP catalogue record for this book
is available from the British Library.

ISBN 0 316 86016 6

Typeset in Bembo by M Rules
Printed and bound in Great Britain
by Mackays of Chatham plc, Chatham, Kent

Little, Brown
An imprint of
Time Warner Book Group UK
Brettenham House
Lancaster Place
London WC2E 7EN

www.twbg.co.uk

for Jane, with my love

PART ONE

Brief for Trial and Appeal

Chapter 1

Mr Reilly was an anxious client, which wasn't surprising. But he kept fighting.

'Never,' he said. 'I've never done that. I wouldn't dream of it. You would have to know me, Mr Scott, I'm no angel and I've done a lot, but never that.' He took a deep breath and said, 'I've never touched a child.'

He had been saying the same thing since Scott had first seen him, but this time he added, and this was different. 'I wouldn't know why I would want to.'

An accident meant that Jimmy Reilly couldn't play in the pub football team any more, so he turned out to help with the juniors until one of them complained and the police had turned up.

'Someone has done this to me,' Jimmy said. 'Someone has set me up.'

But if the allegation weren't true, why could the small boy say such a thing? And, if it were true, then of course Mr Reilly would deny it, wouldn't he?

It didn't help to go over and over it again, so Scott changed the subject. 'Is your witnesses still OK to come?'

'Yeah, Billy's all right. He'll help me.'

Scott was at the back of the court talking to his client, but he was also avoiding prosecuting counsel. This trial was becoming nasty. And here he was, Herbert Skerry, just coming in; Skerry, modern prosecuting counsel, intent on getting a conviction, no matter how – and the same went for the police officer, Detective Constable Michael Reynolds, following him into court. The opposition.

Scott watched Skerry look over at him, then turn and speak to the policeman. There was a moment's conversation, and both looked at him again. Scott didn't stir. Let them make the move. If he went near them then he would have to say something and in a case like this – don't talk unless you have to.

Skerry gave in first. He walked over and stood, silently, some feet away from Scott, obtrusively not interrupting. After a few moments Scott turned and said, 'Do you want something?'

'Of course,' Skerry said.

'Go ahead. Mr Reilly will hear what you say eventually.'

'I want you to tell me whether you are calling any alibi witnesses.'

'We'll deal with that if it arises.'

'You have to tell me.'

'No, I don't.'

Later Scott realised that it was this piece of indifferent rudeness that tipped Skerry into his first mistake, opening the way to the only chance Scott could see of winning this case.

'Then I shall serve the additional evidence and then you'll have to tell me.'

'You're going to serve it?'

'Yes.'

'OK. Go ahead.'

Scott turned to Mr Reilly as Skerry left, and grinned. 'We did it, we tied him down. Now they can't back down from what the child has said. We'd better get the judge in and tell him, so they are really stuck with it.'

It was what Scott had wanted. Here was something he could get his teeth into.

The trial had been going on for two days. It had heard evidence of how Mr Reilly had been a member of the pub social for years, and how he helped with the junior football team. Skerry, opening the case to the jury, who sat looking shocked at what they were having to decide, puffed himself up and said, 'The junior football team, that is, made up of eight- to ten-year-old boys, whose only interest was playing a game of football on a Sunday.'

It was an odd remark, as though he felt he had to exclude the possibility of the boys having other things in mind for Sunday mornings. Like being indecently assaulted.

'So it was, ladies and gentlemen, that the defendant was given the opportunity to take advantage of one young child – his name is Jason.' Skerry had got into his stride now and became expansive. 'It happened on a number of occasions. It is not possible to say with any certainty when this, or rather these assaults occurred, but that does not detract from the fact, the Crown say, that what you will hear Jason describe clearly took place.'

Mr Reilly had been arrested just before one of the Sunday games.

'That day Jason was not playing, he had been kept away,' Skerry said. This obscured what had in fact gone on. The game was cancelled and Jimmy Reilly was marched away in full view of everyone. A meeting was held there and then and the parents were asked, 'Has your child said anything?'

The witch-hunt was on.

Effectively the parents had been deputised to investigate, which they did, panicking, pestering their children for details, but none produced any more complaints, no one

5

came forward. 'You see?' said Mr Reilly. 'There's no one who says I have done it, save this one.'

That was unusual. Scott had done any number of these cases, and he knew sex offenders seldom stop at one – they can't.

At the police station, a video-recorded interview of Jason's complaint was played to Mr Reilly. Over and over again he was asked the only question that needed to be asked, 'Why should he say it, if it isn't true?'

Mr Reilly couldn't answer.

'Why should Jason make it up?' he was asked again.

Mr Reilly still couldn't say.

'Is there any reason why he should want to say this about you?'

The question was asked again and again in different ways, and Mr Reilly looked guiltier every time it was asked.

He said, 'Yes, he has been to my flat. So have other boys. So do some of the parents. I keep some of the equipment there. That's how he knows what the flat looks like. Yes, I've probably been alone in the clubroom with him – and with other boys, and with their parents. No, I didn't touch him. I had no reason to.'

The last remark showed how weak his position was – people know that sexual appetite of this kind never needs a reason, and that it's always furtive.

Mr Reilly was charged. Now he lived a lonely life, lucky to get bail, but unable to go home. The social services didn't allow it; he had three small children and being a possible class-one sex offender, he could not be allowed near them. He was unable even to step from his door without being followed and taunted by groups of small boys who were always waiting. He had become the modern version of an outlaw, fair game, suspected of anything.

Now there only remained the trial – which the police officer in the case thought quite unnecessary. He told Scott what he thought. 'If I had my way, Mr Scott, reasonable suspicion would be enough to put a man on the sex offenders' list. Then we'd always have their names and addresses, and the real value of the list is knowing where they are, the ones who are likely to have done it. We can pick them up whenever we want. There'd be no more skulking around, they'd know they were being watched.'

Scott said, 'If everyone is, can I be on it too? After all, I defend these people, and that must be suspicious, mustn't it? It can only mean I'm on their side.'

Detective Constable Reynolds thought that was odd and not a bit funny. You don't joke about these things.

Scott walked to the front of the court and said to the clerk, 'Could we have the judge in first before the jury, please? I've got something to say.'

The judge came in and the relaxed atmosphere changed immediately; tension filled the room. Michael Meadowsweet sat down. 'Yes?' he said. 'Why haven't we got the jury here, why can't we get on?'

He didn't even look up at the court while he spoke.

Things had instantly returned to normal, the way it would be for the rest of the day, anxious, straining and, above all, tiring. Scott said nothing in reply. He didn't have to put up with being spoken to like this all the time. His silence eventually forced the judge to look up, his thick spectacles glinting.

Just as the silence became insupportable, Scott said, 'Mr Skerry has told me that he now intends to serve the additional evidence that he spoke of yesterday.'

'Yes, yes,' said the judge, 'and I suppose you are going to ask for time?'

'No,' Scott said baldly.

7

The judge was momentarily put off, but after a pause carried on: 'Well, what are we waiting for?'

'Nothing now,' said Scott. 'I've said what I want to say.'

'Was it necessary?' Meadowsweet said.

What was the judge doing in the court, if he wasn't there to be told just this sort of thing?

Scott said, 'Yes. It was necessary.' Necessary since it was now officially part of the Crown case against Mr Reilly. 'Now they are making their allegation quite clear,' Scott said.

The remark passed Skerry by. He hadn't yet understood the damage he was doing to his own case, and he bounced up, making matters even worse. 'I have, as a result of the extra evidence I am going to serve, invited Mr Scott to give me the names and addresses of any alibi witnesses for that particular date.'

The judge lost the rest of his temper.

'This is not a pre-trial hearing.'

'But we need to know.' Skerry's mouth stayed open.

The judge disregarded him. He said, 'You can't just demand that the defence serve things on you. Not now, it's much too late. You should have served it weeks ago. Anyway, this isn't the time to talk about it.'

While he said this he seemed to speak over his left shoulder, as if to someone sitting beside him, someone in permanent agreement with him that he was surrounded by fools.

For once the judge's behaviour was helping the defence. He was right, it was far too late for the prosecution to try to force information out of the defence.

'We'll have the jury,' the judge snarled at the usher.

Wanting to know what evidence the defence was going to call had made Skerry forget the first rule of prosecuting sex cases – keep it vague. Scott had no doubt it wasn't his mistake; the decision would have been driven by the policeman. Reynolds was, like all policemen, unwilling to let the system take its course. Scott knew he wanted the name of any witnesses, since the moment he got it he'd be round their doorstep trying to influence the evidence.

Already one of Mr Reilly's friends had been warned off. 'You wouldn't want people to think you helped a pervert walk free, would you?' Reynolds had said.

The jury trooped in.

'We'll start the video link then,' the judge said.

They waited in silence as it was arranged.

'Now do let's get on, Mr Scott,' the judge said, as if Scott were delaying things on purpose.

The small television screens on the benches flickered on, and then the face of a small child, Jason, grinned out of it.

The judge and the jury each had a monitor. The arrangement had been devised to shield children from the distress of giving evidence, but Jason wasn't distressed. He was enjoying himself hugely.

'Jason, do you know who I am?' Scott said.

'Yeah.' The young boy sprawled in the chair in front of the camera. The time was well past when small children were transfixed by the oddity of someone speaking directly to them through a television screen. He was totally relaxed. 'I know you, you're the man who's going to tell me it didn't happen.'

'It didn't happen?'

'What he did to me. You're going to say it didn't happen, but it did. He's a dirty paedo.'

'They told you that? That I was going to say it didn't happen?'

'The victim people did.'

'The victim people?'

'Them who offered me help. They help victims. I'm a victim.'

'What's a victim then?'

9

'I am.'

Scott left it. He said, 'You watch TV much?'

'Yeah.'

'Videos?'

'Yeah.'

'Grown-up videos?'

'Why you want to know?'

'Just asking.'

'So?'

'Is the answer "yes"?'

'Yes.'

'What kind of grown-up videos then?'

The boy was now obviously uncomfortable. He was being pressed. It hadn't been like this before. He had only ever been praised when he told the story. The more he repeated it, the more people praised him.

'I've seen men.'

'Really?'

'Sexing each other.'

'Sexing each other?'

'Barrys.'

What was this word? Scott hadn't heard it before. 'Doing Barry's?'

'Barrys. Using their mouth.'

'Oh, you mean sucking?'

'Yes. Sucking off.'

'Yesterday we heard you say on the video, what Jimmy Reilly asked you to do.'

'Yes,' Jason had got his jauntiness back. 'That's what happens.'

'Oh really? That's how it happens?'

'Vernon said that's what happens.'

Who's Vernon? Scott thought. 'Oh, that's what men do when they sex each other up?'

'Not just men.'

10

'Oh?'

'Yes.'

'All the time?'

'Yes.'

'All the time?' Scott repeated it.

'Yes.'

'In school too?'

'Yes.'

'Oh, it's done in school?'

'Yes.'

'All the time?'

'Don't be silly.' The boy laughed to his side. 'How could it be all the time?'

'How often then?' Mistake, too direct.

Suddenly the child realised what he was saying. He didn't answer.

'How often?'

No reply.

'So that's what you say you did with Jimmy?'

'It was his idea.'

'I'm going to talk about that in a moment.'

Jason sat waiting for the question. The silence was intentional; sometimes children cannot bear it.

It worked.

Jason said, 'Vernon told me.' So he was staying there, it was at the centre of the story, what Vernon said.

'Vernon told you what it was like?' He'd wait a moment longer before asking who Vernon was.

'Yes.'

'Why him?'

'Why shouldn't he?'

'You got to know about it?'

Again the boy didn't realise what he was saying.

'No, because he knows, and when he told us, so we all knew.'

11

Scott stopped. Even if Jason didn't understand the implication of what he was saying, the jury would.

'Everybody got to know?'

Don't go into it, let it spill out on its own.

'Billy did.'

'Billy did?' Don't ask direct questions. Stay light.

No reply.

'Billy?'

The judge interrupted, and Jason turned as if someone in his room had spoken to him.

'Really, Mr Scott, is this getting us anywhere? The issue in this case is what your client did or did not do. And I haven't heard you ask about that yet.'

For an instant the case had nearly opened up, but the interruption stopped it. Did the judge intend it, or was it that he couldn't see what was happening, right before his eyes?

Whatever he meant by it, what he had done had the same result.

'That man did it to me,' Jason said.

Now Scott had to contradict him. 'That's not true, Jason. He did nothing.'

'He did, he's a dirty paedo and I am a victim.'

It was a kind of status.

Scott said, 'I want to ask you about a television programme you watched.' The atmosphere had changed completely. No more floating.

'Yeah?'

'The film you said you saw, the first time you went to his flat. It was on a Sunday?'

The boy nodded. 'That's the only day I can go there.'

'Sure?'

'Yes.'

'So Sunday. Now, Jason. If I say you're wrong about that, what would you say?'

'I was there. I did.'

'But let's try and work out which Sunday first. Do you remember saying that the TV was on?'

'Yeah.'

'Mr Reilly doesn't have a dish for TV?'

'No, so we couldn't watch football. That's only on satellite.'

That was the information Scott wanted. 'He hasn't got a video either, has he?'

'No.' Jason clearly thought that was bit odd. Scott paused, relieved. He had cleared away the other explanations.

'So you say there was a movie on Jimmy Reilly's TV?'

'Yeah, we watched that for a bit, before he did it.'

'What?'

'Sexed me.'

'You said the movie was about things under the sea?' Scott waited, then he said, 'What you told us, Jason, was this, "It was about a sea monster, and how they had to find the girl, and the sunken ship."'

'Yeah,' Jason said.

Scott produced a poster. He said, 'Perhaps Jason could be handed the folder.' The jury saw the boy being given a folder. Scott held up the poster so the jury and judge could see it was the same. 'Here it is,' he said.

Mr Reilly's solicitor had spent hours trying to work out which film Jason must have been talking about, only discovering it after it occurred to him to ask his young daughter. Now the prosecution had confirmed it.

Jason opened his poster out. 'That's it,' he said.

Scott's pulse jumped, but he kept his reply very steady. 'That's the film you saw?'

'Yes. I remember, the film was boring so we started talking instead.'

Because of what Skerry had done, making it part of the

13

prosecution case that they had watched the film, they weren't going to be able to back away from this, or say it was a mistake. They were stuck with it.

'You did not.'

'What?'

'You didn't see it. What you are saying is made up.'

'I did.'

'You have never watched that film in Jimmy's house. That film was shown on satellite. You couldn't have watched it. You said he doesn't have satellite.' Pause, no reply. 'He has never touched you. You are making it up.'

'He has. I told everyone. He has. Billy knows.'

'Who's Billy?'

No reply again.

'He knows. He told me.' Jason stopped. He said no more.

'Billy told you what?'

'He told me.'

'What did he tell you?'

No answer.

'What did Billy tell you?' Scott said.

Jason was crying now.

'Did Billy tell you what to say?'

No reply.

'Who's Vernon?'

No reply.

'Who is Vernon?'

Nothing.

'Why won't you tell?'

The child turned away from the camera and seemed to speak to the other person in the room. Then he got out of his chair and went out of sight.

'That's enough for now,' the judge said. 'We'll take a break.' The court rose.

The tension lifted, the jury stood up, gathering their

things, but kept their eyes down. Scott noticed that they didn't look at him.

What they had seen was pretty nasty, and at the same time the child's reaction to the questioning was making their decision much more difficult.

For them the boy's evidence, when first played on video tape, had seemed so straightforward. 'Tell us what you told your mother,' he was asked and he had repeated the story. That was so simple, this was different. Now he was being asked questions directly, not in a recording; it was very different. He seemed a different child.

Could he have made it up? But then they asked themselves the same question everyone did. Why should he?

To Scott, the boy's evidence on tape had felt rehearsed, but of course it was very difficult to judge what it would seem like to others. Scott fought to see it in the way the jury must have done. They had never seen such a video before; Scott had seen dozens, and you can never go back. They wouldn't have noticed the child's strange movements, his continually turning, looking away, his compulsively touching his face and mouth, or, if they did, they would think nothing of it.

Scott had talked to Dr Stock about the video tape. 'Listen to the language he's using,' the doctor had said. 'It's all received. It's all adult language. Children of nine, ten years old don't speak like that. He said, "He took advantage of me." Someone told him that, he's heard the phrase and now he's repeating it. And the sexual language, "blow job", that's an age-inappropriate expression.

'He doesn't say he learned it from the defendant, he just uses it. I've heard children say other things, but "blow job" – that's only when there's an adult providing the language. There's either something wrong at home or some other outside influence on that family. I'm sure of that. Of course it doesn't mean your client isn't guilty. That's what makes it complicated.'

Dr Stock was a paediatric psychologist.

She had said, 'Really to know I would have to speak to the mother, but of course in a criminal trial that isn't allowed. Anyone in our business enquiring into this incident, a child psychiatrist for instance, wouldn't dream of making a decision until the whole family had been seen, and all the background notes had been provided. You can bet the social services have got files on him. He'll have been classified as "at risk" for years. I've no doubt about that.'

Both the doctor and Scott knew that Scott would be stopped from getting the real history of the child. That would remain privileged information.

'Of course, it's not easy to say what I am saying in court. These kinds of remark remind people of "know-it-all" doctors. And juries just hate that. Everybody hates it, what with the press telling everyone nowadays that all doctors are charlatans, or worse.

'Anyway, look at the interviewing method. There's no challenge to the story, no alternative explanation is ever examined. Every time the child makes some assertion, however vague, the interviewer repeats it and turns it into something definite.

'Here,' she said, pointing to a passage in the transcript. 'Here apparently the interviewer is only repeating what the child said, "Right, so he took you into another room." But she's not; in fact, the child didn't say that. He only shook his head when the last question was asked, and the question says nothing about going into another room. What was said was, "This couldn't have gone on in the kitchen, could it?" That was a question inviting the answer "No." The child thinks he is expected to say no.

16

'So what starts as an acceptance of something the interviewer said, then becomes solid fact, and provides the basis for the next step in the story.'

She looked at Scott. 'And so on,' she said. 'You see what is happening? The story is developed step by step. And all the time the child is being reassured that if he repeats it, it will be accepted as true. It's called a "culture of confirmation". But juries aren't interested in that sort of analysis, that's all mumbo jumbo to them. All they say is, "Why should he say it, if it isn't true?"'

'This interview isn't an attempt to find out whether the boy is telling the truth; it's only putting what he has said into better order – for a jury to listen to. Of course your real problem is this: the fact it's a bad interview doesn't mean that the child isn't telling the truth. It only means that there's been no proper testing. And if what the child was saying wasn't true, or an exaggeration, now he's been taught he can get away with it.

'When you stand up to cross-examine him, it'll be the first time any one has challenged him. Up to now everyone has said, "Oh, how dreadful. You poor thing," and patted his head.'

Scott knew Dr Stock was right. He also knew juries never listen to this sort of thing.

Dr Stock said, 'And what material have you got to challenge the child with? Nothing. You're doing it blind. The social worker had access to everything, but she's not going to enquire, she's already believed him. That's her mission.

'What she ought to have done was found out whether there was another stranger circling this family influencing the child. Some families attract paedophiles. Paedophiles travel from family to family like the flu.'

Scott asked Dr Stock if she would give evidence. And he got the same reply he always did. 'Not possible, I'm afraid. I'm far too busy. Anyway in our clinic, as a matter of policy we don't give evidence against children.'

Scott tried to find out about the boy's background. He got a little. She was right, the child had been in care. He applied to the judge to get information. It was refused.

The judge said, sucking his teeth, 'I shall order costs against the defence. This is a mere fishing expedition: an attempt to discover whether there is something with which to attack the witness.'

You couldn't say anything to that. Scott thought that attacking witnesses was his job.

The result was that the defence had nothing to go on. They knew nothing of the child. The jury would know nothing. Jason's story would be judged on a video, which didn't amount to much more than a repetition of what he had said to someone else, and then Scott's blind cross-examination.

About ten minutes' evidence for every year Mr Reilly would serve in prison as a result.

The clerk of the court came back from the judge's room and said, 'We're not going to sit for a while.'

Scott went to speak to Jimmy Reilly in a small, smelly conference room. It was almost impossible to talk. Every minute or so the tannoy made an announcement in a slow measured voice, then after an infuriating pause of a second, repeated it. Scott sat silent, facing his client, waiting for the voice to stop. Then he said, 'Do you know a Billy or a Vernon?'

'I don't know a Billy, but I think there was a Vernon who played in one of the football teams.' Jimmy Reilly sat and thought about it. 'No, that was Vincent. Vincent Narriba, the little Nigerian kid.'

'Nothing else?'

'Well, there is one Billy I know. That's Billy Burns, our witness. He's an adult and nothing to do with this.'

'Oh,' said Scott. He had hoped Mr Reilly might be able to help.

Mr Reilly said, 'Why didn't you call him a liar?'

'I did,' said Scott. 'I said that what he was saying wasn't true.'

'He wouldn't understand that, he needed to be called a liar.'

'You can only go so far in attacking a child. We don't want to alienate the jury completely.'

It sounded weak. Perhaps in this case his job *was* to alienate the jury.

'Alienate, rubbish. He needs to be squashed.'

'You don't need to be violent and angry to attack someone.'

'We'll get nowhere like this.'

This was a rare reaction from Jimmy, who was normally quiet, only watching what happened. The perfect client. In fact, he and his young wife were a perfect couple, about as far from this, Scott thought, as it was possible to be. He dreaded speaking to Mrs Reilly, who generally replied to what he said in a low voice, close to tears, looking up at Scott. 'You will help us, won't you?' her eyes were saying. Then she would turn back to the baby and immerse herself in it. Sometimes it was insupportable.

'We will, Mr Reilly.' Scott thought it was about time he justified himself. 'We've challenged him on the piece of evidence we can disprove. That's the way to do it. Shouting at him is going to get us nowhere.'

Scott was facing the dilemma he often faced. From where Mr Reilly was sitting, having a lawyer make a noisy fuss on your behalf at least made you feel good. Perhaps he was right, perhaps he should be more noisy. But that would be betraying everything he had taught himself, everything he had learnt.

19

'I did reduce the boy to tears,' Scott said.

'He was only play-acting,' Mr Reilly said.

Without saying anything, they agreed to leave it there.

'Mary's here,' Jimmy Reilly said. 'She's here with the children. Say hello to her for me.'

Jimmy was obeying the social service ruling to the letter and going nowhere near his older children unsupervised, even now, even at court.

Scott didn't like to think about what that cost him; only that it showed how powerful the authorities could be if you found yourself in their grasp.

Then Jimmy added, 'But don't worry, you're doing really well, Mr Scott.' It came to something when your client had to reassure you. But it was extraordinary how Jimmy kept cheerful throughout all of it. Most people would have started getting spiky by now, but Jimmy tried to keep his spirits up, his own and everybody else's. 'Can I get you a cuppa, Mr Scott?'

This was the area not talked about. All of these people are low-life, aren't they? Scott had heard it said to him.

'That's kind, but not now,' Scott said.

You're meant to be tough and untouched by it, by what you did. But Scott wasn't. Not any more. Everybody he met in the courts was in pain – the time when they had been feeling good was before they met him, and they were looking forward to the time after they stopped needing him, when they would feel good again. Every encounter he had was shot through with tension. He got out of bed and it was waiting for him. His life was full of it, to the brim. The computer people would say his anti-shock mechanism was full, not capable of storing any more bytes. He stood up, just for something to do, left the room and looked around the benches outside, to see if there was a copy of the *Sun* or something to read; but there wasn't. It was a little early in the day for abandoned newspapers.

20

He sat down to wait.

He was sitting a little away from the court door and watched from a distance as a flustered woman appeared, asking the usher where Mr Skerry was. It seemed she didn't want to go into the court, but wanted him to come out to her. The usher disappeared to get him. Skerry came out, followed by the policeman. The three of them walked away, round a corner.

He returned to thinking about the case. Why wouldn't Jason say who Billy and Vernon were? In his experience it was a relief for a child witness to talk about other people. But here, no. He clammed up when Billy's name popped out, and Vernon's even more so. Scott decided that was where he would start again when they went on.

Skerry came round the corner. He was alone. 'Ah, Scott,' he said. It was as though he were addressing a junior officer. 'I am going to raise the manner in which you cross-examined that child witness.'

'Why?'

'I thought you were bullying him.'

'Go ahead.'

Scott tried to imagine what Meadowsweet was going to make of that. If he had really bullied the child, it would have been the judge's job to stop him. Skerry's complaint was a criticism of the judge and would be sure to rebound.

Scott said, 'I didn't ask him any question I haven't asked dozens of children, lots of times.' He nearly told Skerry to piss off, but didn't. That's what had got him a bad reputation.

'Have you anything to tell me about your witnesses?' Skerry said.

'What might I have to tell you?'

'Who they are?'

'Or indeed if I have any?' Scott laughed. 'We haven't yet

21

reached the stage when everything we do has to be inspected by your policeman in advance for reliability and truth. You do it in court, like I have to.'

Skerry sniffed and turned away. By now the policeman was standing right behind him, Scott hadn't noticed him creep up. If the officer didn't regard him with suspicion already, he would now.

The usher appeared at the door of the court, signalling that they should come in. Scott waved to Mr Reilly who was sitting further down the hall and they trooped back into the court.

Meadowsweet came in.

He said, 'I have had a message.' He was holding a piece of paper. 'The young witness refuses to answer any more questions. We shall have to speak to him before we have the jury back.' He gave no time for any discussion of this, but Skerry was already on his feet.

'I should like it recorded that I was going to raise the way in which my learned friend was questioning the child.'

'Were you, Mr Skerry?' said Meadowsweet. 'Well, you needn't do it now, need you? We'll have the witness back. Turn on the video system.'

The picture showed an empty room. The judge spoke into the space. 'Is there anybody there?' he said. It was like an old science fiction film where the scientist tries to make contact. After a moment there was a rustling noise, obviously a microphone being touched. Then a voice said, 'Yes.' It wasn't the boy.

'Who are you, madam?'

A face edged into the picture. 'I'm victim support.'

Scott recognised the flustered woman who had spoken to Skerry.

'Why were you speaking to the child?'

'He spoke to me.'

It seemed a fairly good answer.

'What did he say?'

'He said he refused to give any more evidence. He said he didn't want to speak to that man any more.'

Scott was sure he didn't. He had been far too close to the truth. Now he knew this Vernon connection meant a lot.

'Any questions for the moment, gentlemen?'

At last Meadowsweet was behaving correctly. He clearly foresaw an appeal. Was there anything to be asked? This might be the point when, later, he might wish he had intervened. But he could think of nothing.

Skerry stood up. 'Was the young child distressed?'

'He was.'

'Did he say anything else?'

'Yes. He said it was much worse than we expected.'

Scott thought, *We* expected? Who does she mean by *we*?

When Skerry finished, Scott asked the television screen, '*We*, who's *we*? You said, "Worse than *we* expected?"'

'Did I say that? I meant "he".'

The judge intervened. 'Nothing is to be gained by going into that, Mr Scott.' For a moment Scott thought the judge was going to add, You've done enough damage already, but if the judge thought it, he didn't say so. That was a change for Meadowsweet.

'Where is the child now?'

'Outside. He won't come into the room at all.'

'So we can't speak to him?'

'He won't speak at all, save to say, "I won't talk."'

The judge turned the television connection off. 'Obviously we can't force the child to continue. Have you any submissions?'

'I need to take instructions.'

'Of course. You too must consider the matter, Mr Skerry.'

★

23

The trial had to stop. If a witness won't be called, then the trial couldn't proceed. Either that or a retrial, and they'd see if the prosecution was able to call him again. He went to the back of the court to talk to Mr Reilly.

'They can't let him walk away.' Mr Reilly was angry. 'He's obviously frightened, because he knows he's been caught lying.'

'We can't argue it on that basis. That's a jury point. It's not a conclusion a judge is going to reach.'

'You don't mean this thing could carry on without him?' Mr Reilly couldn't believe it. After all, he had seen the witness give in.

'It might.'

In the moment he had walked to the back of the court he had realised that Meadowsweet could carry on. There was a precedent for it. The case of *McCarthy*, wasn't it? It was extraordinary – soon they wouldn't need evidence at trials at all. Scott had no time to set out why this could be so, he only knew it had been done with an adult witness who had stormed off. And why should it be different for a child? He could hear Meadowsweet saying it.

'I have to ask you formally. What do you want me to do? Do you want me to try to stop the case to see if he'll come back?'

Mr Reilly looked at him astonished, as if he needed to be asked.

'I have to ask, Mr Reilly. I can't do anything without your instructions. The answer is obvious, isn't it? Insist it stops.'

Scott returned to his place. 'We object to this trial proceeding without this witness being further cross-examined.'

'He has been cross-examined,' the judge said.

Here it was, Meadowsweet preparing to do it.

'Not properly. He's refusing to be cross-examined further because of the questions he was being asked.'

24

Skerry was on his feet. 'It was no such thing. You will remember that I indicated I would complain about the nature of the cross-examination.'

Of course it was the woman from victim support who had put the idea in Skerry's head. He hadn't made any complaint until she had appeared. For a moment Scott thought of raising it, but he knew it wouldn't work. It would only divert the argument.

'My cross-examination was nothing out of the ordinary for the situation.'

'I tend to agree,' said the judge. This remark surprised Scott, but only for a moment. The judge was going to use that argument to allow the trial to continue; it was the only way that it could be justified in the appeal court. It also involved siding with the defence. The judge continued and Scott knew he had guessed right. 'Mr Scott put his case fair and square to the young child who answered all his questions. It was only at the end he became distressed. Is that not right, Mr Scott?'

'No, not everything, your honour. I did not put my case completely. Nor did the child answer all my questions.'

He wasn't going to agree that he had finished with the witness, but he knew that Meadowsweet had screwed him.

'Well, we shall have to see what your client has to say, and whether any of it was not put to the young child. And if there is anything that was not raised with the child, then Mr Skerry can't complain, can he?'

'The purpose of my cross-examination wasn't only to put Mr Reilly's version of events, but to examine whether what the boy was saying was true.'

'I think you had sufficient time to do that, and after all' – this was the clincher and it was said with a ghastly smile – 'his very reaction, his refusing to continue, is something you can point to in your client's favour.'

25

'That cannot take away from the fact that Mr Reilly, if this case continues, will only have had a limited opportunity to test the truth of the child's evidence. Cross-examination is a central part of a trial. Without it, the whole process is flawed.'

'I think you are overstating the case. You have cross-examined, and if I may say so, at some length. Often about things that were not relevant. We shall continue, Mr Scott. I shall explain to the jury what has happened and of course I will remind them of how it might affect your client's situation. Yes, let's get on.'

There is nothing constructive to be done with the feeling that it's not fair. It leads nowhere. Jimmy Reilly was furious. 'How could it happen?'

'I couldn't stop him, Mr Reilly.'

'That's it then. What can I do now?' Finally things were getting to him.

'We'll obviously point out to the jury what happened, and say we haven't had the opportunity to deal with the child's evidence.' It seemed a very inadequate response, when set against what the child had said on the videotape.

Mr Reilly thought so too. 'Lot of bloody use that is. I might as well plead guilty.' Then he saw that his anger might upset Scott. 'But don't you worry, Mr Scott, you did your best.' It would have been so much easier if Jimmy had been a complete shit. They were at the dead point in the case, Scott had been there many times, the only response is to push on.

'We've yet to call our evidence, Mr Reilly. If you prove you weren't even in London on the weekend that he says he was watching that film with you, then we'll be showing the whole thing is wrong.'

Mr Reilly was not convinced.

The trial continued.

26

The boy was never tested and Scott was left wondering who Billy and Vernon were. He'd never know where he might have got if he had been able to carry on.

Skerry called his new evidence, fixing the date the boy had seen the film in Jimmy's flat as Sunday 15 August, at 1.45 p.m. It was the only time the film had ever been shown so there could be no mistake. So eventually Scott was able to call an alibi witness to prove Mr Reilly could not have been with the child that day, to show that Jason's evidence must be wrong.

'That very weekend, that Sunday, I was down Jimmy Reilly's cabin, fixing the plumbing. Jimmy Reilly was there with me – all Saturday, all Sunday. He had to be there to let me in and to get me into the main site office in order to deal with the back plumbing. He had to be there to let me out again, to lock up. Sunday lunch we were in the pub. We always are.'

Skerry cross-examined.

He said, 'But it would be the easiest thing in the world for you to say it was this particular weekend that you went, when maybe it was the weekend before, or the one after?'

It was the standard way of attacking an alibi.

The reply was different. 'You accusing me of lying?' the witness said.

Skerry thought for a moment. 'I am not doing that, no.' Although of course he was.

'You mean I've made a mistake?'

'Yes, that's what I'm suggesting.'

'On what basis?'

'I am asking the questions, Mr Burns.'

The witness paused and thought about it. 'Let's get this clear. You're not saying I'm lying, you're saying I made a mistake? If I show you I didn't make a mistake, what would you say then – that I'm lying?'

27

'I don't have to tell you that, Mr Burns.'

'Well, I'd just like to know because as I see it I'm being accused of lying.'

'Get on with it,' said Meadowsweet.

'Do you mean me?' the witness said, looking, if possible, even more relaxed when he spoke to the judge.

'Yes,' said Meadowsweet.

Billy Burns said, 'Then there's no call to be rude to me. I came here to give evidence. What have I done wrong?'

What he was doing wrong was smashing a hole in the Crown case – much to the judge's annoyance. He was also answering back, but Meadowsweet quickly realised he was going to have to put up with it.

'I had no intention of being rude to you, Mr Burns. I only asked you to get on with it.'

Scott watched the jury. They were amused. The witness was pricking the illusion. Judges and barristers only behave as they do because no one challenges them about their manners.

'Apology accepted,' the witness said graciously, turning back to Skerry. 'Now, are you about to accuse me of lying? Because what I say is not a mistake.'

'We'll see,' said Skerry.

'Right,' Burns said. 'Well, we're talking about the fifteenth. That was week twenty-nine of the tax year.'

He produced a file. 'My accounts,' he said. The papers fluttered. 'I have to keep everything absolutely under control, ever since I had a run-in with the taxman, who said I was swapping my earnings from the two companies around.'

He smiled at the jury. They grinned back. They liked him. 'Week twenty-nine and thirty I was in Holland. I left on the Monday. Here's the ferry ticket.'

It was solemnly passed round the court.

A one-way ticket, Mr W. Burns driving a van, a transit, the ticket had the van's number on it.

'The van's outside now. I have all my kit in it. I was away two weeks. So it couldn't have been the weekend after the fifteenth that I went to the hut. That weekend I was in Holland. Yep, here's the ticket back.'

Again the whole court stopped while the return ticket was handed round.

'I suppose you'll say now that it must have been the weekend before?'

Scott watched the witness. He was dressed in a blue boiler suit with a tweed jacket over it. In the breast pocket of the jacket Mr Burns kept an array of pencils. When he spoke, he occasionally took one out and twisted it in his fingers, sometimes using the end to scratch his head. Scott had the feeling he was playing a part, as if the man knew what he was meant to look like, and what he looked like was a good, reliable plumber, the kind of plumber you can never find.

Unusually Scott had received a message from Mr Burns before he came into the witness box. It had said, 'Don't ask me questions, just this, "What do you know about the weekend of the fifteenth?"'

Scott couldn't do that, since to do so would be to ask a leading question, a question giving the essential information to the witness rather than asking him for it, so he said, 'Do you know the date with which we are concerned?'

'Yes.'

For a moment Billy Burns gave Scott a flashing look, obviously surprised that his instructions had not been followed. Scott got the impression that it was something that did not often happen, and he wondered whether the jury had noticed it.

'Yes,' Burns said, 'the fifteenth of August. Last summer. I remember that weekend well. I think you want me to say what I was doing. Well, I was with Jimmy Reilly down at

29

Strafford Park in Kent. We drove down on Friday night and back up on the Sunday evening.'

Scott left it there. He was right to do so since it was only in cross-examination that the evidence really came out. It was almost as if Billy Burns knew that an answer to a hostile lawyer was much more effective than any reply to a friendly lawyer. As Scott watched the virtuoso performance he realised that Burns did know that, and that the way in which he intended to give his evidence had been meticulously worked out. That didn't mean it wasn't true, of course.

Billy Burns went on, putting the Dutch trip to one side. 'And it wasn't the weekend before the fifteenth, because that weekend and the days before and after it I was on a rush job in Waldegrave Crescent.' He named one of the very smartest streets in London. 'I was working for the sheikh. So I was only free on the fifteenth to do Jimmy's job.'

He turned and pulled another file out of the satchel he had carried to the witness box.

'What's that?' Skerry asked this time.

'Invoices and copy outgoings of the other company,' Mr Burns said in a matter-of-fact way. 'Here's the sheikh's bill.' He had consulted a column at the front, and then turned to a divider, at which he opened the file. 'For the second quarter, VAT returns details in the back. Yes. On the weekend of the eighth/ninth till the following Thursday I was in there putting in one of the double pipe feeds. Very tricky job. Involves balancing the water pressure throughout the system.'

He gave the jury this information and then extracted the receipts, and this was what shook Scott, pulled out a stapler from his satchel, clipped the bundle and handed them down.

Skerry looked at the papers.

Then he handed them to the judge, who turned them

30

over slowly. The judge said to Scott, 'Do you want the jury to see them as well?'

'It was Mr Skerry's question which produced them. He must decide.'

'The jury must see them,' Skerry said. He couldn't do anything else.

'Have you copies, Mr Scott?'

'No. But they will be made, your honour.'

'You should have had copies ready. Why have you no copies?'

'Circumstances have conspired to make it impossible for us to do that, your honour.' Scott supposed that was nearly a dishonest reply. He had no copies of the documents because he didn't know they existed. The judge did not notice the way the answer avoided the question, but Skerry did.

'We have heard nothing of this before,' he said.

Scott was about to point out that it was only during the trial that the date had become a definite part of the Crown's case, but he didn't have to.

'I wasn't prepared to speak to that officer,' Mr Burns said.

Skerry should have left it at that, but he didn't. 'What officer?'

'The one that came to the pub to find out about Jimmy.'

'Why did you refuse to speak to him?'

'Well, he came into the pub like he owned it, grabbed the small room at the back and then told us that Jimmy was a disgusting pervert. He said the whole football team was infected. Well, we knew that wasn't true. Charlie Spence said he didn't think that it was true, and the officer told him, "You'll be helping a pervert go free." So I refused to speak to him. If that was a policeman conducting a fair investigation then I'm . . .' He stuttered before finding a comparison.

31

The jury's eyes swivelled to the policeman sitting behind Skerry. Scott was careful not to look, but when a moment later he did so, he saw anger on his face.

'. . . a Dutchman.' It was rather lame when it came.

'All right, all right,' said Meadowsweet. 'Let's get on.'

Detective Constable Mike Reynolds had been in the police force nearly seven years before he discovered what it was he wanted to do.

He wanted to extirpate child abuse. Extirpate was an efficient word, describing his intention exactly – lift up by the root, root out. He had first used the word in a victims' group where he had been invited to speak. The group was against all types of abuser – road-traffic offenders, drunken drivers, doctors, rapists, railway companies, all of them.

At the meeting Reynolds had tried to be realistic. He did not offer an instant panacea for abuse, especially child abuse, saying only, 'I am realistic enough to recognise that in my area – what in the old days used to be called my manor' – they laughed as he distanced himself from the old-fashioned idea of a policeman – 'we will not easily be able to extirpate this type of crime. We must remember that those who choose to behave like this are indifferent to the pain and suffering they cause –' he emphasised the next words – 'because they have been taught to be indifferent to it. We have found that the abuser himself often claims to have been a victim. Why did he not say so before? We should treat that claim with caution, since it is the case that the abuser only uses this claim more readily to disguise himself and his intentions. Remember that, and be on your guard always. The world is divided into abusers and victims.'

It was with profound shock that he had learnt all this, and from a source he would normally have regarded with great suspicion: a lecture from a doctor.

Lectures were generally given, he had discovered in his

32

previous police work, by people who stand up and spout, rather than getting out and doing something about it. The title of the talk had been: 'The Complex Causes of Child Abuse'.

Had it been 'the complex causes of theft' he would have known the thing immediately for what it was, yet another attempt to talk down dishonesty, to apologise for it, and he would have been right. So at first his reaction to this proposed talk was the same: 'Excuses, always reasons *why* we should understand, rather than condemn. A little *more* condemnation is needed.' He felt better saying this, since the home secretary said it.

But to his surprise he discovered that this lecture was different. He remembered what was said, even if he didn't remember the lecturer.

It was the first of a series of talks on sex offenders for the small group of officers joining child-protection teams, taking the course. They had been warned that what they were going to hear would go against many of the things they had previously thought, so until this lecture, he supposed people chose to be what they were, but, as the doctor said, it was how they chose that was interesting.

The abuse of children, she told them, is mostly perpetrated by people who have themselves been abused, people who have in effect been taught to be as they are. So it is the case that women who have experienced violent fathers will marry violent men. Men and women, but most often men in sexual matters, return to the place of their earliest and most intense experiences and repeat them.

Adults who have been used in this fashion when they are children are themselves drawn to children. The hurt child returns in the shape of grown man. What could be more horrifying?

'This is something we can do little about, except attempt to show these men what has happened to them.'

Dr Karenin, who had taken time out of a very busy practice to give this lecture, doubted whether what she was saying was being fully understood by this room full of policemen. It was information she would normally have to repeat again and again in order that it was not misunderstood. Now she only had time to present it. No time even for questions. Even medical students had difficulty with these ideas. She thought of one, destined no doubt to become a golf-playing surgeon, who at the end of his lectures had told her, 'You are teaching us nothing but masturbation, incest and suicide.' He didn't want to know.

The following lecturers picked up on what the doctor had said and expanded on it. Had Dr Karenin heard how what she had said was afterwards interpreted, she would have been horrified.

'So now we know these people had to be taught to be what they were. They are trained to it. That is why they are devious.'

To Reynolds it was a revelation, showing how it was they could be so cunning. Unlike theft, which needs no teaching – dishonest people steal effortlessly, he had seen it – paedophiles are taught by other paedophiles to be paedophiles; taught by people who, in order to do the teaching, were able to disguise themselves as normal people. Their *aim in life* is to teach what they are and they attempted to justify it by saying, I was taught to be this. Had they no choice? Of course they did.

There were whole networks of them. The next lecturer displayed a vast chart. 'Here is an association of paedophiles in one small northern town.' The name of the town had been covered up. 'Every social services department has one of these charts or something like it. Often you will have access to them.'

Reynolds was told that these people would groom young children – a special word for it, 'groom' – over

34

months or even years, to become like them. *Grooming* was itself a crime now. Often it would be done by people becoming the child's step-parent, so they could have long-term contact, or being an uncle or a brother-in-law.

And so, given what the doctor had said, it was not surprising that these people were so difficult to identify; it was no wonder they could infest society, without society realising their presence. They were so invisible, they could almost be called normal.

As other lecturers continued, DC Reynolds discovered that it was worse – child abusers were most often to be found in jobs that involved children. Care workers, for instance. They *gravitate* towards them. It was the same with arsonists, apparently – amazingly, many arsonists are firemen. So those very people who should most of all be protecting children were themselves the threat, the very people who should be putting fires out were starting them. This threat was constant, intense and all-pervading. He wrote down the words. Gravitate, groom, aim in life.

No child was safe, nobody could be trusted. It was wise to suspect exactly those whom you thought you could trust most; indeed, and here was the most astonishing revelation of all, in certain circumstances normality itself was a sign of hidden guilt.

Of course that demonstrated the importance of the sex offenders' register. Although this was a crime that was uniquely evil, it was also a crime that could be combated. Modern techniques of obtaining, collating and recording information were now available. In prison, specially trained technicians would show pictures of child victims to prisoners, measure their blood pressure and plot the engorgement of the paedophile's penis. This information would eventually be included on the new government entitlement cards, identity cards – if they came in. Then the police would have real control.

Anyone near a school could instantly be checked for his sexual orientation, and arrested if his responses were wrong. For certain people it was already a crime to be near a school; soon it could be extended to everyone.

DC Reynolds sat astonished as he listened.

Experts could now know with complete certainty whether a prisoner would offend again, and it would not be long, the lecturer said, before so-called liberal resistance would be broken down and the information used to keep people off the streets, to put them out of harm's way permanently. For their own good.

As the lectures went on Detective Constable Reynolds was shown the ways in which such people might be flushed out. He was taught carefully to watch those whom he interviewed. If someone who was a suspect became distressed at the suggestion that he was a pervert, then it was likely the investigation was on the right track and that person needed watching. Denial of the offence was paradoxically the first step towards proof.

In summary, here was a threat to society that was unparalleled. It cut across entrenched divisions of opinion. It was everywhere. What was frightening was that he had this information while most people were blithely ignorant of it. He felt empowered, ready to act.

He finally discovered this as he sat and listened to a black man, a home office minister, deliver the last lecture. Once the very idea of a black home office minister would have worried him, with its associated ideas of liberalism and indiscipline, but it was almost as though this man knew what might be thought of him, and he had decided to show he was not like that.

'We will build prisons in sufficient numbers to lock up abusers.'

He said there were people crying out to be locked up, and that 'we' – he meant the government – 'will oblige.

We won't fail them. New ways will be developed to iden-tify those who ought to be kept in custody, and we will use them. This is what our party means by attacking the causes of crime. In this case the very freedom to offend is itself a cause of crime.'

What Reynolds was hearing was very reassuring and at the end the audience rose to applaud the speaker. A broad grin broke out across the minister's bumpy face. He had been accepted.

As the course ended Mike Reynolds left, a changed man, to continue the fight. More experienced detectives, men who had worked in the field for years, told him that he would develop a nose: 'You will know them, almost by a sixth sense. They have secret signs with which you will become familiar. And the worse part of it is that many of those people, who to your certain knowledge are abusers, will walk free from court. But just wait, they will come again.'

DC Reynolds decided, as he sat at the back of the court, that this man Burns would have to be watched. He already had his own list of people who supported child abuse and child abusers. He had noticed, for instance, that this was not the first time Scott had defended a pervert. Reynolds had already checked his own sex offender lists, both the convictions and the private lists of acquittals, for Scott. He would have to do the same for Burns.

Mike Reynolds had used the local social services chart, the ChildWeb of Families at Risk, as he had been shown. The chart was meant for children at risk of ill-treatment of any sort, neglect, violence, but of course the cross con-nection with sex offenders was well known. 'Find me a child in care, and there will be, somewhere in the back-ground, perhaps completely hidden, possibly hidden for ever, child sexual abuse,' the psychology lecturer had said.

'That is why we are able to run sub-charts, from which we can merge, import or export congruent data.'

It was comforting to hear the certainty she displayed. She taught judges. This one had known her stuff. She was more definite than the doctor. She said, 'Do not be diverted. We know that over 98.5 per cent of children who complain are telling the truth. And many children do not complain, because they *do not know* they have been abused. It is quite possible all children have been abused.

'The head of the Crown Prosecution Service has admitted, on our behalf, that we are all racist; the next step he must take is to admit we are all child abusers.'

Billy Burns was one of the best witnesses Scott had ever called. His memory was not only faultless, but it was properly supported by other evidence and it didn't seem odd therefore that it was so exact.

The man described what he had done at the weekend cabin in Strafford Park in detail. Skerry had not the faintest idea what Dutch double pipe feeds were. Burns said, 'The Dutch lead Europe in plumbing; the question we always ask in the trade is, "What are the Dutch doing?" The reason, of course, for that is that if it were not for Dutch plumbers, Holland would be underwater all the time.'

He was laughing in Skerry's face. But it didn't matter; the jury loved every moment of it.

Billy Burns joked that the system in Jimmy Reilly's weekend cabin down in Strafford Park was every bit as good as the sheikh's. The only difference was that the sheikh's had to have a third tap for colognes, and that it was gold-plated – 'which from a strictly plumbing point of view isn't necessary, so I don't count that,' he said. The jury laughed out loud.

38

'Yes,' said Skerry, 'I suppose that's right,' trying to get in on the act, but everybody knew it was Billy Burns's joke.

After he had given evidence Billy Burns made for where he had left the van parked. He knew that although it seemed safe inside his van, it was not.

Safety is a fragile, childlike thing. He remembered how – he must have been six or younger, the time when his parents were fighting – he had hidden in a tree near where people were walking. Had they looked up, then immediately he would have been seen, but they didn't. They searched and searched for him, but never found him.

It was the same now: at any moment the van might be stopped, and among the hundreds of little shelves, boxes and cupboards that he had installed, anything he thought he had hidden could be found. He knew the same for his own pockets. They seemed personal, the safest place of all. But they were not, of course. He could be searched.

Anywhere personal could be searched; the more personal, the more pleasure they took in searching, like the man who put his hand up his arse at that borstal. The man wasn't looking for anything, though they called it a routine search; it was just the pleasure of it, showing him he was owned.

Billy had enjoyed spiking that man, in the dark, two blows into the shoulder; no one ever knew who had done it. But he always remembered the lesson that man had taught him. There is nowhere safe. Save in your head, of course; no one can get in there.

Except for a driving licence, an insurance and a test certificate for the van, he never carried anything on him at all. Nothing that would lead someone searching to anything else.

So he was always careful. He always covered his tracks even when it didn't matter. He was never free of it. He had left the court on foot, walking through the back streets, down the long brick tunnel under the railway lines, past the old market. He reached the van and waited for a moment on the opposite side of the road. No one had followed him and, unless someone watching had been waiting there for him, he had led no one to it. He got in, turned out into the traffic and headed east, following the line of the railway, then the river, until he reached the tunnel and was able to cross. He had beaten the rush and was making good time. The traffic began to thicken, but by now he was home, and he turned into one of the dead straight avenues flanked by tall flats that had been thrown up for the new workforce in the thirties. He turned left, left again and then went back on himself, a full circle. Again he was sure there was no one following him, and he turned the van straight into an open lock-up, where he stopped, cut the engine, jumped out and shut the garage door. It was done in a moment.

The garage had a door at the side and he slipped out, turning behind the row and crossing the asphalt playing area, to the glass doors of the block of flats opposite. He pushed through the unsecured entrance, and into the area at the bottom of the stairs. On his left again there was his front door, unusual for its shining paint and letterbox. He pipped the bell and then opened the door.

As he entered the small hall a woman appeared, warned by the ringing, already putting her coat on. 'She's sleeping,' she whispered, and, not pausing, immediately went out. He wasn't a man you would stop and chat to, unless he asked you. 'See you, Mr Billy,' she said, and she closed the door quietly behind her.

Billy Burns stood silently for a moment and then moved towards the room from which the woman had emerged, gently opening the door. He put his head round it and saw the child sleeping on the bed. Softly he entered. He sat in

40

the wicker chair and, leaning forward, smoothed the girl's hair. He started to breathe out softly, a soothing sound, quieting the sleeping body, which, even as he touched it, trembled slightly, soft spasms rippling across the stricken frame. He began to sing softly: '*She held onto me, when she couldn't hold her own*,' and he sat still, his hand touching the tangled hair on the pillow.

'Heeere's Billy! A hundred and eightyyy!' The group of men standing at the bar in the River Anchor pub turned and laughed out loud, one of them shouting and holding his hands up.

'Billy, how are you?' A pint of beer appeared and was passed through the group.

'So, so,' he said. Then, 'Has anyone heard how Jimmy Reilly got on?'

There was an embarrassed silence. Some in the group turned away, but the moment passed. A tall, stooping man leaned forward to speak, 'You're too good to him, Billy.'

'There's no telling,' said Billy. But he stopped and didn't follow it up. Then said, 'And that's true for Telling's Golden Miller.' As he came out with the phrase, two or three of the men joined in, speaking it in unison with him. Others laughed. The group feeling was restored, the volume of conversation increased slightly.

'Dave P. has got some boots. He was down here earlier.'

'Boots, boots, always boots. He's taking a great risk always doing the same thing.'

'I dunno, how about Martin with that Italian whisky? You'd have thought someone would have noticed that.'

'Who looks at the label?'

'When you poke the fire . . .'

'As long as it tastes the same.'

'But boots. He might as well open a shop.'

41

'A shop stays in the same place all the time. Dave P. couldn't manage that.'

'Not when he's out.'

'How's the missus, Charlie?' Billy Burns spoke quietly to one of the group. 'I only saw her for a moment when I arrived.'

'OK. She's good. And how's it at home?'

'Janey's popped in now.' But he didn't go on, and shrugged his shoulders. Charlie didn't make contact with Billy's eyes, but let his gaze go past. He knew not to go any further, asking about Billy's grandchild.

In Billy's line of vision was a television with a split screen showing four pictures, each of them part of the outside of the pub. A police car appeared slowly, tracking down the road. There was silence at the bar. The crowd watched the car as it left the range of one camera, appearing at a different angle on another screen. It slowed. Two police officers could be seen peering up, they knew they were being watched. But the car didn't stop. It made the instant jump to another screen and then, this time from behind, it could be seen creeping away.

The appearance of the police car quietened the pub.

Then someone shouted, 'C'mon, Billy, give us some of your Tommy.' The man who called out leant over the bar and snatched a fez that was hanging on a hook above the telephone. He tossed it to Billy Burns who caught it and put it on. Then turning down his mouth, putting one foot slightly in front of the other, spreading his hands out, palms down, Billy shot his cuffs, rocked slightly on his feet and began. 'Jus' like that . . .'

Two days later the jury went out to decide Jimmy's case.

Scott waited with nothing to do. Sitting and talking with Jimmy could only take so long. This was the worst time, and he could not imagine how Jimmy managed it.

Every time they looked at each other the same question came. How can they accept the evidence of this child? It's been proved he was wrong about one of the allegations. Either one or the other is lying, and it had to be Jason. Meadowsweet had said the same thing, one of them is lying; it was one of the few things he said that had helped. Skerry had tried to disregard it and bluster his way through it, but it stuck out, even in the middle of his argument.

While Jimmy sat with his wife and baby, Scott walked separately in the garden surrounding the court with the two older children. 'Why do you have that thing on your head?' he was asked about his wig. He was carrying it with him. There was no proper answer. 'It shows what I do,' Scott said, spinning it on a finger, the tails of it flying out. It was an old friend, like a part of his personality, but he had come to hate it for what it had turned him into. 'And is there any point to it?' he asked.

'Of course there is,' he decided out loud, making the children look up at him nervously. To get Jimmy Reilly acquitted. His stomach became an even tighter ball of anxiety. What if the jury thought me too glib? Or if I bullied the child like Skerry said? Or they disliked me because of the way I speak?

He bent down and together with the children they examined a mushroom growing at the base of the holm oak. 'No, you better not eat it,' he said. 'You never know what it might do in your tummy.'

'What will it do?'

'I reckon it would jump around a lot.'

They were all bent down over the mushroom when Jimmy's wife came to them.

'We mustn't eat it, Mummy. That's what the man says.'

'I should think not,' she said. Scott could hear her breath as her slight Irish accent softened the T. It made what she said less severe.

Scott straightened up, leaving the children hunched over the caps, their forearms still on their knees as they examined them. He turned to Mary Reilly and was shocked to see tears in her eyes.

'I should thank you, Mr Scott, for what you have done for my husband, whatever the result.' She put out her hand.

Scott had nothing to say in return.

After many hours in the jury room, the jury accepted what Billy Burns had said, and acquitted Jimmy Reilly on the count where his evidence showed he wasn't there. It was clear that the little boy had made it up; he had not been in the flat that Sunday afternoon.

But since they couldn't risk letting a paedophile walk free, as the newspapers describe it, they convicted him on the other charges, those he could call no alibi for. So the one acquittal meant nothing at all.

His Honour Judge Meadowsweet remanded Jimmy in custody to get reports, warning him of the inevitability of a long prison sentence when he returned.

When Scott came up from the cells he looked for Mary Reilly, but she had gone.

Scott had tried to get the judge to certify the case for immediate appeal. It was his one way of protesting in front of the jury about the crazy decision they had made.

He said, 'This verdict is contradictory. The boy has been disbelieved on the only count where there is independent evidence. But on the allegations where the Crown gave no dates, where they were completely vague about when the offences were committed, in other words where it is completely impossible for Mr Reilly to call any evidence to defend himself, the child's evidence was accepted.'

Scott found he was very angry.

'It isn't a case of telling the truth or not,' said Skerry. 'On that occasion the boy was just mistaken.'

44

'That is not what Mr Skerry said in his closing speech,' Scott said. 'Mr Skerry was quite clear. He said that someone in this case must be lying, and he said, "The Crown say the boy is telling the truth throughout." Your honour, if you remember, said exactly the same thing.'

Meadowsweet was so taken aback by the anger in Scott's voice that he was quite meek. If he had behaved as he normally did then there might have been a shouting match.

So the judge, using the phrase that seems always to be used in doubtful cases, said only that he was perfectly satisfied that there was a case proved by overwhelming evidence, and that he would not certify it for appeal.

The jury sat astonished, only now realising the absurdity of what they had done.

Then everybody went home.

Chapter 2

A verdict of guilty is final. Suddenly there's no more arguing. Of course you can appeal. Defendants always say, 'I'll appeal,' or, 'I'll fight it all the way,' but you can't do that, since there is no more fighting to be done. An appeal isn't a rehearing of the facts; you're not allowed to have a go at getting a different verdict.

Scott wrote all this down in an advice for Mr Reilly. Or at least he wrote a version of it for Mr Reilly. He had found from experience that every time he did this he had to spell the law out carefully. People still in shock from being convicted won't understand, or rather, can't believe that it's all over, that there's nothing more to be done.

He wrote, 'An appeal against conviction is restricted only to an enquiry into whether there was anything wrong with the way in which the original trial was conducted. Only very rarely can the argument go beyond that.'

Once you're convicted, the idea that a man might be innocent is a side issue, irrelevant to the argument the court of appeal was set up to hear, which was whether the process was right. But he didn't write that down.

Nor did he write down what everybody, or at least any criminal lawyer, knows about the court of appeal. For many years that court had considered the possibility of an innocent man being convicted as quite inconceivable, though after the appalling mistakes of the seventies and eighties they began to have their doubts. The system had wobbled, for a moment it had looked as though it might collapse, but the old attitudes recovered.

He knew what would happen in this case. The fact that Scott was on the edge of getting the boy to admit he was lying would count for absolutely nothing. How could they listen to that? They would say Meadowsweet was right to let the case go on. They would say the jury was entitled, if they wished to believe the boy on one allegation and not accept the other. They would not interfere.

The appeal courts still do what Pontius Pilate did. He was, after all, sitting as an appeal court judge.

Scott knew the only sensible approach, once a case is lost, is not to waste time over it. But. But that wasn't satisfactory. It's only possible to keep your eyes tight shut for so long. He found he was still angry, unable to shake this case off. This one he knew was wrong. He knew Jimmy Reilly was innocent. He knew that child had been lying.

Cross-examining someone means getting right up close to them. Most often you find when you get that close that the witness is telling the truth, but here it was the other way round, he knew he was lying. Of course what he knew meant nothing. People always asked, 'How do you defend someone you know is guilty?' They never ask what happens if you know he isn't.

He stood up. He looked out of the window. He had always been nervous this might happen one day; he had clients whom he had liked and for whom he felt sympathy, people for whom he was very sorry when the case went against them, but it had never been like this.

He knew Jimmy Reilly was innocent. He knew it like . . . This was difficult. People think most of the things which they know can be demonstrated. But, for example, you can't always demonstrate that you saw something

47

happen. Sometimes you might be able to, sometimes not. But either way you always know whether you saw it.

He got on and sat down to continue writing.

The traffic outside in Fleet Street pottered on. A tourist bus, open-topped, with a guide on the upper deck, passed by. It was raining, but there were still a few hardy people wrapped up, listening to what he said in the wet.

He found he was unable to continue. His careful analysis of the law meant nothing. All he was doing was playing his useless part in the process that had screwed Jimmy Reilly's life up.

He went to the pub, though it was still early.

'I read that one of the most common fears people have is that they might be on public transport when something happens. The person sitting next to you gets attacked. What do you do? Either you get up and do something, or you remember that you did nothing – for the rest of your life.'

Scott handed his friend a beer. They were in the Law Courts Branch of the Bank of England, all of which had been entirely replaced by a modem. Now the huge building where previously litigants' money had been shifted around had become a pub. It was packed, and after buying the beer, Scott had to fight his way through the crowd to where his friend was sitting.

They each drank some and then looked down at their glasses. Scott's depression was catching.

'And if you get up and intervene, you get beaten up, since life isn't like a film,' Scott carried on. 'Well, I'm in that position now. I'm wondering whether to get up and try to do something about it. For years I tried to understand what the law is, and in the end I find out what everybody else knew all along. It's absurd.'

'It's all we've got.'

'That's not much use if you're the one caught up in it.'

48

The conversation around them in the pub was getting louder.

Scott said, 'Maybe that's the real crime for which people are being tried – being caught up in things. Never be caught up. And I'm about to be.'

He sat silently, then he said, 'I'm going to go and find out what happened.'

'What?'

'Yes.'

'You can't.'

'The proper thing to do is to write the advice, go along to the court of appeal, watch them throw the appeal out, as they will, bow and scrape at them and then forget all about it. I know that. Barristers are not meant to get involved, that's not their job. Everything should be done in the correct detached manner. But why do I always have to be detached? Why shouldn't I be angry sometimes?'

'Because you're more use to him detached. That's what he needs, someone to give him cold-blooded advice.'

Scott snorted. 'I could be as cold-blooded as the Lizard over at number six, – the Perfect Prosecutor, eyes veiled, big feet flapping, cold as ice – and it still wouldn't do any good.'

'Do you believe he was innocent then?'

Scott stopped.

'Of course. Haven't you been listening?'

His friend said, 'For me it's never happened. If it's as you say it is, then yes, you're right, you're in trouble. You're in trouble the same way Gareth Pierce must have been in trouble. It took her years.'

'I know he is innocent. It was entirely clear that the young boy lied.' Scott went on, 'The courts are totally incapable of dealing with that. They have always been unable to deal with witch-hunt crimes. Ask Chris Mullins. Think about it. We're not allowed to know anything about the witness; we can't find anything out about his background. Nothing. If my solicitor had gone asking questions about the child, he would have risked immediate arrest for attempting to pervert the course of justice. As far as the defence were concerned the boy might as well have been an actor.'

Silence. Then Scott said, 'The courts seem to have mislaid the whole idea of a trial being a contest. Investigating a criminal offence now involves calling evidence to justify the complaint. When was the last time a policeman in a case like this made any serious effort to check whether the allegation was wrong? No one with an open mind has ever investigated Mr Reilly's case.'

'What are you going to do?'

'I'm going to go down there and find out.'

'I can't see you getting anywhere.'

'Nor can I, but why not try?'

'Do you know where to go?'

Scott said, 'Well, yes I do. I know where all this happened, and I know some people in the area. Also I saw an address. A crime report sheet was given me, and they'd forgotten to cover it up. I can go and talk to people. I think I'm going to go this evening.'

Until that moment Scott had not known that he had decided to do this.

First he took his things home to his flat. He lived on the third floor, behind Sloane Square, overlooking the old barracks. Tonight there was a squad of territorials marching up and down, something he didn't think happened any more.

A drill sergeant was standing outside the barracks building, strutting like a cartoon character. His word of command, ridiculously drawn out, comprehensible by the consonants alone, drifted up to where Scott stood. The small group of soldiers turned and wheeled beneath the window. They resembled a toy car that the sergeant was tentatively driving away from him, testing the limit to which his signal would reach. Each time they reversed, turned inside out and marched away they went a little further. At one point the front ranks even became hidden by a high wall opposite, seeming to leave the square, but at the last moment the sergeant's voice, angry, slightly irritated, like a buzzing wasp, reached out and drew them back.

The light slowly failed.

Above the black, sooty buildings, thankfully not yet acid-washed clean, London's orange night sky replaced the thin evening blue.

It would take at least an hour to get down to east London. He'd better make a start.

The Potato Patch public house, competition for the River Anchor down the way where Billy Burns was, had the same standard brick, the same Crittall windows as a thirties telephone exchange. The proportions were uncomfortable, tall and narrow.

When it was built the only vehicle likely to drive up to it would have been a horse-drawn dray, and the paved area was designed to take only that kind of weight. Now the paving had long been broken and cracked as an assortment of cars had been squeezed onto it.

Scott parked his car across the road. As he approached the pub he wondered whether there was a police video following him. It was that kind of place. He went through the door, tensing slightly at the noise and light flooding back through it, but even then unprepared for what he found. Despite the quiet road outside, it was packed. There was a roaring noise as the crowd heaved. It was hardly possible to distinguish people since, although the room was lit, all the lights were placed low down and were very bright, throwing the ordinary shapes and figures of the crowd into constant relief. Music was booming, and the level of conversation had increased to compete with it.

Momentarily stunned by the sound, Scott stood and stared.

Eventually he picked out a space at the bar and moved towards it, pushing past men holding pint glasses of Guinness. They made way for him. Scott was aware of being different, of being watched. He had brought a newspaper thinking perhaps he would be able to subside into a quiet corner to wait for the people he wanted, but there weren't any corners, and the only quiet place he could see was where two men were slumped, apparently unconscious, over a table just inside the door. Thank God he wasn't pushing through this crowd holding a book, as he had first thought of bringing. It wasn't the kind of place you go to read.

He reached the bar.

The barman jerked his head in acknowledgement.

Scott said, 'Guinness, please.' The only other thing to buy was a thin lager. The barman flicked the tap on the beer. The time it took for the drink to settle gave Scott his opportunity. 'Is John Hector here?' he said. It wasn't such a ridiculous question; if he were here then the barman would surely know. The man said nothing but jerked his chin to the side, towards the group standing to Scott's right. He turned to look, to find a huge man watching him with a broad grin, his arms wide open. 'I thought so. It's the brief. Johnny's brief,' and Scott was crushed in an embrace.

Despite his being lifted off his feet Scott saw, in a moment of detachment, a hand reach out to pay the barman for the beer he had ordered. 'Look, it's Jeremy Scott,' the large man said to the people in the group, releasing him. Some reacted, others just looked blank.

'How are you?' the man said.

Scott hadn't a clue who this man was.

52

'His brother. I'm John Hector's brother. You remember.'

Scott had no memory for faces but he tested out the idea that he knew John Hector's brother and found it worked. 'Hey, I'm sorry. How are you?' He moved into friendly mode, acting out what he had seen others do and discovered – it always surprised him – that it seemed perfectly normal.

'And here's Geoff.'

Scott was being introduced to the group; he said hello.

'And there's old Tom Hopkins.' He pointed out another man behind the bar. The name reminded Scott of the details.

Tom Hopkins had given evidence against John Hector when Scott had defended him. Scott had cross-examined him, and it was Tom Hopkins who had given them the clue to what had happened, how the case had been organised. This time Scott knew what to do. 'Hi, Tom, how are you? No hard feelings then?'

Tom Hopkins acknowledged him with: 'Nothing like that, Mr Scott. To be sure.' An Irish throwaway line. He pulled the handle on a beer, ducking down as he did so, half watching the beer hiss into the glass, half grinning up at Scott.

'You'll be looking for John then? He's in there.' John Hector's brother pointed towards what must be the lavatory, but as he said it, Scott felt an arm clamp round his shoulders.

'Hello, it's my brief.'

It was John Hector. 'What can we do for you then?' The power of Hector's grip reminded Scott, if he needed it, that he had stepped into a different world.

'You won't like what I came for, John.' They were sitting in a large Mercedes car, parked a short distance from the pub.

'You try me.'

'I've got a client. I think he's been had over.'

'Yeah, and by someone I know?'

'Well, it's someone nearby.'

'Where?'

'Over on the Cummin Estate.'

'Oh. There.'

'You know it well?'

'I know it. I don't go there. Used to. But what's it about?'

'It's difficult. He's been accused of indecency with children.' Scott became aware of John Hector stiffening. Of course he would. Scott said, 'I said you wouldn't like it, but there's something wrong with it. It's not an ordinary case.'

'Well, Mr Scott, if it weren't you I wouldn't be listening any more.'

'I understand that. I know it.' Scott stared out of the car window. 'There's something odd about it. Look, if the guy didn't do it, then what he didn't do can hardly be a reason for blowing him out.'

'And you say he didn't do it?'

There it was again, a reasonable enough question. What they wanted to know was whether the guy did it.

Scott turned and said, 'No, John. He didn't, he's innocent. That's why I'm here.'

'What do you want me to do?'

'To begin with I just wanted to run some names past you.'

'OK.'

'Jimmy Reilly?'

'Nope. Never heard of him.'

'He's the man. He spends time at the River Anchor, or used to. Just the other side of the estate.'

'I know it. I've been there.'

54

'It's just an ordinary pub?'

'Yeah. Pretty good actually.'

'He was involved in football there.'

'Nope. Don't know him.'

'A family called Lee? The boy is Jason Lee. He is in care near the pub with foster parents.'

'A boy huh? Nope.'

'A policeman called Mike Reynolds?'

'Out of East Place nick?'

'I think so. He works in child protection.'

'You're asking me to do something I don't want to do?'

Scott said nothing.

'Hurting kiddies – that's different.'

Scott wanted to say, Not this kiddy, but thought he had better not. He said, 'There's another name, Billy Burns.'

'Now that's a name I know,' said John Hector.

Scott knew he was beginning to make connections.

PART TWO

Dr Karenin

Chapter 3

Dr Grace Karenin opened the referral. In it there was a letter from a general practitioner, medical notes, the child's school report and the results of medical tests. In a moment she was going to try to establish a relationship with the mother, starting out on the journey of helping her and her child. She got up, opened the door and looked outside. 'Hello,' she said, smiling brightly. 'Let's sit down.' They sat down and started getting to know each other.

Darren was on the floor playing and his mother, Tina, who had at last, after hesitating for a long time, brought him to the clinic – she could stand no more of it, she was nearly out of her mind with it – sat opposite the doctor.

Tina's face, which had at first been tight and expressionless, gradually loosened. After a short while she began talking more freely and the relief of letting it go began to show. It was nearly always the same; Dr Karenin was used to seeing it happen.

Of course Tina didn't want to be here at all. No, that was wrong (the doctor watched her talking), it wasn't whether or not she wanted to be here, she surely wanted someone to help her, but what she didn't want was what was happening. This was too personal.

The doctor said, 'What you really want to say to me is

that your little boy, Darren, has finally got too much for you?'

'No, not . . .' There was a pause. Then, 'Yes.' Letting her breath out and slumping down.

The doctor said, 'There's no shame in that, everybody feels that at one time or other. Sometimes they even want to hurt the child, but most don't.'

The mother stopped and allowed what the doctor was saying to wash over her. She felt so tired. She was angry too.

The bus journey had nearly finished her – just when she had hoped it was going to turn out easy, he had started playing up and using language. The woman on the seat beside them had started muttering under her breath, pretending to edge away, though of course she couldn't since it was a tight seat and there was nowhere to edge away to. Tina had nearly said something back at her, but had controlled herself. Time was she would have and got into trouble, but she'd learned to manage that now, she had to. Still Darren went on and on, until a man in front had turned round and cussed at him.

She felt everyone looking at her, but then had been saved by the ticket man, the inspector – whatever – coming along, and for once, despite all her clothes and her bags, she had found her bus pass and Darren's ticket immediately. Then Darren had become interested in what the inspector was doing and quietened down, until suddenly they were at the stop, the inspector told her, she didn't have to worry whether it was the right one. She had to get the buggy out to get off, but again the inspector had helped her, so it turned out right in the end.

But the tension of it, it was too much. She knew Darren picked up on it when she felt like that, and still she had to get all the way home again. She had to take the bus – walking that far was out of the question.

It all started to pour out of her. 'It's not normal. I can't get any rest. He . . . it's as though he wants aggression from me. Sometimes I think he hates me. Can children do that? I saw this film where the small child attacked his mum . . .' But she got no further, interrupted by a crash. Her son had dislodged a toy truck from a shelf. It fell to the floor and broke into bits. What he had done didn't seem to affect him, and not even glancing round he carried on climbing up the shelves, intent on getting at the piece he wanted.

'Oh, Dar,' she wailed. 'Come down from there. Just leave it.'

The boy looked round and in the instant before his face snapped shut, the doctor saw an open, unprotected look – was it fear? Whatever it was – fear or maybe the result of being called back from somewhere far away, somewhere almost unreachable – the reaction promptly turned into anger. 'Not me. It weren't my fault,' he said, spitting it out. Then he went back to where the wild things were.

His mother turned back to the doctor again. The incident was closed.

'He's always like that, you just can't leave him for a moment.' The broken truck lay disregarded on the floor.

'You were telling me. You find him . . .?'

'I hoped when he began at playschool things would get better. But no. They wouldn't let him stay.'

Dr Karenin knew from the school doctor who had agreed to refer Darren's mother to her that it had taken only two days for the school to exclude Darren. He had kicked, spat and attacked other children. 'A decision was made that it was not safe to leave him alone with other children,' the report had said.

'You told the school doctor that you had difficulty with Darren from the start?'

'Well, it weren't too bad to begin with. I knew it was going to be difficult, but Ali, I was with Ali then, and he

61

used to drink, you know?' But the doctor wouldn't allow anything to remain unsaid, and she asked, 'And you too? You used to have trouble yourself with that, didn't you? At least I think you said that to the other doctor?'

By referring to what someone else had said Dr Karenin made her questions, even though insistent, less bald, less aggressive. That way, she knew, slowly it would become possible for the mother to talk more easily. Tina Lee glanced up at Dr Grace Karenin but saw no judgement, no disapproval in her face.

'Yes. Well, when I was with Ali I was drinking a lot. But never with the baby, I never hurt the baby. I did it to get out of myself.'

She paused. The doctor said nothing; Tina was encouraged to go on. 'My mum used to help, but Dad objected to that. He wouldn't let her come round to my place, he used to stop her going out, and all my sisters were against me. They said the baby's death was my fault. Though it wasn't.' Gently she started to cry.

Dr Karenin could see Darren listening. He seemed to be indifferent, preoccupied on the floor with the toy he had climbed for, but he was aware of what was going on, not the words, but of the thing they meant.

'It weren't my fault, I wasn't even there. That Roger, he was a violent man, even the policeman said that to me.'

'Why d'you live with him then?'

'He seemed nice enough when I met him. He was older than me, and I wanted to get away from home.'

Dr Karenin had heard this before. It was extraordinary how uninventive humanity was in the ways it brought suffering down on itself. She prodded a little further, knowing in advance what she would find.

'Why did you leave home?'

'I didn't get on with my dad. He was never nice to me. Still isn't. He drank. He hit me.'

She wanted to ask, why marry someone exactly like your dad then? But Tina wouldn't understand that. No, that was unfair, she might understand it, but she would say the fact that she had married a man exactly like her father was merely a coincidence, or perhaps, if she was feeling a little more confident and relaxed, she would say all men are like that, so what's different?

Of course that might be true as well.

'And your mum?'

'Well, she's got problems of her own. What with Dad. And she and I never really got on.'

'What was it?'

'I was always in trouble. At school and that. I never seemed to fit in.'

Darren was quiet on the floor. He didn't try to under-stand what was being said, but he could feel the tension and distress. He drank it in, it gave him energy. For him this was normality. That would never change now, he would never feel easy unless he was surrounded by it, and if it wasn't there he would create it.

'Would you like to come here regularly to see me?' Dr Karenin watched herself asking the question. It was a question she often asked and each time it seemed presump-tuous. Someone, one day, would say, 'Why should I want to come here to see you, to talk to you? Why? What do you think you've got to offer that's so special?' But no one ever did.

'OK.' Not sure.

'And you'll bring Darren?'

The mother paused, unwilling to commit herself. What she wanted was the drug. Ritalin. Give it to the child immediately, get some peace, other mothers did, they swore by it. But she couldn't bring herself to say it out loud. Instead she said, 'What we say here . . . What we talk about, how I get upset, will other people . . .?'

63

'It's entirely private between you and me, although if Darren is in trouble and other people get involved, then I have to talk to them.'

Again it was the phrase she always used.

'You mean the social?'

'Yes.'

'They've never helped me. They took Jay away, he lied and lied about me. He said I used to hit him and made up stories. He made up things about the man I was with, that he did dirty things to him, it wasn't true. Jay admitted he made them up. He did it because he thought then he would be able to go to live with his real father. His real father had walked out on us. Jay took that bad.'

Grace Karenin had seen the summary of the incident in the notes, together with the withdrawal of the child's complaint.

'Well, we'll try and see if I can help you.' Dr Karenin gave her a bright smile, and transferred her attention to Darren, 'All right, Darren? You'll come to see me?'

The child was interested, despite himself. Something slightly different was happening here. He was used to seeing people come to the house, the ones who upset his mother. After they were gone she would shout at him. He had thought this woman was one of them. On the way, his mother had been nervous in the same way, he could tell. But it was different now.

'Yeah,' he said, not looking up.

After the mother and child left, Grace Karenin sat writing up the notes. She chose her words very carefully; nowadays with people getting access to them all the time, what she wrote, although only provisional, could so easily be used to condemn the patient.

The phone rang.

Jennet at reception said, 'There's a man here who wants

to see you, a Mr . . .' There was a pause, and Grace could picture Jennet covering the mouthpiece of the phone, looking up and saying, excuse me, what was your name again? '. . . Mr Reynolds. He hasn't got an appointment. No, I don't know, he says it's business. OK, I'll tell him to come down.' There was silence, obviously giving him directions, then, 'He's coming down the passage now. Oh, and he said he was a policeman.'

Grace Karenin thought, Oh no, Jennet, not again. Almost forgetting the important bit.

There was a knock on Dr Karenin's door. A man came in. 'I'm from the child protection team. We haven't met.' He put a hand across Grace's desk. She shook it. 'I'm sorry I wasn't able to give you any warning I was coming.' He sat down and said, 'Do you mind if I get straight into it? My colleagues are interested in one of your patients. They've asked me to come, and I thought, well, it would give me the chance to meet you at the same time, so I said yes.'

Dr Karenin watched him. He went on, 'At least the child is not a patient yet, but we think the father will come here with the child. The child's a girl. They live alone. He used to work on the railway, a signalman, but now he stays at home. The mother has disappeared.'

Dr Karenin watched the man in front of her. She asked, 'When did this happen?'

'About six weeks ago.'

'That's when the mother disappeared?'

'No, that's when a neighbour called us, saying the wife wasn't there any more. By then she had been gone for some time.'

'And you think he'll come here? Why?'

'The social services have told him to. No doubt they'll be writing to you.'

'And what do you want me to do?'

'Let us know what happens, what you discover. We're

treating the mother's disappearance as suspicious.' It was the phrase that was used on the radio, or in the news. Grace had often wondered if they actually spoke like that. It seems they did.

But she said, 'I don't know if I can do that.' The police officer stiffened at this hint of attitude. 'We should have to see,' the doctor said, softening it slightly.

'See what?'

'See if I can. I can't always, not always.' Dr Karenin was aware of the effect she was having on the policeman, and decided to say nothing more.

'But this is a murder investigation.'

'Oh,' Grace said, and then, 'I'm sorry but that makes no difference.'

The phone rang. Dr Karenin picked it up. She listened and then said to the policeman, 'You'll have to excuse me a moment.' She spoke into the phone: 'They won't take her? Well, there are no other places. All the beds in Essex and Kent are full, and the Queen Elizabeth won't have her. No. It will be very difficult to put her on the ward. We had trouble with a child there last week, throwing herself around. They've got drips and things up in there.' Pause. She listened. 'No, we can't send her home. Her mother can't cope and the child might jump out of a window, or something. Where would we be then?'

She listened again. She said, 'Try her on a little to begin with. Two point five mil. And watch her. Ring me if there's any change. All right?' She listened. 'OK, you speak to them about the bed, if they are on the phone now. I'll hang on for you.'

Throughout this conversation her eyes remained on the detective. He sat quietly on the chair and then, to deal with the lack of activity forced on him, opened a file he was carrying.

She had seen policemen like him before, self-assured

66

because in the end they normally got what they wanted, but at the same time slightly unsure in her presence, since they were dealing with an authority that didn't cater for them. Generally, to compensate, they tried a chatty man-of-the-world approach. This one didn't seem much different.

The junior doctor came back to the phone at the other end. 'No, there is no bed.'

'I thought not,' she said. 'Why don't you ask the prime minister to find one?' There was a laugh at the other end of the phone. 'Or the health secretary, he seems to think everything in the garden is lovely.'

She put the phone down and transferred her attention to the policeman.

'A murder investigation, you said?'

'Well, the wife has not been seen now for some time.'

'Yes?'

She knew that if she said nothing he would tell her everything. She had noticed how policemen didn't consider themselves bound by confidentiality, except when they thought it was to their advantage. Then they'd say, 'I'm not at liberty to tell you that.'

It was curious how unprofessional they were, how they couldn't manage detachment. Policewomen were worse. Almost always they allowed themselves to be caught up in the emotion. It must be very tiring.

Detective Constable Reynolds said, 'She took no clothes, though that doesn't mean anything in itself. But when we went to the house there were no carpets in the bedroom, and he'd replaced the floor boards.'

Grace Karenin said nothing.

'All replaced, the old ones burnt. Now why should he do that?' He expected the doctor to react, and when she didn't, he found himself continuing, 'We want to talk to you about anything he says.'

67

'Well, we'll have to wait. To see what happens.'

She stood up and he found he was leaving without the agreement he wanted.

'Thank you, Mr . . .?' she said.

'Reynolds, Detective Constable Reynolds.' He realised he hadn't fully introduced himself earlier, he'd only said, I'm with the child protection team. He showed his card. He said, 'I've taken over from Tony Windows,' trying to make up for it. 'I think you knew him.'

Yes, she knew Tony Windows.

He tried again. 'We'd like to come round here after you see the father.'

'What would be the point?'

He looked at her. She was in a suit: slim, neat, confident. Hadn't he seen her before somewhere? He thought he had.

'As I said, it's a murder enquiry.'

This time she had to reply directly, 'I'm afraid that still would be no basis for me to tell you what goes on in this room.'

She looked at him steadily. Now it really was out in the open. He wasn't used to having to ask more than once. But what was he to say? We'll get an order? We'll go to the court, and get an order? He wondered what she would say. He was sure that, unlike most people, she would have a reply. Probably she'd say, What order? And he would be stuck, because there wasn't one.

He stood there.

And she said, 'Think it through, officer,' and opened the door for him. What did that mean? He had to walk out. The door was about to shut on him. He wanted to say something back. So he asked, and he surprised himself when he asked it, 'Is it true you can tell how a child's brain is developing by the pictures they draw?'

'Yes, that's true.' The doctor smiled at him, interested for a moment in the new subject. 'That's part of what we do here.' But her phone rang and she turned back into her room. Slim, very slim, and unreachable. He watched her disappear.

When he had come into the clinic earlier, Jennet at reception had immediately spotted him as a policeman. 'What do you want?' she had said.

'I want to see Dr Karenin.'

'She'll be busy for a while,' Jennet had said. She kept her eyes on him.

He was quite good-looking, too, with that suit, all three buttons done up the front and a hard haircut. It was styled, so there was still a feeling of movement in it. They all cut their hair like that lately, and the wet look. Why was that? To show they were tough.

Mike Reynolds watched the girl looking up at him. No, not a girl, not any more, you couldn't call her a girl. Nice face. No wedding ring. 'I can wait,' he'd said, being friendly.

There was a big waiting room with old magazines, and children's things as well, a slide, some toys. At the back there was a view out onto a scrubby piece of garden. He took a copy of a woman's magazine, which told him how to diet, and he sat opposite her desk.

He didn't really trust ordinary doctors. Generally they agreed with defendants, providing sick notes, all sorts of reasons why people should get away with things. The doctors coming to the police station were always going on about whether people were fit to be interviewed, and in court they were a joke, giving reasons why people were not responsible for what they had done.

On his right there was a wall covered with children's drawings.

He looked at them, at first only glancing at them, and

then, as his attention was engaged, he looked closer. They were set out in age group. First, the youngest children. Above each there was an outline drawing, which clearly illustrated what was happening in the real picture below. It enabled him to see a pattern, starting with only a round space and approximate marks for eyes, then a little older, when stick legs and arms appeared.

He got up to look.

Where normally there would be a name on a picture there was only an age. Two years old, two and a half years. After the stick legs, hands appeared, then fingers. He remembered in his own son's drawings, how the small child had stuck fingers on, to begin with, in wild abandon, sometimes not even on the hand, and then later, counting them out carefully – although even then it didn't seem to matter whether they were actually attached to the hand or not.

'Apparently drawings can tell you how much the brain has grown. At least that's what Dr Karenin says.'

He turned round. The girl must have seen his interest and had come out from behind her desk and up near to him.

'Really?' he said.

The words had sounded – what was it? – unlikely in her mouth, because she was only a receptionist, but then he realised there was no reason why she should not be interested. He was, why shouldn't she? He felt ashamed of his reaction.

'Is that right?' he said.

'Yes, they're very important. When the doctors talk about children's development, they use them. They use the pictures they draw. I've seen them in all the files.'

She had walked over to where he stood, why'd she do that? Now he knew why he had thought of her as a girl. She was small and slight, though now, when he saw her

70

move from the desk, he could see she must be in her late twenties, perhaps even thirties. Her attention was on the drawings, so he could look at her directly. She wore a cotton print dress which hung all the way down – he couldn't find the right expression, it swayed with her. She was inside it, not because it was hanging on her like a tent but because it fitted. And it swayed, *like the señoritas who can sway*. The Mavericks said that.

He had seen the same thing happen with his wife. When she wore something she made the clothing look good, not the other way around. But his wife was gone now.

'Some pictures even show you when the child is disturbed.' She pointed at a group of drawings down to the right, showing figures standing in a row, but in each of them, one of the figures had been scrawled over with hard circles. There was one where the face was, well, that was the word for it, defaced.

'They are from a book. They aren't our patients' drawings, we wouldn't be allowed to do that. That would be wrong.'

In some it was the child itself who had been drawn over. For a moment he wondered what that must mean. Looking at the pictures was a revelation. What at first glance had looked like a series of pictures you might see in any nursery or primary school, had become something different. And when you examined the group of defaced drawings, it was a dark, hard piece of evidence.

He realised he was learning something and the girl, woman, there wasn't a good word for her, whom he first had thought was a dizzy receptionist, he was learning from her.

He thought about that.

There it was again, another assumption about another person, another mistake. Why do you do it? You're always wrong; no, not always, but when you're wrong it can show and can reflect on you. Recently he had been thinking a bit, and here it was again. He realised he was getting a lot of things wrong, things didn't look as simple as they used to. Maybe thinking he was right all the time had been the cause of all the trouble.

He looked her full in the face.

'You enjoy your job?'

She retreated behind her desk, as though conscious that she had brought his attention down on her.

'Yes.'

'Interesting people?'

'I've learned things.'

'What have you learned?'

He was very direct, but she didn't mind.

'Well, it's more just another way of looking at things. You don't just look at how they are, more how they got that way . . .' She tailed off.

He guessed she was thinking that she was making herself sound a bit too clever. But he didn't think that, she wasn't. And it was exactly what he had been thinking himself. This was extraordinary.

He changed the subject, and looked round the empty room. 'You're not busy then?'

'Not today.'

'Why not today?'

'Most of them are out today, seeing people. The doctors and psychologists, that is. It's near the end of term.'

'Why should that make a difference?'

'I don't know really. It just does.'

She stood up and walked to a door nearby, looked through it, he couldn't see what at, and then returned to the desk. The phone rang. There was a short conversation, and she put the phone down. They both sat in silence.

'Is that your boy?'

72

'Where?'

'On your desk. The photo.'

'Yes. Timmy.'

'He'll be a handsome one.'

It was a strange remark. At first it didn't feel quite right, but it was.

'He's coming up to ten now,' she said.

Suddenly he felt awkward. 'What's he good at?'

'Games. But in school also, he's good. He does homework. Every time I get home he's finished it, and then we go over it together. Last night he had to write about . . .' She stopped. He didn't want to hear this. Just because he had noticed the photo didn't mean he wanted her to run on about Timmy. She looked up, but he was still listening, he was.

'Yes?' he said.

'Last night he wrote an essay. On his own.'

'That's good. What about?'

'About the park. I take him to the park.' He was still listening. 'I think he enjoys that most of all. When we're together.'

'That must be good.'

He'd never got that far, though he remembered pushing the buggy past where the boys played. He supposed by now he would have been doing it if his child had got older. He'd have made time for him.

'Has he got friends?'

'Oh yes, there's a group of them, and the park's been newly done. It's always full.'

'You mean the one near here?'

'Yes.'

'At the bottom by Chase Hill?' he said.

'Yes, that's it. The park people did it up. The ground's made of rubber now.'

He said, 'So when they fall they bounce?'

She laughed, he did too. It was easy.

'I saw that playground the other day. I thought it had changed.' It had been a rest day and, nothing else to do, he had walked from the top of the park down past the old bird cages, then he remembered being there before with the boy. He hadn't meant to remind himself, so he turned away back up the hill.

'Well, it's great now. Save there's not much place to sit. You'd think they would have done that, for the mums.'

'You should write to the council.'

'Yes. I'd never thought of that.'

'Or even better, write to your local councillor. It's the kind of letter they enjoy getting. No problems, and they can ask a question in the parks committee, so they look good. Politicians like that.' Again they laughed. 'Looking good, that is.'

She said, 'We had a politician here when we opened. Why he came I don't know, we've not seen him since. He put his arm round Dr Karenin. You should have seen her face – like thunder. Never seen her like that before. We thought he was going to kiss her.'

'She's a tough lady?'

'Yes, very. She doesn't like officials.'

'She won't like me then.'

'Oh no. Not like that. I'm sure you're very nice.'

She became confused. 'What I mean is, she doesn't like people who interfere, or who think they are more important than what we're doing and push us aside.'

Detective Constable Reynolds noticed her say 'we' – after all, she was only the receptionist – and then again he disliked himself for it. Why shouldn't she take pride in what she did? Just because she was behind a desk, answering the phone, wasn't she still part of the team?

'You like her then?'

Jennet wondered for a moment if she was being teased.

So what if she was? 'Yes. She's helped me a lot.' She looked at him direct in the face again. He was smiling. No, he wasn't teasing her, he was just being himself.

She liked what she saw, a marked face, a little thin, but big dark eyes, and he held himself still. He looked a bit sad. And then just for something to say, she said, 'Now I have to work. I'm sorry,' and she wished she hadn't.

'OK.' He picked up an old copy of *Woman's Realm*.

She wanted to say, sorry that's all we've got for you to read, or, let me try and find you something better. But she had pushed him away so she couldn't now, and then the phone went: 'They're coming out, Jennet.' Dr Karenin's ordinary warning. 'Fix me a time in two weeks.'

She got the calendar up on screen and switched to Dr Karenin's page. Two weeks from today.

Ms Lee appeared from the doctor's room pulling her child Darren with her. Jennet said, 'The doctor will see you again in two weeks. Would Tuesday be any good?'

The policeman sat reading a magazine, keeping himself to himself. Someone else arrived. It was that Mr Burns. Darren, as she keyed the name in, went over to the toy box and was pulling something out, there was a banging noise as he fought against the jumble of toys. His mother did nothing to stop him.

'All right then, here we are, week after next, Tuesday.' She wrote it down. 'Four o'clock, for ninety minutes. The first time coming proper is just a little longer,' she said to the mother. There was a crash. She didn't want to say anything about it and the mother didn't even notice. The next appointment, Mr Burns, was waiting behind this woman, but he was ten minutes early, and there was still this policeman to go in.

She gave her the card and smiled up at her, and she smiled back. When she had come in, she had said, Call me Tina, but Jennet wasn't going to do that. That wasn't professional, and Dr Karenin would not approve. 'Thank you. See you on Tuesday next but one,' and the woman went to get her boy, leaving the man who had just arrived standing in front of Jennet.

'Could you wait for a moment?' she said to him. 'The doctor is almost ready for you.'

He was always very polite to her, whatever else they said about him. She had typed one of the reports, so she knew what kind of person he was. She picked up the phone and said, 'Dr Karenin, there's a man here who wants to see you . . .' She kept her voice low, even when she had to ask the man for his name again. 'He hasn't got an appointment . . . he says it's business.'

She said to the policeman, 'If you go down the passage, it's the second door. The doctor will see you now.' He got up and flicked the magazine he was reading onto a table. She watched his movement, lazy, like, what was it? – Sunday morning, the advertisement said. Why like Sunday morning? She'd never really understood that.

She watched him go through the door. 'He said he was a policeman,' she said to Dr Karenin down the phone, but quietly, so the other man waiting couldn't hear. Anyway he wasn't looking, he was over in the corner, had his back to them.

That was silly, why hadn't she kept the policeman waiting a little longer? Perhaps they could have talked more. But she was bad at keeping them waiting. She'd always told herself that.

When the policeman came out from seeing the doctor he stayed in the waiting room. He didn't say anything, but walked over to the pictures on the wall. Jennet answered the phone and smiled at the man who was waiting that he could go down the passage now. He knew the way, she didn't need to say anything, and anyway they tried to avoid saying people's names out loud.

And then the policeman turned round. He came over to her and came straight out with it, so she nearly jumped at the surprise. 'Would you go out with me this evening?'

He didn't apologise, or pretend to be embarrassed or any of those things, or be too tough; he just said it. And she was so taken by it, she forgot how to deal with it.

'This evening?'

'Yes.' He said, 'I'm off duty from now,' emphasising what he was.

'Today?' She was making a fool of herself.

'Yes.'

'It's too complicated.'

'What's complicated?'

'I'd have to arrange. I mean.' She realised she had said yes. She had said she'd go out with him without thinking, Who is this man? Though he was a policeman, she knew that much.

'Why is it complicated?'

'Well, I don't know.'

'Is it your little boy?'

That helped.

'Well, yes. You see, Mam can't help today.'

'You mean your mum normally looks after him when you go out?'

That sounded as though she was always out with strange men. 'No. I never really go out,' she said. That sounded worse.

'Bring him with you.'

She was astonished.

'Bring him with you,' he said. 'We'll go to Jelly's. He'd like that, wouldn't he?'

Jelly's. Timmy had never been to Jelly's – far too expensive.

She said, 'He'd love it. He's never been to Jelly's.' Then she realised she'd agreed.

'Where shall I collect you?'

'You'll come to me?'

'Yes. I'll pick you up.' That sounded a bit funny he thought. Pick you up. He hoped she didn't think he was joking with words.

She was staring up at him. He said, 'You'll have to tell me where you live.' She said nothing. 'Where do you live, young lady?' he pretended to take a notebook out, licking an imaginary pencil. They laughed. She watched his face. He had beautiful teeth.

'Near Chase Park.' She pulled herself together. 'I'll write the address.' She pulled a yellow sheet of paper towards her and wrote.

He watched her pen. She wrote a round looping hand, with little circles dotting the i's. But it was still strong despite that, not soppy, weak writing. She gave it to him. 'I'd better come a little earlier because of the boy. What time? Say half past six? We'll just have a hamburger, we won't be out long.'

It was reassuring. He clearly knew about children.

'I'll get you back easy for Tim's bedtime.' He had remembered Timmy's name. 'But I still don't know your name,' he said. 'I'm Mike.'

They didn't know what to do.

'I'm Jennet,' she said. And a little oddly they shook hands.

'We just shook hands.'

'Oh?'

'Timmy's coming too.'

'Sounds a bit too good to be true,' said her mam. Jennet didn't know whether her mam was being serious or not, but didn't stop to think about it. She was looking for what to wear.

Chapter 4

Mike Reynolds had parked his car a little way from the clinic; he had formed the habit of never parking close to wherever he was going. He had learned that, and other things, when he worked with his first detective sergeant, Tommy Storey. You were meant to listen to your first detective sergeant. He hadn't thought of him for years – why was he coming back into his head now?

'You must just build these habits, and eventually you'll find you don't even need to think about them. One day one of them might save your life. Listen . . .' Mike could still hear him speaking. He had a strange lazy voice; he was from Hull. 'It's like –' he was searching for a for instance – 'shutting your eyes and stepping out into the road. You can't *do* that with your eyes shut. Just you try. Even if there's someone there telling you there's nothing coming, you *still* can't do it. Your body says no. Try it; you'll hear that whole side of your body speaking to you.

'Now, does that count as knowledge? What kind of knowledge is that? Is it even knowledge at all? What's George Steiner got to say about that then?'

Tommy Storey was a philosophical sort of bloke, and he always regarded an appeal to George Steiner as the clincher. He never got a reply. He said, 'You've got to build up a series of responses in this job, another set of senses almost. What an epistemologist would make of it all, I dunno, but it's a kind of knowledge.'

He waited until Mike asked: 'What's an epistemologist?'

'Someone who studies knowledge. Someone who knows about what knowledge is.'

'Really? Is there such a person? Where do you find them?' Mike was willing to enter into the spirit of the conversation.

'Anywhere.'

'Could a policeman become one?'

Tommy Storey looked at him, to work out whether Mike was taking the piss, then he decided it didn't matter. 'Why not?' he said. 'If he's given the proper handling.'

Mike wasn't taking the piss. He liked Tommy and wanted him to go on talking, he enjoyed sitting with him over a drink.

'Go on,' he said.

'Well, I think it falls into the category of knowledge about natural phenomena. Like physics, only fewer rules.' The man drank some of his Guinness and looked out of the window. 'If that's possible,' he said. 'I like that stuff. Always did.'

'What stuff?'

'Robert M. Pirsig. Not much read nowadays, if it ever was. What I mean to say is I haven't seen that book for years. *The Tao of Physics*. Or was it *Zen and the Art of Motorcycle Maintenance*? It's all the same. Tao, Zen, it's all about perfection of one sort or another, and perfection is about being open.'

As Mike walked up the hill to his car, he wondered why he had changed from how he was then when he was listening to Tommy Storey. Experience of life was meant to open you up, but he knew it hadn't for him; he felt it had made him closed tighter, like a bud in January, nastier.

Why was that? Or was it obvious? He knew he had become a bitter man, and that others didn't like it. It was like having bad breath.

Tommy Storey had said, 'Since you're stuck with having to listen to me, I'll tell you the story that we used to tell each other when we were students. We'd sit around stoned, and listen to the Grateful Dead, then after a while, someone would put on that fat Irish chap, the one who sings like a washing machine, Van something, followed by Leonard Cohen. You can't lift a finger after Leonard Cohen, "Bird on the Wire", he's so depressing. We'd just sit there and mope.'

He broke off and stared into the distance. 'And then someone would always tell this story; I'll tell it to you. There's a Zen sword fight. The two contestants take up their positions holding their swords, ready to go for it. As the two swordsmen face up to each other, they're being watched by a Zen master. The two fighters are motionless, about to begin, and then the Zen master gets up and walks away. "But, master, why are you leaving before the contest?" some pupil asks. "Because the contest is already over," the Zen master says.'

Tommy stopped, he looked at Mike.

Nothing. Then: 'The point is, he knew, he knew without watching, he didn't have to wait. You should always do it that way, because what you are waiting for has already happened. Probably.'

He knew he had seen the man in the clinic before. He had only the shortest glimpse, but where? He set out to remember. Not trying, but waiting for the information to come, trusting it was there, like Tommy Storey had taught him, because everything he had ever experienced was in his head. Including all the pain and anger.

It was like listening quietly to a jumble of noise, but knowing that in a moment he would hear a name out from the noise. He reached the car, beige-coloured, nondescript, full of papers, paper bags scrunched up where he had eaten a cheese roll. Some plastic cups. He put the key in the lock. Billy Burns. That was it.

He turned the key, opened the door and got in the car. In the witness box. The one who had tried to protect Jimmy Reilly. The man with the bad criminal record. I wonder what he's doing here?

Billy Burns saw the doctor. It wasn't the first time he had been to the clinic, but normally the doctor came to him, to see him with his grandchild.

'I've come about the interim report you gave the social for the court. What you say in it – you can't say that about me. What do you know about it anyway?'

He was angry, trying to get it right, not losing his temper. Dr Karenin looked at him. She had to handle this right.

'Mr Burns. My speciality is children. What children do is, they grow up. That's what your granddaughter is doing.'

'I mean, what do you know about what it is to look after her?'

'You tell me.'

'I already have.'

'Tell me again.'

As he spoke his anger started ebbing away, 'She was up four times yesterday, and she didn't fall over, not once. I've got a really good woman who started with me and she understands her already.'

He carried on, trying to hold it all together, sure of himself, but knowing he was facing something he couldn't really deal with, he had no experience of it.

'How was her temper, Mr Burns?'

'She's the loveliest thing. She really is, Doctor. But she gets angry, you must understand that. Why not? Of course she does, why should she not be angry?'

82

'Who deals with her then?'

'I do. I can't let an agency nurse do that. She can be too strong, though she doesn't look it.'

'And if you're not there?'

'Well, I always am. And if I'm not I have someone.'

'That's difficult, Mr Burns, because you cannot always be sure to be there.'

'I know it. I know it. But that's no reason to take her away. Where would you put her anyway, who would look after her like I do?'

'Have you had any contact with your daughter?'

He looked away. 'No. I haven't heard. Nor from the father. The last I knew, they were staying in some druggy hotel in Brighton.' He sat silent for a time. 'I don't blame them, you know. Drugs. What can you do?'

Dr Karenin sat silent. He was beginning to talk – talk lets the anger come out slowly.

'She was never able to settle down, and then later using alcohol a lot. You know I brought her up after her mother left. When I could.'

'Did you ever talk to your daughter about her mother?'

'I tried to avoid it.'

'Mr Burns,' she said, giving him time to accept a new idea, 'did you know that we find that people repeat the mistakes their parents made – even if they don't know about them?'

'No?' He was surprised.

'They do.'

'Sounds like magic to me. How can they repeat what they know nothing about? My daughter didn't know her mother was an alcoholic. That was years ago, before she was old enough to understand anything.'

'It may sound like magic. Maybe that's because it is a bit like magic, but it's the case. Even if they don't know, they repeat the pattern, it happens.'

'It sounds like rubbish to me.'

'OK, Mr Burns. But you come here, sit here where I sit, and see what I see, and you'll agree, you'll see it. I see it all the time. I don't have to explain things, all I do is take them into account. It happens. It has happened in your daughter's case.'

'You mean you make your decisions based on stuff like that?'

'If you want me to say yes, I'll say yes. But it's based on experience of such stuff as that. What you see depends on where you sit. You know that.'

Billy Burns did understand that. But who has sufficient detachment to allow another person's view of their life to take the place of their own?

He said, 'You'll not take this child from me. Everyone else has gone. You'll not have this one.'

'It isn't me doing it, Mr Burns. It's the judge who decides that.' The case would go to court, no doubt about it.

'But it's you the judge listens to. I've seen that.'

'I tell him what I think. I do not make the decision.'

'I know you doctors. I read about you in the papers. You think you're little gods, but now we know you're not. You'll not take this child. She only has me.'

He stood up, accidentally knocking the chair backwards, but the violence didn't penetrate the steady gaze of the woman opposite him.

'Jennet.'

'Yes, Dr Karenin?'

'Please let me know in advance if Mr Burns comes again. And do not let him in without an appointment. If he stays despite that, then call security.' Dr Karenin watched as the white van left the clinic car park.

'Was he difficult, Doctor?'

'No.' She turned towards the reception desk. 'Not difficult. He was upset though.' Her eyes fixed on Jennet. 'How are you?'

Jennet could never deal with that cool look, it always turned her inside out.

'All right Doctor. I'm all right.' But she had to tell her. 'I've been asked out. I have to tell you, since I met him here. You said that to us.'

'That's good. Someone nice?'

'It was that Mike, that policeman. He asked me out, tonight, to Jelly's. Me and Tim.'

'Jelly's is the children's hamburger place?'

'Yes.'

'How did he know about Tim?'

'He saw the photo.'

'And he said, bring the boy?'

'Yeah. I said Mam couldn't look after him today, and he said bring him too.'

'Well, have a good time, Jennet. Thank you for telling me.'

Dr Karenin wondered what it was the policeman wanted. Was it Jennet? She was an attractive woman after all. Or was it the little boy? Or, again, was it to find out what Jennet knew? There was no reason to tell Jennet what she was thinking and she just added it to the knowledge she carried round with her. People are not always what they seem, you have to be careful, and with her patients and the people she dealt with that was mostly true. Even the authorities were devious. It affected the way she saw everybody – she saw the skull beneath the skin. Who was it said that? Eliot? This knowledge was her share of other people's pain and her share of their confusion; part of the information that was dumped on her during clinics; stuff you can't give away, all you can do is try to wash it off when you get home, hope none of it still

85

sticks when you step out of the shower. Sometimes she found herself shaking her clothes out over the bathtub as she took them off.

She had been taught to do that as a junior doctor, though when she did it then it had been to get rid of the lice that she might have picked up on home visits. Her training had taken her to places so poor that even London couldn't compete, and the habit had stuck with her all these years later. It wasn't that what she dealt with was dirty, but that the burden she was taking on grew and grew, and as it grew it made the world more tangled. So now people, who didn't see what she saw, seemed merely to be sleepwalking among horrors.

Jennet went home. Richard, the senior psychologist, went home.

The secretaries disappeared. The passages emptied.

The lights were turned off. The clinic emptied. Soon the building fell silent. For a moment the alarm began to arm itself, then it stopped and Grace's door opened. Angie stuck her head in. 'You still here, Grace? Richard said you would be. We nearly set the full alarm, but since you're here, we'll only set the main rooms. We're off now. See you.'

'See you.'

She was alone.

Dr Karenin began dictating. 'Mr Burns insists he is capable of looking after his granddaughter. The child is able only sometimes to manage for herself, but otherwise, for long periods of time, she is confined to her bed. She is in constant danger of an epileptic attack and cannot be left alone. Mr Burns receives no medical help beyond a prescription, which helps reduce the likelihood of the child having a fit. He attends to all her needs. It is difficult to overstate his love for her.

'Other influences on her are minimal. Her parents are

86

not in contact. Since she was born, addicted to the drugs her mother took during her pregnancy, they have seen her only a few times. I have not been able to interview them, either for the purposes of my main report, or for the purposes of this interim summary.'

Dr Karenin spoke into a dictaphone while walking slowly up and down her room. The light outside had gone, and now she could see her own reflection in the dark windows. She paused to draw the curtains, aware that she was alone in the building. She went on: 'I am not concerned over the information I have been supplied with about Mr Burns's past, and his involvement in criminal activities. I do not see how this could have any effect upon his ability to care for the child.'

She referred to the question in the letter from the social services. 'I am, however, asked whether I consider the child to be at risk of significant harm.' She had been about to say, I consider there is a danger, when a noise outside the window interrupted her. She listened. Nothing.

Her attention returned to Mr Burns. As far as she could make out he had been a long-term criminal, certainly he had been in prison when his own daughter was born, and for much of her childhood he wasn't there. So whose fault was the present situation? His or his daughter's? Mr Burns's wife had died very young, probably from alcohol poisoning. That might equally be the source of the daughter's addiction. Nobody could say, although if she had to bet on it, she would have said it was. But such a conclusion was only relevant if the people involved are able to use the information to help themselves, to see what is happening to them, to see how outside influences mingle with what they are already.

People don't want to see that, or are unable to.

How could Mr Burns deal with the idea that what he was doing now was motivated by the need to make up for his previous neglect? He wouldn't accept that, why should he? He would say what he felt, what he felt directly. What he felt was love for the child, and for him that justified anything.

She carried on dictating. 'The danger is this: that as the child grows Mr Burns will be less able to meet her needs. She will not remain a child, even though she will not be able to look after herself like an adult. The effect of this relationship, as she approaches adolescence, will be harmful to her. It will significantly affect her well-being. The court will have to decide whether that is significant harm, but I am unable to alter my previous conclusions.'

There was someone outside the window, she thought she heard a voice. The building was set in a patch of scrub on the top of a hill, well back from the road, and beneath it there was a large park. Anyone could get in at the back, there was only an old fence between the clinic and the park. She moved to pull the curtain back, but realised that she would see nothing and would become completely visible to anyone outside.

An object fell to the ground and there was the sound of breaking glass. As the sound died away, it was replaced with the blip, blip of the building alarm. In about thirty seconds the siren would go off. Outside the window she could hear feet kicking in the gravel. Two sets of sounds, two people running. A voice shouted something, it was moving away. She turned the light off and stepped to the window, pulling the curtain back. Nothing.

She tried to remember what to do, the building manager had explained what happened when the alarm went off. The central company were telephoned, and then they rang the keyholders; she tried to remember who they were. Then she remembered. Of course, one of the numbers was her own mobile phone. She took it from her bag, put it on the desk and waited.

Two things happened at the same time. The full alarm sounded as the warning beeping ended, and she heard footsteps in the corridor outside her room. The light in the passage went on. So they hadn't run off. Or at least they had come back immediately and were now inside the building. There was a whispered conversation, and then one voice said, just in a pause during the pulsing alarm, 'With that noise? We could shout if we wanted to.' Another voice said, 'It'll stop soon.'

She knew they were right, that was another thing the building manager had said, the alarm just stops after a while. She sat looking at the mobile phone on the desk in front of her. It was a strange position to be in.

Then the door to her room opened. Two young men stood looking at her. One of them wore a rudimentary mask, which he tugged at nervously. She had been lit up by the light from the passage and they were as taken aback as she was. Each of the men looked a little dazed, and in the one who was not masked she recognised the distancing effect of drugs. She had been used to that in casualty.

One of them swayed backwards on his heels. Then they took a decision and stepped into the room. As they did so the mobile phone rang, vibrating on the desk, slowly beginning to spin. It was the movement of the handset, rather than the sound, that seemed to intrude, as though yet another person had entered the room. She picked it up.

She was aware that the young men would hear only her side of what was said. She leaned back in the chair; they would not be able to reach her over the desk in time.

'Yes,' she said talking straight through the burglar alarm company's routine questions, 'I am in the building now. Two men have come into my room. They do not seem to have weapons.'

The operator who had rung her was still asking her to confirm who she was.

'Yes,' Dr Karenin said, looking up and seeing a metal spike, 'one of them does, he has a steel bar. I would be obliged if you could send the police immediately.'

She found herself very calm, and as long as the calm remained it seemed to act as a kind of barrier between her and the men. Boys, they were hardly men. They were in that indeterminate area where they had more strength than they knew what to do with.

'You'd better leave,' she said to them.

'Why?'

'The police are on their way.'

At that very moment they could hear a siren. She had often heard police cars coming up the hill. This one was.

'Stay if you wish,' she said, 'and explain the broken window.'

In a movement exactly like horses wheeling away from a gate, they suddenly jumped away from her and pushed each other out of the door. She could hear them galloping down the passage. There was a crunching noise as they hit the gravel outside the window and their footsteps disappeared. So did the siren. It was going down the other side of the hill now, exactly as it always did, but the two men wouldn't hear that. She could hear them crashing into the bushes in the other direction.

She sat at her desk, her heart thudding, the phone in front of her. But she had no one to call and she didn't want to speak to the voice that had saved her.

It was still saying, 'Could you confirm your name, please?'

Chapter 5

Scott did not have to wait long for a call from John Hector, it came two days later. Perhaps this was going to work.

'I think I found something about it. There's a group that meets in the Badham Church which calls itself a victim group or something like that. I went there, the pub you told me about, the River Anchor, and asked about a bit, I know one or two people there. I produced the story that you gave me, and one of them told me to go there. There was a bit of joking about money. I didn't go any further. The only other thing was, they said, say Billy sent you. From what I hear it may be something to do with what you are looking for. I didn't go any further, things might have got a bit hairy, it had that feel about it, you know?'

'Billy Burns?'

'I don't know who Billy is. Just that, "Billy sent you".'

'Thanks, John. Thanks a lot.'

Scott didn't think he looked much like a victim, but then what do victims look like? Depressed probably. He went along.

Apparently this week's meeting of the Victims Support Group was not as well attended as usual – to get a real crowd it needed an event, or a headline. Scott was told that the Thursday meeting, the one after the release of the killers of that small child in Liverpool, had been very full.

A man with a badge on his lapel that said 'Greeter' told Scott, 'We sent messages of solidarity. We had a speech from Mothers against Murder, and a short recording of the voice of the dead child's mother – full of anger and, yes, it must be said, hate, but well-directed hate, creative hate, is good.'

He adopted a singsong tone, caused, Scott guessed, by constant repetition. 'We should of course encourage forgiveness, but we also find that weakness adopts the pretence of mercy so often that we must always be on our guard and when we find it drive it out – mercilessly. As was well put, there should be a little less said about understanding and a little more condemnation.'

Scott had been met at the door.

'Welcome to our meeting. Part of the Badham ministry,' the greeter had said. Scott didn't enquire what the Badham ministry was, though the clean-cut, suited figure fitted a clear picture in his mind. Mormons? There was certainly the same sheen about the man, the bright smile, determinedly maintained in the face of a hundred doorstep rejections.

'To hear a mother bewail the death of her child, and maintain such steadfast contempt for the society which allowed that death, which even encouraged it, was most moving. We expected a crowd that day and we got it. Today though is just a normal meeting.'

It was this same man who eventually addressed the group. It was clear he was speaking to people whom he did not think needed converting, only reassurance.

'We are sick of the liberal elite running the so-called justice system. On the one hand a driver who kills three people on the motorway is sentenced to three years' imprisonment, while a farmer merely defending his prop-

92

erty is sent to prison for life. Killers on the roads are let off scot-free, while those merely defending their own are punished. Why cannot a man defend himself? Again and again the victim is unprotected.

'You may remember that we have previously listened to Mr John Bercow MP, a spokesman on home affairs, here is what he has said.' The speaker held up what was clearly a newspaper cutting. '"There are a lot of judges who seem to have not the slightest awareness of, or interest in, the sensitivities of the mass of British people. This is constantly revealed in the judgements they hand down, and in the extraordinary insouciance with which they regard quite bestial activities." These are not remarks lightly made, ladies and gentlemen, but the considered words of a member of parliament. We should take notice.'

Scott listened. What bestial activities were they then?

The large modern hall held about eighty people sitting in six or seven rows, crowded together at the front. It was a simple building, white plaster walls and light timber framing. He judged it might seat at least two thousand people. The design was bland, though as an attempt at acknowledgement of its origins there was a stained-glass window set up high in the roof.

Scott had parked his car outside in the huge car park, more suited to an out-of-town supermarket than a church. It did show, however, the attendance they expected, and presumably got, on a Sunday. The large entrance lobby, warm and beautifully lit, was set with noticeboards advertising meetings – there were three that night: Mothers for Christ, and an hour later, Accountancy and the Support of the Lord, and what he was looking for, the Victims Support Group.

'We welcome you,' the greeter said again. 'Have we

been blessed to see you here before?' The tone set his teeth on edge, but Scott was here to find out what he could, not to feel superior.

'No, this is my first time.'

'An exciting moment for you.'

'I am told that there is a victim support group.'

'Ah yes. The victims, they are meeting in our main hall tonight. It's a little large I'm afraid, but we have no other place. Mothers for Christ, you see, have taken our side room.' He pointed to the board. 'However, if you wish you can also stay afterwards when all three groups assemble together at the end of the evening for a moment of joint and assembled prayer.'

'Us, the Mothers and the Accountants. All three?'

'Yes. And tonight there will be a message from Maurice Badham.'

The greeter finished his talk to the group. 'After this address we students will pass amongst you so you can raise individual concerns. Those who are feeling particularly vulnerable should indicate that to one of our students. We can provide greater privacy if you wish.

'We only want you to know that if in some way you have been hurt, or are the object of someone else's victimisation, then we can help. We have two strong arms and we can help.'

The last few words were repeated, clearly they formed a phrase in the organisation. Scott watched apprehensively as he was approached and then engulfed in sincerity. 'We search out those with troubles.' The young woman who spoke to him was carrying a Bible folded in a cloth. 'We seek to put right the wrong that has been done you.'

Her tone became more practical when he told her the story he had prepared. She said, 'Many people come here on other people's behalf. Of course, I should say –' and she looked invitingly at Scott — 'some say they speak for another when it is in fact their own heart that is bruised.' She paused.

Scott did not say his own heart was bruised, but said instead, 'Billy sent me.'

'Oh.'

There was a change of tone.

'We can still of course refer you. And if need be, we do not have to meet the subject of the attack, the real victim, at all. We can offer a solicitor as easily as we can offer guidance. In certain circumstances we can make contact on your behalf with the police. Indeed if it is the power of the press you seek we can introduce you to a friendly journalist.'

'The power of the press sounds attractive,' Scott said. He immediately regretted the repetition of the inane phrase — she might notice the sneer. But the language was apparently so normal to her that she did not regard it as odd.

'Maurice says it is a power that must be used carefully. But it is nevertheless a part of life.' Her round smiling face gazed at him. 'Maurice Badham, that is.'

'Yes,' said Scott. He knew that the moment he asked who he was, then he would get the whole message. So he didn't.

'Are you in a hurry?' She had misinterpreted his uneasiness.

'Well, yes, I am.'

'Then I can fetch the telephone number. All we ask is that if you or your friend feels relief, as a result of what we have done, then you should contact us.'

'Of course. Of course I shall.'

'I shall be a moment only. I have to get permission.'

She went through a door at the side of the hall. Scott sat watching the others. To his left one of the students was huddled with a couple, leaning forward in what looked

95

like prayer. These were needy people, and there was clearly a demand for remedies. It seemed likely to him that this organisation was supplying them, probably at a profit.

'Here is the number.'

The man whom Scott had first met returned, and handed him a card. 'Thank you for coming to us. Will we be seeing you again?'

Scott said, 'I do hope so.' He had found the right note, a kind of effusiveness. 'I have found you and your colleagues most helpful. I think we will find my friend the help he needs.'

It was clear that the man was struggling to place Scott among the more usual type of visitor. He said, 'If you have any more introductions to effect, then please ask for me. My name is Samuel. We can of course deal on the usual terms.'

There it was. 'The usual terms?'

'If we refer directly to the press, there is generally an agency fee for the introduction.'

Scott left the hall only half understanding what had happened. He turned the visiting card over as the bright lights faded behind him, 'The Maurice Badham Ministry', it said in curly copperplate, and underneath, 'Samuel Theodosius, Student'.

Theodosius. He was an Orthodox Emperor, wasn't he?

And, handwritten on the back, was 'Charles Pope', with a mobile telephone number. Pope, it was an apt name.

Scott looked up and saw a public phone marooned by the entrance. It would be better to use that.

'Hello, Charlie Pope here,' a voice said.

'I've been given your number.'

'About?'

'It's a victim support thing.' Even repeating the phrase was slightly distasteful, and Scott slurred the words.

'From Badham's?'

'Yes.'

'Did they tell you that you needed the power of the press?'

'Yup.' Scott decided to sound hardbitten.

'Well, that's me. Is it urgent?'

'Kind of. I might as well get on with it. Where are you?'

'Wapping.'

'Oh.'

'Not Wapping as in the old Murdoch bunker. I'm at Ma Thompsett's. It's on the High Street, just off Gordon's Lane. How long will it take you to get here?'

'An hour, maybe less.'

'OK.'

'How will I know you?'

'You will.'

Scott drove the road back to London; he turned right just before the Dartford crossing and set off down the old thir-ties arterial road. On the left, huge tin-box buildings had been set down in scruffy parking lots. One had been turned into a nightclub. The transformation had been made by leaning some columns up against the tin front and mounting a huge fibreglass horse over them. A neon sign said, 'Caesar's Palace'. Scott used to go to a court in north London built along much the same lines, only above that door it had been a royal coat of arms, tacked up in the same rickety fashion. 'Courts-R-Us.'

Eventually the old road gave way to modern white con-crete banking and Scott plunged into the empty tunnel leading to the city. He emerged at the tunnel entrance under the same sort of horse that had decorated Caesar's

Palace, and a while later turned left into the cobbled streets of Wapping. The whole place looked as though it had been varnished, no doubt to make it more real, like Disneyland. Above him, serried windows of river warehouses had been opened up and balconied – was there such a word? – with wrought iron and geraniums. Smart wine shops had replaced old newsagents.

Ma Thompsett's was a wine bar, wood, sawdust and low lighting. He picked his way down the cellar stairs and instantly saw a man who must be Charles Pope.

He was huge, sitting on a bench, which by his size he made resemble a chair. He had a table on each side, his bulk not allowing one in front of him; on one table there was a bottle and on the other a mobile phone attached to a lap-top computer. As Scott entered the bar he saw the man's eyes flash towards him. Scott crossed the room. The computer beeped and then produced the regular pulsing noise of interference, a mobile phone preparing to make a connection. Pope reached out a hand, it was as big as a foot, and turned the phone off, or at least diverted it. Throughout the conversation that followed the machine received messages.

Scott said, 'Pope? Are you Charlie Pope?'

'Yes.'

'I rang you from outside Badham's meeting place.'

'Have you got a story?'

'They said I should contact you.' Scott was still in the dark, and it seemed best to emphasise that he was doing as he was told.

Charlie Pope said, 'Well, what is it? Sex? Judges? Doctors? Abuse?'

His lips were like rubber rings, and the words seemed to have to negotiate their way past them. The more he spoke, the more his chin and face shone. Occasionally he shook his head and his chins followed the movement slowly, continuing for a while after he had stopped moving his head. Scott watched him fascinated. A sort of fatty nystagmus.

'You deal in all those categories?'

'And more. Well, that's what Morrie Badham's guys normally send, suburban crap, but it's not all I do. All that stuff is a kind of wanking at the best of times. Making sure the photograph of the dead child's parents shows them looking really, really depressed, like the parents of dead children should. What have you got for me?'

He reached behind him and, not asking, he poured out a tumblerful of wine and offered it. Scott realised he was being treated as a colleague. The next remark confirmed it. 'Who are you acting for?'

'They telephoned you?'

'Of course. I keep a residual security and I only work from an introduction. Now, what have you got to tell me?'

The fat man had a habit of holding his hands away from his body, and then curling and uncurling his fingers. On them were rings, embedded in the folds of flesh. Occasionally he arched his chin to ease his collar away from his neck. His size was a continual cause of movement.

Scott wondered about fat men, and whether what was always said in bad novels was true: 'Like many fat men he was very light on his feet.' He took a quick look, and it was right, the man's feet were small and delicate. His shoes weren't patent, but they were made of soft shiny leather, and his feet were crossed neatly beneath the chair. Occasionally when the man's continual motion reached the ends of his legs, he would sweep the sawdust on the floor into small piles, and then spread it out again with short kicks. Do feet get fat? Perhaps they can't, perhaps there was no mechanism for it, nothing to grow fat on, or, like insects, it all happens inside the structure.

Fat grew on everything else. It hung in folds from under

99

his wrist, there was an extra fold on his thigh, reaching up into the groin, and then an extra fold on that. Scott knew that when he walked, his legs would ripple with a bow wave. His trousers contained so many folds that they looked corrugated. There was an extra panel sewn into his coat under the arms, and when he wasn't opening and closing his fingers, Charlie Pope was able to rest his hands on his stomach, much as another man might put them on a table.

He was smoking, using a cigarette holder. Scott realised he had to since, when he took the end of a cigarette from it to stub it out, it disappeared between his fingers like a pin.

'I tend to sit here most of the time now,' Pope said. 'I find it difficult getting about.'

Scott wanted to say, I'm not surprised, but he didn't know him and it was hardly something you could say. He discovered later that such a remark would not have bothered Charlie Pope in the least. His size was incidental to him, much as the weather was; something to be endured, certainly not something for which he might be held responsible. The only responsibility he acknowledged was to deal with the problem sensibly. 'People come to me, not me to them, though not so much now that we have these machines.' He pointed to the computer, which at that very moment was responding to a call. 'So it's a pleasant change when people who are recommended drop in. As you have done.' He paused, then, turning his head slightly sideways and dipping his gleaming forehead, he looked at Scott from under his eyebrows and said, 'A lawyer, I think?'

Scott was so surprised that all he could say was, 'Yes.'

The man began to fit another cigarette into his holder. He had a pleased look on his face.

'You will have to excuse me my little vanity, but I will go further in my guesswork. You have a client for whom you wish to do your best, and like colleagues before you, you have found your way to me. Am I right?' He sat back in his chair, presenting a huge mound towards Scott on top of which was balanced a vast chin with a broad smile. He puffed on his cigarette and the fingers of his other hand worked among each other.

'Yes. You have it exactly right,' Scott said. Then, taking advantage of Charlie Pope's moment of triumph, he had time to add: 'But I'm not here officially. I haven't even asked the client.'

'Ah.'

'So I can't tell you very much.'

'What's the problem?'

Scott had half prepared himself. 'It seems the police are unwilling to prosecute.'

'Why?'

'Who knows? It's a sexual offence. Normally they can't do it quick enough.'

'Is there a child involved?'

'Young man, not twenty yet. He was a child at the time.'

'Which police station?'

'East Place.'

'I know them. But what do you want from our meeting?'

'Well, what kind of things can you do to help?'

Charlie Pope looked at Scott, and for a moment Scott thought he was going to be discovered lying. But any game of deception involves coping with the feeling that the other side has found you out, and after a moment it became clear Charlie Pope had no suspicions.

'Do you practise in the criminal law?'

'Occasionally.'

'But this is, in your opinion, a criminal thing.'

'Yes.'

'Well, what we do is let the police know that the press

might be interested, and naturally that is to the policeman's advantage, and will in turn stimulate his interest in doing the right thing for society. Are you able to give me an outline of the events?'

'I don't think so, not yet.'

'I understand that. I'll tell you what happens. But your client would have to agree to our terms.'

'Of course. I'll have to come back after I have spoken to him.'

Scott had cleared a space just to chat to this man.

Pope said, 'The only way I could raise any interest would be if we had a contract for an interview with him, or if it's a child, with the mother. And the contract would have to involve the policeman as a beneficiary. If it's a girl of course the offender has to be a celebrity.'

'You mean the police get paid to prosecute?'

Charlie Pope looked at Scott. 'Yes, pay the policeman. Witnesses can always be paid money and often are. After all, we are not paying him to prosecute – we are paying for an interview about the case, allowing him to express his thoughts and feelings of distaste and horror. Of course he won't get to do the interview if there is no prosecution, no successful prosecution, that is. As for payment, the only stipulation the courts make is that the defence should be told that there is a contract.'

'That would make it pointless.'

'No, no. It's not a great problem. It's not our job to tell the defence, so it doesn't affect us.'

'Whose job is it?'

'The policeman's.'

'You mean the policeman you are paying?'

'Yes.'

'But he's not going to tell anyone.'

'No, he's not, is he?' Charlie Pope's grin grew wider at the pleasing simplicity of it. It was extraordinary to hear

102

how what Scott treated as serious and important rules were so easily disregarded.

'But the courts demand—'

'First the defence have to find out, which isn't very likely, but even if they do the courts aren't particularly interested. A conviction is a conviction, and if there is a technical fault the appeal court will itself go on to decide whether the defendant was guilty. You must have heard them say it: "We have decided despite this that the jury would still have convicted . . ." It's only in very unusual cases that they do anything else.' Again he smiled at the simplicity of it. 'Anyway, if they didn't turn down appeals, the court of appeal would have to double in size, the amount of appeals would demand it. And more judges means less status. They wouldn't like that.'

Scott heard echoes of what he had written in his advice to Mr Reilly.

Charlie Pope said, 'When the court does interfere, that's normally because the press have been involved on the side of the defendant.' Charlie Pope leaned sideways and tapped Scott on the knee. 'The odd thing about you lot, the thing you lot got wrong, you lawyers—' He stopped. 'I trust you don't mind me telling you this? I have a bit of a bee in my bonnet about it.'

'No, no,' said Scott.

'Well. You had one thing in your favour and you threw it away. That was your respect for the rules. Everybody knew where they stood. But then you all started bending the rules. The courts didn't think the old-fashioned application of the law looked modern enough, not user-friendly. Lord Denning started it. That was about the time I set out covering the courts. I used to be a court reporter. In those days I got round a bit more. You remember Lord Denning?'

Scott nodded.

'Of course you do. For instance, he knew that nobody likes banks, so who cares if he finds some odd reason to find the case against them. That's how he became the "people's judge". That's what he was called. Bluebell time! The press loved it, I used to write that stuff, but once it had started, it went on, off into the other courts, into the criminal court of appeal 'specially, who now will twist the law to get any result they want.

'Nobody is much interested in someone who's been convicted, so no one minds when the courts say, "He would have been convicted anyway, never mind the rules. We'll bend it a bit to keep him convicted."'

'It's not as bad as that.' Scott was surprised to find himself defending them.

'It is. As I say, I used to cover the courts. In those days, barristers, the police, the whole system was independent, nobody interfered with them. But you've been bought now. The victim lobby, the *Daily Mail*, television reporters – they've bought you out. You're frightened of appearing elitist, or some such twaddle. Extraordinary. The judges are frightened of being laughed at because of the way they dress. Good God!'

Scott wondered what it was that Charlie Pope was regretting, what lost times he was looking back to. Or was his attitude only the normal regret that everybody has for standards that have changed? On the other hand, maybe he was right.

Charlie Pope said, 'Who cares? Victims, that's where the money is. Now I'm on the victim's side and believe me, it's a damn good living.'

Scott had only to keep him talking.

'More wine?' Scott said, and he went to the bar. He ordered another bottle and paid for it.

The barman said, 'Will you be eating?' and then to explain he added, 'We're about to bring Mr Pope his meal.'

104

Scott ordered some cheese, and said to the fat man, 'They told me you were going to eat, so I ordered something.'

'By all means, dear boy. As I said, it's good to have someone to chat to. Where was I?'

Scott relaxed. Not only did he think that this man knew what Scott wanted to know, but he was willing to tell anybody who would keep him company for a while.

'Victims,' Scott said. 'Lucrative stuff. You were saying.'

'Well, it's so easy. If you think I'm a bit angry it's only because it's all changed since I started out. When I was a young journalist I would never have been allowed to get away with what is written nowadays. But national newspapers weren't owned by pornographers then; megalomaniacs yes, but not pornographers. Did you know the *Daily Express* appointed a director, a director mind you, whose only role was to buy snatched photographs of famous people? I ask you.'

His body heaved, perhaps anger, perhaps amusement.

Scott said, 'You were saying about victims.'

'Yes. You've only to turn on a radio to hear it. Some young reporter finds an issue, there's no attempt to say, one side is saying this, the other that . . . all that's old fashioned, who wants to know? So now one side is a victim, the other the oppressor: a surgeon or the doctor. And of course, such people have professional rules, they can't answer back.'

His food arrived.

Scott was surprised to see the restraint – a plate of beef sandwiches, but in moments it disappeared, to be replaced by another.

They allowed the wine to affect them, and Scott began to relax. 'And this victim support group I went to . . .'

'That's not the only one. There are dozens and they all refer cases to me. I thought of setting up a commercial organisation, calling it Victims Direct. But you couldn't really advertise that sort of thing, could you?' Charlie Pope shook with laughter. His shoulders vibrated in waves.

'But this group?'

'The one that sent you? Well, how did you find out about it?'

'Some people in a pub suggested I go.'

'Which pub?'

'The River Anchor.'

'Oh yes?' Charlie Pope looked up sharply.

'Yes. I think it's called that. I was recommended by someone who spoke to someone there.'

'You've never been there?' He seemed to relax again.

'No. Just a pub, isn't it?'

'It was one of the first. To begin with they used to deal in criminal injuries compensation, help present the claim to prevent a knockback.'

'What do you mean?'

'A refusal. The main reason for refusal was that it was your fault you got beaten up or whatever. The association clause it got called. If you associate with people who are inclined to smash glasses into people's faces, then that's your problem, you can't complain if it happens to you. So the claim has to be cleaned up a bit, and for that you need advice. I used to advise. There's a bit of cash in it and it still runs well, though like everything it has its fashions. Sexual assault on children is quite well paid, and nowadays not so difficult to prove. That's something your client ought to know.'

Scott thought it was about time he joined in. 'You know, the way you're talking, it's astonishing, I didn't know I was born.' He slopped his glass slightly, a man a little affected by the drink. The movement encouraged Charlie Pope even further.

'Ah, but that's what we need. We need that, we need you to be naive. It's a market out there, people say it's a

106

jungle, but they're wrong. It's a market. Hayek got it right. Thatcher got that right. Everything is for sale. Ah, here we are.' He looked up, his food had arrived. The plates of sandwiches were only a beginning.

Chapter 6

Two young men were found tied up in the woods beneath Dr Karenin's clinic.

They refused to say who had left them there, or why they should be naked, so by the time Mike Reynolds saw the intelligence circular it had been classified 'no suspect, no crime'.

But for Mike that meant three things had happened, connected with the clinic: the guy who had burnt his floorboards, next Billy Burns, now this. 'If you pay no attention twice, at least do so the third time even if they are all unconnected.' Tommy Storey again. The clinic seemed to be inviting his attention.

Mike thought about Billy Burns. He had got hold of his criminal record after the trial; Billy Burns was the real thing. Now he looked at it again in the light of the tie-up. Yes, there was a connection. Burns had been involved in something very similar in the past. Could the young men in the woods be his work? What was he doing, protecting the clinic?

Burns's contact with the law went back to the early seventies. After the usual juvenile courts, detention centre, borstal training, he had progressed to jump-ups, and then finally the front man, the first man into the bank with the gun. In those days there would be only two or three people operating in London at any one time who were capable of that – it was very special. You need to be a fully in-control psychopath to walk into a room full of strangers showing a sawn-off shotgun, telling them to get the fuck on the floor – and not in a nice way, but in a way they would believe in. Not many could do that then. In some parts of London you would never have to buy a drink if you could do that.

Mike Reynolds read down the list of offences and suspected offences. All of it was professional crime. Two hijacks off the A109, just near the sandwich stop where you could buy and sell the load twice while waiting to steal it.

And there was a punishment beating: a man who had sold Burns a car which was to be used for an armed robbery down Kingston way. The car had been pulled over when Burns was driving it, discovered to be reported stolen, searched and the police found a robbery kit. None of that would have happened if the car had been clean as it should have been. Burns was eventually convicted of handling the car, although he was acquitted of the robbery. But while he was in custody awaiting trial, the man who sold him the car had been found tied to a tree in the scrubby garden opposite the prison. He said he'd been attacked, but he wouldn't say how, nor why he had no clothes on. It was never proved against Burns but it was kept on the file.

Then there was a gap of some years. Burns seemed to have gone silent, nothing had been entered. No doubt a judge would say that for some years he had led a life without crime, but Mike Reynolds knew that doesn't happen. They never change. Billy Burns had only got better, and more careful.

There was nothing known up-to-date, save two things. There'd been an enquiry from Dutch police. Why was that? Reynolds remembered what Burns had said about going to Holland, about their being better plumbers, was that connected? It must be, too much of a coincidence. The message from Holland was a routine request for his criminal record, no reason given.

And finally, and this was an interesting piece, he had informed against his own daughter on a drugs charge. She'd been arrested and convicted of possession of crack cocaine, she and her boyfriend. Reynolds recognised the name of a political family, double-barrelled, very famous. So there had been family trouble, and it was at the family clinic that Reynolds had seen Burns.

Nothing happens by chance.

Mike Reynolds went to see Grace Karenin again – the serious crime squad were insisting.

'Our man, the signalman, has been travelling. He goes out to the country, and wanders around. It seems odd he doesn't take the child. And we still haven't found his wife.' He was still trying to persuade the doctor to help, without seeming to be climbing down.

'What we would like to know is, what was he doing? He's not a man for travelling much. We think he's a black-bag man.'

Grace Karenin had to say, 'Why are you coming to see me? I can tell you nothing.'

'We thought you ought to know about it. Now that the man is actually coming to the clinic.'

'All right.'

'After all, it can't be very nice talking to someone who murdered his wife.'

'That happens,' said Grace Karenin.

'It can't be very pleasant for your staff either.'

Grace Karenin thought about Jennet. This policeman had come on to her, they had gone out together. She hoped Jennet was being discreet.

110

'Please don't worry about my staff. We're trained to deal with these things, Mr Reynolds.'

'Call me Mike.'

She said nothing. She did not say, call me Grace.

He said, 'You mean you train them?'

'Yes, I train them. That's how I know they can manage. And anyway people come here for help, not to harm us. We help them.'

'You don't get any trouble then?'

'Not often,' she said, 'but occasionally.'

'Like those two kids they found in the woods.'

'I heard about that and wondered whether that was anything to do with us in the clinic. The last time you were here, that same night, we had a break-in and that was two young men. The incident down in the woods was only a few days later.'

'You saw the two men at the clinic?'

'Yes. They came into my room.'

'And what did you do?'

'I told them they'd better leave.'

'And did they?'

'Yes, they did.'

'Did they offer violence?'

'What a quaint way of putting it, Mr Reynolds. Young men like that offer violence by getting out of bed in the morning. That's what young men do, unless they have had the luck to have a good father.'

'Did you report it?'

'No, not separately. There didn't seem any point. Nothing was taken, and what could the police do?'

'You should have reported it.'

'Please do not tell me what I should or should not have done, Mr Reynolds. The hospital was fully informed. If the management wish to call the police they may do so. It is not my decision.'

He was a little shaken by that. So he found himself mentioning Billy Burns. It was another mistake. 'Billy Burns was here the night I came as well.'

'I will not discuss people who come here with you, Mr Reynolds.'

'Did you know he was – is a dangerous man?'

'I will not discuss it with you, Mr Reynolds.'

Silence, which she broke. 'The people we treat are sometimes dangerous, Mr Reynolds. Young people we try to help sometimes turn out to be very disturbed. We see people who are hurt, and we see the people who do the hurting. They are two sides of the same problem.'

'I wonder if Billy Burns was anything to do with those two who broke in. Perhaps they were the same two who were tied up.'

Grace Karenin said nothing.

She had talked to the man who was suspected of murdering his wife. He had been seen burning something in his backyard. A neighbour had told the police. The mattress was gone. There were no bedclothes in the house at all, he had no explanation for that. 'They just disappeared with her, Doctor.'

He didn't know where his wife was. 'They think I murdered her, you know,' he said, smiling at the doctor. Grace Karenin sat quietly, taking notes; she had said very little and in the quiet the man had found himself talking.

'They think I murdered her and put her body in a black bag.'

He waited for the doctor to ask, 'And did you?' But she did not; she said nothing. But when later DC Reynolds said he's a black-bag man, she understood what was meant.

'She drank, you know,' the man said.

At a small table on the other side of the room a small child drew pictures of her absent mother, and then tore

112

them to pieces, hiding the bits in corners of the room, behind the furniture.

Over the next few days the doctor found them, and when she did so, she filed them away with the notes she had made of his visit.

Jennet knew Mike Reynolds had an appointment that day. She had arranged things so she wasn't behind the reception desk when he arrived.

She didn't want to see him before he went in to see the doctor; she would make sure she was there afterwards. Dr Karenin had already spoken to Jennet about her contact with Mike. Well, not directly, but she had said something which fitted the subject, and had looked at Jennet as she said it. It was at a staff meeting.

They had all been drinking coffee. Jennet liked this time when they were all together, all part of the team. Then Dr Karenin had repeated what she had often said before, 'We all have complete responsibility for whatever our job is; we are all equal in that, the most important thing of all. And one of our duties is this. Staff must not speak about who comes here to anyone, not even to confirm that someone does or does not come to the clinic. I don't. You don't.' She looked at Jennet, and then she added: 'Nor does Richard here. Do you, Richard?' Turning to him.

Everyone laughed.

It was what Grace had intended and it took the edge off what she was saying, because Richard was the biggest gossip of them all, as well as being the only man, or rather, almost the only man, because there were two male social workers in a different building.

'What, me?' Richard said, understanding exactly what Grace was using him for. He was, after all, a psychologist.

'Yes, you Richard,' said Dr Grace. The others called her

that. 'Now we'll start the medical meeting, so we'll see everybody else later.'

Jennet knew she should not talk about what happened at the clinic to Mike Reynolds. Anyway, that was easy since Mike Reynolds hadn't asked her. But she made sure she was there when he came out from seeing the doctor. He saw her at the desk inside the main door.

'I wondered where you were,' he said. 'I thought you were avoiding me.'

'No, of course I wasn't. I had something to do.'

'Well, we had a good time, didn't we?'

'Tim loved it. I couldn't get him to bed that night, he was jumping around so much.' Jennet hoped she was saying it properly, so he really heard her, and not overdoing it. She worried that she wasn't getting it right. He didn't want to hear about Tim, or at least, she shouldn't always go on about how Tim felt. She had really enjoyed herself, that was the bit she had to get out properly. 'I haven't had such a good time for years.' That was wrong as well, too, something wrong with it. It sounded as though she was complaining about her life. 'You're good company,' she said.

That was right. Her mam said a man likes it when he is praised.

She had already told the others in the office about him. He was a kind man. And they had all agreed how good it is when a man is just kind to you. That's not very common.

He said, 'I'm glad Tim liked it. You tell him from me that we'll go on that water thing again.'

She laughed. 'He was so frightened. It worried me, but . . . but when you took him, he was all right.'

'He was brave, Jennet. He's a good little kid.'

Mike was aware that they were talking at the reception desk in full view and that other people were going to and fro. He wanted to say how good she looked, even maybe

114

touch her arm, but it was too public a place. The phone rang, she picked it up. 'Yes, Dr Karenin.' Her attention went to a file.

He noticed every small thing she did. How quickly and efficiently she dealt with the file. It was in the colours of the clinic, 'Confidential' marked on it, full of papers, letters. As she opened it, the leaves concertinaed back, and he saw some drawings at the back. He liked the way she was proud of her job. He meant as in she took a pride in it, he didn't mean she was boastful or anything. She took a pride in being part of the team, and that was very special.

She was talking, but he wasn't listening, he was looking at her. She was a beautiful woman, but not beautiful in the way film stars are. She was like, like . . .available, but not in the wrong way, not at all, that was the wrong word. In fact, she was very proper. How lucky he hadn't said that out loud. What he meant was, she was not unavailable, like a film star was. No, the word he had meant to find was open – open, honest and real. He could imagine touching her. He knew what would happen if he did, at least to him. He wanted to put his hand on her right now. But he didn't know her well enough yet, it would come later, and anyway that wasn't the most important thing.

Meanwhile he had to get it right, not frighten her away, like the others. So he said, just to say something, even change the subject. 'Does Dr Karenin lecture anywhere?'

'Oh yes, she's always off teaching. She teaches in London and at the College. They call it the College, the Royal College of Psychiatrists in central London. She's a fellow, FRCPsych, you know, one of the youngest they say. I have to type that at the bottom of the letters. They all have to take the exam eventually. Young Dr Usborne is going to take it soon, though at the moment Dr Karenin is our top one.'

'No, I meant, does she teach other people, outside of doctors?' He wanted to say policemen, but he couldn't, he was worried she might laugh and say, Why policemen? Or, What can you teach policemen? Something like that. Why was he worried about that? Then he remembered they hadn't talked about his being a policeman at all.

'Sometimes she does,' she said, frowning as she thought about it. 'She's giving a lecture next week. Now when is that?' She turned to the computer and hit a button. Then a voice behind them said, 'Jennet. I'm sorry to interrupt.' Jennet looked up.

Mike looked round. It was Dr Karenin. She must have seen him getting the receptionist to look in her personal diary. But he hadn't, he had only asked an easy question, and it was Jennet who had turned to the computer.

'Yes, Doctor?'

What had happened didn't seem to worry Jennet.

'I'd better take that file now. He'll be here later and I won't have time to go over it otherwise.' She took the floppy green file from the desk. Mike noticed her arm, brown and slim. She was carrying a fountain pen in her other hand, and she smiled white teeth at him as she leaned over to get it. 'Goodbye then, officer,' she said, dismissing him.

She probably hadn't heard anything, most likely didn't realise that they were talking about her. But what did that goodbye mean? She wanted to get rid of him. He was at a loss. He said, 'Goodbye, Dr Karenin. Goodbye, Jennet,' and left the building.

And as he walked out through the gates he reminded himself that he was not part of this at all. He had his own team, his own place, he needed to concentrate on his own ideas, he didn't need to get involved. He was always telling himself that, he could manage quite happily on his own.

★

116

'What was he asking?' said Grace Karenin.

'He was asking do you lecture.'

'Why did he want to know that?'

'He's very interested in what we do.'

Jennet wanted to tell the doctor how nice he was. But it was difficult, you felt so transparent. Sometimes she seemed to look right through you, and then she did it again. She asked, 'And did you have a good time the other evening?'

'Yes. And he got on really well with Tim.'

'That's good, Jennet. He seems to be a kind man. You can't beat that, can you?'

Jennet felt good all through. She stared after the doctor. She knew about things before you say them, maybe that's what being a psychiatrist meant, but really it was just because she thought about other people.

But she wondered about Dr Karenin herself: was she lonely? She seemed so self-contained – that's a description one of the other girls used. They talked about her, and about how much responsibility she had to carry, and how she did it all on her own. Did she have someone to talk to? No one had ever seen anyone with her. Jennet said to the girls that she thought she was lonely, and the girls laughed. 'No. She's far too much in control.'

But they were wrong.

Dr Karenin looked up at the clock. The clinic was silent again, everybody gone.

In her memory she could replay the sound of breaking glass that had announced the young men's arrival, and she knew that if it wasn't happening here, then the same thing was happening somewhere else, out in the turmoil, as people vented their pain. She began to pack her things to go home.

First her diary with her appointments – pieces of paper

117

with notes, messages, permission requests, telephone numbers, emergency contacts and colleagues' home numbers all spilling from it. Two files for tomorrow afternoon's home visits. Another thick ring binder, one of a set of three, the other two on her desk at home ready for the court attendance in the morning; her keys, a scarf. She paused over another set of notes. The Burns file needed updating with the policeman's visit, although it would be difficult to know how she should record it. Since they were public, in certain circumstances patients could demand to see them. But if she left it out, what would happen if it became known that the police had been, or if she needed to confirm she had said nothing? She didn't take the file; the problem would have to wait.

The most urgent thing she had on hand now was the child, admitted by the registrar that day. He had been put on the ward, and there would be difficulties, he would cause trouble, she could see that coming a mile off.

She checked: the registrar had her number and she had his pager number. He had rung to confirm the contact, which at least showed he was alive to the problem. She had those notes as well. She would almost certainly have to prescribe, so she made sure she had the MIMS directory with her.

She stopped for a moment, thought: everything OK. She turned the lights out, balanced the papers on her knee and using her free hand locked the outside door and then, carrying a good part of her teeming medical practice with her, she went out to the car and off in it, down the hill towards London.

She fed the car gently into the traffic and followed a large lorry carrying glass. The image of the child she was going to have to speak about tomorrow came back to her; her report was already with the lawyers for the court hearing.

The mother held the baby carefully. She watched her movements intently, then put her down and arranged her on the floor. The baby picked up a toy and shook it. The baby smiled at her mother. She smiled back. She picked up the baby again, and let the child touch her face. Both laughed out loud. The baby was confident and relaxed. The mother looked at the baby's hands and decided her nails needed cutting. She took off the child's socks, and holding her firmly she carefully undertook this delicate task.

Grace Karenin didn't want to think about her recommendation. She stopped for a light, a long trail of traffic crossed from her right. She knew she would have to say out loud that the court should take this child away. It was inevitable.

The mother is a heroin addict. Her partner is a heroin addict. Heroin addiction leads to failure in care. The mother lives in a chaotic household. Other addicts, often strangers, come to her home. There have already been episodes of violence, which will recur. There will be confusion.

The baby will be at risk, as were her previous children before their removal. This mother cannot change in a time scale sufficient to enable her to help the baby establish and maintain a first attachment. Without the proper formation of this primary attachment, the baby will be at substantial risk of significant harm.

She would have to justify this opinion, and already she could hear the lawyer for the mother asking her to set out the detail for her reasons. She'd like to reply, 'It's all in the report, I wrote it all down, Mr whoever, or Ms . . .' Most of these barristers were women now. But of course the system demanded that she should justify her advice out loud in the presence of the mother. That wasn't unreasonable. Think of the pain. The child was going to be taken away because of what she said. Mr Burns storming out in a temper was right. It was she who took these children from their mothers, not the judges.

The road was white in the evening lights, hard, unforgiving; the traffic whirled indifferently around her, each person separated off in a small steel cabin.

But then sometimes she would hear on the news of those cases where the social workers or doctors hadn't intervened in time. What outrage there would be then! Maybe a child had been killed. She'd been to a house once with a pathologist, and the mark on the wall made by the baby's head was still there. The wall was actually dented. There was a hole in it. Good God, how had that been allowed to happen? No wonder questions were asked. And she pictured another child who had been tied to a table leg. It had eaten its own nappy.

She gripped the steering wheel and switched her mind back to the next day's hearing. How far they tested her would depend on the judge, and how much information was needed to make the decision.

'Could you tell us in a few words, Dr Karenin, what you mean by 'attachment?' The judge was bound to ask that, they always did; again it was done in order that it should be said out loud for all to hear, not because the judge didn't know the answer. All right then, I'll try to say it:

For a hundred years now psychiatrists have been watching children mature. Then attachment theory . . . A van started tailgating her car. She pulled further to the left and saw the driver go past, grinning at what he had managed to do. Bullying her.

Once you saw it, of course, a baby demonstrating good attachment, you don't forget it. It's obvious. It sticks out like a sore thumb, was the English phrase for it. This child has a good attachment, that child does not. Plain and simple. You can't argue with it any more than you can argue that a bandaged thumb is not bandaged. *Kao sto, se vidi*, was what she ought to say to them, that sums it up better. Plain as the nose on your face. But then of course they would just say to themselves, these foreigners.

But the difficult bit was forecasting the result of a bad attachment.

The van had slowed in front of her now. Now he was forcing her to pass him, so he could do the same thing again. No problem, she wasn't going to get involved in this. He wasn't moving very fast, and she was driving a very powerful car indeed; it was just that she didn't use its power very often. She waited for the right moment, and then shot past the astonished driver, leaving the van a hundred yards in her wake before he had even changed gear. She slowed for a traffic camera, then put her foot down and, as far as the van was concerned, she disappeared, filtering left down into the tunnel, and then, after the Highway, turned left into Wapping.

She dawdled down the cobbles, nothing behind her now. The gates to the garage beneath the block hissed shut behind her, and she turned left into her parking space, free, just by the lift. From the lift it was only a step to her front door, short enough to manage her papers easily.

She disarmed the alarm and with one switch turned on all the lights. She had herself insisted on that arrangement, no more groping into a dark flat. The bookshelf accommodated everything she was carrying, including her bag. In her previous flat the files would have stayed in the hall, on the floor where she dumped them, for hours, getting progressively more untidy. This was a much better arrangement.

121

She dropped her scarf and headed for her bedroom. She took a shower. Some mother's son had been driving that van. All men were some mother's son, and then women criticised men for the way they behave. But who first taught them? Boys were becoming so much more difficult. Could one say that? Changes do happen. Things shift.

She noticed now that at least once on every car journey she took, someone, deliberately or ignorantly – in east London ignorant means deliberate – broke the rules. They cut you up, or jumped the lights, or pushed into a queue. It wasn't always the case. It used to happen, of course, but not with such regularity. The structure – can you call the rules of driving a structure? Of course you can – seemed to be fraying at the edges. But maybe it always does, that was the nature of change, that's how things change.

But there must be societies where it moved the other way, where rules get tighter, where society gets more cohesive – horrid word – coherent is better. In this society there seems to be a value in allowing things to become less coherent. The odd thing is that when the fraying at the edge is complete, and what was once there has been completely obliterated, even then the secondary effects of the loss don't become immediately apparent. It's only slightly later on.

She turned the television on. A large room with some listless people sitting in it appeared.

You had only to read the lectures and research papers of the late sixties and seventies – they comprised complete records of the breakdown of family life. No-one cared then, or maybe there was nothing that could be done about it. The economic pressures were irresistible – fast food meant less cooking at home, easier transport for young people to get out and away from home, more activity outside the home to replace being in with the family.

She found a skirt and a good sweater.

122

But now the effects were becoming obvious. Her present patients' grandparents were the first generation to grow up with no grandparents at home or nearby. Then husbands started leaving home in significant numbers. There was no extended family to stop the men going, no peer-group control over their behaviour and nothing to replace them. Black men were often not at home. Mothers were left entirely on their own. Children grew up isolated. More work for her.

One of the people on the television screen moved across the room scratching himself. It was odd. Had Beckett or Pinter written this, it would have been art, but this, it was complete rubbish.

The kids who were brought to her now were strange, detached entities, small atoms of feeling in a wasteland. They had no connections, save their harassed mothers, and maybe some complicated stepfather relationship, which changed every year or so.

An argument broke out in the room on the television. One of the women objected to the habits of one of the men, but she quickly found herself in a minority. There was some discussion. The others decided: 'You can do exactly what you want. If you need to fart, then fart – as long as it doesn't harm anyone else you can do what you like.' They left it there.

She wriggled her feet into a pair of shoes.

But that was the difficulty. These mothers did exactly what they wanted. They would form any attachment they wished, without a thought to whether it harmed the child to have a series of relationships with different men. So the child never learned to settle. That this sort of thing caused harm to the child was unarguable, but you weren't allowed to say so out loud. If you did you were considered a dried-up harridan, and if you were a man you wouldn't dream of saying such a thing. That a woman should be more careful about the relationships she forms if she already has children was obvious; but you weren't allowed even to acknowledge it. It would be seen as a sort of fascism, restricting the liberty of young women – quite wrong.

She wondered about Jennet. Her Jennet, everybody's Jennet, they all liked her.

The scene on the television became more bizarre. Someone was jumping on and off a plank, while the others were counting out loud.

She turned it off. Dressed now, she looked round.

She walked into the large room. The picture window looking out over the river was a black, reflecting block in which she could see her own image. She turned the light out behind her, and stood, allowing her eyes to become accustomed to dark, gradually seeing out over the river.

'And this place too was once one of the dark places of the earth.' Marlowe's boat must have swung at anchor not far from here; the financier, the lawyer, all smoking their pipes, unseen in the dark. But now the darkness seemed to be gathering again. Perhaps people always thought that? Well, Marlowe didn't, his generation thought they were pushing the darkness back, and yet they were now universally reviled.

She could now make out the shapes of the buildings across the river, lights moving, and to the right, the bright colours of a restaurant. The unfinished files beckoned her; she ought to sit down and work, but she found she was hungry, or at least wanted to sit quietly for a while. Undecided, she paused in the middle of the room and then, collecting her keys, she went to the door.

Her mind ran on, churning over the problems of the day. She had had a meeting with a young woman doctor, overworked and in trouble in her private life. She had seen it before, it was quite common. For some reason young women doctors refuse to find men who are capable of looking after them. She remembered the phrase in Paul Evans's poem, 'For Paddy':

I want to place a man at the heart of me,
Who will burn with a steady flame.

What they do instead, they find a problem, which they think they can fix; they find some unreliable man they want to put right, then there's a baby, and of course they don't want to stop being doctors. I mean, who would? But they have to find work somewhere different, because there aren't that many posts available. And the man doesn't want to move. It was all so inevitable.

She left the block and, turning to her right, she took the steps down to Ma Thompsett's.

And everybody thinks these women are so in control. But no, they are as much out of control as anybody else, and they need just as much help as anybody else. Which of course people won't give, since doctors are meant to help other people. And young women doctors don't know how to ask for it.

She had recently sat at a school leavers' assembly, handing out prizes – 'We are privileged to have Dr Grace Karenin here' – and occasionally a young girl would come up to the platform: 'Here is Jean, she hopes to read medicine at Imperial', and Grace's heart went out to the child. She wanted to say, 'Do you know what you are putting aside in order to do this? The freedom you are forfeiting? Now's the time you should be enjoying yourself. Instead you will be taken up with hours on duty, off duty merely waiting to be on duty again, clinics, exams and crippling responsibility, when you should – just look at you – be enjoying your wide open eyes, your best time.' But she didn't, she just shook her hand, and smiled, like doom, into an unsuspecting face.

125

She sat down in the bar and looked around. From where she was sitting, she could see the fat man talking to someone.

Or they get involved in some sort of religious fiasco. I mean, I ask you, look at this Alpha course thing. Not surprising; Alcoholics Anonymous had been declared a religion by the courts in some parts of the United States, and Alpha uses the same twelve-step method. The American judges were right, after all, there's not much difference between admitting, 'I'm an alcoholic', and confessing, 'I'm a sinner'. One of the results of AA being recognised as a religion was that people who confessed to crimes in the meetings were protected by privilege. Was that a U.S. federal decision or a state decision? She had read it somewhere.

Was what her patients told her privileged? Obviously private and confidential, but privileged? It was one of those things that she had never cleared up properly. She ought to find out really, ring the BMA, no, the MDU, the Medical Defence Union. Especially with that policeman snooping around trying to find out about – suddenly she couldn't remember the man's name.

There was no doubt she was very tired, she had no control over her thoughts, they raced on. She'd better not drink anything. The bar manager appeared and sat down opposite her. 'Hello, Grace.' She was a woman of about her age and they often sat together.

'You OK?'

'I'm tired tonight.'

'You look it.'

'Do I?' Grace reacted and started to straighten her hair.

Annie laughed and stretched out her hand to touch Grace's arm. 'No, no. Don't. Not so's anyone would notice. I notice because I know you.'

Grace smiled. The simple movement her friend had made seemed to release her from the load, and she let the

126

mask slip. She was able to relax a little. 'Have you been busy?'

'Yes. Numbers are up. Definitely.'

'All round?'

'Not in the evening. No.'

'That doesn't mean you're going to shut the place in the evening?' This was important to her. Here was, extraordinarily, a restaurant where it was possible for a woman on her own to sit in a corner for a quick meal, quite undisturbed. In fact, there were two or three who regularly did so.

'Oh no. It's part of the lease. We have to open in the evening, so you the residents have somewhere to go. Anyway what would Charlie do without us?'

She looked up at the fat man.

'Who is he? I've often wondered.'

'He's a press agent or something. Actually very influential. I've seen top people from the *Sun* at his table.'

'Does the *Sun* stretch to having top people?' Grace Karenin laughed.

'There's another world out there,' Annie said.

Grace looked at her.

'A place where not everybody depends on you, Grace, or is demanding things of you. You should join it.'

Chapter 7

Scott prepared a rudimentary file which he could take to Charlie Pope. He would have to have something to show if he were challenged, and a solicitor's file wasn't difficult to organise, and when you look at them, they are all curiously anonymous – often they do not even have the company name on them.

He would only need a few papers, notes of the complaint, perhaps a copy letter, since the claim had not got very far. On the other hand, Charlie Pope looked as though he knew what he was doing, he'd be suspicious. Well, Scott could do that too. He thought about it, then marked the front 'Copy' and blacked out the name, and did the same to the papers inside. Eventually it showed nothing at all, but like all censored papers it bristled with life. He had noticed that, when dealing with prosecution disclosed material – the act of concealing something always made it look much more interesting.

He had bought a pay-as-you-go phone just for the anonymous number. He contacted Pope.

'I have my client's permission to go further,' he said.

'Right.'

Pope didn't sound very interested, so Scott cut it short, businesslike. 'I'll be over later,' he said, and rang off. Why not be brusque? This was a market; and market traders are

128

not interested when people turn up saying, 'I might have something to sell.' They are only interested in immediate sales. In some ways that made it easier. He put the documents and the phone in a briefcase with all his other papers and set off for court.

Scott hadn't wanted to work and had tried getting out of the case. What he was doing seemed much more important, but his clerk had said, 'You can't be doing that, sir. People are depending on you.' At court, however, he felt detached. Never before had the plain oddity of court procedure so struck him. The occasional moments when a decision was made that directly affected someone stuck out, but they were surrounded by a fog which obscured all motives, so decisions seemed to arrive out of nowhere, preceded by incomprehensible signals.

He found exactly the right person to talk to about it. Moggy was tall, lugubrious. For him it wasn't just a word. His face was long and deeply lined. His eyes were sad and mournful. His whole body seemed to sag from his shoulders, like a suit on a hanger. He was always willing to agree that everything around him was absurd. Indeed, unless everything you said assumed that, you could not talk to him. Other lawyers skittered away, unwilling to risk their preconceptions.

Moggy had sat down next to him in Counsel's row. 'Hi,' he had said sliding in. 'Are you in this?'

'No, the next one,' said Scott.

'Who are you against?'

'Jane Christabel over there, she's prosecuting me.' They both looked over at Jane Christabel, who was simmering at the end of the row.

She was married to a banker and was surrounding herself with a larger and larger family. Scott guessed that on their joint income they could well afford to amass children,

129

and every two years or so she took a couple of weeks off to have another.

'She's back already?' said Moggy.

'Yep. And totally untouched, look at her figure. Perhaps she collects the babies from Peter Jones.'

Jane Christabel looked up, aware that she was being discussed. She saw Scott and Moggy talking together and looking at her, so she flashed a grin. Her short sight made her all the more attractive, adding a slightly puzzled aspect since she wasn't always clear what she was looking at.

'Jane Christabel, Jane Christabel, the girl of our dreams.'

'C'mon, Moggy, you're well looked after,' Scott said.

Tom Mogg had married a girl whom he had met on voluntary service in Africa. Now they lived near this court, and Moggy was able to go home to lunch every day. His excuses for inviting the court to rise a little early and sit a little late after lunch were famous.

'Mr Mogg, have you an engagement at two o'clock?' Mac the Hat, who knew about Moggy's domestic arrangements, used to ask. He was the judge in court seventeen. 'I understand you do.' The judge never waited for a reply, so Moggy never had to mislead the court. 'Well then, this court will have sit a little later after the luncheon adjournment, but longer in the afternoon to make up for it.'

The jury were so bemused by the break being called the luncheon adjournment, or even sometimes the short adjournment, that they didn't notice what was happening. Moggy used to come back with a dreamy look on his face. It wasn't luncheon he had been adjourning for, Scott thought.

Scott told Moggy about Charlie Pope. He said, 'I couldn't believe what I was hearing. I have to tell you about this, but keep it quiet.' He kept his voice low since the court was sitting and the judge was addressing a very junior barrister who was on her feet next to Scott. Attacking was a better word, Scott thought. Why doesn't he try to bully someone his own size? But then it was none of Scott's business. 'This character, what was he? A press agent. And he said things about the law I didn't believe. His speciality was the manipulation of criminal trials—' A voice interrupted what Scott was saying. Scott looked up and saw the source.

Bernard slid into the seat next to them. 'Bernard, we're discussing Jane Christabel,' said Tom Mogg, changing the topic back.

Bernard started making movements with his mouth as though he were tasting wine. He had a full florid face with a large forehead, and his eyes shone at the mention of her name. Jane Christabel looked up and noticed that now there were three of them. She groped around to find her spectacles, to see who they were.

'Ravishing,' Bernard said.

Jane Christabel found her spectacles and put them on.

She looked at the three of them, and then, there can have been no reason for this since without them her long sight was quite useless, she pulled them slightly down her nose and looked at Bernard over the rims. Scott felt Bernard quiver.

A note found its way to them along the bench. 'A little less excitement, please, gentlemen', it said in spidery handwriting. No one knew who it was from. They considered it for a moment, then Bernard wrote on it, 'Then Jane Christabel Belair must be invited to leave the court for a moment. Her presence is disturbing.'

They watched as the note made its leisurely way back along the bench, each hand automatically returning it to the hand that had originally sent it. About halfway along, it popped forward to the front row, where it continued along Counsel's benches. It reached the end. It was passed to the probation officer. He held it for a moment then he

131

passed it to the usher. There it became becalmed on her clipboard for a while, until she got up and walked to the back of the court.

The judge continued to deal severely with the very junior counsel. 'Miss Ticehurst, what you think is not relevant. What I need to know is why your client did not attend court for his trial.'

The usher stood for a few moments then circled Counsel's benches. She handed the note to the clerk of the court, who waited for a few moments and then stood up and interrupted the judge.

The judge read it.

'Miss Belair,' he said.

Jane Christabel stood up.

'Miss Belair, I understand your presence is required outside.'

'Oh,' she said, mouthing her reply.

Jane Christabel managed to resemble at the same time both an intellectual philosophy teacher at a French lycée, and a vamp; leaving the observer juggling uncertainly between the two possibilities.

'I wonder who could want to see me?' she said.

'I don't know, Miss Belair. I don't know at all,' said the judge.

Jane Christabel threaded her way out. 'If any other counsel wishes to leave us, then now is the moment to reduce the noise level,' said the judge.

Scott, Moggy and Bernard all got up, and the judge returned to his attack on the junior counsel.

'You are not attempting to suggest, are you, Miss Ticehurst, that the fact that this offence is really not very serious makes your client's failure to attend his trial somehow understandable?'

'Tell him that it might have served to concentrate his mind less,' said Scott as he passed her.

The young woman was standing, quite silent, unable to deal with this curmudgeon on the bench.

'It might have concentrated his mind less,' Scott heard a strained, small voice say as he left the court.

'Now that *is* an interesting proposition,' the judge said. The door closed behind Scott and the argument disappeared.

'Hello, Bernard. What have you been up to?' Jane Christabel said.

'I've been in Wolverhampton. And you? What have you been doing?'

Scott listened with interest. How would she put it? No doubt in between selling bonds, or whatever bankers do, her husband, if asked, would have talked about producing another sprog.

'A baby. We've had another baby,' she said. She was surprisingly coy about it, she almost blushed.

'I didn't know that,' Bernard said.

'You were in Wolverhampton, Bernard, defending the waste merchants. You're not even in the frame.' Jane said. It was odd. The remark didn't fit, especially after the blushes.

The usher interrupted them. 'Your case, Mr Scott. You too, Miss Belair.' Clearly the young barrister had been quickly vanquished.

Moggy came up to him in the bar mess later. 'You wanted to talk about that person you met, but then you stopped.'

'I didn't want to talk about it with people who were obviously going to say, What are you on about?, and then tell everyone what I was saying. I know Bernard, he'd just say it was the facts of life or something.'

Mogg said, 'You'll have to tell me about it first. Then I can decide whether to agree or not.'

133

They were moving to a table at the large picture window in the big room overlooking Penrhyn Road. The room was packed, a Turkish heroin case had camped in the court for months. It needed nearly twenty counsel.

'That's some gravy train,' Scott said as they sat down. 'The only way the Lord Chancellor would get his money back on that one would be to sell the heroin on.'

'Would that cover it?'

'Twenty-five million pounds' worth? Should do.'

'That's street-level prices. He'd need a small army to sell it for him and they all need paying. Anyway, what about the prison costs? Nine men, two women. An average of twelve years' sentence, at how many thousand a week? It's thousands, isn't it? Say quarter of a million a year each. That's three million each, not counting parole – no parole for drug dealers to please the hangers and floggers in the Labour party – that's thirty-three million for a kick-off. Leading counsel, junior counsel, solicitors, policemen – not counting their sick leave at having to work so hard – judge's pension costs, court staff, appeals, the court of appeal straining every nerve to uphold the verdict, though they'll knock off eighteen months from the sentence to show they understood the case. The Lord Chancellor would have to import another truckload of stuff at least, to pay for all that.'

There was a flurry at the door and a group came in talking loudly. Two of them came to the table next to where Scott and Moggy were sitting. A voice said, 'I don't believe it!'

'What is it?' Moggy said to one of the men.

'Natasha says she's going to apply for the case to be stopped and retried. A retrial! The whole thing over again. The judge threw a wobbly about the Tiddler's cross-examination, and Natasha thinks she's been prejudiced by the judge's behaviour.' He turned back to the other man and said, 'And you have to agree that what the judge did was pretty odd.'

Another voice broke in, deep – oysters and Guinness deep. 'I am not going to drive here from Blackheath every day for another eight months.'

'Well, that'll double the cost,' said Moggy to Scott. 'Is there any reason that case should ever finish? Now, you tell me about this man you met.'

Scott said, 'He was a court reporter, used to be one of the people who hang around the Old Bailey, but has retired now because of his size.'

'What?'

'Yes. Don't ask.'

'Hi, Jeremy.' Another of the Turks' counsel had passed their table.

Scott said, 'Anyway, he's doesn't get out to the courts at all now, but he's using his knowledge. You know, I think he was more than a court reporter.' He stopped.

'I can't help you on that since I don't know the first thing about it,' said Moggy.

'It's just that this chap knew so much about the law and the way the system works, more than a journalist would want to know. Anyway, what he has done is to work up a business selling people's stories. Organising criminal injuries applications. Taking a cut from the press payment. And this was the stunner.' He heard himself use the words – where had that expression come from? Was he trying to act out astonishment or was he really amazed? 'He'll even undertake to start a prosecution on your behalf by paying a policeman to get it going.'

'What?'

'Yes. He calls it an interview fee, nothing to do with the decision to get the case going. Perfectly legal, though I suppose police regulations would have something to say about it. He offered to do it for me.'

'Why should you want to start a prosecution?'

'That's different. And this, after a few drinks he really got talking. He can help the case along, getting prejudicial information before the judge using the disclosure system.'

'How can he do that?'

'Easy, or he says it's easy. Imagine someone is arrested as a result of his manipulated complaint. He then rings, or gets someone to ring, the policeman involved, anonymously of course, pretending he is an informant. That's normal, it happens all the time. Then he gives information about the man arrested. It's very prejudicial, stuff like, he's done this before but we can't tell you exact details. The information doesn't take the case itself any further one way or another, so it's never revealed to the defence. But the judge has to see it of course; come to that, prosecution counsel sees it, and the case becomes a different thing then.'

'Why did he tell you this?'

'Complicated. He was drunk and I think he was lonely, in the sense that he liked talking and as far as I could make out not many people sit and talk to him. He seems to work from this wine bar, like Adam Faith did from Fortnums.'

'Who?'

'Doesn't matter. But he guessed, or knew, I was a lawyer; I don't know how, and I think he wanted to score over me, or over the whole lot of us. Prove how smug we are and how we haven't a clue what's really going on. He's about right too, if you ask me.'

At the window further down the room most of the counsel in the Turkish case had gathered, each trying to digest the effect of what Natasha was about to do. The noise of laughter and complaining got louder. Then Natasha came in: 'Oh, Oh,' they shouted. 'Don't do it, Natasha.'

136

Natasha stood smiling, one foot forward and turned out. What poise she has he thought. Knee slightly bent, and her hands palms up, awaiting her moment. She had been downstairs to the cells.

'I am instructed,' she said, '*not* to ask for a retrial.' A cheer went up. Scott could see someone in the street outside look up at the window.

Scott said, 'If what this man said is true, then he's completely right. All this is rubbish —' he gestured towards the group of advocates now deciding what they wanted for lunch — 'this whole thing is a complete charade. Or at least even more of a charade than we thought it was.'

Tom Mogg said, 'You've got it bad.'

'Moggy, you know I'm right. It's all going anyway. Jury trial is being attacked on all sides. In a few years it will be no more than a single judge, rubber-stamping what happened at the police station.'

'Maybe it'll last us out.'

'I don't know if I can be bothered to wait and see. The only hope is that there will still have to be proper trials for serious offences. But don't count on it; the accountants can't quantify the value of that. And if people like Charlie Pope have their way the whole thing will be run like a version of that TV show *Big Brother* — parcelled out for entertainment, and sold to whichever newspaper needs some copy.'

'Who's Charlie Pope?'

'Who's Charlie Pope? The fat man. The man I met last night.'

'I knew a Charles Pope, he was the managing clerk of that firm, what were they called? Dustin's. Was that it? I'm not sure. They were down Romford way, they were shut down. That was twenty years ago. I used to work for them when I began, they still owe me money. But Charlie Pope wasn't fat when I knew him, or at least not that fat. Monty Bach knew him. I think they were friends.'

Scott decided he should find out as much as possible about Charlie Pope before he got in deeper, so he went to see Monty Bach. He found him in the Clock House, just off Peckham Rye.

Monty was a stately man, getting on now. Scott judged he must be in his seventies at least. But he still went to work; Scott had seen him once or twice, driving an old white Rover 90. It was a car Monty had bought in the sixties, and Scott doubted he had ever driven it at more than forty miles an hour. He only travelled about four miles a day, from near the cemetery beneath One Tree Hill, down to Peckham, and then back in the evening to his wife. So, maybe forty miles a week if you threw in the odd visit to one of the central prisons. Twice a year he took his wife to Herne Bay for a fortnight, so it was about three thousand miles a year at most. The car was probably good for a few miles yet.

Scott saw the car outside the pub when he arrived, parked at a slight angle to the kerb. Those models were made before power steering, and he guessed the wheel was probably getting a little heavy for the old man. It had a note under the windscreen wipers. Scott took it, went into the pub and handed it over. 'Hi, Monty,' he said. 'Do you mind if I disturb you?'

Monty took the note and read it. He said he regularly got messages from enthusiasts asking to buy it. 'But what would I do with a new car? In this car people stay away from me, and they don't mind if I go slowly. They expect it. Anyway, thank you for bringing it in. No, I shan't sell it. Now, what can I do for you, Mr Scott?'

Monty bought Scott a drink.

'I don't really have to buy drinks here, but it's good to

138

do so occasionally. A lot of my clients come here, and they often say, What are you drinking? And then they leave one behind the bar. I've got a little stored up.'

Scott could see why. Monty was sitting with a small glass of port in front of him and for the greater part of the time Scott was there, he didn't touch it at all.

'Do you know a man called Charlie Pope?'

'Ah,' said Monty. Then he said, 'Charlie Pope. Yes.'

Scott waited.

Monty said, 'What's he been up to now then?'

'You knew him then?'

'Yes, he was in a number of firms and ended up at Dustin's. I haven't heard from him for some time, though I did hear that he was still around.'

'Who was he?'

'He was one of the old-fashioned managing clerks, in the days before there weren't enough solicitors to go around. Or rather when solicitors didn't do this work.'

'Yes?'

'In the end he was struck off. If you can strike someone off who was never on in the first place. The firm was shut down. Two of the principals went down at the Old Bailey.'

'What for?'

'Gold bullion. It was one of the first cases where modern money-tracing techniques were used.'

'Charlie Pope had gold bullion?'

'No. I don't think he did. But what harmed him was people thought he was in a much simpler business – writing defences.'

'Did a lot of that happen?'

'Much less than you would think. After all, look at all the silly defences you've had to put forward for people. Do you think they were written for them? No. But it did happen. Supplying alibis too. That's what was said about Charlie.'

'Was that common?'

'Not often. But it's easily done. It's happened to you, I should think. You point out the stupidity of the client's explanation, you have to do that and they say, What should I say then? I've even heard someone say that to a policeman. It's not a real question. But some people answer it for real; it's not difficult to take the next step.'

'Charlie Pope did?'

'Who knows?'

'But people thought so.'

'Everyone thought they knew.'

'Everyone?'

'The same way everyone knew the police made up evidence.'

'Everyone knew?'

'Yes, even the juries. Verbals. Everybody knew they were nonsense. They represented what *would* have been said if the defendant was guilty and he had been honest about it. It was a kind of fiction. The really bad bit, though, was then if you denied the verbal strongly enough, it always counted as an attack on the police officer's honesty and your bad character went in as evidence. That doesn't happen now. Of course, the police only really verballed people with bad characters, so it went with the territory.'

Scott liked hearing Monty talk, so he just waited.

'I don't know about Charlie Pope. Myself, I think he was honest, but he was working in a system that was dishonest to the core.' Monty looked at Scott and said, 'Mr Scott, sir, what are you doing? You're making me go all philosophical. Let me buy you another drink.'

'No thanks, Monty. Look, it's interesting.' He wanted Monty to carry on.

'Once a process like this relies on dishonesty anywhere, it becomes dishonest everywhere. Or at least it breeds dishonesty everywhere. Dishonesty isn't intentional when

140

it comes to systems, it's accidental. Accidental in the proper sense. You know the technical meaning in logic?' Monty laughed. 'You didn't know I studied logic, did you? Worker's education, a bit unfashionable now. It's called the Open University now. Accidental means something that's not inherent. Colour is accidental, unless it's an orange of course. Where would an orange be that wasn't orange?'

He moved his small glass of port, folded his spectacles and pushed the *Evening Standard* aside. Scott knew he was a good listener, and listening makes people talk. Monty said, 'That Jeffrey Archer case is a good example of inherent dishonesty, but not in the way people think. The judge's summing up in the original libel case was so biased that counsel for the losers, the *Star* or something, wasn't it, actually got up to complain. And then, believe it or not, he was attacked, not the judge, for having the bad manners to suggest that the judge was not acting fairly. What does that tell us now?'

He answered his own question. 'If you have a system that sweeps anything under the carpet, then naturally things will happen under the carpet.'

It happened under the carpet – it sounded to Scott like a phrase from a Turkish court.

'But what do you say about how it is now?' Scott asked.

'It's dishonest, yes, in the accidental sense again. Prosecutions are not enquiries into whether somebody committed a crime, but into whether the police can prove that some particular person whom they suspect committed it. Proof that someone did something is not necessarily proof they did it. Paradox. Because the other side of the question, whether they didn't do it, isn't examined at the time that counts – during the investigation. It's only examined months later during the trial, often too late. The police look for evidence to prove what they think is true, and that's different from looking for evidence.'

141

'But that's unavoidable, isn't it?'

'They used to say that about verballing. It may be unavoidable but it's still the cause of grief.'

Scott was hearing what he said being played back to him. But perhaps he was feeling particularly susceptible. What he really wanted to know was how to live with the disillusion. 'What do you do with this information, Monty?'

'I don't know. I don't think there is anything to do with it. People don't believe there's a problem for two reasons. One is that it doesn't matter much, since the people who get locked up deserve it anyway. But the second is more difficult. Any information you have depends entirely on where you stand. That's why I like defending policemen occasionally. You should hear them squeal about how unfair the system is, when it's used against them.'

'Is that what Charlie Pope says?'

'I doubt it.'

'He was telling me how lawyers don't know what's happening.'

'You met him?'

'Yes.'

'Charlie Pope is a very angry man,' Monty said.

'How do you know?'

'I defended him on the bullion charge. Got him off. I briefed Victor.'

'Why should that make him angry?'

'Because he was nothing to do with it. I knew Dustin, and I know that what he took he wasn't going to share with Charlie. Charlie knew nothing at all about it.'

'But he got off.'

'After waiting fifteen months in Brixton Prison to be tried.'

'Oh.'

'The others got bail.'

142

'Why didn't Charlie Pope?'

'Because the officer in charge of the case didn't like him.'

'Just that?'

'In those days that was enough. It still is.'

Scott listened.

'His wife left him. His kids went with her. He lost his house. Had no job, nothing. After his acquittal he had to start again, selling stories to journalists about the courts. I remember him asking me for stuff.'

'Did you give it to him?'

'Of course I did. He was bitter, deep down bitter. But I liked Charlie.'

'But you don't see him now?'

'I heard he was around.'

'What did you hear?'

Monty did something Scott hadn't seen for years. He tapped the side of his nose, like Disraeli.

'There are things instructing solicitors don't tell counsel. Especially impressionable young counsel like your good-self, Mr Scott, sir.'

'Would it be like providing witnesses for cases?'

'I have heard. I have heard. But I had better be getting back now, hadn't I, Mr Scott? Don't you yourself have a home to go to?'

In the end Monty's mannerisms always became annoying, but mostly he came through with what mattered. Scott went to Wapping better equipped. He felt he could deal with Charlie Pope. He would go as far as he could in setting up a prosecution similar to that against Jimmy, to see how it was done and discover some of the other people involved.

Scott said, 'I have my client's permission to take the next step. You read it and then let me know what exactly you would want.' Then he added, 'And what he should be saying.'

Charlie Pope didn't react. He only opened the file with one hand and looked sideways down at it. 'How did you meet him?'

Scott was prepared for that. 'In a matrimonial case. You'll see I have crossed out names and things like that.'

'You do matrimonial work?'

'Mainly. I do some crime occasionally, but there are others in the firm who do that for me, when it's more complicated.'

'Is the matrimonial case in this file?'

That was why Scott had chosen matrimonial work – he needn't say anything about it. 'No. I would have to get the court's permission for that as well, even if I had the client's.'

Silence.

Scott controlled the impulse to say something. Now was the time to leave it and go, look indifferent. He said, 'I'll be in touch. If I don't answer then leave a message.' He scribbled a phone number on the back of the file.

Charlie Pope was quiet for a moment then he obviously took a decision. 'No,' he said, 'we can start now.' He handed the file back.

Scott said, 'You don't need to read the file?'

'Not really, you've already told me most of what I need. Now, what will this cost you.'

'Much?'

'You needn't worry about the amount, since anything you pay virtually guarantees you a profit.'

'Who do I pay? What am I paying for?'

'You're paying for the story to be made sellable. At the moment all you've got is a vague complaint.'

'How can you guarantee it?'

'Because when Vernon writes one of these, it always sells.'

144

Vernon. Scott's pulse jumped.

'How much?' he said.

'Some down and a percentage.'

'How much down?' Scott suppressed the desire to apologise for being so hard-nosed.

'I'll speak to him and tell you when you come again.'

'I would have to see him first before paying anything,' Scott said.

'You know, Mr Scott, that doesn't normally happen. But you seem a nice enough sort of chap. I'll ask him.'

Charlie Pope had warned him.

On the way back to his flat Scott worked out what he was going to have to do. This was becoming serious. The coincidence of the name was too great. He must be some sort of ghost-writer. Newspapers have reporters who look after people whose stories they have bought. What kind of people are they? Is it something you are taught about in media studies?

Anyway, if he was going to meet him he'd better have it well prepared. And he'd have to see a matrimonial court, he'd never even been in one. When he got in he telephoned Maryanne.

Chapter 8

He discovered that family division courts are different from criminal courts.

There is no bustle. They have the detachment of the area in a hospital which is set aside for death. Those who attend these courts ostentatiously carry files, papers which demonstrate they are on the way to somewhere else, the whole event merely another stop in a busy day. Matrimonial courts are doubtful, morose and there for only one purpose: finally to extinguish what happiness the marriage ever had.

'The trouble is that there are no winners,' Scott said.

'Everyone says that. A bit trite if you ask me.' Maryanne was nothing if not direct. 'All events have their legal aspect, in the same way that all objects have colour. Think about that.'

She paused to allow Scott to think about it.

'The idea that law is some dishonest confabulation of the lawyers, spun out in order to exploit the long-suffering public, is tripe. Law is a way of looking at things, and a method of settling arguments. If the public wants to stop lawyers existing, I suggest they stop arguing.'

'Now?' Scott said. 'Immediately?'

Maryanne laughed with abandon and suddenly looked like a schoolgirl, not Maryanne Tutton QC, doyenne of

146

the family courts. 'Yes, right now,' she said, stopping and turning. 'Why not?'

But she had another reason for stopping. 'That's my client,' she said quietly, indicating with her chin over her shoulder. 'The droopy one.' Scott looked and indeed there was a woman sitting on the bench. Droopy described her exactly.

'I'll leave you for a moment, I must have a chat with her.' She descended on the woman, who drooped a little further.

Scott wandered over to the door of the courtroom. It was locked. An usher standing inside regarded him suspiciously through the small pane of glass. 'Hello,' mouthed Scott. The usher did not respond in any way, save to look at him with even greater suspicion. Scott turned aside. This was odd. He felt out of it, and yet this was an ordinary division of the courts, a division of the same courts in which he practised. In theory he should feel at home in any court, but here he didn't.

He had explained to Maryanne. 'I have to do a perjury case, and the offence occurred in a family division court.'

'Oh what fun,' she said, 'we don't get much perjury. Or at least we don't pursue it with the vigour that you lot do.'

'I'd like to see a family court in action, so I can picture the whole business. I mean, do you all sit round a table in suits or what?'

'Sometimes,' she said. 'Have you never been at all?'

'No, never.'

He wanted to say thank God. It wasn't the kind of work he fancied. Even the titles of the Acts of Parliament had put him off – Matrimonial Causes and Finances Procedure Act, No 3. Who thought up these titles? Even the Children Act, which pretended to be simple, was designed to catch you out: 'No, no. Not the Children's Act. It doesn't belong to them, you know. It's the Children Act, 1990.'

147

You were made to feel a careless and indifferent dilettante right from the start. At least the criminal law stuck to the same name, the Criminal Justice Act, each with a different date, each changing the one that came before it. Everybody got them wrong and no one felt superior about those mistakes at all, since no one really cared any more.

Scott walked away from the court door. He was trying not to walk over to where Maryanne was sitting, not wishing to interrupt her conversation, but he found that, unless he made a conscious effort to go in another direction, he always seemed to end up going towards her. He turned and went deliberately to the other end of the hall and found himself stopping opposite a young woman, the only other person there. There was huge space to walk in, so why had that happened?

'Hello,' she said. 'Are you in this case?'

Scott was surprised. People don't talk to each other at criminal courts much, at least not to strangers.

'Not really,' he said. 'I am a lawyer though.' As if that were a recommendation.

She smiled. 'I could see that.'

'How?'

'You look like one.' And stopped.

They looked at each other. Scott hadn't seen such a beautiful woman for a long time.

'Is that good enough?' she said.

He said, 'Not really. I might be a father.'

'No, you're not a father. And certainly not the kind of father who comes here. They're mostly distraught.'

'Who are you?'

'I'm a doctor. A psychiatrist.'

Scott wanted to say, 'You're too young.' Instead he said, 'You're not.'

'Why shouldn't I be?' She laughed. Her teeth were white.

'I didn't mean you're not, I meant you're *not*.' Trying to emphasise it differently.

'No difference,' she said. 'Try again.'

What I meant was *here are intelligence and beauty both combined*. Shakespeare. He didn't say that though, instead he said, 'You don't look like a doctor.' But that was wrong too. It was only a matter of time before she took offence.

'Oh?' she said. 'How?'

'I don't want to offend you,' he said.

'Keep trying,' she said. She smiled again.

He fell in love.

You can't cater for that. Things weren't in order. He was in his thirties. Not very successful, and as far as he could make out he might be about to abandon his career. Even when he was working he was busy doing damage to his prospects every time he was rude to another judge. 'You're insufferable, and you're getting a reputation for it,' Suzanne, the dragon judge, had said to him in private.

He said to the doctor, 'What I meant was, I assumed you were another lawyer. I mean, the way you look.'

'This is my court suit,' she said.

He was suddenly avid to hear about her. He said, 'Very nice.'

They spoke at the same time. He let her go on.

'Are you a barrister?' she said.

'Yes.'

'But you're not in this case?'

'No.' He decided to venture something. 'I'm a criminal lawyer. I do crime.' What would she think of that?

'Oh.'

'Yes, crime,' he said.

'You're becoming alexythymic,' she said. It was a word that had become lodged in her mind because of what she was going to have to say.

He thought, What on earth does that mean? Shall I ask her?

'Hello, Grace.'

Maryanne had walked over. Now he wouldn't find out what alexythymic meant. How do you spell it?

'Have you two introduced yourselves?' Maryanne spoke as though meeting this woman were an everyday thing. Silence.

'No?' Maryanne didn't notice. 'Grace, may I introduce Jeremy Scott.'

The detached part of Scott's mind noticed the correctness with which Maryanne did it. Always ask the woman's permission to introduce a man to her. It was her breeding: she was as upper class as it was possible to be without disappearing entirely off the top of the scale.

'Jeremy. Dr Grace Karenin. Grace is our psychiatrist.'

'Are we allowed to talk?'

Grace Karenin's white teeth appeared again. Was she laughing at him?

'Oh yes. Everybody talks to everybody in the family division,' Maryanne said. Then, 'Grace, I have to ask the judge whether Jeremy can come into court, so I'll be off for a moment.'

She walked away.

'We have to ask whether a member of the public can come in,' Scott explained to Grace Karenin. 'These courts are normally private.'

'The public?' she said to him.

'Yes. That's me.'

'Jeremy, come on,' Maryanne called across the hall. 'Do stop dawdling. What's holding you up?'

Good question.

'He'd better sit with me,' said the judge speaking about Scott in the third person, 'so there'll be no doubt about

150

who he is. We wouldn't want that.' They both looked at him.

What might people think I am? Scott wondered.

'Will you organise the permissions, Maryanne?'

'Yes, judge.'

'He can wait outside.'

Scott was sent to sit in the passage outside the judge's door. He felt he was being tossed to and fro. People walked past him as he sat still. He kept his knees together.

The passage stretched away to his right and left. Where could he get a dictionary? Alexythymic. Grace Karenin. Grace, what a beautiful name. He had never thought about it before. Had he ever met a Grace before? No. The Three Graces. They had always sounded as though they were a pop group, but they were a statue, women with particularly female bottoms. Then there was Grace, Grace who wouldn't wash her face. But none like this Grace. What grace! There he had said it. Graceful. He was graceless. And what a difference it made.

'You sit there.'

Again Scott was told where to sit.

'Now, where were we?' the judge said to the court.

'I was about to call the evidence of an interview with Miss Poole. You'll remember we had hoped to get to it yesterday, but then Dr Karenin agreed to delay her appearance till today, so perhaps we should deal with her evidence now.' Scott gathered Miss Poole must be the mother involved.

'Well, let Dr Karenin come in.' There was the same delay while the witness was fetched. That at least was normal.

Maryanne sat with her client. The droopy woman was not, as Scott thought, the mother of the child whom the case was about, but the local authority lawyer. 'Totally worn down by it,' Maryanne said later. 'She'll have to go back to New Zealand soon.' They all did, apparently.

The mother of the child sat next to her own counsel. She didn't just droop, she had collapsed already. Scott didn't need to read the files in order to know her story, he'd seen it often enough. The files would only provide the specific details. Heroin, violence, the wrong men, more babies, more heroin.

The judge spoke to the mother's counsel. 'You do have the doctor's report, Mr Hinchcliffe, don't you?' She emphasised the word 'have' as though Hinchcliffe, being particularly obtuse, was bound to have forgotten it, leaving it at home with his maths homework.

He got slowly to his feet, saying, 'Yes, milady,' and sat down again. He looked as though he was about to start a particularly heavy day at the office and wished he had not got out of bed that morning.

'Good, good,' said the judge. Then, as Dr Karenin entered the room, she added, 'I should say that Mr Scott here, who is himself counsel, needs to observe some matrimonial proceedings. Everybody has agreed, I understand, that he should be here? I thought it would be better that he sat here by me to keep him out of the way.'

How could he get in the way? Perhaps if he didn't sit up here he might start moving around the court, interrupting people, saying, Look, can I see what it says on that piece of paper? If I could just reach over perhaps? The image made laughter well up in him, and he found his eyes seeking out Hinchcliffe, the only other man in the room. Their eyes met. It was always going to be the case, there was a secret language available to them. It was only a flash, but enough. Life married to this judge passed through their minds at the same moment. The horror, the horror. Scott sat contemplating the court.

If there was a secret language for the men, then what

152

were these women saying to each other, with their hundreds of signals and moments of understanding? He and Hinchcliffe would be left entirely out of it, which of course in the end was just what they wanted. Then perhaps they could go off to the pub together and drink a beer in total, blessed silence. He shook the idea away from him. Here was the last place in the world to be male chauvinist. It would be flushed out, the consequences would be unimaginable.

He looked around. Both Maryanne and the judge were looking at him. Perhaps they already knew what he had thought.

'No, he hasn't got a copy,' said the judge to Maryanne.

The judge was answering a question which hadn't been asked. It was already happening.

He was handed a copy of the report. He looked at it. A thick report, it must be fifty pages long. There on the front page was her signature. Grace Karenin. Black ink, strong writing. Someone who, when she signed her name, meant it. What does that mean? He didn't know, he knew only that it was what he thought.

'Now we'll begin,' the judge said, again looking at him. Did he have to stop thinking so they could get on with it? This was paranoia.

'We all know Dr Karenin, but perhaps you had better introduce yourself, Doctor.'

Scott looked at her. Not so tall, but slim and a little older than he had at first thought, but not much, perhaps a little younger than he was. She spoke with a slight catch in her voice. But she remained very still, stood very still. She occasionally moved her hands, opening and searching for parts of the report, but otherwise she waited and listened to find out what was wanted of her.

When she was asked a question that mattered, she thought about it; once she stood and reflected for a minute at least. During the pause the court waited for her in absolute silence. Scott was transfixed.

She said, 'There will be violence, there has already been violence. Yes.'

Hinchcliffe went at it immediately. Despite his assumed detachment he knew exactly what he was doing. 'First, why do you say there has been violence?'

'I have read of it in reports.'

'Has Miss Poole ever told you she was involved?'

'No.'

'Do we have any indication that she was involved?'

'No. Only that there is violence in the house.'

'You are saying that this violence will follow her wherever she goes.'

'No. Not wherever she goes, but as long as she lives the chaotic life she has described, there will be violence. She knows this.'

Scott noticed that while speaking of the mother as 'she', Grace Karenin looked the woman in the eye when she replied. That was brave. These were the answers that would take the woman's child away.

'It is not violence for which she is responsible, then?'

'She is responsible for her child, and that child is present when violence occurs. She has failed to protect the child from witnessing the violence. She is still at present unable to do so.'

Scott wondered whether Hinchcliffe would challenge the doctor's right to speak in such final terms. The challenge did come, but it came gently: 'How can you be sure? On what basis do you make this judgement?'

'It is not for me to decide. I only offer you an opinion. But since you ask, I have seen many children and mothers. Please read the report. I have put in it what I saw. I have remarked upon her achievements, and her failures. Attachment, for instance.'

154

The judge asked, 'Perhaps you could tell us what you mean by attachment.'

Scott thought he saw a flash of amusement in Grace Karenin's eyes. He guessed she had been asked that question before.

'Yes. It is that period when the baby begins the long, long business of making relationships; the business that occupies us for the rest of our lives. If it is not done properly then yet another damaged person will grow up and bring with him or her all that unhappiness. Other people will suffer as a consequence.

'Amongst other things it is the start of the development of the language of feeling. If it does not develop, the child can grow up without awareness of shared feelings. It will affect his or her ability to form social and emotional relationships, or even, at its worst in adulthood, make him alexythymic – the state when he or she has no language for feelings, and is consequently unable to express them.

'Attachment theory argues that most things depend upon that first attachment. A child looking around for its mother, and then seeing her and feeling secure, is the basis of all our later experience. I know this is true.'

Maryanne was a very good lawyer, which is why she had got so far. All she asked the witness was, 'Could you take us through your report again, to the passage when you watched the mother and baby together? I think it's at page eighteen.'

She knew perfectly well it was at page eighteen.

Dr Karenin read out what she had written.

'Yes. Paragraph eight, point two: "The mother held the baby carefully. She watched her movements intently, then put her down and arranged her on the floor. The baby picked up a toy and shook it. The baby smiled at her mother. She smiled back. She picked up the baby again, and let the child touch her face. Both laughed out loud.

The baby was confident and relaxed. The mother looked at the baby's hands and decided her nails needed cutting. Then she took off the child's socks, and holding her firmly she carefully undertook this delicate task. While she did this, the baby peered about the room, occasionally gurgling with pleasure. 'The mother always likes to cut the baby's nails,' the foster carer said. 'She does it every week.' At the end of the contact visit the mother left the foster carer's home.

"'The mother did not separate from her baby easily, but the child did. She transferred her attention to the foster carer immediately.

"'The mother walked down the street away from the house, then she crossed the road, came back and walked past the house again. She looked over at the window of the house where I was standing. I think she was in tears.'"

The court room was entirely silent. No one who had watched the mother with the care Grace Karenin had shown would wantonly or indifferently wish to harm her. It was impossible to disregard her judgement, which was of course the conclusion Maryanne intended should be drawn.

Scott wondered: How do I get to see her again?

PART THREE

The Crack House

Chapter 9

Mike Reynolds hadn't meant to drive past Timmy's school, at least he didn't think he had, but he was aware of where he was, and he kept an eye open for Jennet's boy. Then he saw him, being led down the street by an older woman. That must be his grandmother. Mike pulled to the side of the road and got out of his car. The old lady stopped. He could see she was apprehensive. Then the little boy spoke to her, still holding her hand and looking up at her face, telling her who he was; but it made no difference to the look she had. Mike Reynolds could read faces.

'Hello, Timmy.'

'Hello, Mr Reynolds.'

Mike was impressed by the way the little boy spoke up for himself.

'Now you have to introduce me.'

'Grandma, this is Mike. He and Mummy and me went to Jelly's.'

'You have to tell me Grandma's name,' said Mike.

'I just did,' said Tim. 'It's Grandma.'

'Hello, I'm Mike,' he said.

But the little pantomime had not reduced the old lady's suspicion of him one bit. He put his hand out. She was obviously not used to shaking hands, and offered only a limp touch. Mike Reynolds picked up on a tightly controlled life, fashioned in the face of adversity, not willing to accept intrusion.

'Well, what are you wanting with my Jennet? A fine man like you,' she said.

Surprised, Mike snatched a look at Tim. But the little boy seemed to think this was a perfectly reasonable question and waited, like his grandmother, for a reply.

'Well, your Jennet is a fine woman.'

'I know it,' she said. But he thought she seemed a little influenced in his favour by the directness of his reply.

'And a fine man like me would be a fool not see that. Isn't that so?'

Stalemate. Both of them thought she was a fine woman. Where do we go from here?

Then he made a mistake.

'And a fine son Jennet has too.'

'And it will be a foolish man to say such a thing in his presence', she said, shaking the little boy violently, as if to get the idea immediately out of his head.

Again the child was obviously used to this behaviour and, when the storm had passed, he continued to watch the contest between Mike and his grandma gravely. She was not to be won over easily. Finally Mike said, 'I have a small gift for your grandson.' His driving around with a gift in the back of the car for the boy made her all the more suspicious. It was only his having said it in the boy's presence that forced her to accept. It was a kite.

'I thought we might go to the kite festival this Saturday in Streatham. You ask your mum. Tell her I'll telephone.'

It was too much for Tim's grandmother. 'Now what opportunity does my daughter have to refuse to take her son, without his railing against her and spoiling the day?'

The moment she said it, he realised what he had done. She was right and his best intentions were no excuse. Of course if you are as ham-fisted as that, you will even doubt your own intentions. Why should he be bothered about the child after all? He just knew he was.

They walked away, only the little boy looking back, to be shaken straight again. He still waved at Mike though.

Mike Reynolds continued on to East Place. Fulton, Detective Sergeant in the serious crime squad, had asked to see him again. Fulton was as awful as he usually was.

He said, 'We particularly asked you to speak to that doctor, since you cunts in the child protection team claim to have special relationships with doctors; you spend all that time with them, at meetings, gabbing away. So, you say to us, If I ask her she'll do it. And what happens then? She says nothing and this cocky bastard sits there laughing at us.'

Detective Sergeant Fulton, scratching his neck as though what he was saying was difficult to get out, went on, 'I don't know as I'd want to have to go to tell her myself. I might just have to. To tell her what we really think.'

Mike Reynolds wondered whether Fulton wanted to avoid going because he knew he would get the same answer as he himself had, and that wouldn't help his dignity. Maybe that was the reason. He said, 'I was quite clear about it and she didn't want to know.'

Fulton looked as though he was going to lose his temper.

'What's she in the job for then, if it isn't to protect children? Shit. That kid is living with a murderer, and she's pissing on about medical confidences. The only fucking confidence I have is, I'm confident she's a pain in the arse.'

Fulton's temper was well known, but Mike Reynolds didn't care. All he wanted Fulton to do was to stop swearing. In the murder squad and the robbery squad it was

161

'fuck this', 'cunt that', all day long, even when they dealt with the lawyers and the pathology people. What was that about? And what could he say to shut him up? 'Watch your language with me, Fulton, you fuckwit?' Would that work? Probably not.

'The trouble is, we don't own her,' was all Mike Reynolds said. 'I'm going down there anyway and I'll tell her again. Anything more I should know?'

'No. Save that chummy's murdered his wife and is just sitting there laughing at us.' Mike Reynolds knew that 'being laughed at' is as bad as it gets for a policeman.

'Billy Burns,' said Reynolds out of the blue. 'Do you know Billy Burns?'

'Yeah, I know Billy, or knew him, rather. Don't know him now. Why do you ask?'

'He's stuck his head into something I did. Is he still active?'

'Not so you'd notice. But I have my doubts. Old men turn to drugs nowadays – it's a pension thing.'

Fulton picked up a golf ball he kept on his desk. He thought it made him look expansive. He tossed it from hand to hand. 'I know that Poseidon looked at him a while ago. There was a Dutch involvement apparently. I can't say any more.' Fulton didn't gab away, giving information out to any old person. No.

Reynolds thought, Another Dutch connection. He looked at Fulton's golf ball. When he first came to East Place, Fulton used to say to him, 'Why don't you join?' And he'd say, 'You're looking at the ball which Colin Montgomerie put down in one, on Camber Sands. Won it in a raffle.'

'Oh,' Reynolds would say.

Now Fulton said, 'Have you got something on him, Burns, that is?'

'Same as you. Not so you'd notice. He just stuck his

162

head in where he wasn't wanted and I was curious about him. Who is he?'

'He used to be a front man, though he was never nicked for it. He worked with Batty George, he was good. He wasn't a whiner. Did what he had to do and then shut up. Enforcement as well.'

'Nasty.'

'Yeah. People didn't cross him.'

Fulton looked up from his trophy. He remembered what things were like, and became angry again. 'But that was the old days. It was clean enough then, none of this weirdo stuff you lot go in for. Or at least if they did then people kept quiet about it. They didn't ponce around in medical conferences, asking some social worker what she thinks.'

He started making a face, but Reynolds stopped him. 'OK, Fulton. You do what you're good at.'

He turned to leave, expecting Fulton to go on about it, but he didn't. Instead Fulton said, 'If you want to know about Billy Burns speak to the Darkie. He knows him.' The Darkie was Detective Inspector Abbott.

Nobody liked him because yjey thought at one time he had got where he was because he was black, and once, without thinking about it, Mike Reynolds thought the same. But he was changing his mind. He had noticed that change – another one, with all the other changes that were happening to him. He was getting a different point of view. Why?

Now he was beginning to realise Abbott was a good man, careful, quiet – and with people like Fulton on your case, he could understand why. Anyway, contacts, and how you use them, the people you know, and Abbott knew black people – that's what made you a good officer. Frank Abbott had used what he knew to his advantage. And what did Fulton know? He knew about bars in golf clubs.

★

163

Frank Abbott said, 'Yes, we had Billy Burns's name come up from Holland. I asked Fulton about him, but in the end we decided it was only because he travelled there a lot and the computer had picked him out as frequent flyer. And he had paid his own way, not a company cheque; paying your own way is shown up as suspicious. Or at least that's what the computer thinks. We were monitoring things because a huge amount of crack cocaine seems to have started coming in from Holland.'

'Does the computer record all arrivals and departures?'

'Yeah. We get that now from Europol. In usable form too, so we can run it past the central intelligence computer and it picks out what we want. It'll pick up the new personal cards if they ever come in, so wherever you go you'll be listed, with your car numbers and whatever.'

'What did it say about Billy Burns?'

'That he had a criminal record and that he goes over to Holland a lot. Once he travelled on the same ferry as a Jamaican gang member we're looking at, a man called Gargie, known as the Spaceman. But it could have been a coincidence. Three hundred people travel that ferry every time. Maybe it's just because he works there a lot.'

'He does – plumbing, he says.' Reynolds didn't say what he thought about coincidence.

'They probably need a lot of plumbing in Holland.'

'Yeah, right.'

'What with the water.'

'Yeah.'

'Billy the plumber.'

'I wonder if it runs in our system?'

'What, Dutch plumbing?'

'No. The Europol information.'

'What system is yours?'

'Child crime, sex crimes.'

164

'Is it a web pattern?'

'Yeah, that's what they call it. ChildWeb.' Reynolds noticed that Abbott knew about web pattern investigations, he didn't have to be told. That's why he was a detective inspector, and why Fulton was still poking around in his golf club, being introduced to people who sold sporting goods. Reynolds said, 'Billy Burns spoke up for a nonce. And to me that spells involvement.'

'What? Just speaking up?'

'Yeah.' Reynolds felt backed up a bit, but then, even Abbott didn't know what was really going on. He remembered how he had been taught that a denial can be an admission. In fact, especially a denial. Again he was reminded how his work was a hall of mirrors; what was normal was abnormal, what seemed ordinary was designed to conceal the thing beneath. Would, for instance, Frank Abbott understand collusive periods?

'Yeah. These people,' said Frank, 'I suppose they hang together.'

'Well, at least they don't use guns and machetes.'

'No.' Frank Abbott laughed. Frank Abbott worked in Yardie country, crack houses, Jamaican gangland, where they did. They always had.

Today Alleycat was driving the black jeep. Sitting high and looking down, delivering product for Spaceman Gargie. She had to do it now the previous arrangement had broken down.

Wicked Man better be there to take it in, not like last time when she had to wait nearly half an hour in the open. She shifted the package in her mouth. It weren't nothing. Just like chewing gum when you got used to it.

She pulled up at the lights at the turn into Burrell Road. You always had to wait here, unless you were lucky or you nicked the lights. But today Gargie had said, 'You be

Miss Law-abiding today. What you got is worth more than that car, so don't mess.'

She was not about to mess with Gargie. She had seen what had happened to people who did, and she didn't kid herself she was special just because of Little Gargie, because in this business nobody counted more than product.

But you never know what changes a man. Little Gargie was in the back – she was going to deliver him to school. Maybe that would change him. Maybe they soon could live a normal life – they had the money.

Out of the corner of her eye Alleycat saw the black woman in the car next to her look up at her. Plain dowdy. What did she see? What did she say when she saw it? A star? Alleycat knew she looked it all. She knew that. She stretched her hand on the leather steering wheel, and spread her fingers to give her nails out a little. She didn't need to look down again, one glance had been enough. Because that woman didn't have it, she didn't look to herself properly.

The woman in the car next to her said to her driver, 'She clocked me.'

'No, she didn't,' the man said. 'All she did was think how much better she looked than you do.'

'Thanks a lot. She hasn't been sitting in this piece of junk since five in the morning with only you and your body odour for company.'

He laughed.

She went on. 'Anyway, since when did these people start to work shifts? They'll be paying national insurance next.'

The jeep took off with a jerk, they could see the small child's head whip back with the movement.

'Just look at that. OK, let her go. Next stop the school, and she'll spend at least ten minutes there, coffee-clatching with the mums. We can follow her from there.'

★

Gargie had got to number 15 before Alleycat. He had decided to come early because she had told him that nowadays Wicked wasn't always there when she arrived. And today he wasn't there at all. The place was empty. That meant a delivery hanging round and waiting on the street. That was no good. When the stuff was on the streets it was at risk. Anyway, it was part of the deal that someone had to be in the house all the time. Twenty-four hours a day. 24/7. He'd have to speak to Wicked, but it would have to wait, since he'd have to choose his moment.

He looked around for signs of where Wicked had gone, and waited for Alleycat. She should be here any minute now. No-one would come buying yet, though in an hour it would be different. They'd rouse themselves and then they'd be over to see Gargie with their money.

The door bell rang.

He went to the iron gate in the passage. 'Yeah?'

'Is that you, Gargie? Where's Wicked? It's me, Alison. It's cool.'

He allowed the door to open, it opened outwards. 'Stand back, won't you,' he said.

Alison stood back, so he could see the whole entry hall. He didn't trust her not to bring someone. She came in and he locked the outer door with a remote. Only then did he unlock the inner gate.

This was the weak point. A sudden rush through the outer door at just that moment could take him out while the inner gate was unlocked. He sometimes lay awake and wondered how he could fix that. It would need a much stronger lock on the outer door, but he had been told that anything bigger would be too much for a remote to handle.

Anyway he couldn't get no professional locksmith out to do it. He could just see him asking, 'Hey, Mr Banham, would you just come and fix my security system?'

Banham's did the Queen's locks. The Queen – he remembered the picture of the Queen in his old schoolroom, with that diamond thing on her head and those white shoulders.

He was the clever one then. Teacher's favourite. Still am the clever one, he said to himself.

But he needed a stronger lock to give him a minimum of five seconds, even if the inner door didn't stop them – five seconds to get to the john. He thought about the system. The weak bits especially. In the end they would try to get him. He knew every time he sold to a new contact he was increasing the likelihood of a bust. No one can be trusted. In the end someone whose need for stuff was great enough would sell him, to another dealer, or to the police.

The Queen's police. What would happen if they stuck a gun through the bars? Dunno. But they wouldn't, they wouldn't shoot, so even with a gun they'd never get the product. He went to the john with what Alleycat had brought him and put it on the shelf, just above the water. Go in that room without pressing the switch and it would be thrown from the shelf and automatically flushed away. And not into the main system which the police could block. It went into a system where it could be retrieved, if you did it right. If you didn't it went down next door's sewer and off to the sea in barges. Pretty good. It was part of the deal with Billy.

He went back to the main room to see what Alleycat had to offer him.

Chapter 10

'It's Thursday so I'm having some people to dinner, perhaps you'd like to come. Tonight at eight. Grace Karenin will be there. I could see that you rather approved of her.'

The matrimonial case was finished, the judge had gone to write up her decision. Maryanne and Scott were standing outside the law courts in Fleet Street. Maryanne turned and climbed onto a number 15 bus. 'Altogether the best bus in London, much better than the number eleven, you don't get that boring bit behind Victoria station,' she spoke from the open platform. 'You know where I live, off Knightsbridge. And none of your surly behaviour tonight, Jeremy. Don't worry about dressing, come as you are.'

Jeremy was already wearing the full fig, dark suit and stiff collar, correct for being a guest in court, so 'come as you are' didn't offer him the freedom which the expression usually implied – although could that mean that the others might come in dinner jackets? You never really knew with Maryanne. On the other hand it didn't matter since this was an opportunity to meet the doctor again.

Scott got there about half past eight, calculating he'd be just a little late, but the party was already in full swing when he arrived. Not that being late seemed to matter – he was given the next place at the empty end of the long table. During the next half hour the table filled up, so by now he was near the centre of the group, which, like sediment laid down over time, demonstrated who had arrived first and who later.

He looked around to find Grace Karenin but she didn't seem to be there. He waited. Food would occasionally appear, accompanied by small shrieks from the door which led immediately into the kitchen. The meal seemed to have no pattern, and for a while all Scott had near him was a large meat platter full of roasted carrots.

'Very good,' he said to his neighbour to the left, senior in time.

'Do you think so?' she said.

The words were not intended as a putdown, nor even to indicate world-weary disagreement, but it was clear, now that his approval of the dish had been given, it would soon appear at her own dinner parties. Then she turned away to her other neighbour, a thin nervous man to her left.

Wine was elusive, until Scott realised that the knack was to capture a passing bottle and hang onto it. Slowly, in this way it became possible to build up a complete meal. Meat entered his orbit, then some figs, a gravy-like substance – delicious – followed by potatoes, which upon being discovered to be undercooked, were carried back to the kitchen with shouts of disapproval: 'More time, give them more time, Maryanne.'

Maryanne's face, hot and beaming, appeared for a moment at the door. 'Do eat up,' she cried, waving a spoon, 'we're expecting the vicar.'

'The Vicar of Harrods, that's who,' called a stout, red-faced man who had been laid down in the earlier ages of the dinner table accretion, and who from this position of seniority dominated the conversation.

Then the thin man leant across the woman sitting between him and Scott and said, 'I concern myself with the notation at the bottom of Johnson's dictionary. There are numbers on some of the pages in the bottom left-hand corner. Shall I go on?'

Scott did not respond quickly enough to stop him.

'We know they are folio numbers or printers' marks, but we don't know how they work. Why should one particular number be where it is and *not somewhere else*?' As he spoke the last words, the man tapped the table sharply with his middle finger. A small butter dish leapt away like a tiddlywink. Then, 'Thank you,' he said, and he took Scott's bottle.

'That's OK,' said Scott and, waiting till the man had poured some out, he took it back.

Scott offered it to the woman between them who had not reacted at all to what was happening across her, but she refused, or at least Scott took it as a refusal. 'One hardly ever drinks,' she said.

The man with the dictionary in mind said, 'I became aware of the problem while proofreading. It was clear to me that the chappie who wrote it, who said he knew it all, had got it completely wrong. Shall I tell him, dear?' He spoke across the table to another guest who had seemed to be deep in conversation with her neighbour. Despite this she was in fact also monitoring her husband's behaviour closely, 'Not now, Charles,' she said without pausing.

This deflated the thin man and, giving a small groan of dismay, he tapped on the tablecloth for a moment as though to get rid of the stored-up points he had wanted to make. He returned to what was on his plate, crestfallen.

'I think it is such a pity that there isn't more of this.' The woman next to Scott spoke.

Scott looked round for more carrots. There were none since the plate was travelling down the other side of the table, disappearing from sight occasionally when it went behind a particularly large candelabra.

'Can I offer you some more sprouts?' Scott said, looking at them doubtfully. They had achieved a curious blue colour.

'People used to entertain so,' his neighbour added, explaining her last remark, it was nothing to do with food, 'but now we don't go out. We sit at home watching *Big Brother*. Except when we go out here, of course. At Maryanne's', she added to make it entirely clear where she was.

'I did so love Leslie, he was totally yummy,' the woman seated next but one down said.

'But gay, totally gay right through, like a stick of rock,' the large florid man said sadly. He took off his spectacles as though more easily to shout, and put his head back: 'Maryanne, where is the wine?' He held his bottle entirely upside down to demonstrate.

'In the cupboard, but not the St Estephe, that's for Jeremy.'

Jeremy was looked at.

'That's the wine he wants. He said so. I got it up specially.' Jeremy looked around to see if there were another Jeremy at the table who had specified the claret he wished to drink. Apparently not.

'This is Jeremy, by the way, everybody. He's a jolly decent criminal lawyer. Took a first at Cambridge, but not in law if you please, Tit' Hall, even though that's where the lawyers go.' Maryanne appeared wearing an apron over a black silk evening dress and pointing with a wooden spoon. She held it overhand, pointing down slightly, the same way people hold guns in Tarantino films.

'No, I didn't,' Jeremy said, denying the first-class degree. But he should have waited a beat. As he spoke everybody had turned to their neighbour and said, 'Jolly good,' and his denial was offered up to an empty table. Then everybody turned back to face him.

172

'Pass Jeremy the St Estephe!'

A cupboard in the wall panelling was opened. The interior was dark ruby with bottles of red wine.

'At the back,' Maryanne's voice called from the kitchen, 'and cooking red for you, Toby.' Toby was obviously the senior man with the spectacles. 'Can't tell the difference myself,' Toby said, 'save tomorrow, when I'll have a thick head.'

'Anadin.'

'Sebroputanamol.'

'A corkscrew, get him a corkscrew.'

'Jeremy's is already open, so it can breathe.'

'Peter failed his membership one year, and the next he was top. How do you account for that then?'

It was a bottle of St Estephe, first growth. It would taste of oysters and the sea. Scott couldn't have afforded to buy it, even if he could find the kind of shop that might sell it.

'Decanter, decanter.'

'Let it breathe.' The man who was involved with Johnson's dictionary got up and took a decanter from among the silver pheasants and china on the sideboard behind them. 'Let the dog see the rabbit,' he added.

He decanted it for Scott. It bubbled, blinking at the brim.

'Peter just worked hard the second time around. I've seen that sort of thing happen before.'

The conversation became general again and Scott was left with the decanter. Drink it immediately? Why not? It could only get better as he went along. He offered it round, but was pleased when they refused. That's for you, they said, as though they themselves had been part of the decision to treat him to such luxury.

Maryanne interrupted, 'But do give Grace some wine, Jeremy. Now that she has arrived. She's starved for good wine where she comes from.'

173

Scott instantly looked to his right, later in time, and saw Grace Karenin. He had not seen her arrive though he had been watching carefully. She leaned out to look towards him, and he saw her face, shining, smiling, her cheeks round, full of life. 'Hello,' she said. A hello face.

'And Grace is to sit next to Jeremy —' again Maryanne burst from the kitchen door into the room — 'and you, Sophie, are going to sit next to the vicar.'

The word vicar received the same response as before. Everyone shouted, 'The Vicar of Harrods!' It reminded Scott of an audience at a television game show.

Sophie seemed to think it perfectly normal to be moved on. 'All move round,' called Toby. Without a word she picked up her plate and Grace Karenin slipped into the seat next to Jeremy.

Scott always remembered that the first moment he had Grace Karenin to himself was in the midst of the general turmoil of moving and shouting, laughter and a sprout being dropped and retrieved and dusted down and eaten; all of this carried on over their heads as they sat and looked at each other in near silence. They had no need, no wish to move.

'Hello,' she said. 'You looked very grand today sitting up there with the judge.'

'But you dominated the court,' he said.

Her clear pleasure at being complimented showed. 'Did I?' she said. 'That's nice.'

'People must have said that to you before,' he said.

'I don't talk to people about it.'

'You just do it?'

'Yes,' she said.

'You've changed from your court suit.'

'Yes,' she said, and sat with her hands in her lap, her back straight, turned in her chair slightly towards Scott, making

174

no attempt to eat or drink, looking at him, waiting for him to speak again.

What could he say?

'That's a lovely dress.'

'Yes,' she said.

'Grace, Grace,' a voice shouted. 'The man's come about your tickets.'

'Oh, right,' she said.

She got up and went away from him. He felt alone. What tickets? She had a complete life, which went on perfectly well without him.

'Here's the vicar. Here's the vicar.'

'The Vicar of Harrods.'

She had gone.

Scott didn't find her again until late in the evening.

Twice he changed places at the cry of 'all move', each time clinging to his decanter. He discussed recent changes at Holy Trinity, Brompton, banking law, why Maryanne did not eat anything, and was pursued for a while by the man who wanted to tell him about Dr Johnson. But Grace Karenin did not come back into the room.

He could see that there was lots of comings and goings in the hall outside the dining room, and after a while he got the impression that there was another party going on elsewhere in the house.

That became a certainty when screams of laughter began to interrupt the flagging conversation at the long dinner table. Certainly the food seemed to have stopped arriving. He decided to investigate. Clutching his wine he stood up and left. It seemed to be a perfectly acceptable thing to do. At least, no one said anything.

He found his way into a long hallway, which opened up into a tall room. No, not a room, it went up for at least three stories into a kind of atrium, the nearest thing to the

175

book-lined rabbit hole in *Alice in Wonderland* he had ever seen, shelves stretched upwards, crammed on the lower sections with law reports and textbooks, and above them copies of *Punch*, novels, almanacs. He could see a set of Wisden, a complete Dictionary of Biography, and then the light failed. On the far side of the room there was a door, lined with shelves, standing open, revealing another room a few steps lower. It was almost bare, with only a large desk against the far wall, but brightly lit. In the centre of the room Grace stood surrounded by men, each of them taller than her, each of them leaning down slightly, talking to her. Scott stood above them on the step. He needed to get to her.

He stepped down and joined the group. A laugh greeted him. He wasn't really aware of what they were saying, but he said something in response. There was a flurry of conversation. He turned away, but when he looked round by a mechanism he never really understood there she was standing at his elbow.

The other people in the group were unaffected, indifferent to his taking her away.

He said, 'Did you get your ticket?'

'Hello,' she said. 'I was waiting for you to come through.'

'To rescue you?'

She laughed. 'Is that what this is, a rescue?'

'Yes,' he said.

Chapter 11

Mike Reynolds couldn't get the information he had about Billy Burns out of his head. An ex-con, willing to give perjured evidence for a paedophile. The Dutch police enquiring about him, and the evidence he gave in the trial based upon his being in Holland. The abuse of children is an international business, and Holland is a very liberal place, so there might be another reason altogether for Billy Burns's going to Holland. He went back to see Frank Abbott.

'You say you made a connection between Billy Burns and someone you were working on, but it seemed to lead nowhere. You put the connection down to chance. Could I see it? At least see the summary, it might be something up my street.'

Frank Abbott liked Mike, though he thought he was too involved in his subject. But then, who did anything well by not caring about it?

'Yeah. Look at the intelligence summary. All we know is that maybe he and Gargie, Gargarin that is, travelled together. When I say together, they were on the same boat.'

'Gargarin? Unusual name.'

'Yes. Russian name, though they got it wrong and spelt it with an R. An intrusive R is what they have got in

Jamaica anyway. But it was a fashionable name in intellectual circles there for a time, since it meant taking the Russian side against the colonial oppressors. It was our Gargie's grandfather's name. Our Gargie himself couldn't have been more normal to start with. He had a Jamaican university education before he started working to improve his CRO number.'

Frank Abbott was remembering.

'Perhaps they should have worried less about colonial oppression and more about controlling the posses. But that's probably something one's not allowed to say.'

Frank Abbott was allowed to be rude about Jamaicans, since he was one.

'Why should this Gargie be travelling anywhere?'

'Drugs. Everything Gargie does is connected with drugs, except sex. He runs a crack house. Anyway, you read the report. I'll get it.'

'Was he carrying anything when he returned?'

'No, we stopped him on the way back, at least customs did. Of course he gave off lots of fuss: you're doing this 'cos I'm black. Blah, blah. Which was both right and wrong, of course. We stopped him because he runs a crack house, and he's running a crack house because he's black. Not the other way round, so don't think it is. If he weren't black he'd be a banker or something, with that brain. No, they found nothing on him.'

Frank Abbott went to a filing cabinet, one of about twelve lining the side of the large room where they were speaking. He riffled through one of the drawers and pulled out a folder; it contained a series of plastic envelopes, each labelled, and bound together so they could be read like a book.

'All he had were these papers. We copied 'em. I haven't examined them.' He looked at the folder. He said, 'It's an outline franchise agreement and some technical documents.'

He dived back into the filing cabinet. 'Let's see what he said about them.' He ran a finger down the page. 'He said he was hoping to start a franchise in Kingston when he got the money to go home. Said he had been to a franchise exhibition. Got the plumbing stuff at the same place.'

'I'm surprised he talked at all.'

'Well, it was customs, a woman. I was watching her through the glass, she made it seem like a piece of routine. "Sorry, sir, we just have to stop so many" – you know? When he got over the black stuff he started coming on to her.'

Mike was looking at the plumbing documents, at least what he could see through the cover of the sealed plastic wallet. They said '*doepplepipe foet*', which it wasn't difficult to think might mean double pipe feed, just what Burns had talked about.

'We thought the only thing he'd want to franchise were crack houses.' Frank Abbott laughed. 'Anyway, here's the relevant intelligence. At any one time there are about twenty crack houses in London. Average life about five months, but Gargie's places always survive longer. Twice we've taken him or his people out, and both times we've found nothing. No gear, no stuff, nothing. And always an explanation for what the flat was being used for. And the steel gate? "Well, if you can't stop them burglars, officer, then I have to get my own safety organised." Who can argue with that? They're right. Everyone has a security gate now, save that normally they put them outside the front door. He always puts them inside. It's like the joke about Superman's tights, only the other way round.'

He handed Mike a document. 'And then he moves on and opens another one. Same thing happens. Here you are. Sorry, but you'll have to read it here,' he said. 'Nothing's allowed to leave.'

The document was entitled 'WRS.x.257. *Operation Fishhook*'.

'Fishhook?' Mike said as Abbott moved away.

'Yeah. Poseidon has got lots of operations attached to it, so the computer chooses a name that fits.'

The document was a jumble of subheadings, computer classifications. There were lines of numbers, and then meaningless phrases. 'Suspect not yet eliminated.' Mike knew some of the phrases from his own work, but even then it did not always make sense. He scanned through the jumble looking for a simple passage of narrative. And there it was.

15 Burrell Road. Crack house. Open twenty-four hours. First floor flat. Downstairs beneath is empty, but still rented. Council confirm this. Tenant away in India. Target flat property of Tyrone Williams, long-term occupant. Returned to Jamaica leaving flat for son. Son not seen.

Occupants/users. Gargarin. See CRO number IC3, smart appearance. Intelligent, university dropout, very violent; Firebird posse. Lives out of London, drives in every day to deliver son to private school in Blundell Park, then on to Burrell Road. Either a black jeep, rhinoceros mating, or a red Land Rover. Carries about twenty wraps in his mouth at any one time.

Alison, Alleycat, baby mother (Little Gargie, boy, 4yrs) sometimes delivers. Never deals. Always well dressed, looks like Baby Moon.

Wicked Man (Esau McLaren, see CRO number) works as his foreman during the night. Whoever on during the day, not yet identified. House works on a shift pattern.

Security. Buyer must be known to seller, knocks

180

at front door, left hand of the two after a flight of stairs. It is opened remotely outwards into hallway. There is a steel reinforced security gate 6 feet into flat entrance passage; again it opens outwards. Double recessed hinges. Buyer does not enter the flat beyond the gate. Security at rear complete. Effective and efficient system. No weaknesses identified.

It was a standard crack house description, nothing remarkable save that it was open all hours, and people seemed to work shifts. Gargarin sounded interesting.

'Who are the Firebird posse?'

'They were one of the posses that grew big after the last set of wars. But they are so violent that the politicians don't use them, so they are outside the loop. Firebird since they mainly burnt their victims − alive of course. They used petrol, hence Firebird, the logo for National Diesel.'

'Who's Baby Moon?'

'A singer in one of them girl bands. You haven't got children?'

The question hurt Mike. He wanted to say yes, but instead he said, 'No, I'm not lumbered.'

'Look,' Abbot said. 'I think there is a connection between Gargarin and Burns. I don't know what, but I think there is. You want me to tell you why I think it?'

'OK.' Mike was tempted to say, Don't laugh, it's not very strong, but he knew Abbott was a good police officer. 'This,' he said, pointing to a phrase, 'this means reverse gravity connection. It's something that Burns said once. He spoke of going to Holland and he used this same expression. You see it's nothing really, but it's a coincidence.'

Frank Abbott knew what he meant.

★

181

That weekend at the kite festival Mike Reynolds said to Jennet, 'Who's Baby Moon?'

'She sings with Mercury, that girl band, don't you know her?'

'Not my music,' he said.

'What's your music?'

'Grace Slick,' he said.

'Who? Who's Grace Slick?'

'She sang with Jefferson Airplane?'

'Who's Jefferson Airplane.'

'My dad's favourite band.'

'Your dad's favourite band!'

'Why shouldn't I like Grace Slick? Fantastic stuff. "Ballad of the Chrome Nun."' He turned, looked over to where the child was running, and shouted, 'Pull it, Tim, harder. Run, run! It'll come down otherwise.'

Then he leapt to his feet and chased after Timmy.

The little boy was running desperately downhill, trying to keep his kite afloat. Mike caught him, snatched him up, grabbed the string and raced uphill against the wind. He was able to get some lift into it, and the little kite, instead of fluttering on the brink of dropping from the sky, suddenly soared higher, and then higher, and the wind caught it, and it towered upwards.

'Wow,' said Timmy. 'You're good at this.'

Streatham Common kite day. The bands were out, although they had to compete with the Grateful Dead, who, long now after death, were blaring out from Bob Colover's tent, pegged out near the children's swings.

'How did you know about this?' Jennet said.

'Bob Colover sent me a flyer.'

'No, I meant the park.'

'It's where I grew up; down there.' He pointed to Abbotswood Road.

182

'I've never been here before.'

'You mean Streatham?'

'No.'

'Never?'

'No, never.'

'Amazing.'

'Are you laughing at me?'

'No.'

'You are.'

'No, I am not.' He put his arm round her shoulders and hugged her. It was the first time he had touched her with abandon. Before it had always been careful, polite. He had wondered about how to do it. Once or twice he had tried. But now it came so naturally, there was no fuss about it, no hesitation. Maybe this is how it is meant to be. No embarrassment.

'I like you the way you are. Why should I laugh at you?'

'What way am I?'

She sat down, then lay on her back, a piece of grass in her mouth, looking up at the blue, blue sky.

'Dark star, dark star . . .' sang Jerry Garcia.

'What are you?' He sat down and looked upwards with her. A huge multi-coloured kite, three tails, each thirty yards long, drifted into their vision. It rippled like an eel, like three huge eels; each ripple took seconds to travel its length.

'Here it is, the big one,' said Bob Colover on the PA system. 'It's the one we've been waiting for – The Kraken Wakes. One hundred and thirty-two feet long, it needs three people to fly it, each displaying skills learnt over generations of kite flyers.' He got into his stride. 'This, ladies and gentlemen, is the largest flying man-made object that it is possible to get into the boot of a Morris Minor.'

Timmy's kite nudged beneath it.

'And beneath it there is Timmy's pilot fish kite, allowed by the Kraken to clean its teeth. Careful, Timmy, it doesn't get eaten.'

Timmy cried over in dismay at Mike.

'Don't worry, it's only Bob. Take no notice,' Mike said.

He looked at Jennet again. 'What are you?' he said. 'Is that what you asked me?' He thought about it, he said, 'I know you're an open door.'

'A what?'

'Meeting you was like opening a door.' He rolled over onto his stomach. 'I found an open door and through it I saw a garden.'

She had turned over too and was looking at him. He could see she didn't understand what he meant, though she knew it was good.

'What I mean is you're so natural,' he said. She was still not satisfied, she wanted more. 'And since you ask, you're beautiful, and intelligent, and kind. What more do you want?' He kissed her.

Timmy was watching someone kissing his mum. 'Don't you worry about me. Your mum's safe with me,' Mike shouted. 'But you're not!' He got up and ran after the little boy, who screeched and scampered up the hill, this time pulling his kite into the wind. It went higher and higher. Jennet watched them laughing and she thought about it.

Next they were sitting in the box compartment at Joanna's Restaurant, at the top of the hill. When Mike was young this place had been, for him, the height of sophistication. Timmy had seen the little compartment and had begged to go in there, but the moment they took the table he fell asleep. A hamburger sat disregarded in front of him.

Occasionally Jennet took a guilty chip from the child's plate. 'I know I shouldn't,' she said.

184

Mike looked at her. He thought, How do people have the courage to be themselves? Of course it was a stupid question, since people are lumbered with what they are and they make the best of a bad job. But some are brave about it. Jennet was one of those. Where did she get it from? Of course, from her mother.

He thought about Tommy Storey, who had told him, 'Most people lead lives of quiet desperation. Thoreau said that,' and for the first time Mike thought he understood it. Till then it had just sounded like another excuse.

'But your mum doesn't approve of me,' Mike said. 'She said so when I met her outside the school.'

Jennet got her chance. She'd been wondering about that meeting, wondering what her mam had said. Her mam might have driven this man away. She had done that before.

'Please don't worry about my mam.'

He put his hand on hers. She let it stay there since Timmy was asleep and he wouldn't see. He had seen him kiss her earlier, though it was just a peck.

Mike said, 'Now, don't you worry about your mum, because it's not me that's worrying about her, it's you. I like your mum. You wouldn't be you, if it weren't for your mum, and I think it's right that she looks out for you. She doesn't want any old person stepping in and hurting you.' He added, and then immediately wondered whether he should have done, 'She's not going to frighten me away.'

Jennet didn't say anything more. How was it he always said just the right thing?

'I tell you what you do, Jennet. You make me feel a better person. I understand more when I'm with you. I am a better person when I'm with you.'

Her eyes brimmed with tears. Nobody had ever said anything so kind to her.

185

'C'mon, Timmy,' he said, and he scooped the child up like a feather. 'Let's be getting you home then,' and Timmy's head fell back against his shoulder, completely relaxed.

Chapter 12

Billy Burns went to see Charlie Pope. He needed to warn Charlie what was going to happen. After all, Charlie was the main investor and ought to know about it.

'Wicked Man has disappeared, at least that's what Gargarin thinks. He doesn't know what I know. He was picked up, outside the house. Only a routine stop and search. He didn't get bail because he was carrying – I'll be able to fix it. But it might be preliminary to a raid. If he's talked, that is.'

'Is the place being run according to the House Rules?'

'Yeah. Gargarin is very good, to the book. If he is raided it will be clean, nothing, no wraps, no equipment, no trace. Just like you designed it.'

Charlie Pope had done what comes naturally to someone after sitting through so many drug trials. He had designed a foolproof system, one that would not provide the police with evidence to prove the case. He only needed a plumber to design it, and then as long as the franchisee stuck to procedure, the house might be raided but the franchisee could not be prosecuted, because nothing would be found. So no torn bits of wrapping paper, no jeweller's scales, no lists of people or chunks of unexplained money – nothing to tell a story. A raid would only be an inconvenience.

'But there is a problem. The amount of stuff they're taking has dropped off. They must be buying in. It's happened since the delivery system changed – after Jimmy. It's either him or Wicked doing it. We shall see. I'm gonna go and talk to him, have a franchisees' meeting. I thought I better warn you.'

'Don't let the twins get out of hand.'

'No, that's next time. This is the first warning, like it's set out in your manual, Charlie.'

The next day Billy Burns, carrying his plumber's kit, wearing a flat hat, stopped Alleycat as she was about to drive out of the school gates.

'Hi,' he said.

She recognised him despite only having seen him once. He had guessed she would; he'd noticed she always watched what was going on around her.

'I need to see Gargie.' He had to mouth what he said through the car window. She said something in reply and he didn't have to pretend not to hear it, because he couldn't.

He stood in a such way that made it difficult for her to move the vehicle without hitting him. She was stuck. People were piling up behind her. There were often arguments about the cars in this school entrance. She said something again, it sounded like 'come round later'. This time he did have to pretend not to hear. He knew she wouldn't want a fuss at the school gates, so when he made 'open it' signs at the car door she did so.

She had broken the rule, never open a car door when you're carrying. Never, even for me, he had tried to teach them. To illustrate it, he used to tell the story of how Saxby drove off, leaving his wife screaming, which wasn't surprising, since the Taylor brothers had her. It was all there in the training manual.

188

He got in the car.

'What do you want?'

She still had the sense to be suspicious. She didn't just accept what was happening because he was someone she knew. But by now it was too late.

'Never mind,' he said. 'I want to speak to Gargie.'

'Get in touch in the normal way.'

'No, I need to see him now. Something urgent's come up.' Might as well reassure her.

Reluctantly she drove off. She should have got out of the car, just left it and dumped the stuff.

Billy didn't speak, he watched the road. This was where he had grown up. Those days he would have been amazed at the idea of being driven like this, with this black woman in this ridiculous car, a big jeep with pictures on it. But things had changed. They left the school behind them. She drove carefully.

'Where is he now?' Billy said. It did no harm to make her think he wasn't quite sure where they were going.

'At the house. He won't gonna to let you in there.' She was nervous enough to have it affect her speech.

'Why not? He knows me.'

'He'll speak through the gate. He's never let anyone in there with him save me and Wicked. I'll go in and tell him you're outside.'

'Something's come up. I need to show him something.'

'It was you fixed up the place?'

'Yes.'

She didn't say anything just kept on driving.

When they stopped Billy said, 'I'll come with you.'

'No, you mustn't.'

'You can't stop me, can you?' He knew he would get nowhere unless he was with her. She had parked the car a little away from the house, but that would make no differ-ence if police were watching. The essence of this system was not to prevent the police knowing where they were, but to make sure that even if they did, they could do nothing about it.

They crossed the road. It was the first time he had been to one of his houses while it was operating, but he reckoned that what he had to do could only be done in the house. He carried a workman's bag, some sort of reason for being there. The chances were he would go down on an observation sheet as 'Unidentified man, ?workman. In at 9.15. Same man as above, out at 9.45'.

'This man came with me. I couldn't stop him,' Alleycat said.

'There's a problem,' Billy said immediately.

Gargie looked very doubtful. 'What about our system?' he said.

'We've got a problem with Wicked. Why do you think I risked coming?'

It was enough to convince Gargie and he swung the gate open for Billy and Alison to come in. 'What you got?' he said to her.

She spat into her hand, and handed over what there was.

Gargie said, 'OK, see you later, I'll put this away first.' He disappeared through a door, returned and let Alison out through the gate. Billy went ahead into the other room.

'You said you would never come here.'

'This is different, Gargie.' Billy turned round from where he had bent over the TV to turn it off. Now he had a gun.

What happens when someone pulls a gun on you: time and space is warped in your head. Things sway. The *North American Journal of Psychological Studies* has published on it.

190

Prison had taught Billy to spend a lot of time in libraries and he had found it there. If you – when you are the guy having the gun pulled on you – can force your way out of this warp, then the guy holding the gun, who is in the warp just as much as you are, can be surprised. Use the bend in psychological time to speed yourself up, like a slingshot.

When he first read this, instead of laughing at it, Billy Burns knew it was true. He had felt it often enough. It's like stepping on a step that isn't there. If you know you're about to do it, there's no problem, you just count a beat as your foot goes down the extra distance. But if you're unprepared, you fall on your face.

So when you're the guy producing a gun, the best way is to count one, two, and say, just at the right moment, 'This is a gun, Gargie.' It puts everything back in its place again. This is what he used to do when he did it in banks. When he did the same to Gargie, he knew Gargie wasn't about to jump anybody. Instead Gargie stood still.

'Sit down.'

Gargie sat down.

The abreaction was coming. Billy had read about the 'abreaction' as well. That's the moment most people get shot, according to the magazine. Gargie, in control now, was about to come up out of the chair and at him, so instead Billy Burns said, 'I want you to count to five, Gargie, or I'll shoot you in the eye.'

He pointed the gun directly at Gargie's eye.

He knew that in the guy's brain the muzzle hole of the gun would expand like an image in a concave mirror until it filled the whole of his vision.

Billy said, 'One, two, go on, count, Gargie.'

'Three,' said Gargie.

Now he had him. Billy knew he was all right now.

This was the bit the magazine called 'the chicken and

the white line'. As long as the chicken looked at the line, it wasn't about to move. In the banks he had done this by making people hold their shoes. They'd stay reached down, holding their shoes, for minutes after he had left. He saw it on a video once.

Billy said, 'You're gonna put these on.' He threw some handcuffs in Gargie's lap. 'We need to talk, and although I can hold this gun steady for a long time, I don't want to have to stand here like this. That way there could be an accident.'

When Billy breathed in he could feel the oxygen at the tip of his nose. Apparently this was the result of adrenalin expanding the blood vessels. Maybe that was rubbish, but it was a good feeling. He hadn't had it for a long time.

'Through the arm of the chair first.'

Gargie put the handcuffs on. He was either very angry, or very frightened; the veins at the edge of his eyes were showing. Billy had chosen that chair for that reason. Gargie was tethered. Billy could now let the gun fall.

'We have to talk,' he said. 'I'm told that things are not being done correctly here.'

Gargie said nothing. Billy fetched a chair and sat opposite Gargie.

'Look,' he said, 'if I hadn't pulled the gun on you, you and I wouldn't have been able to talk easy. You know that, you'd have thrown me out, maybe worse. Now nothing is gonna happen. Soon I'm going out that door, leaving you this key on the mat there. We may well not see each other again.'

He paused to let it sink in.

'So what I say is, you talk, and I'll talk. Sensible. No disrespect.'

Gargie's voice was thick. Billy recognised the anger compressed in it. 'What's this, if not disrespect?' He held up his handcuffed hands.

'That's not disrespect. That's because I'm an old man now, and I need the space. Think about it. What could I do in here on my own against you? You're still young, you've got life ahead of you. What have I got? Cocoa and Viagra. So let's talk.'

Billy watched him. Gargie was an intelligent man. Billy had guessed he would get through to him, which was why he came himself. Not sent the twins looking for him to bring him in. He said, 'Look, I came here because I can talk to you, not like with some of the others. With them it's like working with a child. With them you have to be rough.'

Gargie nodded and came to a decision. 'Right,' he said. 'You tell me, what's the problem you came about?'

'As I see it, the problem is you're not opening all the time.'

'I know that.' Gargie was quick. It was clear he was telling the truth. Obviously he was relieved that this was all that was worrying Billy. 'I know Wicked Man is leaving early,' he went on. 'He's done it a number of times. I've spoken to him already. And now he's gone. I'm looking to interview a replacement.'

'You know the agreement? Otherwise neither you, nor I, will get the proper return on our investment.'

'Yeah, yeah. That's all that you came for?'

Billy said, 'Wicked Man has disappeared.'

'OK, OK. I'll replace him. The take is only down slightly.'

'Is it, though? One of your men going home early, or not working any more, that's for you to deal with, not my problem. What I came for is more serious.'

Now the tip of Gargie's tongue showed at his lips. Gargie was very nervous.

'What I hear is you're selling product that's not Dutch stuff. Our agreement was that you would only bring stuff

193

into this house bought from me. None of this falafel rubbish.'

Gargie didn't answer. That was enough for Billy. He'd been told this. Now he knew it was true.

'What are we going to do?'

Nothing.

'Do you want to go back on our deal?'

Billy knew he might have to get angry. He didn't want to.

'Look, let's lay this out, let's think why we have an agreement. If you run this house on your own you'll make some money. For a while. Then you'll be busted and the chances are you'll go down for it. You've already got a conviction for class A drugs, you told me, and anyway dealing on this scale is worth five years minimum. More like ten, there being no exceptional circumstances in your case that your lawyer will be able to find. Not that exceptional circumstances would help, running a crack house being exceptional in itself.

'But if you run the house my way, you may be busted, but you won't be convicted. There will be no evidence to prosecute you with. You won't lose your drugs and you can start up again. I'll have another place for you within – what did we agree? – five weeks. But only if you stick to the rules.'

Gargie stared at Billy. Nothing there for Billy to see behind his eyes.

'And another thing. I helped you when you had a problem with your neighbour Jimmy, didn't I? If you'd hit him like you said you were going to, there would have been trouble, but he's away now, isn't he? Much less messy, you'll agree. So I've helped you. Now take my advice.'

Gargie stared at him. This wasn't going in.

'Take a holiday, then come back to work. And we can work together. This is a service I provide.' He looked

194

round at the standard suburban room, the *TV Times* on the hearth, the ghastly picture on the wall. 'This is the service you buy. You've moved twice now, and how did it feel? Was it much of a problem? Better than prison?'

Gargie still did not respond. He looked at Billy like he must have looked at his first probation officer, unable to deal with someone telling him something he didn't want to hear. Maybe he wasn't as bright as Billy thought. Billy knew what it was. Gargie's injured dignity was getting in the way of understanding what must be done to make things work. Who would have thought dignity would matter so much? That was black all over, of course. Always looking for an insult.

'But you have to keep your side of the bargain. It would be stupid not to.'

Billy stopped speaking and there was silence.

'Go on,' he said, 'talk to me.'

Billy knew what Gargie had been thinking. He had been thinking the same as any man who ever takes up a franchise thinks. Once the system is up and running, he thinks to himself, Why should I sell their stuff and not my own? Look at the price of it. Tied houses say it about the beer. Chicken bars say it about the chicken. And now he had crack houses saying it about the crack. Anyone selling a franchise will tell you it happens, it's one of the headaches.

He knew now Gargie was not going cooperate, even if he said he would. Billy said, 'Gargie, I'm going to say one thing. I'm going to threaten you. You shut this house, till you come back to me and agree you'll only sell my stuff. Then I'll start you up somewhere different.'

Silence.

'I'm gonna let that sink in,' said Billy. He waited thirty seconds.

Then he said. 'Here is the threat. If you don't, I will

have you fucked. You're fucking me over, and I'll do it in return. And I mean just that. I won't have Alison Alleycat fucked, that's unfair on her, though no doubt she's used to it. I'll have you fucked. And I'll let everyone know about it. And the film will be available for hire.'

He got up.

'That's all I've got to say to you. You listen. You know what happened to Rootsie. I know you do, because he still walks funny. And all the ladies laugh.'

Billy went to the door. He put the keys to the handcuffs on the floor. 'I'll give you one piece of help. I'll deal with Wicked Man for you. As an offering.' That was easy to say since it had already been arranged. Gargie still said nothing.

'Nobody but you and I know about this, Gargie. Think of it – I could have said all this in front of Alison but I didn't. Remember that. I'm showing you some respect. It may not look like it, but I am.'

PART FOUR

Sentence

Chapter 13

When he looked back on it, Scott realised that this was the day when things became both serious and confused. It should have been straightforward.

The sentence hearing for Jimmy Reilly was fixed for the afternoon, but had got mixed up with another case his clerk, Terry, had found for him to do. 'Mr Scott, you know you're a regular there and if there's anything spare you're one of the ones they ask for – there's a plea on in the same court after yours, and the CPS has no one to cover it. They need someone senior because it's a text case.'

'They told you that? Texts are meant to be secret.'

A text is the document telling the judge the defendant is an informer, and for obvious reasons they are kept very quiet.

'Not to us, sir.'

'Where is it now?'

'Here.'

'And?'

'We were hoping you would come in and collect it.' Terry sounded unusually meek. For good reason. The detour would at least double Scott's journey.

'No. You bike it to the court.'

'But the security.'

'It hasn't been very secure so far.'

'All right then. It'll be in the list office.'

Scott had to set off much earlier than he had planned since he still needed time to see Jimmy Reilly. On the way he remembered he had not rung Charlie Pope. Today was the day he was going to see him. After he had told Jimmy Reilly what he was doing.

He called while sitting at an interminable red light. No reply, then a click and a voice machine: 'Leave your message.' For a moment Scott wondered, then he hung up. You don't leave messages if you're involved in this sort of thing. Eventually he would even have to junk the pay-as-you-go Sim card. He remained sitting at the red light.

When he got to court, he went straight to the list office. Then he found a place in a conference room, opened the new papers and tried to soak up the story as quickly as he could. Esau McLaren had been stopped in Burrell Road by a police constable in the act of lighting a spliff.

When he was told to put it out, since he was in public and there was a school nearby, he sucked his teeth and told the officer to fuck off.

Even that was not enough to get him arrested. It only resulted in a request to search him. He refused and tried to run off. If he had made it, no one would have been any the wiser, or cared very much. Life would have carried on much as usual, but a police car happened to stop right behind him.

And then he was arrested.

He was found to be carrying twenty-one packets of a 'rock-like substance, believed to be crack cocaine'.

Esau told the custody sergeant to fuck off as well, so he didn't get bail, losing his next chance of running off.

He couldn't have done better if he had been trying to make it worse, which he wasn't. He was just being himself – dumb. All this was just another story to Jeremy

Scott, who had read literally thousands of such cases. Esau hadn't handled himself well, but not much worse than many do.

Scott did not know then that this case would engulf him.

He always read briefs backwards: the main evidence first, only then find out what he is charged with. That way, if the charges were wrong he would see it more easily. This was a good example. Esau McLaren was only charged with possession of crack cocaine, not with possession with intent to supply. The difference was massive. He had not been accused of being a dealer, which he most obviously was.

Scott turned to the scientific analysis.

Only five of the wraps had cocaine in them. The others were baking powder with gunk mixed in. That nearly explained it, but even the wraps that weren't cocaine were still good evidence of intent to supply. But the instructions were clear, proceed on possession alone. Scott knew what it was that had caused this. It was the text. This Mr McLaren must be a valuable man.

'Prosecuting in court four, McLaren?' A face appeared round the door.

'Yes,' Scott said.

'I was told you were in here.'

'Yeah, I was just getting the brief up.'

'Fulton. DS Fulton.' The policeman stuck his hand out. 'I'm here with the necessary.' He pulled a brown envelope from his pocket. He didn't offer it to Scott, and held it as though wary it might be snatched from him. 'Our Mr McLaren has been very useful to us. He has to be very carefully handled.'

It was odd how accurate the terminology was. Handling him as though he were a package. An informer did not come into the category 'person' at all.

'I bet.'

'We don't want to lose him now. It took a long time to turn this guy.'

'Do you want me to say that to the judge?'

'I'll say it if I have to.' Then he seemed to take a decision. 'I'd better tell you about what we've got here.' He waved the brown envelope. 'His tag name is Wicked. He provides us with top-class information. He was picked up by a uniform patrol by chance, and if he hadn't been prosecuted, then it would have seemed odd. So the case had to go on.'

'For possession with intent to supply?' said Scott.

'The charge is only five wraps now, which isn't enough to show he intended to supply anything. Since the rest of the stuff luckily turned out not to be cocaine.' He smiled.

So, the forensic report had been interfered with, or perhaps what arrived at the laboratory was not what was seized. The idea that a top-grade drug dealer would go around with imitation drugs was ridiculous. He'd be risking his life.

'He was stopped just outside the crack house. We're asking you not to give the address. It's in the papers, we couldn't take that out, but it's not important.'

'That's all right. I can do that.'

Fulton said, 'The officer who made the arrest doesn't know we are involved and he mustn't know there was a text.'

That would be difficult. How would Scott justify accepting the plea? Something was wrong here. 'How can I do that?' said Scottt. 'What if he asks?'

'Say it is another operation. We'll fix that. I'll get this to the judge.' He held up the brown envelope. 'I'll deal with the officer who's coming. His name is Carr.'

Fulton's system relied upon counsel doing what they

202

were told, and they always did when it came to disclosure.

Scott found PC Carr by asking the usher. 'Reilly will be on at about three and McLaren after that. There's your officer,' he said, pointing at a policeman sitting on a bench.

'Are you in McLaren? My name is Scott. Shall we talk?'

The officer didn't waste any time. 'This is a serious case. I know that this man is a major supplier, I can smell it.' What for him had been a chance encounter had turned into quite a catch.

'We can't say that. He wasn't carrying much,' Scott said. 'Not enough to demonstrate an intention to supply.' He had to say it, though it was ridiculous.

'Five is enough. Especially since he had sixteen other wraps. They didn't come up as cocaine, but he obviously believed they were. Even if he was wrong it shows he was intending to supply.'

This wasn't going to be easy – the officer was completely right.

Scott said, 'My instructions are to offer a plea to simple possession, and I'm stuck with that, I've no choice in the matter.'

'Typical.' The policeman wrote something on a clipboard. As he took his hand away Scott could see what he had written: 'Accept plea to possession', it said, and after it added a big exclamation mark.

'I can understand why you say what you do,' Scott said. Then he wished he hadn't said anything.

'It's obviously a perfectly good supply case. Chummy had a wad of money in his sock. How do you get that much if you are an unemployed IT student like he says? He had a list of people to whom he sold, or at least he had a list of people. And the place he was heading for, everybody knows it's a crack house.'

'Well,' Scott said. 'It's not my decision. Weren't you told? After all it's been listed for a plea.'

Of course the policeman must have realised a decision had been taken elsewhere, but that wasn't going to stop him complaining about it. He probably associated Scott directly with the people who had made it.

'At least he'll do time for it. Look.'

PC Carr unclipped a wad of papers from his board. It was McLaren's record. Two offensive weapons, a possession of class A drugs and two cautions for cannabis. For someone who had only been in the country for two years, he had done pretty well. Normally with that, he would have served a sentence already.

Well, Scott knew why he hadn't.

The policeman said, 'He's obviously a Yardie. They come over here—' He broke off. This was a dangerous thing to say. A complaint of racist language could be more damaging to his career than hitting a prisoner. It was odd really, since he wouldn't have liked Esau McLaren even if had he come from Dorset. He'd still have said, 'They come down here.' The courts still say that in Kent about Londoners.

'Came over here, did he?' said Scott. It was better let him blow off steam.

The policeman was reassured. 'Yes. They come over here. Well, I don't mind the ones who behave themselves, that's OK, that's the way it goes. But these ones. They cause nothing but trouble, and they go to and from Jamaica, you know, like they owned the place – which they do, Jamaica that is, no problem – and every time they do it they recruit another flood of women coming in carrying cocaine.'

Scott nodded.

'Bloody violent they are as well. We had one the other day who threw his woman out of the window. Luckily it

204

was Myatt's Fields, and that's only two stories high. Of course he shot her in the mouth beforehand.'

'Oh,' Scott said.

'Shooting in the mouth is the way Yardies deal with women. It started with Mrs Penny, the wife of the Chairman of Air Jamaica: Don't talk, it means.'

Scott nodded.

'There's no doubt in my mind—' The policeman began and then he stopped. 'My name's Carr. Good to meet you.'

He stuck out his hand, interrupting himself. Scott shook it.

'There's no doubt in my mind, there's something funny going on here. I don't know what it is, but, you know –' he sucked his teeth, and bent his head towards Scott, as if to say mark my words – 'you know, mark my words, there's funny business with this chief, here.' Then he nodded.

Scott nearly said 'Chief?' but he didn't want to stop the man in his flow.

'The Firebird posse. I reckon he is, there are signs. And if he's not the chief, then he's close to him.'

'Right,' Scott said.

'They set fire to people.'

'What?'

'Yeah, that's their method. Did you know that an old Volvo 244 can produce enough heat completely to incinerate a body? Leaves nothing behind. No remains at all, better than a crematorium. That's why they like Volvos. Especially the Firebird posse.'

For once Scott blessed the loudspeaker in a conference room. 'Call for Mr Scott of counsel.' He had left a message with the desk to be called when Jimmy Reilly was brought to the court. He looked up and said, 'That's me. We'll have to talk about this later before the case comes on. I've got something else now.'

He escaped PC Carr.

★

205

At last Scott got down to the cells. Jimmy Reilly said, 'You did your best, Mr Scott, but how they convicted me on the ones they did and acquitted me on the other one beats me. They were frightened I might be who that Reynolds says I am.'

As a summary of what was wrong with the conviction it couldn't have been bettered.

Scott said, 'I've got the report from the probation service. It's together with a psychology report.'

'I know it. I saw the guy. He kept saying I had no feeling – what did he call it? No empathy, for the small boy and his awful experience. And I said, "Well, since he didn't have an awful experience, I can't, can I?"

'And then he says I was wrong to put him through the ordeal of giving evidence. And I said, what do you want me to do? Admit something I didn't do? Anyway, it wasn't an awful experience, he enjoyed it. And he said victim support had rung him up to say the boy had cried in the video room. And I said it was because he had been caught out lying, wasn't it? And then the man got up and left.'

No wonder the report said what it did.

'Do you want to see it?' Scott said.

'No,' said Jimmy. 'Why would I want to know what that moron thought? He knows nothing about anything.'

Just as well. The report had been written on the basis of the prosecution papers, and everything that had happened in the trial might as well not have taken place, save of course for victim support ringing up and saying how upset the child was.

'It's not going to be good, Jimmy.'

'I know it. But they are not going to have me admit I'm a nonce, because I'm not. Look.'

He rolled up his sleeve. His arm from elbow to wrist was a livid red.

'Good God, what's that?'

'Hot tea. And if I hadn't been expecting it they would have got my face.'

'You haven't been segregated then?'

'No. I'm not. I'm not going that way. That would be admitting it, and it would mean having to associate with nonces, wouldn't it?'

The irony was that Jimmy would probably still approve of the throwing of boiling water over sex offenders.

'You can manage that?'

'Look, Mr Scott, I've been around. I've met every sort, and I know that what gets through is standing up for yourself. So that's what I am going to do.'

Scott wasn't listening to ordinary bluster, the kind you can hear in any golf club from men standing slightly back on their heels, legs apart, clasping a jug of beer to their chest. This was real. Jimmy wouldn't go to any open prison. He would spend years having to watch out for revved-up young men, wanting to vent their anger. Scott had seen this sort of courage before, but never so clearly as now.

As if he knew what Scott was thinking, Jimmy said, 'Now, don't you worry, Mr Scott. And you tell Mary not to worry either. I'll manage this.'

Silence, then astonishingly: 'Mr Scott, you did as much as any man could have done for me. The way you fought. And you refused to give up despite that judge. But then that's your reputation, I know, I asked around.'

Well, that was a character reference to put alongside the dragon judge Suzanne's spiteful little remark.

From the moment the hearing began, Scott said to himself, He's seen my grounds of appeal. The judge, Meadowsweet, was a changed man. He was hedging his bets. He said that he was not going to take any account of the psychologist's report. Scott didn't even have to push the point and for a moment it was so surprising it nearly threw him.

'No, Mr Scott, you're right. Sometimes I think one should take a broader view.'

Scott had no idea what that meant, but he knew when he got to the court of appeal they would be thinking this was a reasonable judge.

'Four years.'

It could have been worse; on the other hand, this was an innocent man. Scott was entirely sure of that. He dreaded the meeting with Mary Reilly.

Mike Reynolds sat at the back of the court. He noticed the change in the judge as well, but he put it down to the way the lawyers always pull together eventually. Scott even seemed to expect it.

The clerk of the court was about to call the McLaren case on when she was interrupted. 'We'll sit in chambers first,' Meadowsweet said. 'Are you prosecuting this next matter, Mr Scott?'

Scott had to turn back from telling Jimmy Reilly that he would be down to see him after this next case.

'Yes, your honour,' he said and he saw Fulton moving away from the front of the court, the brown envelope being passed up.

'Who defends?'

'I think it's Mr Street.'

'Does he want to be here?' And then with a flash of his normal self: 'No? Well, we'll carry on without him.'

The judge spoke to the court usher at the door of the court. 'Bar the door. Don't announce the case.'

The usher shooed people out. Scott saw Reynolds turn to look at him as he left. Well, at least that meant that PC Carr could not come in; though what Scott was going to

208

say if he was asked about what was happening he still didn't know.

'There is a text in the case? Yes? Who is bringing it?'

Scott indicated the detective.

'You need this man on the street, do you?'

The officer only had to nod his head in answer to the judge.

'All right then.' It had been done in a moment, hardly noticed, even the defence were not there – and all quite lawful. In the moment the usher walked to the back of the court Meadowsweet said, 'Mr Scott, I don't see the value of psychological reports like that one.'

The judge had acted on a visceral memory that people ought not be sentenced on the basis of some expert's opinion.

The doors were opened, the case was called on and twenty minutes later, much to PC Carr's disgust, Esau McLaren was on the street.

PC Carr started to complain. 'You didn't say how much money he had on him, or about the crack house nearby.'

'I couldn't,' said Scott. 'Neither were anything to do with the charge of possession.'

He should not have been so brusque; but he had Mr Reilly and his wife on his mind and he wanted to get downstairs before security took Reilly away.

PC Carr, like most disappointed litigants, naturally blamed the lawyer.

Mike Reynolds saw Fulton as they were leaving the court afterwards. He asked, 'What were you doing in the court when it was closed for a moment?'

'What do you mean?'

'In with the judge.'

'Nothing really,' Fulton said.

Fulton didn't think he had been seen. He covered up. 'I

209

was in the next case. The one before had been some sort of sex case, and the barrister was talking with the judge about taking no notice of the report. They agreed on that. I just happened to be there.'

It ought to have struck Reynolds as a bizarre answer. Why should Fulton have been present when a case, not his own, was being discussed anyway? But the reply was so exactly what he had expected, confirming that Scott was up to something, that the question never formed in his mind.

'What was the judge like?'

'Like? Working on the side of the lawyers, as usual, what do you expect?'

'Yeah,' Reynolds said, 'too true.'

He was going back to East Place with Bill Carr and he told him about it.

'That's OK, Mr Scott. I can do that on my head,' Jimmy said. It was always said. It was a strange expression. Where it came from Scott never understood and Morton's glossary only made a guess.

Scott wanted to tell Jimmy what he had discovered. Nowhere near anything definite yet, but beginning to confirm what they knew was true, that Jimmy had been set up.

'Is there anything? Any reason why they should pick on you?'

Jimmy Reilly was sure there wasn't. 'I keep myself to myself now, Mr Scott. I had enough trouble before I met Mary. But now I have to look out for her. Life has changed for me.'

He told Scott the story again: how he had settled down, the three children, and then his accident and no work for six months. 'I lost the van, and all my kit, since it wasn't paid for yet. I only got by through a bit of ducking and diving. I got work out of the boys in the pub.'

'Did you know about the victim compensation business which was being run at the pub?'

'That's criminal injuries stuff, not theft or anything. I'd heard Billy helped people, but it was only because he knew a little about it, that's all. And he'd help anyone out, Billy.'

'And Vernon?'

'No.'

'You remember that was the name the little boy used?'

'Yes.' But nothing, Jimmy could add nothing. He didn't know a Vernon.

They talked about his family.

'It's the kids, Mr Scott. For a while the wife didn't know whether she could even bring the kids to see me. She did, though, and no one has said anything. Do you know the rules?'

Scott didn't even know how to find out, and they both agreed it wouldn't be wise to speak to the probation officer about it. Mary might be stopped from bringing them. Jimmy Reilly remained outside the system, with no help at all, and he would do so as long as he denied the offence.

'I'll go and speak to Mary then,' Scott said.

'I said to him, to Jimmy when I saw him, Mr Scott will help you. Don't you worry. But all the same it's a nightmare.'

Scott knew that this belief in him was pure accident, that if by chance he hadn't been free to do the case, and Brian, or John, or anyone else in chambers had done it, then it would have been they on whom Mrs Reilly depended. After all, Mrs Reilly needed to believe someone was on their side, so it wasn't personal. But it was a burden all the same.

'The children have started saying, Where's Daddy? When is he coming to put us to bed? And one of them came home from school and said, What's prison? One of

211

the other kids had said it to her. She didn't know that the place we went to see Jimmy was a prison.'

Mary Reilly started crying. 'And I can't talk to anyone. Not anyone. They all think it's my fault for choosing a pervert to live with. A pervert! Sheila Kenny said that. When I heard it, I nearly went round there. It wouldn't have done any good.'

What do you do when this happens? You sit and listen. Perhaps they train young lawyers in it now. It's odd how the complaint is that barristers are cut off from life. Scott wished he was.

'And I keep saying to Jimmy, you know why this happened. You know.'

What was this?

'But he's such a fool. He's got a temper on him, and that's got him into trouble in the past. But deep down he's a decent man, that's his problem, he doesn't know how to deal with people like that.'

'People like what? He said he didn't know why this might have happened.'

'Oh yes he does. He thinks that Billy Burns is such a wonderful man, and that his evidence would do it. But I bet it's him that did this all along. He's a pig. Everyone knows it.'

Slowly Scott got the story.

Jimmy had been approached in the pub and agreed to take a parcel in, look after it, till it was collected. £50 a week, and they could do with the money to get back on their feet again. But Mary was suspicious. The guy who collected it didn't look right, all the gold and that, so she followed him, and it went to the crack house. The one in the street, the cause of all the trouble in the area. The place was notorious, but even the police couldn't touch it.

So the next time the man came for the parcel Jimmy

212

knocked him over and threw him out, parcel and all. She told him it was a silly thing to do, but no, he would do it. He was a strong man, Jimmy, he knew no other way. And now this.

Scott didn't leave the court till the rush hour had begun.

The traffic approaching the flyover was backed up already, but just far enough to give Scott a warning and he was able to pull off at the tight turning next to the scrap merchant. The road took him round in a small circle and dumped him onto the back roads near the park, but at least it was away from the jam.

It began to rain. He managed to cut through some of the back doubles before the traffic closed in on him again, but then found himself stationary outside a huge Victorian church in Hackney. It rose up into the night sky to where a great lantern adjoined the roof of the house next to it. I wonder what goes on in there, he thought; what girl's prayers?

He stared at it for five minutes, while a truck in front of him inched forward. A large lady, with her small daughter in tow, threaded her way between his car and the truck.

So Jimmy Reilly said no one had done this to him. But more is going on all the time than we know. We can only guess at it, we haven't a clue. Stuff is served up to the courts and the lawyers play silly games with it, imagining that what they are working on is real and has not been predigested. Perhaps he had been silly to think he could interfere.

Good God! The very forensic scientist's report in that drug case had been fixed.

The traffic began to move again.

And if you can fiddle it in favour of a defendant, why can't you fiddle it against him? In what way is that different from the judge disregarding that vicious psychologist's report? On the basis of that report Jimmy Reilly should have been locked up for ever. And then the drug dealer, McLaren, eventually gets a fine. A fine! For heaven's sake. The police officer, Carr, was livid. Quite right too. What a day. You only just get over handling one weird thing, and another comes along.

A side road looked open and he slid down it.

The road took him across two main roads. Both were full, snarled up in each direction, so he continued cutting across the traffic towards the river.

As Scott crossed Commercial Road, PC Carr saw him. He sucked his teeth. 'There's that barrister,' he said.

'Where?' Mike Reynolds hadn't noticed.

'Going down that one-way street.' They looked to their left, and Reynolds saw a car disappearing. Silence.

Mike Reynolds said, 'Don't tell me it's a coincidence. He was in both cases. Both cases he discusses with the judge; in mine they agree to disregard a medical report, and in yours he fixes a plea.'

'What do you mean, both cases he discusses with the judge?'

'Didn't you know?' Reynolds was quite surprised. 'Your case was called on behind closed doors. I heard the judge say so. It must have been discussed, defence counsel was not even there. I thought you would know.'

'Good God,' said Carr. 'Nobody told me that.'

'That's no coincidence, then. In each case, in front of the same judge, he talks about it without telling us?' Reynolds thought about it. He said, 'Was Scott the lawyer who dealt with your case to begin with?'

'No, I was given a different name,' said Carr.

'He was brought into the case then?'

'Must have been.' Then Carr said, 'How do you know they disregarded the medical report?'

214

'The judge said he had. From what I gathered there was something in it the defence wouldn't have liked. But of course we're not allowed to see them.' Mike Reynolds thought it through. 'I thought there was something suspicious about Scott, and if I hadn't seen him getting involved in your case, I would have thought it was a kids' thing. I mean, he's obviously involved in assisting paedophiles. But now I think it's more than that. He must be in much deeper than that. There's more going on than we know.'

Carr agreed. He enjoyed a conspiracy – and a chase. 'Well, we know he's off somewhere now. Driving across London like he knows exactly where he's going.'

So they followed Scott down the one-way street.

At the end of the road Scott had to choose, left or right. It didn't really matter which one he took; he didn't know which went which way or where he was at all. He swung right and suddenly found himself in Wapping. The street turned into cobbles, and on his left he saw the converted warehouses with their expensive balconies. The door to the basement wine bar was wide open and light was spilling out on to the pavement.

He'd driven straight to Charlie Pope's without knowing the way.

Reynolds stopped the car outside the wine bar. Carr said, 'Shall we follow him in?'

'Why?'

'Let's just see what he does in his spare time. I have a feeling about this place, it rings a bell.' Carr's feelings about things were a legend, at least to him. He reached over to get his ordinary jacket to replace his uniform.

'No, not this time,' Mike said. 'Let's go.'

'Get the name of the place at least.'

'All right.' Reynolds took down a note: everything – time, car number, address, even that he had a clear and unobstructed view – CAUOV.

215

As they drove away Carr was quiet. Then he used his phone. 'Could you get me Frank Abbott?'

'To speak to?'

'To speak to. What else is there?'

Abbott picked up the phone.

'Frank?'

'Yeah?'

'Do you remember that wine bar in Wapping, yeah, near the newspaper factory?'

Frank Abbott said something.

'Didn't we go there during that investigation into the information that got out? The leak of information enquiry.'

Silence.

Then Carr said, 'Charlie Pope. Yes.'

He slapped the palm of his hand on the dashboard. 'I knew it.'

He turned to Mike Reynolds as he flipped his phone shut. 'That's the pub that Charlie Pope uses.'

'Right. Who's Charlie Pope?'

'He's a fixer.'

'What?'

'If you want to fix something in the press or in the courts, or in this job even, at least if you're dishonest, you contact Charlie Pope. Do you want to turn round? It sounds too good to be true.'

Mike Reynolds repeated the sentence. 'If you fix something in court you go see Charlie Pope. OK, that fits. I think we've got ourselves a dishonest lawyer.' He turned the car round and immediately they became totally stuck in the traffic.

'If you don't want me to know what happened, Mr McLaren, then I won't ask,' said Tony Street. Esau McLaren, Wicked Man, looked at his defence lawyer. Too right. He

216

didn't know why this had happened either. He was going to say nothing.

'Right,' he said, and put his hand up for touching. Give some respect.

Wicked left the court. No way was he going to go back to Myatt's Fields. So he was going to make for the Shakespeare estate. Larbey would help him. Whatever it was that had happened, and he didn't know what it was, he knew people would only think one thing about him now.

There's only one reason why someone who is carrying like he was walks away from court.

But he didn't make it. Fulton saw him leave and pointed him out.

Whichever way he went they were prepared and an arrest near the court would not strike anyone as odd. He was walking quickly, and they followed. 'It's what you would expect from someone like him,' one of them said.

Although Wicked Man was expecting something, who would have thought it would happen so soon? For a moment he took no notice of the two white men who stopped beside him in their car, asking the way. He just didn't expect white men. Whatever.

He didn't answer their question, but just kept going. They kept on at him. 'How do we get to Amberly Crescent?'

'What's it to do with me, bro, which way is which?' he said. 'You go find out.'

Then the men got out of the car, one in front of him, one behind. They weren't upset by his walking on and talking at them so, although some might have thought what he said was ignorant. They just put him in the back of the car.

It was an old tough Volvo. The locks on the doors had been taken off. So he had to sit, unable to do anything, thinking for a moment of putting his feet through the

217

window, waiting his moment. But one of the twins said, 'We need you out of the country, Wicked, and the best way is Luton airport.'

Then as they drove off Wicked Man saw Fulton standing a little further down the road watching, now turning away, and thought, They're police. Of course.

So he did nothing. Nobody said anything. The car got stuck in traffic for a while, but then they got onto a straight road.

'We have to stop here to collect some suitcases, you'll have to have them to travel with. You don't want to attract attention by walking through the airport empty-handed, do you, Wicked?'

Wicked Man felt a cold wind, but still he trusted the police. They pulled into the car park beneath an old estate.

'First you are going to have to come up the stairs with us, and the only way we can do it is like this.'

The passenger produced some handcuffs.

'That's cool,' said Wicked Man, who knew otherwise it might be difficult to walk through this estate with two white men, obviously policemen. But they didn't have to walk far. The old lift picked them up right from the car park. As they came out of the lift, the flat was one of a few not boarded up. They went inside.

When Wicked Man realised what was going to happen, the handcuffs that he had agreed to wear made it impossible to do anything about it. Billy Burns said, 'This isn't for your own good, Wicked, but I want others to know what happens when you sell other people's stuff in one of my houses. Even if it wasn't you, you were the man who put up Jimmy Reilly, who had done nothing, who knew nothing. Why – because he damaged your dignity. You nearly got him killed. I had to intervene. Jimmy Reilly was a friend of mine. It cost me a lot of grief with the Dutch boys that did, and money. You were warned when you

218

came into the trade, this thing doesn't work if it isn't tight, if people play games.'

He pulled the curtains even closer shut. 'Go on,' he said to the twins, and he left.

Chapter 14

Scott looked for Charlie Pope in the wine bar, but he wasn't there. The two round tables were empty, pushed back, creating an odd effect, as though they were merely pretending to be normal, but still waiting for Charlie Pope to sit at them. It seemed absurd to ask whether he was in – his absence was so obvious.

'No,' the woman behind the bar said, 'he's not in tonight. He may come in, but I doubt it now.'

The basement was dark and warm, sawdust on the floor. At the back, where the room curled round into another area, there were some more booths, each softly lit in among the shadows – inviting in their seclusion.

'Would you serve me a drink?'

'Of course.'

Always the same problem, one glass would not be enough, but to ask for two glasses outright would be clumsy, and if he bought two he might as well buy a bottle. But one thing was right: he said, 'May I take one of these?' and picked up a copy of the evening paper.

'Red wine?'

'Thank you.'

Scott took the paper to the table and the problem of the wine was solved when a bottle was brought over to him.

'There are still two glasses in there if you want another.' This was like a wine bar should be.

He read the paper.

One or two other people came in and disappeared into the other booths, but it was still very quiet.

In front of where Scott sat the bar was lit up, and anyone turning from it to carry a drink to a table had to peer into the darkness. So when the policemen arrived they looked as though they had walked onto a stage. They turned and looked over to Scott, who, seeing them, sank a little further back into the fold of the settle. He thought it was fairly likely they couldn't see him.

They turned back and waited at the bar, and when she came over, spoke to the same woman who had served him with the wine. She looked up and spoke. Scott could tell that she was saying no to something. Carr turned to Reynolds. Was he suggesting a drink? If he was, then Reynolds refused it and they left.

What were they doing here? It set him thinking.

The woman, Scott guessed by now she was the manager, since no other staff had yet appeared, brought some cheese biscuits over. 'Were those two men looking for me? I thought I recognised one of them,' he said.

'No, not you.' She lingered a moment sorting out Scott's table. 'Perhaps you did know them, though. They were asking for Charlie, too. But I don't know where he is tonight.'

'He's normally here?'

'Yes, normally.' She turned to her right, attracted by something she saw at the door. Scott couldn't see what it was. She went away.

So that's why Reynolds was here. He came to see Charlie Pope, and that was too great a coincidence, just after Reilly's case, wasn't it? Was it so unlikely he would be in contact with him? Pope said in this very bar that he

221

could fix cases, had offered to do so, and did so by paying policemen – so Reilly is set up, and the one person who could easily have done it would be Reynolds. Now here was Reynolds to get his payoff.

The whole thing seemed outlandish. But . . . but. He was always suggesting such things in court, not, it must be said, with much belief in them, but why shouldn't it be true for once? Maybe Reynolds was a corrupt cop.

He knew the reason why Jimmy was done and the way it was done and now he was getting closer to knowing who did it.

He had finished the two glasses and knew he was close to the driving limit, if not over. Why wasn't there a way of drinking and getting home OK? He got up to go, but as he did so he thought, why not stay for a meal and get a cab home? He had a book in his car outside. He could get it and be lost in it for the evening. This was as close as you could get to total self-indulgence.

He walked over to the bar; the manageress was serving a drink. He waited until she looked up at him and he said, 'Can I start another, and order something to eat? I'm just popping out to my car.'

Outside he fished around in the rubbish that had gathered in the boot. It was somewhere here; he pushed a scarf and a boot aside. Here we are: *Joseph and his Brothers*.

Very deep is the well of the past.

He could feel the loosening of the day's tension that alcohol gives, when you can subside into familiar ideas and rhythms you are used to repeating. He found his way back to the cellar, almost having to grope in the dark. On the table there was an open bottle of the same wine. Amazing. He poured himself a glass, settled his back into the corner of the seat and, holding it up to the light, opened his book. It slowly engulfed him.

★

222

As Grace Karenin talked to Annie her eyes became accustomed to the light and she became aware of someone sitting in the far booth reading a book while eating.

'Who's that?'

Most of the evening customers were regulars, and it wasn't someone she recognised.

'Not one of ours. He came in looking for Charlie and stayed.'

'What's he reading?'

'I was curious about that too. I looked: Thomas Mann.'

Single men reading books in public places are a provocation to women. Do they think they don't need anyone? If the two women thought this, then it was only just far enough below the surface not to be spoken. Certainly they both felt it, perhaps not enough to think it.

'Oh.' Grace watched the corner for a moment and naturally the man looked up, feeling himself being looked at.

Their eyes met and after a moment they recognised each other. Scott put the book down. He didn't wonder why she should be here. Rather he experienced the feeling, having lost something, of finding it again. There was no difficulty in approaching her because she was already halfway across the room.

He stood up as she slid onto the bench opposite. Here was Grace.

'Grace,' he said. He sat down again.

'Yes.' She smiled.

'What a coincidence.'

'Nothing happens by chance,' she said.

'You don't accept coincidence?'

She said, 'I work with it all the time. Things don't happen by chance, except when there's no one to see it. Thinking something is the result of mere chance is only a way of not staying alert.' She looked at him. 'What are you

223

doing here – other than reading a book?' She reached out to look at his book, but before she took it, she said, 'Thomas Mann?'

'How did you know that?' She couldn't have seen the title.

Grace wasn't above a bit of artifice. She said, 'That would be about the kind of thing you read. You think too much. What are you doing here? Are you following me?'

'How can I do that? I don't know where you live.'

'I live here, upstairs.'

'So you come here?'

'Yes, it's a kind of canteen for the block of flats, and I know Annie, who runs the place.'

'Do you eat here?'

'Yes.'

He took a breath.

'Shall we eat something together then?'

'Of course,' she said. She waited a beat, then, 'I thought you said you would ring me.'

'I did. You didn't answer.'

'No?'

'Do you listen to your answer messages?'

'No.'

'Why not?'

'When I get home I'm all phoned out. I don't want to listen to messages.'

She found his concern about his court cases unnecessary, or at least that's what she said, and she seemed amused to see him a bit disconcerted. She teased him. 'They're not serious enough to worry about. It's all a game.'

He said, 'That's easy to say, just because there are rules. After a time it's difficult to walk away. Or at least –' he thought about it – 'you can leave most of it behind every

224

time, but the little bits that stick keep adding up, until eventually you've got a heap, and you're carrying a great pile around with you. Like tiny bits of mud eventually clogging the brake.'

He was silent for a moment. He said, 'I think I may have had enough of it.' That sounded overdramatic. He tested the idea, though, and thought it might be true.

Then she said, 'What I do is I shake my clothes out over the bath. To get rid of it all.'

'That's odd.'

More silence, then.

'Things go wrong for people,' she said. 'That's no different from having a road accident. What are accidents about? Are they fair? Sometimes they are fair, you drove badly; sometimes they are not, someone drives into you. Your clients have had an accident with the law, there's no pattern to these things.'

He didn't know what to say, perhaps she was right.

She said, 'Look, I'll tell you a story, obviously I can't give any names. I've got a patient, he's pleasant enough, at least he is to me – though in real life, I think he's pretty nasty, maybe even a psychopath.'

She was a psychiatrist, so the word meant something. He said, 'You mean that?'

'Oh yes. But let's not get too worried here, not all psychopaths carry knives; most of the ones I saw don't. Mostly they just drove home to their families after seeing me. I don't see them much now, dealing with children mainly.

'So this guy lives a pretty disgraceful life, but also he loves his granddaughter. The only problem is that his granddaughter is severely disabled. If I listed everything she's got wrong with her you'd think I was making it up. And he wants to look after her.'

'What's wrong with that?'

225

'Well, he snatched her from a hospital to do so. It took months to find her.'

'Oh.'

'They decided they can't just snatch her back. I've been asked to say whether she is being harmed by his behaviour. And of course she is, she'll grow up wrong – or rather even more wrong. He's damaging her, not intentionally, of course, but he won't accept that, since this may well be the only time in his life he has ever felt he was doing a really good thing. The only time in his life when he has done something entirely for someone else.'

Her finger had found a drop of wine on the table and she was spreading it round and round. She said, 'Where does that rank in the justice stakes? Even when he *knows* he's doing good, we don't accept that he is.'

They sat there.

She said, 'I've got families that have had so many things go wrong in their lives that the only way to deal with it in referral meetings is to laugh.'

A long silence.

'And who did it to them? God, or someone organising things on his behalf? Your clients are the lucky ones, they've only got the law to deal with.'

What could he say to that?

Annie brought them some supper.

'Here's my friend Jeremy Scott,' Grace said. 'I met him at court.'

'Very nice,' Annie said. She looked at Scott as though wondering whether to buy one too.

They ate the food.

'Let's have a different wine,' Scott said.

This time he ordered a really good bottle. Grace thought it was good too. He knew it. He watched her. She didn't seem to mind him watching her. They both started speaking at the same time, but it didn't matter. They were

226

enjoying being together, but they didn't say so out loud. It would have been better if they had done so, now, while they were still talking to each other.

At about the same time Wicked Man had to be carried back to the car. The twins had taken their time, but now they had to be back in time for late supper, or people would be annoyed. Wicked was still alive, though he wasn't enjoying it. They set fire to the car, but despite the care they took, it didn't burn right through – perhaps because of the closed space – and when the firemen found him, Wicked was still in a condition to be identified.

Later when he heard about it, Frank Abbott thought it was unlikely that Wicked had been killed, black on black, for being a police informer, although it was a good explanation.

Bill Carr and he were trying to work it out.

Abbott said, 'I don't know that Wicked was not an informer, all I know is he wasn't mine, and I think I would have known if he was working for someone else. But then again, maybe not.'

This was getting too complicated for PC Carr. He said, 'Then what was prosecution counsel doing seeing that judge if he wasn't giving him a text?'

'Maybe just explaining why he was going to accept the plea? After all, it needed explaining, didn't it? You say he went in there with Fulton?'

'Yeah, I'm fairly certain of that, but I still don't know Fulton was there for this case. He could have been going to get a search warrant. I don't know why he was there. I'm just guessing.' By this time Carr was completely lost.

Abbott said, 'Maybe the killing wasn't connected with the guilty plea. It doesn't have to be, it could be that some-one said, If he gets out, we'll get him then. Maybe Scott just didn't want to fight the case, and the killing is a com-plete coincidence.'

Carr said, 'That could be so. But when defence counsel turned up, he was surprised about the plea. He didn't know about it. If it had been decided in advance he would know, wouldn't he? So that means it must have been decided at court. But. But –' he was thinking it through – 'Scott couldn't drop the charge of supplying on his own say-so. He'd have to clear that kind of thing with the prosecution solicitors. After all, he said it wasn't his decision.'

'That's right. He has to get CPS agreement. But what does that mean? Not much. You've seen it done, the person who is in charge of the papers is never there, so someone else has to decide. Someone who knows nothing at all about the case, except what Scott tells them. Anyway, does he even have to speak to someone? Does anybody ever challenge or check these things? All he has to say, if asked, is that he did. I doubt if they even make a note. The guy at the other end of the phone doesn't necessarily have the file to make a note on.'

'So you think Scott was in on it?' Carr said. 'He doesn't normally prosecute, you know.'

Frank Abbott was not sure. 'No, not very likely. But if what you say is correct, then Scott is up to something. It's quite possible it's to do with Wicked – after all, drugs get everywhere.'

Chapter 15

The next day Grace Karenin sat thinking about their meeting. He was a nice guy, different, different enough to make her stop during her dictation occasionally and look out of the window – which wasn't like her. Perhaps it wasn't too late to take a risk, to let someone close.

She continued setting out her conclusions. 'I have spoken to Mr Burns about his attempts to care for his granddaughter and about his circumstances. He spoke of his own childhood, which was marked by violence and anger. He was removed from the family as "impossible to deal with" and lived in a series of children's homes and approved schools.

'Mr Burns told me it was at that point he realised that no one would help him. He could only help himself. He thinks all agencies are biased against him, and told me he did not trust me. I pointed out that I had no reason to be biased against him. He said, "You'll be the first who isn't, then."'

Perhaps she shouldn't have dismissed what Scott was saying about his work last night so easily. But then he deserved it. Good to see if he could take it and still come back. She thought he would; he had a sort of dogged certainty. But why did she always try to drive them away? What caused that? Was it because not one of them was as

229

good as her father, is that how these things worked? That's what her business told her.

She continued: 'I asked again how he would manage when his granddaughter approached adolescence. He was unwilling to discuss these difficulties.'

Grace Karenin paused, then clicked the button on her machine to continue and said, 'He is an intelligent man. In many ways he is self-aware, but nevertheless it is my opinion that it is not possible for him to undertake the care of this very sick child, and he will not accept this.'

The care hearing was only days away and she had to get her decision on paper for the court. It would be the same as she had given the local authority. And she had been told he didn't have a lawyer and he was going to represent himself. So she would have to answer him, face to face.

He had already said to her, 'You'll not take the child from me.'

She had said, 'It isn't me, Mr Burns. It's the court.' But they both knew that wasn't true. He would hold her responsible, and that might cause problems.

She looked out of the window. The trouble with men is they have it so easy. They need to be tested, they should expect it.

The phone rang. 'Yes, Jennet?'

'That policeman Mr Reynolds wants to come and see you. He wants to come with someone.'

'When?'

'As soon as possible.'

'What is it about?'

'He didn't say.'

'How long am I free?'

'Until three.'

'OK, give me ten minutes. I shall have this report ready for typing by then, Jennet. How are you set to do it?'

'I'll be able to do it immediately, Dr Karenin.'

Grace Karenin turned back to the problem of Billy Burns's granddaughter.

After receiving the phone call from Mike Reynolds saying he was coming round in a moment and could he see Dr Karenin, Jennet found herself becoming flustered. She was conscious she wanted to think about something else, but found herself nevertheless getting up and going to the staff lavatory. There was a mirror there. She touched her face, pressed her hair, checked her collar. How ridiculous! She went outside and stood in the door that separated her reception desk from the main office.

Through it she could see three of her friends working, typing up notes and filing. How organised they were getting everything! The office had been completely rearranged recently; they each had had to take part. Even Claire, who complained all the time, even Claire had done some filing. Jennet stood and watched them, and it was only the movement of a shadow that made her realise Dr Karenin had come up behind her. She was bringing the dictation tapes.

'Not like you to be just standing, Jennet.'

'I was just watching them, Doctor. Look at them all working to get it better. It's so nice here,' she said, turning.

'You're in a good mood, but I'm afraid you won't be when you see this.' She held out the tapes. 'Two full tapes, I'm afraid.'

Jennet took the tapes and went to her desk, pleased to have something solid to do. 'I'll get on with it now.'

Dr Karenin stood at the door, looking out over the scruffy car park, tapping her pen on her teeth. She saw Mike Reynolds appear in a car with another man. 'Of course, you've got a good reason to be cheerful,' she said to Jennet.

She had noticed that last time he came on foot. Why

231

was he interested in Jennet anyway? Two worrying possibilities there – access to the department records, or worse,
access to Jennet's small child. She saw so much nastiness
of that kind that it was difficult to get it out of her head.
Of course, maybe he just liked Jennet, why not? But it
didn't fit easily, he didn't quite seem the type. She turned
round, 'But who wouldn't?' she said as she saw Jennet
working.

Jennet smiled down at her computer keyboard.

Fulton was apparently not at all affected by where he was,
nor did he seem to care to whom he was talking. He
wasn't going to be pushed around in someone else's room,
so he only sat down reluctantly, even then leaning forward
as he spoke, moving a box on the doctor's desk around
with the tips of his fingers.

Fulton said, 'You know, we're sure he did this. He murdered her, cut her up and spread her around, and I am not
going to have him sitting there taking us for fools.'

Set it out, make them realise how devious and difficult
chummy was. Once they understood that, they would be
through in no time. Mike was familiar with his style,
though he didn't like it.

Fulton continued: 'The wife is gone. Where is she?
People don't just disappear. What we need is some sort of
lead, some indication. And it's probably there in your files.
Some little thing, something that you'd not notice yourself
probably, but we would. We would. We'd fit it all
together.'

Mike Reynolds watched him talk to the doctor and
began to wish he hadn't agreed to come along with him.
It was not a nice experience to see this oaf at work, to see
another policeman with the eyes of an outsider.

'This is all bloody nonsense,' Fulton had said to him as
they set out. 'I'm not letting some namby-pamby, trick-

232

cyclist doctor get in the way of this investigation. The father is probably interfering with the child as well, so she should be even more concerned.'

The idea had obviously jumped into Fulton's head from nowhere while he was talking to Mike. It must have seemed a clinching argument for him, and Mike knew he would try it out on Dr Karenin.

Mike Reynolds gritted his teeth; here it came.

Fulton said, 'And what about the child anyway? A father like that, how do we know what he is doing with that child?'

The remark was met by complete silence. Grace Karenin did not even respond. Suddenly Fulton was struggling.

'We know that these things go together,' Fulton said. It sounded lame even to him.

'Do you?' Grace Karenin asked it as a question, clearly wanting a reply.

Fulton said nothing. Then he said, 'We know that most women who are murdered are killed by their husbands.'

'I know that,' Grace said, 'but what I was curious about was how you know that it is coupled with the likelihood of sexual abuse of their children.'

'Well, it would have to be, wouldn't it?'

'Not necessarily.' Grace Karenin's eyes left him and she spoke to Reynolds. 'Have you told your colleague what I said when previously you came to ask me for the same thing?'

Mike Reynolds started to reply, and as he did so Fulton realised he was about to be left out. He interrupted. 'Mr Reynolds here gave me your message, but I didn't find it satisfactory.' Reynolds cringed inside. 'So I have had to come.'

'But the answer I am afraid is the same as it was before, Mr Fulton. The young child is my patient. I have a duty of confidentiality towards her, and unless I think that she is at

233

risk, legally at risk, I cannot break that confidence. At the moment I have seen or heard nothing that suggests she is at risk of any harm.

'Were her father accused of murder then of course we would immediately reassess the case.'

'We can tell you—'

'Is there anything you have to say to me beyond what Mr Reynolds has already said?'

Of course Fulton knew there was nothing.

'If anything changes, then I shall be in touch with the local authority, and the social services will immediately call you.'

Fulton said, 'We'll have to do it on our own then.'

She was used to that kind of response; it was the kind of thing a child might have said. 'I suppose you will,' she said, 'but you are not without resources, are you?'

It was the only time she showed any reaction.

The strained silence in the car as they went back to the police station eventually made Mike Reynolds, for the want of something to say, ask a question. He said, 'Did you hear what happened to that dealer?'

Fulton was very angry. He had not expected to be shown out of the clinic so smartly. He had expected to be treated with some respect. After all, this was murder squad stuff, not some plodding enquiry about stolen cars. When Mike spoke it broke the spell. 'She just turfed us out,' he said. Then he lapsed into an angry silence again.

Mike Reynolds tried again. 'You remember, that Yardie dealer, when we were at court. Did you hear what happened to him?'

'Yep, I heard. Got roasted, didn't he?'

'They say it was the Firebird posse,' Reynolds said. He said it more to demonstrate he wasn't going to be shut up by Fulton's bad temper than anything else.

'Yeah, he was set up, I guess.' Angry silence. 'I'm going to go to the hospital authorities about her.'

Mike nearly said, Grace Karenin *is* the hospital authority, but thought better of it. He said, 'I was told it was a revenge killing.'

Fulton wouldn't have said it had he not been furious with the woman doctor, and had he not needed to be seen to be in control, showing that he knew more about what goes on than this wanker Reynolds. The moment he said it he regretted it, but he didn't think it would matter. He said, 'Sounds like strike three from Billy Burns and Popey to me.'

Reynolds said nothing in reply. But when he got free he went straight to see Frank Abbott. Frank Abbott listened to Reynolds carefully.

'Yes,' he said, 'I think we can use it now. What do you know about Burns?'

'Only that he goes to the River Anchor, the pub where the paedophile I put away was operating. I told you Burns gave evidence in the case. And that was odd in itself. What ex-con ever gave evidence in favour of a nonce? Even odder if he was lying for him.'

It was a remark that Mike Reynolds, when he made it, didn't understand himself, but it made some sense to Frank Abbott.

Scott had to go back to Ma Thompsett's the next night because he had left his car there. When he and Grace Karenin had eaten supper together, he ordered wine for them, which they had drunk. Then he had ordered wine for himself, which he had drunk as well. By the end of the evening he had drunk far too much. Maybe it was a celebration.

Is it wrong to be attracted to someone because they are so intelligent? Wasn't it a little suspect, like being attracted to a person for their money? Intelligent and beautiful anyway. Occasionally he had tried to pay her a compliment, but she had always seen it coming and started laughing as he tried to get it out.

He had got home by cab.

While he was arranging this, Grace Karenin had offered to let him wait upstairs, but he had been sensible and said no. He had only made her make a promise that they could have supper together again. 'Where would you like to go?'

'You choose,' she said. 'That's what men are for. But somewhere full of people, *u zivot*, not the kind of place you go to read a book on your own.'

Scott didn't know any places that were full of people; all the places he went to he went to sit and read. But he did know to remind Grace that he would have to come back again to collect his car and maybe see the man he had missed. 'I wouldn't want Annie to tell you that I was chasing you around,' he said.

'Would she think that?' she said and smiled.

'Yes,' he said.

'Would I mind if you were?' she said. 'Here's the number of my mobile.' She didn't take his.

So Scott returned to get his car the next night and this time found Charlie Pope straight off.

'My client has made up his mind. He would like to go ahead. I'd like to contact Vernon,' Scott said.

'Well, that's fine. I've made my enquiries too.' He didn't say what the results were.

'What's next then?'

'You tell me the story.'

'His name is Anderson.' Scott found himself nearly tripping over the name even though he had prepared it all.

'How old?'

'Just twenty. Unemployed.' He took out the solicitor's file. It was odd how difficult direct lying was. 'These events happened a little time ago,' he said.

236

'All the better.'

'Why is that?'

'It makes them almost impossible to disprove.'

Scott digested this.

'No, I suppose you're right. But my client is still affected by it.'

'Has he had medical help?'

'No. But he once made a suicide attempt.'

'How?'

'He cut himself.'

'Grand. That's the stuff. Was he treated?'

'Yes. Five days in hospital.'

'No? Well, it won't go to the proof of the crime, of course, but it would affect the amount of the criminal injury compensation.' Charlie Pope obviously remembered his law of evidence.

Scott said, 'It happened when my client was staying at one of the houses the football club provided for young players.'

'What happened?'

'Well, sexual activity. Some mistreatment. Beating, standing in the rain.'

'Well, even standing on the touchline can amount to child abuse nowadays.' Pope began to ripple with laughter. 'Is your client a footballer?'

Scott took a deep breath. 'He would have been. If not for this.'

Pope grinned. 'Ah. Were there any other players in the same house who are playing now in the league?'

'Yes. At least one England player.'

'And is the man who did it still working with young players?'

'I think he is.' Scott was worried it might be too neat. All he had to do was not go too far. 'There's one thing.' He leaned forward. 'I am not so sure of my client's steadiness.'

It was an odd word, but conveyed exactly what was needed. He had prepared it.

'So.' Charlie Pope rubbed his face and his other fingers twirled around his cigarette holder. 'Does he need rehearsing?'

'Well, sometimes he'll tell it and it sounds like the kind of thing that happens to anybody, just an unhappy kid. And other times he'll include all the lurid detail.'

'Without the details of course he doesn't have a case.'

'Isn't that what Vernon does?' Scott hesitated. Was he being overenthusiastic? But Pope seemed to disregard it. Scott's hesitancy seemed to work for him. He said, 'What I am saying is, he'll need firming up.'

'Firming up? After Vernon has had a go at him, he'll be describing it like it happened yesterday. And with Vernon it probably will have. But that's what I mean, unless you're one hundred per cent sure you are word-perfect, don't go. The police aren't interested otherwise.'

'But why?'

'Because everything that is said to them should be made available to the defence. Most of the time, of course, it isn't. After all, why should the prosecution harm their own case by showing their witness is unreliable? But it does happen, when you get a judge who applies the rules. So we have to make sure the complaint arrives in police hands completely clean. All the rough edges snipped off.'

Scott was seeing the other side of the barrier against which he pushed so often. He changed the subject, not wanting to seem too interested in Vernon. 'What about the press connection?'

'The press reaction will be pretty strong, so I'll probably auction it.'

'Auction?'

'Yes, a bit of a grand word, but I'll call the red tops one

238

by one, and let them know about it. When I see what Vernon's got.'

A plate of sandwiches arrived. Scott took another glass of wine. The whole thing was so baroque, he already felt a bit light-headed.

'This is astonishing for me.'

'First time you ever dealt with the press?'

'Well, I was once involved with the *Independent* over a case. I wrote—'

'No, I mean the real press. Where the money is.'

Scott poured some wine into Pope's glass. The man slurped at it, the perspiration gleaming on his huge forehead.

'What sort of money are we speaking of here?'

'You're sure your man is perfectly happy to be interviewed?'

'Yes.'

'Photographed?'

'Yes.'

'Ten to fifteen grand for starters. Depending entirely on what names he can give. If there are big names it could be more.'

'Good God.'

'Give him five.'

'Five?'

'Yes, you give him five of it. That'll be enough. He'll be amazed by five, and anyway he'll have his criminal injuries compensation application, and he's probably got an action against the football club. You've obviously thought of that?'

Scott tried to look as though it were obvious.

'A criminal conviction of a member of the club staff responsible for the young players would make a civil action impossible to defend. The club will certainly settle, and they'll pay a premium to make sure there is no publicity beyond what was in the original story.'

More wine.

'What more publicity would there be?'

'There doesn't have to be any. The club only has to think there might be. So that could be another few thousand for your client there.'

The torrent of money was quite staggering.

Scott said, 'You told me the whole court process was for sale. I didn't really believe you.'

'And it always includes agents' fees. Of course, you are the agent.'

Scott said, 'I'm still not sure about the preparation of the complaint.'

Pope said, 'Don't do it yourself, you'll make less money. Vernon is the best, but he'll charge you.'

'How much again?'

'You'll have to ask him. You said you wanted to meet him. It's unusual but he's agreed. Here's his number.' Charlie Pope handed Scott a visiting card. 'You'll find him at the Piano Factory. Not very salubrious I'm afraid. At least, that's what they tell me, I've not been there.'

The piano factory? Scott decided not to ask.

'And do I have direct contact with the police?'

'Yes, when the complaint comes it has to come from you, or from the victim himself. After you have contacted the police formally you don't see me again. But I'll always be in touch with it. All you have to do is let me know where you are going.'

'Well, I'd assumed East Place?' Hoping for a name.

'OK. And I need to know when, because then I will be ringing the editors.'

Charlie Pope groped inside his jacket and produced a fountain pen. He scratched on the back of the visiting card. 'I'll give you a name and telephone number. This guy has a contact in the child protection team. Once they go in, they go trawling for other cases. Remember the

240

Jonathan King case? You watch, the moment the man is arrested and his name is announced, all sorts of crazies will turn up on the police doorstep. Which of course is why they announce the name. The only pity is that they are not allowed to send them on to us. We could go into the wholesale business if they did.'

More wine. Charlie Pope was getting expansive.

'You have to be a bit careful with Vernon. He lives in a bit of a fantasy world. He thinks he is on a mission.'

'What's the piano factory?'

'It's a charity. You'll see, he'll welcome you like a customer. You wait.' Charlie Pope started wheezing. Scott could not work out whether he was laughing or not. It was time to go.

Scott said, 'OK, I'll tell you when we approach the police.' Scott stumbled over the man's first name – after all, he wasn't a friend or anything: 'Thanks, Charlie.'

On his way home, held up at the long traffic lights just past the Royal Mint by Tower Bridge, he unfolded the note. The policeman's name was Fulton.

He drove on down, past where the Old Billingsgate market had been.

Wasn't Fulton the name of the officer in the crack dealer's case? Unlikely; though Fulton, if it was the same Fulton, knew Reynolds. Scott had seen them together talking in the court that day. So if that was the connection, he could be the 'contact' in the child protection team. And Scott had seen Reynolds at the wine bar.

It was amazing. He had never thought he would get this far; but now that he had done so, what was he going to do with the information? So far, what Charlie Pope was offering wasn't illegal. He was only putting people in touch with the right people; and arranging for the press to pay someone for their story isn't a crime. Charlie Pope wasn't

241

to know whether any particular complaint was true or not; he probably didn't care. The same position as any solicitor, or any policeman come to that.

So who would be interested in what was going on? How could it be used to help Jimmy Reilly?

Not the press. The only people of whom the press is frightened is the press itself. Even the *Independent* or the *Telegraph* won't take the *Sun* or the *Mail* on – maybe because that would make it more difficult to get a job with them when the time came. Perhaps it was the only area where real self-interest corruption still exists – as a matter of policy.

He had managed to confirm what he already believed – that Jimmy Reilly had been set up. But he was no nearer to any information that he could actually use in a court. No one else was going to believe it; on the other hand, now he had names. He'd see Vernon before deciding.

PART FIVE

Costs

Chapter 16

'Jus' like that.' Billy Burns had his fez on. The bar rocked with laughter. He opened the box with a flourish, but the rubber ball was still inside. A look of astonishment and disappointment crossed his face and he shut the box again, tapping the lid dramatically with a wooden wand.

'It'll go, mind you,' he said, 'it always does. Eventually.'

He was standing in the pub. 'Go on, Billy,' they had said, 'do us your Tommy Cooper.'

He held the box up and the audience's eyes followed it, delighted, knowing what was about to happen.

'I told my old lady. It'll go . . . like it always does . . . jus' like that.' He repeated the phrase in a low breathy voice and made a sideways movement, shooting his cuffs, holding out the box. Obediently the audience's eyes followed the movement and he went to tap the box again. But there was nothing to tap it with, the wand had disappeared.

The audience, surprised at the sudden switch, howled as Billy held up his empty hand, examining it, turning it over, looking underneath it. 'Where did that go?'

Billy shrugged, resigned at the obstinacy of things, reluctantly transferred his attention back to his other hand, and found that now the box had disappeared – leaving behind it only the rubber ball.

And lifting it up, that disappeared too.

There was a roar.

'I could do with another beer,' he said, taking his fez off and turning to the bar. There was a rush to buy Billy a drink. Conversation became general, although one or two people were still laughing, some even wiping their eyes.

'That'd be the way to go, like Tommy, right in the middle of a show,' a man leaning on the bar said.

'Yeah,' said Billy Burns. The old master. Even his death, he even made that work. Now you see me, now you don't. But Billy said nothing out loud. He was wary of strangers.

The man leaning on the bar was PC Carr. He had discussed what he was going to do with Abbott. He had done a bit of homework, watched a video and got hold of Jeanette Winterson's biography of Tommy Cooper. It was bit slushy, he thought. He carried on. 'But how do you get the time to practise? I know Tommy used to practise for hours at home, in the kitchen. In Fulham, weren't it?'

Bill Carr had dressed for the job, wearing a plastic jacket and trainers. He had combed his hair right up and got hold of some glasses. He wouldn't be recognised.

He often wondered about that. If film stars can act sad, ugly people and then turn themselves back into beautiful people, why can't sad, ugly people turn themselves into film stars? Or maybe they do.

But whatever he thought, despite physical change, you can't change your personality and Billy Burns sniffed him out.

'What the fuck's it got to do with you, what I do?' he said, looking PC Carr directly in the eye, and turning his back on him.

He walked away, leaving the policeman transfixed, holding the same position at the bar.

'That's Billy Burns all over,' said the fellow next to him. He had seen what had happened. 'It's all very well, his

246

funny man stuff, but underneath he's an evil bastard.' He dropped his voice to say it.

This time Carr got the reply just right. Perhaps the surprise of what had happened had taken the wind out of him, and along with it the bit that always made what he did ridiculous, 'You can say that again,' he said.

'And when I say evil, I mean it.'

PC Carr had found someone with a grudge.

'Is that so?'

'Yup. And there's many here as would say so, if they weren't frightened.'

'I didn't know that.'

'There's no reason why you should. It doesn't get out much. He doesn't look the type, after all.'

PC Carr moved so he shielded the man, making it easier for him to talk.

'People do what he says, or they get it.'

Suddenly they found themselves surrounded by a scrum trying to get a drink. The man stopped talking. Carr used his position next in line to order two more beers. For once they came quickly, and the next moment they were heading for a side table, out of the way. Carr knew well enough not to ask directly for more information. He said, 'That may be so, but his routine is good. He should be on *Stars in their Eyes*.'

The man was not to be deterred from what he wanted to say.

'Routine? He can manipulate anyone. His team, the guys that work for him? He's got young people round here would do anything for him, anything. And if you don't like it, you'll get it. He's got policemen eating out of his hand. He can even manipulate the courts. I said, he's an evil bastard.'

Carr didn't know where to start.

'The courts,' he said. 'How do you manipulate the courts?'

247

'There was a guy here recently, he did something to cross Billy. I don't know what it was he done. You know, I don't think even he knew he'd done anything, at least he never said anything to show it, or that he thought it was Billy who caused the trouble. But I know Billy got a case up against him and had him sent down. And all the time Billy was pretending to be his friend.'

He dropped his voice even lower. Carr knew the need to get rid of a secret was often overwhelming; to keep a secret can be the same as being complicit.

'I know because one of my kids was told about it, a friend of his was talking. That was recent, but he's done worse.'

They both drank the beer, calm now that they couldn't be overheard. Billy watched them from the other end of the room.

'And now he's working with the blacks, and you know, they're even more frightened of him than this lot. Dunno why. It's surprising because they are pretty violent among themselves. Maybe it's because he's on his own turf.'

Carr nodded. Now was the time to seem uninterested, or bored. Of course, it spurred the man on. 'People say he has two things he does, either he fucks you, or he burns you.'

Carr said, 'If he's that much of a nasty bastard, then I don't think I want to know any more.'

'You're right there.'

'Let's change the subject.'

PC Carr knew that if he left it unfinished, with the real grievance still to come, he would get a chance of starting the conversation up again. In fact, he would have difficulty stopping it. For the moment he had plenty. 'Fucks you or burns you,' the man said. What was it exactly had happened to Wicked? Both? 'You don't want to know,' Abbott had said, showing him the photograph of the burnt car and holding the pathologist's report. 'But I doubt he was walking properly after they did it to him.'

Billy Burns knew something was happening. He was standing in a crowd but watching the man who had asked him the questions on the other side of the pub, sitting with Joe Took. That pisshead, he'd say anything for a beer. They were discussing him, it was obvious the way they didn't look up. That man was the filth, he could smell it. Nobody spoke to him like that round here.

When he left he'd see if he was followed.

'Must be going now, look out for yourselves,' Billy said.

He tried the pub persona on, felt how well it fitted. One of the two others around him glanced at the clock, their movements copying his. The man next to him opened his mouth and words came out, 'Goodnight, Billy.'

Slower than normal. Billy knew what that meant, when it seemed it was slowing down. His muscles were going.

But these were special muscles. For as long as he could remember, keeping things normal for him had been an act of will, a matter of tensing the right muscles. Once he had wanted to ask if this was true for everybody. But how do you find that out, though? What question do you ask? He remembered the woman on the radio who had described having what she called tunnel vision. She had not realised she had it till her thirties. What he wanted to know was, how did she notice she had it? What do you compare it with? And there was another guy on the radio and he had been asked, 'How does it feel to be the son of someone so famous?' And he had said, 'How does it feel not to be? Is it different?'

The woman with the funny eyesight said she knocked into things occasionally, but not so's anyone would notice, and she had become expert at avoiding things that came at her. She had assumed everyone was the same.

So how did she find out?

The question he wanted to ask was, Does everybody else have to hold on when the world slows down? Maybe it was normal, everyone has it, so it was something you don't talk about.

He said, ''Night then,' to some faces that swam in and out of his fishbowl.

The cool air felt good. But now his back felt tight. He didn't need this now. The spat with that guy at the bar had caused this. He dropped his shoulders and rolled his head to free himself from the pressure. He had discovered that this movement helped when he had been boxing. He took a few steps and jabbed a little to help it on. He could still move the moves. And he noticed that other people commented on it. 'Hey, Billy's going for it.' How come they knew that about him, when he didn't know it about them?

He reached his flat.

Same every night, quick tap on the bell, and as he reached the inner door to her room, the woman was leaving. 'Goodnight, Mr Burns. She's been restless tonight.'

He touched his granddaughter's forehead. Slightly damp, but not too much, her eyes opened and closed once or twice, her eyeballs turned away. He knew what that meant. He could judge that. A difficult night coming, an exception occurring.

He turned her pillow over, and held her head steady while he did so. A spasm rippled through her body. Then he pressed the back of her neck and she moaned softly, returning to deep, deep sleep. Who else could do that? Send her back straight to sleep? No one. What would happen if he didn't do it? Who would?

He slipped into night clothes, went to the loo, kept his slippers near him for when he got up, and arranged a basin and a towel near the kettle. Then he lay down beside her. She would wake in a couple of hours and he knew that if she touched him, or at least felt he was there when she woke, she wouldn't sit up screaming and reaching her arms out to the door, where her mother wasn't standing.

Where – he was falling asleep now, careful not to touch her even with as much as his heel as he lay there – where his own mother had stood, and not moved towards him as he sat up in bed reaching out to the door, which seemed so far away across the room, and getting further and slower all the time.

'He sleeps in the same bed as she does.' The meeting fell quiet.

Grace Karenin sitting at the main desk watched what was happening as the pre-trial meeting started reacting, moving towards a shared balanced opinion, but about to be derailed by this intervention.

'I could tell. I was there two days in a row and it was obvious. His night things were in one place in the bedroom and the next day in another. He was sleeping with her. And I could see through to the back room; his own bed was untouched.'

'Are you prepared to say that?' said the solicitor, but then he fell silent, a little embarrassed by the eagerness in his voice. The question was ignored. For a moment the group savoured the luxury of what was little more than gossip.

'If it's a sexual matter we have to intervene immediately.' There it was, someone has said it.

'Are we going to let the child protection team know?'

'We must.'

'Is he a section-one offender? We have checked, haven't we?'

'Of course. Nothing for sexual offences. Plenty of other things, but no notifiable offences.'

'If the child protection team get involved, it will only

slow us right down. We'd have to start again with a formal section eight enquiry.'

'But if it's sexual, there's no alternative, she's so young.'

'Even to hesitate is to show him favours. What if he were some black guy? Just because he's white.' Sarah said this.

Silence. They wouldn't admit it, but the meeting knew this would have to be said, it always did. As if it weren't difficult enough already.

'I don't think that's right, Sarah. I really don't.' Grace intervened. For a moment Sarah subsided.

'So we're going to have to contact that Reynolds man.'

'He probably knows already. He's going out with Jennet.'

'No!'

'Yes he is. And why do you think he is?'

'Why?'

'So he can find out what's decided here.'

'Jennet doesn't know what goes on.'

'Of course she does. She's extremely bright and she types all Grace's reports.'

They all turned to look at Grace.

Someone added, 'Of course, Jennet has a small child. We've seen that sort of thing often enough.'

'People who work in child abuse, you should never trust them.'

'Very doubtful.'

'You would have had Lewis Carroll on the sex offenders' list.'

There was laughter.

'Naturally.'

But then, 'I don't think Mr Burns is a sexual problem,' Grace Karenin said.

'Why not? Seems a classic case.'

'The damage he is doing to the girl is not to do with sex. It's to do with control, his excessive control of her.'

'It's still too dangerous to risk.'

Grace went on, 'The moment she's away from him, she'll begin to grow, she may even begin to deal with some of her problems. The hospital reports prefigured that.'

'I agree.'

'No, we have to let the police know what we suspect.'

'I don't suspect anything,' Grace said. 'I've spent some hours with him now. Here's a man who loves his grand-daughter, probably out of guilt. He knows that if he'd been around to stop his own daughter getting involved in drugs, then this child would not have been born so. And his feelings are all the more intense because of what happened to him as a child. His love for her is an honest feeling for him. Our intervention proves to him that the authorities will do anything to get him. Like they always have, for as long as he can remember.'

Billy Burns lay down next to his granddaughter hearing her move restlessly in her sleep. He had to be near to judge when it happened. Tonight he would get no sleep.

It was extraordinary. In one way she never slept; always, always there was a slight tremor running through her body, vibrating, so that it was always fragile, as though it had never yet set.

He searched for an image, and recalled a television picture he had once seen of solid ground trembling slightly, just before an earthquake. The camera had focused on what seemed like packed solid earth as it began to ream and crawl; still in fact firm enough to support things, but rippling like disturbed water. Beneath this child's skin there was this tumult all the time.

No wonder she sometimes could no longer stand it, crying out, unable even to recognise him, so he had to hold her. That's all that could be done, hold her.

What did they, the doctors, know?

He lay on his side, uncomfortable, as close to the edge of the bed as he could, so as not to disturb the trembling thing next to him. There was a sudden movement. He had been told the word for it. What was it? A myoclonic jerk – it heralded the discharge of pent-up energy.

There was another. The fit was coming on. Once this was over, she'd sleep the night through, maybe even be quiet the next day or two, but the next hours were going to be difficult. He got up, groping for his watch in the dark. Sat on the bed a moment, doing up the strap, collecting his dressing gown before going to get hot water and the large flannel. She jerked again.

That guy in the bar, some jerk he was. Billy had always wanted to call someone a myoclonic jerk, just to see their expression. He noticed that he was still angry, though this with his granddaughter had distracted him. That guy was a policeman. He was sure of that.

He was fully awake now and he began thinking about Gargarin. Not only had he not done what Billy had said, closed down, but he was behind on money. It was as though they never had that talk, as though he hadn't helped him with Wicked. He was right to do something about it.

She had begun to tremble violently and he realised he had not even got the kettle on yet, he'd let his attention go to other things. He got off the bed and hurried out of the room, leaving the door open; he'd hear it if she kicked off.

The kettle started to hum and he stood with a bowl waiting. The dark of the room and his recent near sleep contrived to make his thoughts drift away; he felt the warm flannel in his hand and remembered the touch of it on his skin.

Then he remembered the beating that made him run away that time. It wasn't the only time he ran, but it was the only time he had found anyone who had helped him.

What a beating. Terry, tall, well built, red-headed, a bully, a good foot taller than himself, acting out the ridiculous idea that you could give the older boys authority over the younger without damaging both.

The kettle boiled. He dashed some of it into the basin, and plunged the flannel in. It had to have a little cold, but the hotter he could make it the better.

He had sworn at someone in Terry's hearing, nothing special, only 'fuck off'. Someone had been teasing him, like they always did, and that was it, enough for a beating.

He carried the basin back into her room. He was right, now she was moving; about to scream he'd say, he'd got there just in time. He put the basin down and turned her on her front, unbuttoned her night dress, so he could put the hot flannel on her back. He began slowly to rub and press, smoothing away all the pain.

He smoothed and pressed – a big angry man.

They had taken him from his bed, walked him downstairs. He had remembered being cold, feeling the pyjamas on his skin, pulling the old dressing gown round him. They had taken that from him, not taken it as in snatching, but just got it off him. He had refused to let them take the pyjama bottoms. If they were coming off he was going to do it. They bent him half naked over a chair.

The first blow; he had not believed it.

Was it possible to feel such pain? And five more to come. He knew the group were standing watching him. His hate was solid, he could still taste it now, but of course hate was no protection.

Another cut, he could hear the cane coming before it hit him. From the corner of his eye he could see Terry's feet as he shifted his weight with the blow. He thought of moving, but knew it was no good, they would only hold him down, their hands all over him. That would be worse.

255

Of course he would heve to run that very night, what else was there to do? He would never submit.

His granddaughter cried out. It was like a peacock, like a peacock noise. He remembered the sounds from the zoo near the school. He rubbed her back, the hot flannel gave her pale skin a tinge of red.

It was the marks on his skin that the woman had noticed while he was coming out of the bath. 'Oh, you poor child, what have they done to you?' And instead of resisting – he had not understood why, normally he would have fought back like a monkey (that's what they called him), spitting and scratching – he had allowed her to lie him on a bed, naked, and bathe the pain. 'What on earth?' she said. 'Who did this to you?'

He had run from the school. Managed to get some clothes on and a blanket to wrap round him, he knew he would be cold. But anything was better than staying in that bed, the humiliation, the violation, the sniggering from the other boys.

He had jumped from the window. It was a place he had noticed before, and he went straight down into a bed of flowers that were always carefully dug, so he knew it would be a soft landing. He wrapped the blanket round him and set off down the yellow lit road.

It was the most extraordinary escape he ever made. About five hundred yards away there was lorry, the driver taking a slash, the engine running, a tarpaulin over the back. He had time to get himself comfortable on some sand before the lorry took off, he even fell asleep for a while. When he awoke, it was nowhere. Again the lorry was stationary and he could jump out. The driver was nowhere to be seen. He got down and slipped away into the trees. But then it got difficult. Cold, wet.

He relived those two days.

As he did so he poured more hot water in, soaked and

wrung out the flannel, and kept the rhythm going. The longer he could keep it going, the shorter the attack would be when it came. Up and press, up and press.

Eventually he had to come out of those woods, just to get something to eat. He had seen the back garden, there was some bread on a bird table, he crept through the hedge but as he took the bread someone spoke to him. He expected a blow and he put up his arm to protect himself. But instead of a blow there was a soft voice. 'I'm not going to hurt you,' she said. He looked past his protecting arm. An old woman.

As he squeezed his granddaughter's back, he laughed to himself. An 'old woman' – he remembered his reaction! Now he knew, she couldn't have been more than forty, but then at the age of fourteen that was old, old.

'I can give you something to eat.' Normally he would have hit out and run, but she clearly wasn't frightened of him and she just turned away. 'Come on into the warm,' she said. He followed her into the house. As he stepped in he was overwhelmed. It was warm and soft, even just standing there. Things around him were brightly coloured, there was carpet everywhere. If he took a step it didn't ring on the floor like it did at the school, endless concrete and metal. He sat down in a chair with a cushion. It still hurt to sit. As he sucked his breath in he realised she had noticed the small movement.

She would look at him, not just look at him, but really look at him, as though he were actually there, in the room with her, not just a body. They went into a kitchen and she busied herself at the stove. She said, 'My boy's away at school. He's just your age, so I know what you'd like to eat.'

Already the pan was sizzling. 'Here we are,' she said, going to the fridge.

He had never seen a fridge in a room like this before.

257

The fridges at the approved were vast, full of plastic boxes, but this one had things laid out inside it; he could see it all, a chicken, some other things.

'My Nicky always loves this,' she said. She cut slices of bread and put it on to toast. 'Scrambled eggs, lots of butter, a bit of pepper.'

Butter – he never tasted butter as butter, only something they called butter. The boys called it marge.

'Will you eat a mushroom? I picked it this morning from that field, just by where you were hiding. That's when I saw you.'

No one had ever asked him if he wanted something. Was there a choice? Could he say no?

'I wondered if you would come out, you know. I was watching you.'

She turned and smiled at him, holding out the plate. Creamy yellow eggs, piled up on toast, he could see butter melting on it, pieces of a big black mushroom, a sausage, a beautiful plate, flowers on it, her hand holding it out towards him.

'You mustn't be frightened of me.'

She was beside him, putting the plate in front of him, shifting a knife and fork for him, and putting a napkin on his knee, a thick hard piece of white cloth, stiff like the shirts they had when they were new, but softer somehow. Putting a napkin on his knee. He felt the soft touch. This woman didn't hate him.

'Now you just eat up, I'll get you some things to change into.' And she left the room.

He picked up a knife. It was heavy, silvery, shining, clean. And the fork. You wanted to use them, you actually wanted to use them.

She had gone to get the police, no doubt. But he might as well eat. He put some egg and toast in his mouth, and his whole body shifted. He had never tasted anything like it. This wasn't egg, not the egg he was used to. He tried the mushroom. He had never eaten mushroom before, save in some soup they used to serve, but that was a yellowy pale sort of liquid, with a dull taste. Now his whole mouth exploded with the flavour.

He ate.

'More?' she said. 'My, you were hungry. No, no more? You're full up and tired, I should say. Judging by what my Nicky is like. Now you get upstairs. I've got a hot-water bottle in his bed for you, there's some pyjamas, and I've drawn a bath.'

He remembered that phrase. It was the only time he ever heard those words used: 'I've drawn a bath.' He thought about it sometimes later. From things he had heard read out in cold chapels on Sundays, he knew it was something you did with water, you drew it. A hewer of wood, a drawer of water. Odd idea at first, but then the memory of her saying she drew a bath, and the person in the Bible drawing water, seemed mingled in his memory so they became the same thing.

He climbed the stairs. She was right behind him.

The house had the same warmth everywhere. When he went from place to place in the school, he had to go outside, or through passages that were as cold as if they were outside. But here there was none of that; everything was enclosed and opening a door didn't let some cold gust of air in past your legs. The whole place was warm.

She reached past him and opened a door.

It was a bedroom. A boy's bedroom, he thought. There were pictures on the wall of people sitting in rows, one of them held a big ball with a date on it, one a cricket bat. And there was a train set on a shelf. Neatly lined up. But the bed, a big snowy-white bed.

He didn't mind, she could fetch the police, he wanted to lie down.

259

'Now first a bath. I know what you're going to say, you don't want to have a bath. But I am going to insist.'

He found himself being propelled into a bathroom. Extraordinary, it was attached to the bedroom, and it had a carpet in it too. It was full of steam, and there was a big bath full of water. This one just for him, on his own. He stripped off and got ready to get in it. No one already in it, grabbing at him as he lifted his leg over the edge to get in, reaching right in there, painful, so painful he had to let them get on with it, there and then in the bath.

He hated baths. He never washed if he could help it.

From outside, where she had shut the door and gone away, he heard her say, 'The pyjamas are on the bed. I'll collect your clothes for washing when you're in bed.' And she left him alone.

For a moment he was suspicious, but there was silence, she had gone. He climbed into the bath, lowering himself gently. But however slowly he tried it, it hurt, the dull throb became a screech of pain. He tried again, but couldn't manage it, so he stayed standing, and wiped himself over with the sponge thing she had left.

For the first time in many years he started crying, silent in there, private. Then he managed to sit down.

He was dry now, he draped the towel round him, and slowly opened the door, looking out. No one there. On the bed were some pyjamas, lovely mustard yellow and soft. He crept out and put on the jacket. It was warm, and he saw that underneath them was a rubbery bottle that was hot to the touch.

He had the jacket on, he dropped the towel and hopped on one leg to get his foot into the pyjamas, when the door opened. He was bent over naked. He spun round holding the pyjama trousers in a bunch before him, ready to fight.

'Good heavens, what are those marks on you?' She strode over towards him and took hold of his shoulders.

'Oh, you poor child, what have they done to you?' He struggled to cover himself up.

'Now don't be silly, I'm a nurse. I was in the war and I've seen much worse than this. Come here.'

She led him to the bed. 'Lie down,' she said. 'No, no. Like that. I want to look at you.'

He found himself lying on the bed.

'You're running away, are you?'

He said nothing.

'So this is why there's blood on your clothes.' Still he said nothing.

'When did this happen?'

Nothing. He felt a warm towel taking away the cream she had been rubbing onto him, and the pain lessening. Slowly she spread the movement of the towel up his back, up and press. The sheets around his face smelt sweet, and the pillow was so soft, he remembered how his tears made it wet, and how eventually she wiped his face and ran her hand over his forehead, smoothing back his hair.

He fell asleep.

His granddaughter became more agitated. The only real way to keep her from a full-blown fit was to rub and press. It was almost as though he were squeezing something out of her. He would take a line, up her spine, round over the shoulder blade, down her arm, and then out the pain would go, out of her fingertips. He knew that this last part was what mattered; as though the pain, the devil that had her, was being squeezed out, and if it weren't squeezed away, then it would flood back in through the fingertips, back up through her arm again.

He had done this many times, for many hours at a time, slowly, methodically, fighting to mop up the distress brimming out of her. As he repeated the movement he remembered that house again.

261

In his sleep he had dreamed he was running, and worse. Wherever he stopped they seemed to know where he was, and as soon as he tried to settle he had to start running again. He woke with a start. It was quiet, the room was filling with morning light. He lay listening and remembered; she had said, 'You're running away.' She knew what he was. He got up and looked out of the window. In the road outside there was a man in uniform looking towards the house, walking to the front gate and coming up the path. They were coming for him. Billy had never seen a postman before, they never saw them at reform school.

He spun round and saw clothes laid out on a chair. Grey trousers, a shirt and a rough-haired jacket. He pulled them on, not bothering with any underwear. Grabbed some shoes and quietly opened the door. He went downstairs.

The same smell greeted him in the warm kitchen, sweet, smelling of bread. On the table were some biscuits, and there was money there also. He stuffed his pockets and made for the back door. As he did so he noticed a small wallet and he picked that up as well, into the breast pocket of his shirt as he ran to the woods.

It was wearing shoes without socks that did for him. He was noticed by a policeman who knew instantly that it wasn't right. They cornered him, and so many of them he didn't stand a chance. Eventually the school came to get him. They couldn't prove the theft of the clothes and the money; he said nothing at all. But they knew.

He was driven back.

It was the flower bed that had really upset the head, almost as though running away might not have been so bad. A school beating. In front of the whole school, immediately on his return. And a woman present. There wasn't even time to get him changed into ordinary clothes, so when they stripped him he had no underwear.

That destroyed any sympathy he might have had from

262

the assembled sullen boys. Suddenly it became a sport, and they hooted with laughter as he tried to twist to cover himself up. He was held down this time, the grinning stupid face of the gardener near his, as his arms were pulled forward, the gardener whose flower bed he had ruined.

But this time he wasn't going to take it.

When he spat full in the face of the gardener, for a moment he was released, and this he still remembered – he raised his head for a moment as he massaged his grand-daughter's back to picture it – he remembered the blow he gave the headteacher. It nearly broke his hand. He could still feel the crunch of bone, and see the blood and teeth come from the headteacher's face.

He remembered the shouting.

From then on nothing again, only that, as he sat that night in a police cell, he felt in his shirt pocket and pulled out the little paper wallet. It said 'passport photograph' on it. He opened it. It was that woman, her face staring out at him, half smiling. He stared at it.

After a while he spoke to her. 'I'm sorry I took your things.'

She had a jacket on, with a sort of collar, and a scarf with a brooch. Her hair was waved and grey, like he had seen. She forgave him.

Always afterwards, when he looked at the picture, she forgave him.

It took him two hours to calm his granddaughter. Twice he had to change her. Once he prevented her from biting him with a cloth between her teeth. He had to change the pillow case. Eventually he managed to soothe her.

There was no point in going back to bed. He knew she would sleep solidly now. He sat down in the kitchen and sipped at a mug of tea.

He felt like getting on with it. Gargarin, he had to do

263

something. Well, he had it all arranged. He started to dress, taking his tea with him to his bedroom, and then called Sharon, who ten minutes later appeared in her dressing gown.

'That's all right, Mr B. I'll lie on the sofa. She'll be all right.'

He was able to leave.

London was not yet awake. The air still smelt clean. He could cross straight over to where Gargie lived, doing it in twenty minutes, when in an hour's time it would take three times as long. By the time he arrived, the others, telephoned to get ready, were there. He pulled in on the other side of the railway tracks, padded quietly through the foot tunnel and they set off together.

'Give me the video,' Billy said. 'No one else is to speak at all. Not a word, you hear me? Have you got the camera?'

Gargie was still in bed, Alleycat beside him.

'We can't find your child,' said Billy. He said it softly since Alleycat had not woken up.

'He's not here.'

Gargie was staring at the muzzle of a gun.

'Get up.'

Gargie slid out of bed. He reached for some clothes.

'You won't need them,' said Billy. 'You stay here for the moment,' Billy said to one of the twins. 'You can come in later.' He knew he had to let each one enjoy himself, or they became difficult to handle.

Gargie walked ahead of them into the front room.

'I didn't want to do this,' Billy said. 'But now you're costing me money. I warned you.'

Gargie was unable to move, bent forward by the tether and the piece of wood. As a gag was put on him his eyes grew wider. 'Have you seen this?' Billy said, and he put the video on.

Gargie couldn't reply because of the gag.

'It doesn't matter.'

Gargie had seen it, and his skin crawled as he watched it again. Wicked Man's body jerked convulsively. The twins had enjoyed themselves that day.

'Now they are going to do the same to you.'

When they left, Billy went and spoke to Alleycat. She lay awake, frozen with fear. She had heard some of the noises from the next room, especially the exhausted cries of pleasure the twins let out. Billy sat on the bed and said, 'Alison. I've got some money on deposit from Gargie. Quite a lot.' Her eyes grew wide. 'It's yours, you only have to ring me for it. You can keep both the cars, though he must have bought them with money stolen from me. And I've got a concession free now, it's yours if you want it. To begin with, I'll help you run it.

'All you have to do is go to sleep again, and wake up when the police get here. Say nothing. If you say anything, you'll get what he got. OK?'

Alison was not stupid. Billy was making a good offer. She nodded her head and turned over to pretend to sleep.

Chapter 17

When Vernon answered the phone Scott couldn't place the type at first. The man's voice was high and fluting, precise, choosing words with particular care and yet, when they came, the choice was quite ordinary.

'Yes, I had been . . . ah . . . notified . . . of your possible arrival.'

It was the voice of someone who regarded himself as detached, distancing himself from what was ordinary, imbuing himself with a magisterial quality, not appreciated enough by those around him.

He had heard such a voice before. Where was it? Then he remembered, exactly similar to a judge in a court near London, and when Scott remembered that man he understood the present voice.

Well educated – in the judge's case very well educated – but not as successful as he thought he deserved. The result was a man who had to bear the burden of what might have been, and of what others, less well endowed, had managed to achieve. Why should people who were rougher than he, and, let's face it, he must be saying to himself, not so refined, have got what he had not? An unhappy man.

Scott was being given directions. 'As you approach East Place on your left you can make quite a sharp turning into Burrell Road north. Take the . . .' Here it was again,

266

the man paused in an exaggerated fashion, though he must have said this dozens of times before – 'the penultimate turning to your right. Follow that road down and you will reach The Drive. We are opposite you.'

Scott wasn't looking forward to this. He would have to defer and flatter, and laugh at the jokes and whimsy, show he appreciated the breeding and intelligence; at least that's what he had to do with the judge.

He was near the place already and would be there in ten minutes. 'I look forward to seeing you,' said the voice. Scott cut through under the motorway and immediately his surroundings changed, the way things can in London, moving from wealth to poverty in a hundred yards. This was the Cummin Estate, the kind of place where it would be better not to stop the car if you were a woman on your own.

The road reached a crossing; on the right there was an area for buses to pull in, with a vestigial green patch, now rutted and bare, and on the left a row of shops was set back behind a slip road. It was the tattered remains of the town planning of fifty years ago. He could see the local mayor, his mouth wide open, his wife in a fox stole sitting behind him, effusively welcoming the advances that such a public-spirited enterprise would bring, as the local slums were decanted into 'houses fit for the future'.

There was just such a picture of the Lord Chancellor opening Inner London Crown Court new extension: morning coat, striped trousers, the lot. What was his name? The Original of Widmerpool. Bullying manner? The same wife.

Now the place, for all the good intentions, had become another slum. Scott swallowed and dragged himself back to the present. It was reflecting on the man's voice that had set him off. He had better get his mind on the job, go over his story and his tactics once more before he got there.

He guessed this man's personality would make it easier to play the professional game. 'I can't give you too much detail, Mr Day, you will understand my position.' Vernon Day didn't sound like the man who was going to reply, 'Come off it, mate, you're in this for the money, as much as anyone.' And what Scott said wouldn't matter much anyway, as long as he flattered him by deferring to quality. That was the way. Was it possible to tell so much from a voice? Yes.

He'd better be completely clear though. He pulled the car over. The guy would want to know details, want to know background, so he could calculate the amount of work. He'd want a promise of cash, and of course Scott needed to put off the paying of cash as long as possible, because the moment he wanted paying would be the end, since Scott could produce neither client nor cash. But that wouldn't be today.

What Scott would have to do was pretend the client was nervous of meeting him, so he could get as much detail as possible, get what information he could, in advance. Of course, as it turned out, he was quite wrong about all this — save the voice, that is; the reality is always so much more overwhelming than the idea.

There was a tap on the car door.

He looked up, a woman police officer. He reached to his left to press the button, and the window slowly lowered itself; he knew that from the outside that always created a feeling of condescension.

If it did, it certainly worked on the officer. 'C'mon then, out of it, let's be rid of you,' she said, hoiking her thumb over her shoulder.

'What?' said Scott at a complete loss.

'What?' The woman imitated Scott's voice. What she would have no doubt called a posh accent.

'What? What, what?' Shaking her head from side to side: 'Now out of here before I nick you.'

268

'Oh, I see,' Scott said, opening his mouth to protest, but then he thought better of it.

He drove off. He got control of himself, letting the anger trickle out, imagining it draining out of him, running off him, leaving him untouched. He was untouched. He was only amazed again at the power such a person had at her command.

She supposed she knew exactly what he had been up to, crossing the tracks, and he also knew that what she would put in any arrest note would have reflected what she knew, not what had happened. And the publicity. 'Judge stopped for kerb crawling.' Even the most minor recorder, which he was, would be described as a judge.

Scott shivered. He was out on a limb anyway, why get more involved?

Number 24, The Drive was as anonymous as it could be. A large house on the edge of the bad area, trying to inch away if it could. Chance had put it this side of the estate. Had it been on the other there would have been poets for neighbours. If you stood at the door and looked to your left, resentfully, you would see the concrete encroaching on the leafy street, but it was well screened by laurel that had been allowed to grow, and there was some attempt at gardening, where a flower bed of salvias followed the front path.

The moment you stepped through the gate you were in a completely private area. A milk container was marked at 'six pints, please, Milky'. Someone had changed the six to sex.

Scott paused at the door. The brush with the police and the tension of the visit had increased his anxiety. He felt his heart beating. It was beating as had other men's hearts, standing at that door for the first time.

Once inside it didn't take very long for Scott to realise he had come to a male brothel.

'Welcome,' said Vernon Day dramatically, standing back and waving Scott in with his other arm. 'Our visitor. Our professional visitor.'

Day was not a tall man, slightly built, neat and carefully dressed. He wasn't big enough to dress informally. He stood to one side, allowing Scott to pass into the hallway. 'May I take your coat?' As he did so Scott noticed the man's eyes slide past him to the wall.

He took the hint, and as Vernon Day took his coat, no doubt inspecting the label, Scott examined the pictures, the kind of pictures you see on the walls of an Italian restaurant. Someone shaking hands with someone; he could see, on looking closer, that it was Vernon Day. A scrawled signature. A cheque being presented to Vernon Day, turning to the camera and smiling. Always men; men who were a bit famous, a one-time politician now a journalist, a singer. A member of the House of Lords, a jockey. Later Scott realised the pictures must have been there for protection, to remind Vernon Day's guests that they were involved. Getting your picture on the wall would be a potent threat.

He turned back. 'Very impressive,' Scott said. 'You are clearly well supported, and obviously well thought of, if I may say.' He spoke with a precision of which Vernon Day would approve. And did. It was working already.

The man was wearing something that approximated to a dog collar, a black shirt with a Nehru collar. He obviously liked the ersatz spiritual feel of it. He had beige trousers and a jacket without lapels. The material sparkled slightly, Scott could not work out why. Was it called shot silk? The kind of coat you might bring back from Bangkok. He said, 'Welcome to the Piano Factory. Although by now of course you must wondering what pianos have to do with anything.' He laughed deprecatingly, tipping his head back; a slight, musical laugh.

By now the smell had got to Scott. From previous experience he knew the only way to deal with this was to breathe right through it, however sick it made you for a few seconds. He gulped and his eyes bulged. 'Yes,' he said, letting his breath out like a cannabis smoker. 'Yes, I was.'

An urge to laugh out loud followed, but Vernon Day didn't notice. He didn't notice much of what others felt, unless it involved him.

'Well, originally we were a charity over Crystal Palace way. Quite a history we had; in the early nineteenth century we were paralleled with the Salvation Army, the same sort of work with foundlings and, ah, vagabondage, though that was years ago. But we did not grow in the same way, we stayed local. In the end the charity was based just up the road from Foresters Hall, in a place called the Old Piano Factory. It had continued there for a long time, eventually outliving its original purpose. So rather than have the commissioners – the Charity Commissioners, that is – close it down, I moved it here, on an undertaking to carry on the same work.

'I changed the name to remind us of where we had come from. Originally we were the Metropolitan and Area Good Works Association. Not a modern or, ah, *charismatic* name, I think you will agree.'

He laughed in his voice. Scott's skin crawled.

He ended this speech with his hands pressed together before his lips, clearly reflecting with pleasure on what he had just said, inviting admiration. 'Not of course that we are charismatists. We leave that path for others to tread.' Again he laughed his musical laugh, at his private joke. 'Now do come this way.' He stopped and paused, adding theatrically, 'The old place, now it's a Safeway. Thus do things change.'

The hall opened out into a large area with a staircase going up to the next floor. It resembled the stage set one might have expected at a West End play in, say, 1955. The smell got worse. Scott found he was beginning to be able to guess at bits of its composition: bodies, adolescent shoes, unwashed plastic sheets; the central heating on too high, perhaps with sealed windows – although surprisingly, underneath it all he thought he could distinguish what seemed to be Mansion House polish.

The next moment he saw why: a huge polished parquet floor that had, in the front of the hall, been covered with a carpet. It led into the drawing room through a wide open double door.

The room still had some of its original furniture, a grandfather clock, a barometer, lampshades with tassels on, a standard lamp and two large sofas facing each other, a Russell Flint print; but in the fireplace, instead of a blazing fire, a large ugly television set, and on the sofas eight young men, trainers scattered round them, feet up, smelling.

'Some of our guests,' Vernon Day said airily. They ranged in age from very young to perhaps twenty, maybe a little more. Some of them looked up briefly, otherwise they were engrossed in the television. One was sucking his thumb, taking it out of his mouth to wipe it on his shirt, before gazing indifferently at Scott.

'Here's Joey,' Vernon Day said, obviously feeling he had to say something, rather than, as he would obviously have preferred, saying nothing at all about them.

'Charlie and the twins.' He waved his hand vaguely towards the group. The ones whose names had been called looked at Scott. Joey worked up a sickly grin. Scott wondered whether this was the look he gave when the member of the House of Lords or the jockey was brought into the room to choose who it might be this time.

The twins looked at him: murderous, shaven-headed, blank-faced.

Vernon Day moved on, but not before, at the far end of one sofa, hugging a cushion, sitting with his head drooping forward, his mouth open, vacantly drinking in what was on the screen, Scott saw Jason – Jimmy Reilly's accuser.

'Christ!' he said, stepping forward out of sight, putting his hand to his eyes. He felt he had been struck.

'We'll go in here.'

Vernon Day had been preoccupied in unlocking a door and had not noticed Scott's reaction. He opened the door to the next room and hung Scott's coat up. 'Better not leave it outside,' he said. 'These young men have not necessarily learned the difference between *meum* and *teum*.' He laughed, his mouth open just so, his eyes veiled with memory. 'That was an expression my father often used to use. This was his room, I keep it exactly as he left it.'

Scott took the chair placed before the desk. The desk was decked out in the equipment of a first-class male of the fifties or sixties: letter opener, inkwell, calendar holder, even a pipe stand, and in pride of place a regimental mascot in silver. On the walls there were formal group portraits, a series of caps with tassels and, above the fireplace, an oar.

So Vernon Day was that sad creature, a disappointment to his father.

'Now what can I do for you?'

Scott was cautious. 'I was advised to come to see you. I have a client who wishes to make a complaint about some ill-treatment he received when he was a young man.'

He needn't have been tentative. Vernon Day was quite willing to explain what he did. 'You want me to interview him. Of course I'll do that. It's part of what we do here. Since anyone who stays with us has to tell me his story.'

'You will have talked to many young men?'

The man almost hugged himself with pleasure. 'You

273

could almost say it is what I do. Often the biggest problem these particular young men have, those who have been dreadfully abused, is a difficulty with sharing their pain. It is something our whole group has in common. How old is your client?'

'Twenty, just twenty.'

A flicker of disappointment seemed to touch Vernon Day's bland face, and the tip of his tongue appeared momentarily at his lips. 'Still young, still young though,' he said, 'and has he suffered much?'

Scott felt himself being drawn in to a ghastly, second-hand confessional. The atmosphere was stifling. The temptation to get up and start doing something vigorous to shake it off was very strong. That must be what the Victorians had in mind when they advocated strenuous exercise in place of masturbation. Instead he said, 'He says so.'

'You won't have enquired? Understandable. I myself deal with this a lot and it is difficult to know where to begin.'

'I see you do have older –' Scott tried to find the word – 'youths. The twins?'

At the mention of them Day looked positively apprehensive. 'Yes, yes. Two severely damaged young men when they came here. Each had spent time in custody, and they do not like being separated. Their father was a very violent man. He used to beat them, until one day they turned on him. It was a very traumatic experience for –' he paused, as if puzzled whom to include – 'all of them.' He leaned forward. 'Mr—' he stumbled because Scott had not given his name, and was not going to. Vernon Day swallowed the rejected attempt at some intimacy with difficulty. 'They can be very violent. I have experienced it myself. But they are safe.'

It was an extraordinary thing to have said, and Scott

guessed was the result of great strain, since it was clear that safe was just what they were not.

'Unless roused,' Scott joked in an officers' mess manner.

'I have to protect the younger brethren from their attention. And to begin with the only way to do so was to draw their anger down upon myself –' he stuttered, and this was not for effect – 'u-p-pon my own p-p-person.'

What did that mean? The sooner Scott was out of here the better.

'Would my client need to stay here while this is done, or can he just visit?'

'I am afraid we should have to ask him to stay.'

'He is apprehensive of that.'

'Has he experience of staying away from home? So few young men have nowadays.'

'Yes. When these things happened – what has made him have to come here – then he was staying in a house with a group.'

Vernon Day simpered. 'Well, he will have understood, what those of us who went away to school understand. We all have to, ah, *muck in* together, though in our case there are no cold baths.' He laughed again, inviting Scott to confirm the reminiscence.

Scott guessed that many people sitting where he was sitting would allow themselves to be drawn in for what Vernon Day would call a, ah, little chat. Leading where?

'I think it may be just the group aspect that worries him.'

Vernon Day was adamant. 'But I am afraid it is vital for the communication which we attempt to stimulate. We would expect him to join in the group sessions. And that' – he changed the subject drastically – 'does, I fear, cost money.'

'And how much would that be?'

Now very businesslike.

'Well, for a week's work, and the presentation of a report, say to the criminal injuries compensation board, or to others, it would be in the region of one thousand pounds, plus incidental expenses. The report would be sent to you, and you would also receive a videotape of the . . . well, we call it the disclosure interview, though modern thinking discourages that expression. For why, I do not understand.' He stopped. 'Do you follow me?' he said.

'You are being very clear,' Scott said. They had come to an understanding.

Vernon Day said, 'Of course, that tape is solely yours, and your client's property.' The atmosphere changed back. 'We would like him to stay for at least seven nights. I would see him, it may be others would help him. We often . . .' He stopped. Scott could see he only needed encouragement, permission even, to carry on.

'It must be difficult?'

'Yes.' Vernon Day let his breath out, and got down to it. 'We rely to a certain extent on re-enactment and role play.' The whole lumber of modern psychology began to appear, perverted to his purpose. 'Even handling the original instruments of pain can help a young man get over the memory.'

Scott's eyes followed the man's gaze. There was a rattan cane in the umbrella stand. 'My father's,' Vernon Day said with a cold smile. 'Was there any such a thing in your client's past?'

'I really don't know,' Scott said, then, feeding the man a morsel, he said, offhand, 'Maybe there was a slipper.'

'Oh, the slipper? Our old friend.'

'A thousand pounds.' Scott changed the subject back again. He was safe now. 'And for that he would be much clearer in what he was saying happened to him?'

'Clearer, yes, since he will have re-enacted it, released it, and thereby to an extent freed himself of it. Certainly he would be able to talk about it much more clearly. I have had customers – clients,' he corrected himself, 'who have been able to speak to the police afterwards in a way that they were not able to do before. It's the re-enactment that does it.'

Now Scott understood Charlie Pope's phrase, 'It'll be like it happened yesterday.'

Vernon Day said, 'We have some knowledge of the local child protection team, including one Mr Reynolds, and we know what they regard as important, what their methods are. The detail of the assault is what matters, not so much the time and place. That is what is compelling for a –' he nearly said jury, Scott thought, but did not – 'the, ah, tribunal of fact.'

'Of course, one presumably has to be careful?' Vernon Day froze for a moment, before Scott released him: 'One of my partners ran up against the problem of recovered memory. There were allegations of memory implantation. This I understand can be a problem with those whose experiences occurred when they were very young. It is something I know little about.'

'Yes, yes. But we have no problem with such a thing since those who come to us by definition have had bad experiences.'

He had avoided the question. Of course, here it wasn't implanted memory at all. It was all too real, it happened here, only the place was changed. Scott imagined what must have happened with Jason.

'What is a greater problem is giving the very young an adequate language to describe what they have suffered. I call it the language of abuse. I have a young child here for instance at the moment, whose difficulty was in speaking of his experiences, since he had no real language to describe it. His friend Billy was the same.'

That was it. Scott stood up. He said, 'Do you have a card, Mr Day? So I can write to you, with a formal approach as it were, and I shall then be able to give you the details you need.'

But Vernon Day didn't want to stop. 'We should remember this. We all have had these experiences. I myself – do you mind me speaking about myself? That is why I took up this work; I was at the mercy of a larger child for some years. It gave me insight, because I believe, and find, that most children have these experiences; certainly Billy and his friend did so on a daily basis at school. It is only when they are told that they come to realise how damaging it was, how unnatural, how abnormal.'

He got up. 'There you have it. The philosophy behind the Piano Factory. Our mission.' He put his hands in prayer beneath his chin; a modern Mrs Jellyby.

They left his room, Scott apprehensive of being seen from the sofas. As Vernon Day locked the door, Scott put his coat on, turning away from where Jason was sitting. The moment the people in the room heard voices appearing from the study, the picture snapped off, but not before Scott had seen on the screen one of the twins, shaven-headed, stooping over what looked like a prostrate, splayed body. Naked, Scott thought. Maybe it was a television film. No. A videotape slid slowly out of the slot. It must just have been turned off, tipping itself out, just like Vernon Day's tongue, darting out between his thin lips, and just as revealing.

Scott walked past, his head turned away from the big room, made the door and, keeping his hands firmly in his pockets so he did not have to shake the man's hand, escaped into the fresh air.

He was that much nearer to getting Jimmy Reilly free.

Chapter 18

Now that he had definite information he needed to act. He immediately contacted Colin Nicholson, a solicitor used to dealing with the intricacies of corruption. He was able to move through it untouched. 'What do I do now?' Scott asked him.

Colin didn't answer him. He said, 'It was very unwise to go anywhere near a place like the Potato Patch. The next thing you'll find is, there you are, in evidence, on a police video.'

Scott realised that there were rules for what he had been doing. There always were rules, and he was going to get advice that he didn't want.

Colin said, 'Never go anywhere like that without a written appointment, or at least a note in the appointment diary. Then you are covered. I always tell Jan and she types it up for me.' Jan ran Colin's office in smoke-filled clamour.

Colin had been slow and deliberate, smiling at the idea of what he had heard. It was how he always reacted.

'I know it goes on,' he said. 'I know the whole witness thing can be very lucrative. Look at that football person. £75,000 payment to someone who claimed his hand was on her knee? That's four times the annual salary of a nurse, maybe more. How the press must hate him.'

Then he was serious. 'Solicitors have to be very careful. When you get the papers as counsel, all the sticky bits have been dealt with. You don't know how lucky you are.'

Colin listened to the visit to Vernon Day. 'I have to say it again,' he said. 'What if there was observation on that house? What would that have made you – a customer?'

Scott realised that having your car window tapped by a policewoman was not the only danger.

'What do I do now?'

'For someone who has been so adventurous, it's rather boring advice.' He stopped. 'You're probably not going to accept it.' Again he left a gap for Scott to fill in.

'OK, Colin. I understand. If you go to a solicitor for advice, you don't disregard it without a good reason. All right, I think I know what you are going to say. Say it.'

'You go the police.'

'But which police? They themselves are involved.'

'I know someone at East Place I can trust.'

'He's not called Reynolds, I hope. Taking arranged stories and prosecuting them for money. Vernon Day actually mentioned his name.'

Colin said, 'No, it's not Reynolds. We'll meet at my office. Give me twenty-four hours.' He laughed. 'Alternatively, you could go to the press.'

'They're complicit,' said Scott. 'They're players themselves.'

'I know,' Colin said.

'And they know the public wouldn't believe it. It's not what people want to hear.'

Mike Reynolds said to Jennet, 'I'll look after him. I'll look after Timmy for the afternoon.' He was sitting with her in a Café Rouge, a French restaurant, good, even though it was a chain. He was eating nothing, just drinking coffee.

She was eating a chicken baguette, with mayonnaise, tightly packed. She didn't like to eat in front of him like this, him watching, that is. You couldn't control the situation; it was easy to look silly if it squirted out the side of your mouth.

He watched her.

To eat a chicken baguette like that one, you have to open your mouth wide, and even then it's too big. She was going to be embarrassed, she probably already regretted choosing it. He turned away and poked about amongst the newspapers on the shelf next to them to give her a moment to deal with it.

She was still nervous about her body, he could tell. It was as though she was ashamed of it, as if it were something which might suddenly get out of hand.

He wondered what it would be like when it did, and hoped he would be there to join in. He told her that, and she blushed, embarrassed. On the other hand he knew she enjoyed it. Like 'Manuel and Manuela' in the trailer park.

'He dr-inks te-qui-la,
and sh-e – talks di-rty – in – Spa-nish.'

He said it out loud with a steady beat, and she paused, still with a bit of mayonnaise on her lip, brushing it off.

'What?'

'Nothing. "Manuel and Manuela". They play it on Ritz radio 1035, the Cutting Edge of Country Music,' he said.

'You think I'm stupid.'

'No I don't.'

He knew he didn't think that. She wasn't stupid, she was just not concerned with some things, things that didn't really matter.

'I said, I'll look after Timmy.'

'Will you really?' Eager. Then she was cautious. What

281

Dr Grace had said about young women with children jumped straight into her head. Men and small boys.

'Of course. What else is there to do?'

She wanted to say thank you, thank you. But you can't say that. She had to be a bit careful. She said instead, 'Where will you take him?'

'On the country walk.'

'Where?'

'In the big park. If you go further down towards the train station, you can turn off through that gate. Then we can walk the walk.'

He grinned. When he was with her it was as though he freed up.

'I won't drop him,' he said. 'At least not on his head.'

Some bit of her trusted him completely, and that bit was gradually winning, so she couldn't stay cautious all the time. She knew he was all right.

'There's a rope there, attached to a tree, and you can, I mean he can, swing on it. He'd like that.'

Her eyes brimmed. This was what it was meant to be like, what she had read about. It was silly to be so affected by something so small, but nowadays she was easily moved. The strain seemed to be lifting; things were opening up after the tight, closed life she had had.

'I do,' he said. 'I enjoy it, I mean. Swinging on the rope.'

He took her hand and she let him hold it.

'You take your mum to the hairdresser,' he said. 'She'll enjoy that, with you to look after her.'

'You make it all sound so easy,' she said.

'It is.'

'Not for me,' she said.

'That's because I'm the first person who's loved you properly.'

Nothing for a moment. She swallowed; nothing to say to that.

282

'I'll tell you what. I'll run you two to the hairdresser's now, and then I'll take Timmy to the park.'

She started to pack herself away, self-conscious, relying upon him, but taught to be cautious, not relying too much in case the ice broke and she fell through again. She didn't agree out loud, that would be too dangerous, she just went along with it.

'Don't be frightened,' he said.

She looked at him and said nothing. He was in there, right in there, the place where she felt things. It wasn't right to say he was just looking about. This was more like the song said, he was making himself at home in her heart.

Mike and Timmy crossed the road to the park.

'Now,' Mike said. As he got ready to move forward he felt the small boy's hand slip into his. It shook him for a moment. Was this what it was like? No doubt the child had never crossed a road without holding someone's hand. The hand felt warm and it trusted him completely.

'Now,' he said, and, in breach of everything a policeman should do, they ran across the road.

They wandered down the wide path. On both sides huge beech trees clung to the disintegrating bank, plain and beautiful. Nothing grew beneath them. 'Cheap furniture used to be made from beech trees, by people who were called Bodgers. That's where we get the word to bodge something,' Mike said.

'Bodgers,' the boy said. He threw his head back, laughed and said it out loud again.

They slid down a bank. Mike fell on his backside, his feet slipping as he followed down the steep slope, and they both laughed again. A fox appeared – in daylight! And Timmy just saw it. Above them a bird sang, and in the distance they saw a train chugging down the branch line.

They were no more than five miles from the City of London but they might have been deep in the country.

Timmy slipped and fell. His knee hurt, but he knew he was with a big man and he didn't want to seem to be a baby. He bit his lip.

'Do you know the best way to deal with that?' Mike said, his hand on the boy's knee.

Timmy said, nearly crying, 'Wh–what?'

'Take no notice at all. Just march right through it.' And Mike stood up and said, 'By the left, qui–ick, march! Left, right. Left, right,' and the boy followed him, single file, both swinging their arms, marching across the field, a little army of two.

And the pain started to go away for both of them.

'Wow,' said Timmy. A great thick rope hung down from the beech tree, the kind of rope you use to tie a ship up. It was attached with a chain to a huge bough; you could have hung a car on it. The rope was knotted at the bottom, a knot big enough to sit on. The ground sloped sharply down, away from the knuckled roots of the tree, so, ten feet out from the tree, the knot would be twelve feet up in the air, and that was even before the rope really began its upswing. Twelve feet!

'Wow,' said Timmy.

'Now hang on tight.'

Timmy didn't appear to hear him. 'Wow.'

Was this a good idea? They could fall.

'Right, let's get on.'

You had to reach up with a stick and push at the rope so it swung back up the bank. A couple of goes and they grabbed it, and managed to hang on as they scrambled up to the top.

'I'll get on first.' Mike sat on the big knot, and then, 'You climb on here, on my lap.' The small boy climbed on.

'Wow,' he said.

284

Mike backed up, forcing his way further up the slope, his feet slipping and digging into the earth for grip, then, taking a tight hold on the rope and squeezing the small boy with his elbows, he lifted his feet off the ground.

'Hold on very tight, please. Ding, ding . . .' In a singsong, like a bus conductor, then Mike let go. They swung out into the air in a huge arc, up into the trees, continuing on and on, and then lazily twisting, back down at speed and up the bank again. He kicked the earth where they had started and they swung back out.

Time stopped.

'Wow,' Timmy said. 'This is fun.'

When they drove back to the hairdressing salon they were early and had to sit outside in the car.

Through the window Mike could see Jennet's mother sitting in the chair, what remained of her hair being teased and puffed back into a confection.

Here was an elderly lady, careful of how she looked, although she was for the most part invisible. No one noticed her much, a little, old person, making her way down the street, but her daughter was standing behind her, directing the hairdresser, caring for her mother. That made her someone who mattered.

The little boy sitting next to him was preoccupied with a comic.

People had such courage to be themselves. Mike watched them and as he did so his heart seemed to swell, and his mistrust of people peeled away a little more, and he knew he was rejoining life, after all this lonely time.

Scott said, 'Am I doing this officially?'

'No, no. Nothing like that yet.'

'So I can just talk?'

They were sitting in Colin's car the next day, just arrived, not far from Colin's office. The display panel of

285

instruments glowed in the dark. 'Look,' Colin said. 'The computer can pick up what we are saying.'

'What now? It's recording?'

'Not now. I have to press the button.' He leaned forward and touched one, and a wavy line went up and down.

'I thought that was the tyre pressure, or something.'

Scott was joking, but he was nearly right.

'No, this is the tyre pressure,' Colin said. He flicked another switch, and a series of numbers marched up and down the tiny screen.

'Would I be an informer?'

'Kind of. But not registered or anything, nothing so dramatic. Billy Unknown you'll be, to begin with.'

'What?'

'Billy Unknown. The expression began up north. Up there you can't tell the police from the faces, they're so mixed up.'

'What's this guy's name?'

'Frank Abbott. He's running Operation Poseidon. He works near East Place police station, at least that's where his office is.' Colin leaned forward, flicking buttons. This car was so sophisticated that you had to close it down when you parked it, like a jet plane.

'Billy Unknown. If he makes no notes then you stay completely out of it, and if he writes anything down he has to reveal the existence of the notes, so he won't. But you know that.'

He turned and grinned at Scott. He had one of the broadest grins Scott knew, it was very reassuring. They got out of the car.

'The effect of what I'm saying is that two police officers are corrupt, you realise that?'

'They won't be the first.' Colin pointed his key at the car and pressed a button. It played a tune back at him before subsiding with a sigh. 'Certainly not the first.

286

Nothing surprises anyone any more. Not much that is.'

'Colin, there's one thing.' Scott stopped on the pavement. He wanted to say this. 'I am not interested in what these people are doing. It's irrelevant to me. I am only interested in Jimmy Reilly. He was innocent. He is innocent. And on that evidence, innocent or not, he should never have been convicted. He was had over by the system, and I'm part of the system, so that matters to me.'

He continued: 'I only want Jimmy Reilly out. I've got no vendetta against anyone, they can do what they want, I'm sick of them.'

'Well, we'll see if Frank Abbott understands that. He probably won't. After all, he isn't a lawyer, is he? He's never had a client to look after. That's something we do, policemen don't.'

They plunged into a concrete tunnel, coming out on the other side of the square.

'We'll go in the back way,' Colin said. They cut past the side of the red cathedral and crossed a small park. 'That way no one can connect you two,' he said.

The first thing Scott noticed that was different about Abbott was that he didn't react when Scott said that Jimmy Reilly was innocent, nor when he told him what the offence was. It was clear this man had no fixed ideas to get in the way; for him everything was possible. He was just what Colin had said.

Scott said, 'Jimmy Reilly was fitted up and what I've found out proves it. After the trial, I began by going to the Potato Patch to see if there was something about the pub, the River Anchor, or the people in it that I could discover. Or whether I could find a Billy or a Vernon.'

There was a slight tension. It must be the reference to the Potato Patch.

He said, 'I only went there for information. I know

287

someone there. Then I was directed to another place, further out of London, a kind of evangelical church. I was told to mention Billy, but it seems that was another Billy. These people run a victim support group, but when they heard what I had to say, they told me to go and see a man called Charlie Pope. Obviously by this time I had managed to get across to them that I was wanting to do business with them.'

Scott gained the impression that the names were familiar to Abbott, since there was no repetition, no asking him to repeat them or to say anything more about them. On the other hand, Abbott didn't seem to react to anything. What Scott was saying was going to be considered, nothing was going to come back to him in return.

'Pope offered a deal. If I provided a complainant, he would arrange a prosecution, and the publicity money from the press, exclusive stories and things, the fees would be funnelled through me. The complaint which I ended up describing and offering, of course, was a sexual assault on an apprentice footballer in a league football club.

'I was given the name of a police officer, and told that he had a colleague in the child protection team who would take it up. Presumably they work together, that's how the prosecution would be arranged. I have the name of the officer here.'

Scott produced the card. He put it on the desk. Abbott leaned forward to read it. Fulton.

Scott noticed Abbott didn't touch it.

In the moment that Abbott's eyes were not on him, Scott noticed Colin mouth the words 'slow down' at him. He stopped.

Abbott leaned back. 'Anything else?' he said.

Scott wondered if it was all a damp squib. In the silence he wanted to say something, to ask, What do you think? But

288

he knew that he wasn't going to get the small reassurances that you get in ordinary conversation. He said, 'These were the people who fitted Jimmy Reilly up. I know it.'

'You haven't rung this man?' said Abbott, pointing at the paper.

'No. That would be going too far,' he said. But his opinion was of no relevance. Again he had the feeling of having entered a world where things were serious, and didn't need emphasis.

'Did Pope say anything more about the people he dealt with?'

'Yes. He said it was all up for sale, the whole system. For instance, he could use the informer text system to get private information to a judge to help defendants, or get privileged material before a judge to affect the way a case was treated.'

'Did he ask you if you wanted that done?'

'No. I just got the impression he was –' Scott paused, was this relevant? – 'he was boasting to me what he could do, that sort of thing. He wanted to show me how little lawyers knew of what really goes on. All of us, lawyers and judges, of course.'

Abbott listened.

'But he also told me the name of the person who would arrange the story.' Scott had kept the best bit to last.

He realised he wanted to convince this man more than he had thought. It must be because he was used to the idea that if the police accept a defence, the case is won. But of course the court of appeal, they were the real barrier. No doubt things look different from an expensive room in the court of appeal, they have a whole system to protect: the one that pays their salary and gave them a knighthood.

'There was another name. Vernon Day.' He turned the card over and told Abbott about the visit to the house –

and this was the only time that Abbott interrupted. 'The twins?' he said.

Scott finished and waited.

Then he was swept away.

'What would you say, if I said I didn't believe you, Mr Scott, sir,' said Frank Abbott.

'Not believe me?' It wasn't possible to imagine someone would not believe what he knew was true.

'Yes,' said Abbott.

Again Scott said, 'Not believe me? Why should I ask to see you then?'

'I don't mean not believe that you did what you said you did. I mean not believe what *you* believe. You believe Jimmy Reilly was wrongly convicted. You believe the witness Jason Lee made up his story. You believe that Charlie Pope invents the stories he sells and manipulates the courts. You believe that this Vernon Day is running a male brothel, when he could equally well be what he says he is, a charity working with the local authority and the police. You believe, to cap it all, that Fulton and Reynolds are corrupt. Have I got it all?'

Scott sat – as far as he could remember when he thought back on it – with his mouth open.

'Now let me ask you some questions,' said Frank Abbott. 'A man called McLaren was prosecuted for drugs. He was allowed to plead guilty merely to possession, despite his clearly being a drugs dealer. Why was that?'

The change of subject threw him and Scott struggled even to remember the case.

'You were prosecuting the case. You don't often prosecute, do you?'

That was easy to answer. 'No.'

'But on this occasion you did, and a man who had two thousand pounds from selling drugs concealed in his sock went free with a fine. Not your decision?'

290

'No. But it never—'

'Hang on. This man McLaren was murdered within minutes of your releasing him. He was employed by a man called Gargarin, who himself days later was murdered in the same way. Both were impaled, I won't tell you on what. We think the person who did this was an associate of Charlie Pope.'

Scott was struck dumb.

Pause. 'Who was it you went to see immediately after McLaren's case that day?'

Scott tried to think back. Which case was that? He couldn't immediately separate from all the others. His very failure to reply seemed to tell against him. He looked at Colin for support. Colin's face said nothing.

'You went to see Charlie Pope. If Charlie Pope was, or is, involved with the man or men who had McLaren killed – then one' – Abbott numbered it off on his fingers – 'McLaren could only have been killed if he was released from custody, which he was, against all the odds; two, we think Charlie Pope was connected with that; three, Charlie Pope's business is, as you say, manipulating the courts; four, how much of a surprise is it that prosecuting counsel – who spent time with the judge in private – went to see Charlie Pope immediately after the plea was offered to McLaren?'

'I only got the brief the night before.' Scott was dragging the events back. Of course he should have said, Stop, stop talking for a moment, so I can remember and let it sink in. But how many clients had he himself represented who should have said that and did not?

'OK. But let's think about this. You went to see the judge. Did the judge say anything about why he gave Jimmy Reilly such a light sentence?'

Again Scott was completely flummoxed. It was like trying to say exactly where you lost your keys – with a gun

291

at your head. 'I don't know. I don't know that the sentence was a light one, anyway.'

'You were there, privately with the judge. I believe they call it "in chambers".' He used the phrase with contempt. 'Why did he say he had disregarded the adverse medical report? Because he had, hadn't he? And when he disregarded it in court, it didn't faze you in the slightest, did it? People watching could see that. Were you expecting it? Had it all been arranged on Jimmy Reilly's behalf? By Charlie Pope? And are you trying to do the same thing now, by shopping Charlie Pope? What do you owe Jimmy Reilly?'

'Nothing. I owe him nothing. He was just a client.'

'He's only a client, Mr Scott. Clients mean nothing to you. They are ten a penny. And you've done all this for him?'

This was something Scott had thought about and he was suddenly able to fight back.

'Look, Mr Abbott. That conviction got to me. It shouldn't have happened, nor should I have reacted, but I've had enough of walking away and forgetting about things like that, like we're meant to. Can't you understand that?'

'I'm just asking you some questions, Mr Scott, sir, at your own request, you'll recall. Now. What about Billy Burns? You called him to give evidence?'

'For Jimmy Reilly, yes.'

'And what did he tell you?'

'I have never spoken to him in my life.'

'What, and you called him?'

'Those are the rules, Mr Abbott.' Scott was finding a breathing space.

'Did you not know about his background?'

'What background?'

'No one told you?'

'No. I am only told what he tells my solicitor.'

'So he concealed his convictions from your solicitor?'

'If he had any, he must have done. We don't have access to your computers, Mr Abbott.'

'But Billy Burns knows Charlie Pope, doesn't he?'

'Not that I know of.'

'Billy Burns is a target criminal, Mr Scott.'

'What?'

'We think he may have killed at least two people, probably more in his time. We think the twins you met work for him, to put it gently, hurting people. We are not surprised your friend Mr Reilly was accused by that boy. Billy Burns probably arranged it.'

Suddenly the atmosphere changed.

'Mr Reilly used to take goods in for Billy Burns's crack houses. Mr Scott, your great witness Billy Burns is a franchiser of crack houses. Now that's marketing innovation for you.'

In the midst of this Scott clung to his reason for seeing Abbott at all. 'What about Jimmy Reilly then? That means he was innocent?'

'Just because he was set up, doesn't mean to say he isn't guilty, Mr Scott, does it? Why should it?'

What could you say to that?

'I told you he was a good policeman,' Colin said.

Scott laughed. 'He knows a man was set up and still he doesn't think that shows he is innocent?' He felt wrung out. Extraordinarily, he didn't just feel he'd been under attack, he felt guilty because of the questions. But guilty of what? It wasn't clear to him.

'You didn't think going to the police was going to be like a cosy chat, did you, Jeremy?'

Scott felt he had just climbed off a big dipper.

Colin said, 'You have to agree he'd done his homework, hadn't he?'

Scott said, 'Did he really suspect me of being involved in something?'

'I don't know. Perhaps you were. On the other hand you reacted pretty well when he attacked you.'

Scott was amazed. 'Did I?'

'But you might have been involved. He has to find out if you are playing a double game, doesn't he? But maybe he wouldn't have told you what he did if he still thought you were. It'll be interesting to see what happens now. Of course, these policemen don't like barristers much.'

'Unless they are prosecuting for them.'

'Even then.'

Scott said, 'He's not concerned for Jimmy Reilly though. Jimmy is going to get lost in the wash.'

'There is that danger,' Colin said.

'Is that it, then?' Scott said. 'I leave it now? Not get involved any more? Just wait to see if they help Jimmy? Or are they going arrest me for something?'

Because of what Abbott had said about lawyers not caring tuppence for their clients, Jimmy Reilly's unjust conviction was more important than ever.

Colin said, 'I think I had better buy you a drink.'

Chapter 19

The next day Scott fought a case, which pleased his clerk who thought he was getting back to his old self, bringing the work in.

'You win some, you lose some, Mr Scott. That Reilly case, I know it got to you, but you have to move on. Anyway, those solicitors still brief you, so it hasn't all gone wrong.' He didn't know how wrong it had gone.

Scott grunted, gave him the brief and went down the steps, making his way through the arch into Fleet Street, where he bumped straight into Maryanne who seemed to be carrying everything she owned, and, astonishingly, was wearing leather trousers.

She said, 'I saw Grace today, we were in court together.'

Scott said, 'In court, in those trousers?'

Maryanne looked at him and carried on.

'She told me that you two had dinner together.'

Maryanne was exhibiting all the signs of a woman on the scent of a new relationship. 'Yes, we did. She's an amazing lady,' Scott said, giving her something to go on.

'Where did you go?'

'I bumped into her in a wine bar. We ate there.'

Maryanne inspected Scott, wondering whether he would do or not. 'Very domestic. And what are you going to do next?' When Scott hesitated, she said, 'Well, you must have thought about it. You have to get on with things, you know. You're no spring chicken.'

'I got her to agree to come to dinner, but she said it has to be somewhere lively.' He was going to ask if Maryanne knew anywhere, but Maryanne was probably a member of a gentleman's club. She surprised him, 'I used to get taken to the Valbonne. That shows my age. You couldn't hear yourself eat there, and that's probably what she wants. Ring her. She needs taking out of herself. Have you got her mobile number?'

'Yes.'

'Well, there you are then,' as if that clinched it. Then Maryanne said, 'I'm a bit worried about her anyway.'

And without Scott knowing it, the whole business started up again and he became involved.

'Why?' said Scott.

'It's a little unlikely, but it's to do with the case we were in today. Do you mind if I tell you?'

'Why should I mind?'

'Because all I'm doing is spreading the worry. Telling someone takes the edge off, but it hands the trouble on as well.'

Maryanne stopped at the end of the number 15 bus queue.

'Where are you going?' said Scott. 'Can I give you a lift? My car's in Essex Street. It's much too wet for the bus.'

Maryanne settled herself comfortably in the car. Now all Scott had to do was listen. 'I shouldn't tell you anything that happens in the matrimonial courts, but this is OK, I'm not in breach of the Matrimonial Causes Act.'

She paused. 'In this case I'm acting for the local authority again – child custody work. It's fairly unusual since it concerns an older man; normally we're all years older than the parents. Anyway. This man is the grandfather of the child and the child is sick, really sick, and he's looking after her, and of course he's not up to it, she's far too ill. It's not that he doesn't love her, he does, she's the most important thing in his life, that's the problem. But he can't manage, she needs specialist nursing. He can't do it.'

Scott had heard this before from Grace's point of view. For a moment he felt intimate with her, sharing part of her world; saying nothing, not saying 'she already told me', was like being close to her.

Then Maryanne told him something new, 'So who ends up having to tell this guy he can't manage, but Grace? From the witness box. And what makes it worse is, he's unrepresented. Of course, he starts shouting. He feels he's being cheated. Ooh, watch that van. And by all accounts he's a nasty piece of work.'

They became stuck in the traffic approaching Trafalgar Square.

'Apparently he is a career criminal, or at least that's what the local authority has been told, but nothing relevant for us. After all, you can be a bank robber and still be a loving dad. Probably goes well together.

'So Grace is the person who has to stand up and tell him they are going to take the child away. It's not her final decision, naturally, but it doesn't look like that to the grandfather. The court has asked her opinion, and she's giving it. But of course as far as he's concerned, it's she who's taking the kid from him.'

'That's better.' They ejected into the Mall behind a taxi that had broken loose from the pack and left a space for him to squeeze through.

'Of course when we, I mean us, the lawyers,' she said turning to Scott, 'when we do this sort of thing no one knows who we are. Just some dope in a wig. But a doctor is right there giving a personal opinion. And with Grace Karenin – well, you don't find many judges who disagree with what she says.'

★

297

'I know who you are,' Billy Burns had shouted. 'Don't think you can get away with this. I don't know why you are doing this to me.'

The judge tried to intervene.

'Mr Burns, Dr Karenin is only giving her professional opinion.'

He shouted at the witness box. 'Professional opinion, crap. I thought you would help me.'

Grace Karenin said, 'Mister Burns. I am not here to help or to harm you.'

It was useless.

'I helped you once,' he said. 'I punished those boys who threatened you.'

In the court the remark was meaningless, but Grace understood it. She said, 'All I am saying is that the child is too much for you to cope with. You have every good intention, I know that. But your granddaughter needs specialist care.'

There was no talking to him.

'She's just going to do what you say,' he said pointing at the judge.

Everybody knew he was right, which made it worse.

Maryanne said, 'The best way through is up behind Harrods.'

Scott turned out of Belgrave Square and pulled past Halkin Place. '*Sally used to live here,*' he said.

Maryanne said, 'Grace tried her best, but it was useless. Oddly enough it was clear to me that she rather liked him, no, not liked, respected him for what he was doing. No, not respected, liked him. Something.'

'Make up your mind,' said Scott.

Maryanne disregarded him. She went on. 'And she didn't go in for all that neediness stuff, which she could have done. With some of them you would have expected it.'

'Neediness? What's neediness?'

'Oh that: it's the standard tosh the family courts use against men. If a man gets upset by not being allowed to see the child, then he's accused of being too needy and not being a good influence, and then you've got a good reason for not letting him see the child. So he gets more upset. It's all circular.'

'Who wouldn't be upset if your child was taken away from you?'

'Of course.' Maryanne closed the subject. 'And that's what was so difficult about this case. There's nothing wrong with him, he's a good father, I mean grandfather. If he'd had a good lawyer, he might have understood how it has to go this way. Now that's the house I would really like to live in, look, the one on the corner. But you can't get that across in open court. These specialist care places are able to give stimulation that he can't begin to give. The girl's going to waste away as long as she is with him.'

She finished, slowing down in a reminiscing tone, and seemed about to stop, forgetting how she had started.

'Well then?' Scott said.

Maryanne picked it up immediately.

'Yes, sorry,' she said. 'Well, I'm worried about him. He's dangerous I think. We've been told he's violent. He actually said –' she turned and poked Scott on the shoulder as though he weren't listening – 'he shouted it out during Grace's evidence, something about pun- ishment. I don't think he is very stable at all. Barking mad.'

'So?'

'I'm worried.'

'That . . .?'

'He might do something.'

'Like what?'

'Well, he knows where she works from.'

'She works in a clinic.'

'I know.'

'Which is full of nurses and staff, and whatever else happens in clinics.'

'I know.'

'So what can this man do?' said Scott.

'You're right. Nothing.'

'Well then.'

'OK, that's what I meant. Right here, turn right here.'

'I was going to.'

'OK. I told you, if you tell someone what you are worried about you've shifted the burden. Oh golly, it's still raining.'

'I see.'

'So there's nothing to worry about?'

'Did I say that?' said Scott.

'No. Not really,' Maryanne said, 'but I've told you about it now, so at least I can stop worrying.'

'Who is this guy?'

'He's a strange one,' said Maryanne, forgetting the rules. 'His name is Billy Burns.'

'Good God,' said Scott.

'Is that such a strange name?' said Maryanne.

On her way back from court in the pouring rain, the same rain that made Scott give Maryanne a lift, Grace Karenin received a call on her mobile. She pulled over from the traffic and her car rocked as large trucks thundered past her down the dual carriageway. She looked at the flat panel on the phone to see who it was. Withheld number.

'Hello, Grace Karenin here,' she said tentatively.

The signal wasn't good and the voice at the other end was reedy. It came and went. But it was distinct. It said, 'My name is Fulton. We have met, I'm a police officer.'

300

For a moment she could not recall him, and until she was able to disentangle the memory she was thrown off balance.

'We've arrested him.'

'Who?'

'The husband of course. The railway porter. The one I came to see you about. His wife turned up in a black plastic bag, or at least her head did, near a layby on the A126.'

'Where?'

'That's the road to Southend,' he said. 'We told you he had done it.'

'Oh, yes.' Everything settled back into place. 'I know what you mean.' It was the case they were pestering her about.

The voice seemed to come closer.

'We're talking to him now.'

'Oh.'

'We told you,' he said again.

She had gained her equilibrium again. Why was he ringing? 'Yes, you did,' she said.

'And you wouldn't believe us.'

What did he want? Was this some sort of game of 'I told you so'? It sounded like it.

She said, 'Believing you or not didn't come into it, Mr Fulton.' She wanted to ask how he had got her private number. God, she could do without this after a long day.

'I need to speak to you.'

'Why?'

'To take a statement.'

Of course he was allowed to do that. The BMA had told her that the police may approach anyone for a statement, but it's up to you to decide whether you want to speak to them, or what you want to say.

'Can't it wait?'

'No.'

301

'All right. But don't get too excited about what I'm likely to say. I won't tell you anything about a patient without checking first.'

'We only want to speak to you about the black plastic bags.'

'What bags?'

'Apparently he told you about them.'

'Did he?' Again she tried to work out what he was talking about. The car rocked and what seemed like a bucket of water hit the windscreen. The rain was so heavy it was now bouncing up from the road.

'Don't play funny with me, Doctor. He told you about the plastic bags.'

'I'm not sure.' She couldn't remember.

'He told us he told you.'

Grace Karenin's head was swimming. She had been in the witness box most of the day. Mr Burns had been enough, and now this fool. She pressed the off-button and finished the call. He'd ring back and she could answer it or not as she wished.

She eased the car forward to where there was more space at the side of the road. On the left she found there was a canopy leading into a garage and she parked the car under it and sat.

The rain stopped drumming on the car and it became comparatively quiet. The phone rang. Again the screen said 'Withheld number'. She took a breath and answered it.

Before he could say anything she said, 'You got cut off.' Make it seem like something that had happened to both of them.

'Yes.'

'How did you get my private number?'

'That's not relevant.'

'It is if you want the conversation to continue.'

It was curious how, sitting quietly out of the way of the

302

pounding traffic, she could take control again. He was just a bully. She could be that too if necessary. 'No—' he said, getting no further before she interrupted him.

'Please tell me how you got this number.'

'From your secretary.'

'Oh.' Jennet again. How many times? But then it was in her nature, always trying to be helpful.

'I insisted,' said Fulton. Somehow that came over as an apology, which changed the whole thing. Or had he got it because Jennet was going out with that policeman?

'Now what do you want?'

'We want a statement.'

'I don't see why you don't get in touch with me in working hours. It's very late.'

'We need it while chummy is still with us.'

'Oh, you need to interrogate him with it?'

She was back on top of it enough to follow what was happening.

'Yes. We need to see you this evening. Where will you be?'

'OK. I shall be at the clinic. I shall be there 'till eight, eight thirty, probably later.'

'Will the clinic still be open?'

'I'll be there, but there'll be no other staff. You'll have to knock on the door really loudly.'

She put the phone down, and as she did so thought about what she had just said. There can't be any harm in telling a policeman you are on your own, can there?

Fulton dialled Billy Burns. 'OK,' he said, 'I did it. She'll be at the clinic. Yes. She'll be on her own.'

The rain poured down and the traffic rocked Grace's car as she waited to pull out. It was odd how such an ordinary thing as going to work involved taking your life in your hands. She waited for a gap and then accelerated the car, her wheels spinning momentarily, acutely aware of a huge lorry, water spilling from its tyres, bearing down on her.

Bill Carr phoned Abbott. 'I've just been called by the surveillance group. Two of them have stood down, but one lot is still there. Something seems to be happening with him and his child. They got him when he returned from wherever he went. He's got his van out in front of his flat instead of in the lock-up. He never does that normally. And he's carrying bedding out. They reckon he can't go far with her, so they'll see where he goes then stand down themselves probably.'

Abbott said, 'That seems reasonable.' It was, surveillance teams cost a fortune.

Carr said, 'I'm away now, I'll get in touch again tomorrow.'

'Does he take her out much?'

'Never. She's pretty nearly bedridden.'

'I didn't know that.'

'Well, at least we know that while he's with her, he's not going to be up to any trouble.'

'That's true. You're finished now then. Where are you off to?' said Abbott; it never harmed to chat.

Carr paused for a moment. Then he thought, Why not say it? 'I'm giving a lecture,' he said,

'Oh,' said Abbott. 'What on?'

'Delphiniums. Soot and delphiniums. How they like soot on their feet. But not before August.'

'Interesting?' said Abbott.

'I think so,' Carr said.

Frank Abbott put the phone down. 'Delphiniums,' he said. 'Bill Carr is a delphinium fancier. He's going to give a lecture about them.'

Abbott was talking to Mike Reynolds.

304

'Yes, that lawyer Scott came to see me, or rather we met. It was pure luck he happened to come to me, introduced through a solicitor I know. He had some story about people being given favours in court, and cases being fixed.'

Abbott wasn't sure how much to tell Mike Reynolds. After all, given what Scott had told him, Mike Reynolds might himself be involved with Fulton. But already he had decided he wasn't. He knew Reynolds well enough for that. He went on, 'And Billy Burns's name came up. Along with Charlie Pope's.'

'Did he admit he had been to see Pope?'

'Yes.'

'Well, that's it. We saw him there.'

'I know. I knew that and that's when I decided to call you.' Abbott shaded the truth a bit. Then he asked what, for him, was the central question. 'Just how far did the connection with Fulton go?'

Reynolds was genuinely puzzled. Abbott could tell it. No, he decided, Reynolds wasn't lying. It was obvious that he had no idea what Abbott was talking about. He had been right in deciding to trust him.

'Fulton? No. I don't see Fulton. Hardly ever, thank God. We just had that conversation, and he made that remark.' Mike thought about it, trying to allow things to surface in his mind. 'But I did see Fulton that same day in court. He was with Scott. He went in to see the judge.'

'Exactly.'

'In the dead man's case. Wicked's case.'

'And in your case? Did he see the judge in Reilly's case?'

'Reilly? Well, I don't know. When I spoke to Fulton he told me that Reilly's case had been mentioned. But only that. No, looking back, I don't think he had contact with the judge in Reilly's case.'

Frank Abbott said, 'Billy Burns was a witness in Reilly's case. And we've seen Billy Burns with Pope.' This was the difficult bit to work out, but Frank Abbott thought he knew the answer already.

He said, 'Scott was telling me he thought that Pope was the channel for setting people up. Through Fulton.' He counted off the connections on his fingers, his old habit. Then he said, 'So my real question is this' – he bent another finger back – 'How did the child in Reilly's case come to see you?'

Reynolds was silent. Then, 'My God, you're right. Fulton. Fulton gave me the number to ring. It wasn't Fulton seeing me directly, that's why I had forgotten. I found a number and a note on my desk; later I was told Fulton had been in. I never even got back to him about it. It happens all the time. I left it, assumed he didn't want to be involved.'

'Well, there it is. I think that small boy was a set-up.'

'No way,' said Reynolds.

'Billy Burns did it with Pope, and a man called Vernon Day.'

'Impossible.'

'Through Fulton.'

'No.'

'To punish Reilly.'

'Ridiculous.'

'Reilly was known as the Postman. He accepted cocaine for Burns. And when he discovered what he was doing he wanted to stop. He had an argument with Wicked Man and some stuff went missing. Normally he would have been taken out, but my guess is Burns decided to get rid of him like this, rather than let anything worse happen. Since he was a friend. Odd sort of friend.'

It was a complete explanation but it seemed Reynolds still could not accept it.

'That child was telling the truth.'

'Maybe he was. I don't know. But we reckon what happened was that when Wicked Man threatened Reilly, Burns calmed it all down by agreeing to put Reilly away. Bill Carr may look a fool, but he's put the information together.'

'That child was speaking the truth,' Mike repeated.

'I didn't say he wasn't, but it was very convenient at the time. It gets worse. My guess is that it was Burns who killed Wicked. And I don't think you know this, some days ago a group of men arrived at Gargarin's in the early morning and stuffed *him* full of . . . well, you don't want to know what they pumped him full of.'

'Same as Wicked?'

'Yes. Almost the same, but they set light to Wicked to make it look like a Firebird posse killing, to make everybody think Gargarin did it. Burns has a pair of twins who work for him. They are even more psychopathic than he is. If you can be more or less psychopathic.'

Reynolds said nothing now.

'And who pointed Wicked out after the court hearing? Fulton was there and arranging for him to be released. Fulton must be in Burns's pocket.'

'No!'

'I'm not going to be able to deal with this, I'll have to refer it to internal investigation. But there is one thing I have to say first. Scott thinks you were involved in it. At least, that's what he told me. Because he assumes you were in on setting Jimmy Reilly up.'

'Does he?'

'That won't go anywhere. I think you can be assured of that.'

Reynolds said, 'But what about Scott? How do you know he isn't part of it?'

'We'll see about that,' said Abbott. 'But at the moment

it's Burns we're worried about. We're following him now.'

When he got home Scott wondered whether to tell Abbott about what he had heard. Tell him what Maryanne had said. From what Abbott said, the man was serious bad news. He thought back with astonishment at the naiveté with which he had got involved.

He tried to remember where Abbott's phone number was. He had written it down when they met, but couldn't recall where. He disentangled the events that surrounded the meeting with Abbott, to try to work out where the number had gone. He had been with Colin and had been carrying a blue notebook, like he always did, the one he had been using today. So it would be with today's brief. That case had finished and he had left it at chambers for costing. It would still be in Cliff's pile next to his desk, so that was no good.

Was there any other way to get in touch with Abbott? He thought back. No, Abbott had emphasised his was a private number, and Scott remembered then how at the time he thought he wasn't going to get involved with Abbott any more.

The memory of that decision made him think again about whether to get in touch. It wasn't a good idea. Once you get entangled with the police, it becomes a habit. He had seen it happen both with barristers and judges who show too much interest. They end up riding in police cars; they become police groupies. No, he had gone far enough when he went to see the policeman in the first place.

Grace was all right anyway. She did this all the time in court. She didn't need him barging in; she wouldn't thank him for getting the police involved.

He started to look for a bottle. There were several places

in the flat where he might have left one. He took off his jacket and began to wind down. He'd see Grace soon enough, maybe this weekend. No wine. He checked his post. Two letters this time from the immigration appeal authority with directions to adjudicators. He received at least five a week and he was only part-time; what must their post bill be?

Yes, this weekend. He'd ring tomorrow. He'd try to find a good busy restaurant. Forget about the whole business, just see what the police produced. He opened a bill. From Butterworth's, for a law book. They called it a pro-forma invoice, which, oddly, meant not that he had bought a book but that they wanted him to. He threw it in the bin.

Why not ring her now?

Of course, you don't want to go pestering her, but if she wants to say no, there it is. After all, what did she say when he said she wasn't to think he was following her? She said, 'Why should I mind?' That's encouraging.

He turned the television on. The group of people who seemed to live in a room together were sitting round doing nothing. Then the picture switched to a bathroom where a girl was helping another girl wash her hair. What's all that about? Washing your hair is a one-person activity, isn't it? He watched, fascinated for a moment, then repelled.

He had punched Grace's number into the phone already and now his attention returned to it. He pressed the dial button.

The phone on Grace's desk started vibrating, then, as it struggled on its back like an overturned beetle, it started ringing.

'I'm going to have to answer that,' Grace said.

Billy Burns sat in a chair on the other side of her desk. Across his knee, her head cradled on his shoulder, was his granddaughter. In his hand he had a gun, he was pointing it at Grace. 'Leave it,' he said.

Grace was trying to establish a position. She knew that her grip of the situation depended on the degree to which she prevented this man's crazy world from enveloping hers.

'I can't just disregard telephone calls. I'm on duty,' she lied. 'If I don't answer, then someone will come looking for me.'

'Let them,' Billy Burns said. Of course he knew she was going to be on her own; Fulton had told him.

The phone stopped struggling, solving the problem. Grace's glance shaved the phone, the screen was still lit. It hadn't rung for long enough for the call to be switched to the messaging service, so the number would still be retained on the missed-call record.

'Can I see who called me?'

'Go ahead.'

Grace scrolled through and pressed select. A number came up. 0207 730 . . ., then figures she didn't recognise. She didn't know who it was. She put the phone down, the number still showing. 'I'll just lock it,' she said. 'I always do,' and as she said it she realised what a stupid thing it was. To ring out, that was what she needed to do. She left the phone unlocked and put it in front of her, near her car keys, her discarded dictating machine and her pen. Occasionally, as they spoke together, she moved the small pile of objects on the desk in front of her about, apparently at random, but eventually she pressed the green call button, allowing it to engage and recall the number and then immediately she cut it off. She only had to toggle her fingers on, off, and she could go on doing it without being seen.

'Go on, you cure her. See if you can do any better than I can,' Billy Burns said. 'You doctors, you think you're so bloody marvellous. I'm taking her away. You won't find me this time.'

310

The detached part of Grace's mind noticed the old-fashioned swear word. Things used to be 'bloody' this, 'bloody' that, in old films she saw, but the word was much too weak now for her modern patients.

'But first I'm going to deal with you,' he said.

'You know she can't be cured, Mr Burns. She is chronically sick, she will not get any better. But we can offer relief for the symptoms.'

'You say that, so you can slide out of what you're doing.'

It was strange this, the new belief that illness was the doctor's fault, that not being able to cure it meant you were incompetent, or worse, responsible.

The cold pressure of the situation seemed to give her more space to reflect on irrelevant things. In a moment of time her mind could burrow deep into other ideas.

The notion that mental illness was some sort of doctor's trick was common amongst the medical students she taught. When she lectured, she found that many of them believed that it was not really illness, even that mental illness was something created by the medical profession, or by society; certainly they were often determined that it was something they weren't going to be taken in by. She would be grimly amused when one of these students first came across one of her sick children, sick beyond reach, beyond comprehension. Then they would turn to her, wanting help.

'No, that's not so, Mr Burns. I'm not trying to slide out of anything. I am always honest. I am not like a surgeon. I can't just cut the sick part out.'

But she could touch people. She was astonished when she first discovered the gift, feeling the heat, actually feeling the heat of the pain under and out through her hands, and the hotter it was, the more it was released. It was a frightening occasion when it first happened, and she tried not to think she could ever do it on demand. She had

311

never told anyone about it. Anyway, psychiatrists don't touch people.

He said, 'But you are going to interfere with me. You want to take away the one thing I have.'

There it was. The child was a support to him; she had no separate existence, save as something to extinguish his pain. But why shouldn't she be? Maybe that's part of life. How many women were called Betty in the nineteenth century as a signal that they were born only to look after their mother when the time came? It's only the modern conscience that insists on the right to self-determination for everyone, even the profoundly sick who cannot determine anything for themselves. What did it matter to Billy Burns's granddaughter if she was used as a salve for her grandfather's guilt? There was nearly no reply to that.

'Mr Burns, your child can be helped. Her life can be improved. She need not be what she is when she lives with you. Now she is almost a – a dare she say this, something she would not normally dream of saying? – 'almost a vegetable.'

Burns shook right through, as though he had received an electric shock.

'She needn't be,' Grace said.

Scott had cut off the call he was making to Grace. What was he going to say when she answered: 'I'm just ringing to say hello'? Their relationship had not reached that point yet. No, no good, he had to have something positive to say, so before he rang he had better find a restaurant. *The Good Food Guide* – where was it? He had one a couple of years old. He put the phone down to look for it. Eventually he discovered it, behind the table.

Now what would she like? Somewhere crowded: the Oxo Tower? A Russian place, or would that be trying to say something? The Ivy? He'd never get in. How about the

Gay Hussar? The trouble there, it's so uncomfortable. Rules? That was the kind of place the head of chambers took people, very nice but a bit too pompous.

Then he realised that if he wanted to get some wine he'd better go get it immediately while he was still up and about.

'Yes, Mr Burns. I'm telling you that you are not doing her any good. You love her. You feel for her. But that does not mean that you are the best person to look after her.'

She pressed the call button and then stopped it after it rang for a moment.

Billy Burns sat looking at this woman in front of him. It was an odd experience because she wasn't frightened of him, nor, he noticed, was he nervous of her. She was speaking to him as an equal. He wasn't cowering in front of her like he did with that woman on the parole board, or that woman who had supervised his beating at the school.

A woman, a woman standing by, watching him stripped and then beaten. That had been more demeaning than the event itself. Middle-aged, middle class, the type who scrapes the butter back off the bread with the other side of the knife in the same moment as putting it on. The ones who peered down at him from the magistrates' court bench, to the left and right of the magistrate who was sentencing him. The dumb ones, the know-nothing ones, who had no idea of what it meant to have to fight, to fight all the time just to stay afloat. He felt the anger well up in him and he gripped the gun.

His phone rang. Scott turned towards it. Nothing. It had stopped. He looked at it for a moment, then started to find his coat. It rang again. He moved towards it, then it stopped again.

He remembered that if he was going to buy wine, he

would need his credit card, which was still in the top pocket of his suit. He went to the cupboard in the bedroom. The phone rang and stopped again. What was going on here? He shrugged his coat on and opened the front door.

The light on the stairs was out, so he left the flat door open while he went to the light switch. The phone rang again and stopped. What is this? He went back to the flat and pressed the return call-button; the phone clicked its way through its decisions, and then connected and rang.

'I'll really have to answer that,' said Grace. 'It's the same number, a colleague ringing about a patient I have on his ward.'

'OK. But say nothing.'

She picked up the phone, wondering who it was; would the caller understand something was happening? 'Hello,' she said. 'This is Grace Karenin.'

Scott heard her.

As he drove fast towards her clinic, Scott wondered what it was that had made him immediately ask, 'Are you all right?'

'No,' she had said.

The answer shocked him.

'Where are you?'

'Yes,' she said. Wrong question.

'Are you at home?'

'No.'

'At your clinic?'

'Yes.'

'Someone is there?'

No reply.

'Is it Burns?'

'Yes.' She must have wanted to say, How did you know?

'Has he been violent?'

314

'No.'

'Will he be?'

'I think so.'

'I'll call the police.'

'Not necessary. Maybe later.'

'Shall I come?'

'Yes.'

'I'll get the police,' he repeated it.

'Not yet.'

'I'll be there as soon as I can.'

'Bye.'

He ran downstairs. Thank God he had found out where she worked. From what he knew of Burns, he ought to call the police immediately. But she had been quite clear. 'Not necessary.' Anyway, let's get there and find out.

Grace put the phone down. How on earth did Scott know about Billy Burns? She looked up at the man opposite her. 'Someone needs to collect a document,' she said.

'He'd better not come here,' he said.

She asked a question that she knew would attract his attention. 'Mr Burns, when was the last time anyone discussed with you what is actually wrong with your granddaughter?'

'I don't think they ever have.' He thought back to the curiously inconclusive conversations he had managed with doctors and nurses. No, he was right, they never had, they had only been vague, trying to be comforting.

'Well, it's about time someone did, isn't it?'

She remembered telling Scott about Burns's case, but not in detail and certainly she had not given any names. How did he know?

'I've got a copy of her medical notes here.' She pointed to the documents she had brought back from court. 'Shall I get them?' She knew she could handle him, but still she wanted someone to know what was happening. On the other hand what she didn't want was people blundering around.

Mike Reynolds had left Frank Abbott and gone to collect Jennet. They had arranged to go out to dinner, but he found her distracted by something. She said, 'I left early and there was something at work I didn't finish.'

Mike said, 'That's OK, what is it?'

'I'm sorry, Mike.' He could see she was nervous of asking him a favour.

'It doesn't matter. Look, it's not the dressed-up-you that I enjoy being with, it's the ordinary you; the one who worries about her work, and wants to get it right, and wants Timmy to do well and who looks after her mum. And the one who asks me to help her.'

He knew the pleasure she felt when he spoke like that. He wanted to say, What do you like about me? But wasn't sure he could say that out loud yet. He knew she was still frightened at the idea of this man saying he was in love with her, still not certain she could manage it.

He said, 'How else do people grow old together, unless it's the real person they are in love with?' She wasn't yet confident enough to let go; she must have been hurt once. 'If we had to put on an act all our lives, we would never come out of our shells, we'd always be frightened. There has to be a person we can be ourselves with. Completely.'

'Do you think so?'

He wanted to say, Well, of course I think so. But that wasn't what she was asking.

'Now listen to me,' he said. Quite gruff, but OK he thought. 'You are a very special person and I'm not saying that just to make you feel good, but because it's true. Look what you've done. You've got a really nice kid, he's polite, he's bright. You really look after your mum, so she is OK and has a good life. And how many do that? At the clinic everyone likes you.'

She listened.

'If there's a problem, if someone wants something done, they know they can rely on you, they ask for you. You're steady, you're reliable. You're a real person. And the only person who doesn't respect you and treat you properly? You know who that is? It's you, yourself!' He smiled and laughed to make it sound less threatening, but she wasn't threatened, she was pleased.

'Let's go to Joanna's again,' he said.

Since they had been there with Tim after the kite festival, they had gone back twice. It was their place. They liked the pictures. 'They are by Chloe Cheese, she's a local artist,' the manager said. They liked the staff, who were simple and unassuming. The food was good. But mostly they liked it because it was their place, which they shared.

'Go on, have the pudding thing,' he would say. She had always refused it.

'If I want to stay this shape, I mustn't eat puddings.'

'We'll go for a walk tomorrow, get the weight off. We'll take Timmy and I'll show you the swing.'

This time she said, just as they were on their way in the car, 'Will you do something for me?'

'Of course.'

Jennet said, 'Will you take me past the clinic? If I pick up the tape, I can do a bit on it tonight and it'll be ready tomorrow when Dr Grace gets in.'

'OK. Of course. Now I know what you've been worrying about. You've been worrying about your Dr Grace. Look how conscientious you are. There's no need to worry about her, you know. She can look after herself.'

Grace Karenin believed in the power of talking. 'I'm a talking doctor,' she used to say to little children.

317

Just the day before she had a small boy sitting in front of her in the room on his own. He sat, screwing up his courage, and told her about his toys, about his world – all the time keeping a wary eye on her in case she advanced on him with a needle. 'When do we start talking?' he said eventually.

'That's what we've been doing,' she said.

'Oh,' he said, thinking about it. 'Am I better now?'

'Are you ill then?' Grace said, smiling, and the little boy's life opened up like a flower.

Even this man, sitting where that little boy sat – older, angry, damaged and violent, and, she thought, danger-ous – even he could be reached, if she found the right words. But first she had to engage his intelligence. She got up before he said anything more, and went to get his granddaughter's notes.

'Here we are, the copy notes from the hospital, and let's use this.' She picked up a book. '*The Handbook of Infant Mental Health*, Charles Zeanah. He'll tell us exactly what it all means. These Americans know everything.'

She sat down. The child shivered in her grandfather's arms, and made a faint noise.

'Now, Mr Burns, I am not a paediatrician, but I know enough to talk about it sensibly.'

She turned over the notes. His attention was engaged now, he had stopped fiddling with the gun. The first step.

'Your granddaughter was born prematurely. It says here the probable cause of that was her mother's addiction to drugs. Now let me tell you what that means for the child.'

'I was in prison,' he said.

She let her eyes rest on him. Go on, they said.

'I was in prison,' he said again. 'I applied for compas-sionate leave, but that's nothing. They just said well, where's her fella then? He's the one should be looking after her.'

'Of course that was upsetting?'

318

'What isn't, when you're serving time? But I was used to it.'

'Yes?'

'That's what it has always been like, my life.'

'That's what you feel?'

'Yeah.'

He was subsiding into an ordinary talk. It wasn't what he had meant to do when he came, though, of course, he wasn't very sure now of why he had come. He just felt he had to. Billy Burns felt very tired.

Grace sensed a lessening of tension. Keep him talking. She had seen this many times before. His defences were beginning to ebb away; all in all this was just another session, unplanned and with its dangers, but then that was what she did.

She decided to change the route. After all, he was an intelligent man. 'But you have insight, Mr Burns, you don't need me to tell you why you are so angry.'

It didn't work. He wasn't used to that kind of analysis, or maybe she had got the language wrong.

'Angry! Why wouldn't I be angry?'

She smiled. 'You didn't understand me, Mr Burns. I didn't say you ought not be angry. I said you don't need me to tell you why you are angry. Anyway.'

She didn't go on with it or let him reply. She left it hanging.

'Here are the notes. Now do you want me to talk about it, or will you find it too distressing?'

'No,' he said. 'Tell me.'

It was beginning to work.

'Well, it starts, doesn't it, with your daughter's heroin addiction.' She didn't pause; this was not the time to wait for the normal responses. 'Here we are. Zeanah says, "Psychoactive substances cross the placenta, and the blood-brain barrier, potentially affecting the developing CNS

319

directly." ' She explained, 'CNS means the central nervous system.' She read on, ' "Some drugs indirectly decrease maternal nutrition and/or vasoconstriction." That's the blood supply to the child's brain. "Which results in . . . decreased nutrient transfer. A consistent, specific insult to the fetal CNS has not been well documented, however." That means they cannot point precisely to the damage, but that there is damage, they know that. Here we are. "Neonatal neurobehavioural disturbances which may reflect direct CNS effects *are* consistently found in heroin-exposed newborns." That means they have found something. They know it does affect the central nervous system. It has done so with your granddaughter.

'He then goes on to point out that heroin users generally have a particular lifestyle which may contribute to the damage as well.' She had reached the page she knew well now. She had often used it in court. ' "Infants prenatally exposed to drugs are in double jeopardy. They are biologically vulnerable . . ." ' – she began simplifying the language as she went along – and are made worse by parenting dysfunction associated with addiction. There is a whole catalogue of adverse events: depression, irritability. The mother is likely to suffer spousal violence. She will be prone to accidents.'

It was the clarity of the original language which pleased her, but used with lay people it seemed like gobbledegook. Ordinarily people don't want to look directly at a subject like this, imagining somehow that it isn't anything to do with them – whereas of course it is. It's all part of being human – as was the uncontrolled, inexpressible anger of the man sitting in front of her.

He said, 'It's true, she was beaten the night before she gave birth by that man.'

Grace waited but he didn't say anything more. He was lost for a moment in the uncontrollable past.

'Your daughter was gravely addicted, Mr Burns. According to this, she was using well over 20mg a day, which is actually the cut-off point for any management. Mr Burns, we were not allowed to take people into protective custody for their unborn child's sake. That is what you should be complaining about. We are here all these years later because we couldn't do that. Your granddaughter suffered a neuro–developmental delay. But her mother convinced the social services that she could manage, and of course she couldn't. She only made it worse. The baby was suffering clonic jerks and that wasn't picked up, because she wasn't receiving constant attention.

'She was given paregoric, that is, denatured tincture of opium. Studies have shown that 93 per cent of people benefit, but she was one of the seven per cent that doesn't. And it got worse. It became clear that there had been other problems at birth.' Grace said, 'Who knows what caused them? Here we are.' She turned the pages of the medical reports and read out: '"These problems, together with an already restricted blood supply, caused the damage shown in the scans."'

Suddenly his head came up, his thoughts had caught up. 'What do you mean, I must know why I am angry? Who says I am angry? Anyway, I have the right to be angry.'

'Well, you are, aren't you? Look at you, in here with a gun. And I didn't say you had no right to be so.'

'Of course I'm angry. You're telling the judge to take my kid away.'

'Mr Burns, I didn't mean that. I mean angry, like you've always been angry. I'll tell you what, one of your poets –' the free part of her mind noticed that. Odd, she didn't often let slip that she didn't come from this strange country. 'The poet said, "Those to whom evil is done, do evil in return." And pointing that gun at me is a kind of evil, isn't it? Who did the evil to you in the first place?'

Billy Burns looked at the gun in his hand, almost surprised that it should be there.

'Things that frighten people are evil, aren't they?' she said.

'You don't seem very frightened.'

'I am, Mr Burns.'

'Well, you needn't be,' he said, putting the gun down on the desk.

Grace knew this didn't mean much, but it was a start.

Scott found the entrance to the clinic, which let him into a large dark car park, overshadowed by trees. To his left, as he got out of the car, a wood stretched away and up the hill; behind him was darkness. There was no one in the car park and only two vehicles. A transit van and a sports car. That fitted. He parked right over out of the way, no point in looking obvious.

The watchers outside saw his car go in. Normal traffic, they thought. They could see Billy Burns's van through the hedge. As long as it went nowhere they could just sit and watch it.

The clinic stretched down one side of the space. There were no lights, it looked deserted. Scott picked his way to the front, nearly falling down the broken steps. The door wouldn't open and rattled as he touched it. He thought of knocking but decided against it. To his right there was a path, a gap between the building itself and the level of the car park. It looked as though it might surround the complete building. He set off.

It was simple enough. The path must have been designed as a damp course, or runaway, and as it came to the back further down the slope, it became more shallow until it was level with the surrounding ground; and there, there was a lit window.

He crept up to it and peered in. Through the slats in the

blind he could see a desk and a pair of hands turning over some documents. It was Grace. He could even pick out the pitch of her voice through the glass. There was someone opposite her, on the other side of the desk. He could see the side of a jacket, and an arm. Then a hand came in sight. It put something on the desk and withdrew.

It was a gun. Scott froze. His hand went to his pocket, but he had left his mobile phone in the car. Slowly he backed away from the window.

Mike Reynolds said, 'It's no problem, it's not even out of the way.' He took Jennet's arm. 'It will only take a moment.'

Jennet felt better. She hadn't wanted to waste his time or annoy him, but he didn't seem to mind. Not mind at all, not like Elroy would have. He would have stalked off, complaining she had spoilt the evening. She hadn't told him about Elroy. Mike had merely said, 'Look, you don't need to apologise. If it's something you have to do.'

'I've got the key,' she said, 'but I don't like going in on my own, not in the dark.'

She dived into her bag, shifting piles of stuff. Mike stood and watched.

'Here they are.' She produced the keys to the clinic, holding them up.

'What have you got to get?'

'Some letters. Dr Grace did some letters this morning before she went to court, and I said I would have them ready for her tomorrow morning, but I didn't finish one of them.'

She left out the reason why she had not finished; she had not concentrated on her work because she was thinking about going out with him, worrying about being on time. Someday, she was sure of this, someday he was just not going to turn up, and she didn't want it to be today. If she was late he might just walk away, like Elroy used to.

'No lighting of any sort in the car park,' she said. 'We've been trying to get maintenance to do it for months.'

In the car park she could see a white van. 'I wonder who that is?' she said. 'It's probably security from the main building up the hill. Look, there's the doctor's car, she's here, working late.'

They walked down the steps to the front door. 'I'll go and tell her. She may have been looking for the letters I did.'

She opened the door and, leaving Mike by the fish tank where some goldfish were flopping about, she went down the passage. Mike watched the fish.

Scott found his way back to the steps and saw that the door was now open, and the light in reception was on.

He stepped inside.

By the far wall he could see a figure peering into a fish tank, apparently studying them. The door behind him creaked as he took his hand from it and the figure turned round. It was Reynolds, the policeman.

They stared at each other.

Scott understood why Reynolds was here immediately. He had been right about Reynolds. Reynolds was bent. Reynolds was here with Burns.

On the other hand, we all trust the police. Even if our eyes or heads tell us not to, we want to, so Scott asked the question which, if the answer were yes, it would have been silly to ask. 'Are you here with Burns?' he said.

Mike Reynolds didn't say no. He didn't even understand the question. He was still placing where he had seen this man. Then the recognition showed on his face. 'What are you doing here?'

Scott decided he'd have to go along with the man's apparent denial. After all, he must have just arrived. Scott said, 'Listen. I'll try to be clear. That guy Burns is in there with a gun, threatening Dr Karenin. I have just seen it with my own eyes from the back window. That's why I just came in. I came back, found the door open and assumed you were here with him.' He got it all out in one go, which was more difficult than he thought.

'Down there?' Reynolds said.

Scott turned to get his bearings, 'Yes,' he said. They set off down the passage.

'I'm a policeman,' Reynolds said unnecessarily.

'I know that,' said Scott.

'I mean, do what I say.'

'I will. Don't worry.'

Any chance of doing anything was cut short by an angry shout from further down the passage. 'Get down. On the floor. On the floor.'

Grace Karenin's voice: 'Mr Burns. She is my secretary. She hasn't done anything to you.'

Scott and Reynolds got to the door of the room from where the shout had come. It was slightly open.

'Are you here alone?' Burns said.

Jennet said, 'I just came in to collect some papers for the doctor.' She was crying, terrified for her life.

'Are you here alone?'

Scott felt himself pulled by Reynolds through the door opposite just as the door to the doctor's room opened. Burns had been delayed by his child and it had given them time. Burns looked out. He stood listening.

Scott and Reynolds tried to be still, which only emphasised the breath in their throats.

'Is there anyone else?'

'No, I'm alone,' said Jennet.

Scott saw Burns move his chair to a position which gave him a view of the passage and of the door to the room he and Reynolds were in.

'Mr Burns, what do you want?' he heard Grace Karenin say.

'I want my child. I want you to leave us alone.' Then, 'What are you doing?'

'I'm not having Jennet treated like this,' she said. Scott heard her move. 'Go in there, Jennet. Why don't you make us something to drink? Some tea or coffee.'

Grace Karenin was obviously trying to calm the man.

'It's a sluice room, Mr Burns, from the time when this was a small hospital. There's no other way out of there. She can make a drink.'

Scott and Reynolds looked at the equivalent door in their room. Reynolds padded across to it. It was locked. Scott looked out of the window. They had a view of the car park from here.

'Mr Burns, there is only so much we can do about the things that have made us what we are. Circumstances teach us. What happens to us when we are young, it gives us a set of responses which we then repeat and repeat . . .' They heard Dr Karenin start her sentence, and then only some parts of what she said were audible, she must have turned her head away.

Mike Reynolds suddenly recognised something about the tone. This was the lecturer he had heard; so he was right, he had known Grace Karenin all along.

Her voice became clear again. 'I am not interested in the morality of it all, Mr Burns, only in the practical effects. A person hurts you, and all your life you hurt that person back. It's not surprising, is it? It's what you would expect.'

There was another sound, someone else speaking.

'Sugar, Mr Burns?'

Scott thought, What we have here is some sort of armed tea party, mixed in with a psychotherapy session. An armed, psychotherapeutic tea party. There was a clink of china.

326

Scott and Reynolds were trapped. There was no way past the open door in the passage. Burns would see anyone immediately, and it was clear that Grace Karenin's ability to control the man would not survive another shock.

'What kind of gun?' said Reynolds softly.

'I don't know. A handgun,' said Scott.

They examined the metal-framed window. It had two small openings at the top, too small to squeeze through. Then they saw a car come into the car park, driving slowly through the gates, and as it did so a reflected light from the street shone onto the driver's face. It was Fulton. They waved, but standing at the unlit window they were invisible as the car swung towards the clinic's main doors.

Fulton saw a white van, and near it a sports car. Two other cars way over the other side. Burns was here and that was probably the doctor's car. The others looked parked well away. He was going to have to go and find out what was happening. Billy Burns was not a person to be alone with late at night. He let his car drift to a halt. He got out and walked softly towards the open front door.

Norman Fulton — they never called him Norman or Norm, generally just Fulton, or 'that shit Fulton' — was not an honest man, nor was he a generous or a public-spirited man. On the other hand he had two commendations for bravery: one for tackling an armed man on the top deck of a bus, when he had stopped and written the man's description on the leg of his own jeans in biro just in case he couldn't describe him later; and the other for taking a broken bottle out of someone's hand as it was held to a brief's throat in a holding cell at a magistrates' court. 'Don't know why I did that for a brief,' Fulton joked. 'Should have let him get on with it.'

The newspapers linger on this kind of discrepancy, a policeman who has commendations getting into trouble. It

327

is presented as odd, as though courage ought more readily to co-exist with decency or honesty rather than with any other attribute. But courage goes just as well with being a bully. Indeed, it may fit rather better. Certainly Fulton was a bully.

Fulton, stupid Fulton, had not seen where it would lead. But now he realised, too late, that he had gone too far in giving Burns the doctor's movements. At least he had the courage to do something about it.

He went through the open door of the clinic and into the passage where he knew the doctor's room was. He walked softly up to the door of the room opposite where Reynolds and Scott were hiding and walked straight in on Grace Karenin.

He saw the black woman who was Grace's secretary, the one he thought of as a bit tasty, if she hadn't been black, that is, and in the same moment he saw the gun.

He said, 'Billy don't,' just loud enough to put Billy Burns off his move. Fulton broke free of the bubble first, exactly as the *Journal of Psychology* said he should, and stepping forward he pushed the gun upwards.

It went off. The first time it was over Fulton's shoulder. There was a struggle, and a second shot, which happened after Fulton got his hands on the gun properly, pushing it under Burns's chin. He pulled the trigger. It blew the top of the man's head off, all over Grace's bookshelf.

Fulton would not have managed to do this if Burns had not been distracted by a convulsive movement from his granddaughter. He had grabbed at her to prevent her falling, so in a way it could be said she killed him, or at least helped cause his death. Scott was in the room ahead of Reynolds and saw it all, Fulton killing Burns.

Jennet started screaming. Mike ran to get her.

Grace Karenin bent over the sick child, and Fulton turned round, now holding the gun, and said to Scott and Reynolds, 'No one move until the squad get here.'

328

He had killed a man and he wanted every little piece of evidence to show just how much of an accident it had to be.

'You,' he said to Scott, 'sit down.'

He put the gun on the table. 'I got it from him and it went off as I did so. He would have shot me.' He turned to Grace and said, 'Let me use your phone,' and then, regaining his normal poise, he said, 'Do you see *now*, Doctor, just how nasty these people can be?'

Scott went cold at what he had seen. Eventually he said, as they waited for the police cars: 'Billy Burns worked with the police to invent evidence against my client.'

'Just how do you expect to prove that?'

'Obviously I can't. But a man called Vernon Day concocted a story with a child called Jason and Fulton was involved. So was Billy Burns.'

'That's nonsense,' said Reynolds. 'Burns gave evidence for him.'

'It may sound like nonsense,' said Scott, 'but you would say that.' He pointed at Fulton. 'You both know what Burns did. That's why you just killed him.'

When the squad arrived Fulton had Scott on the floor and had his knee on his back.

The watchers outside saw the police cars screaming in and they said, 'Well, that's not normal traffic.'

Chapter 20

Abbott said to Scott, 'Your evidence would never survive close examination. There was a struggle, and, never mind how clear you are about what you saw, a struggle is always confused. You claim you saw him turn the gun on Burns, but no jury would ever accept that. Fulton's a policeman, and a brave one. He saved Grace Karenin's life.

'Your version of events is already being discounted by the prosecution service. Neither the doctor nor the secretary saw what happened and you were standing in front of Reynolds, so he didn't see anything. And where's the motive?'

Abbott began to enjoy himself. 'You have some over-complicated story about a case involving a convicted child-sex merchant. Can you imagine what good counsel would do with that? He'll say, "Well, Mr Scott, not only do you say that my client, Sergeant Fulton, a man with two commendations for bravery, a man who took the killer out while you were hiding in the next room – not only do you say he shot this crazy hostage-taker in cold blood, but you say he did it – for what? To kill a man who gave evidence for your client in a sex case involving small boys? The same man he was working with to frame your client?"

'If he is any good, he'll go on to say, "Perhaps you could explain to us simple folk why that would mean he should want to kill him – because your client was innocent, or guilty?"

'Mr Scott, sir, I don't think you will even be called at the inquest.'

It seemed to Scott that Abbott's voice had lingered slightly on the words 'good counsel'.

Scott said, 'But you know what I am saying is true.' He wished that he had not said anything to Fulton; but what he had seen had been so cold-blooded.

Abbott said, 'All I know is that Billy Burns knew where the doctor was and Fulton knew as well. So the information could have come from Fulton. On the other hand Burns might just have chanced across her there. I know Fulton had good reasons for wanting Burns out of the way. But that's unprovable now. We all know he shot him. I don't know he did it intentionally. I don't know anything else.'

'Well, I'm telling you I saw him force that gun into Burns's throat and pull the trigger. Mr Abbott, you know I don't give a damn about Burns, or Fulton or Reynolds. I don't care if he did kill him. If I had the chance again I would pat him on the back and say nothing. What I care about is Jimmy Reilly.'

'Jimmy Reilly had a bad accident with the law. These things happen, nothing can be done.'

Scott remembered the expression. He had heard it before, and it had upset him; perhaps it was right. It was certainly accurate.

'Well, I'm going to—'

But he knew there was nothing he could do now. The whole thing would disappear in the fog of the death; he had known it as soon as Fulton had had him dragged from the doctor's room, Grace looking at him, astonished at what he was saying about the policeman.

'I wouldn't,' said Abbott. 'It's been explained to

331

everyone that you went a bit crazy and that you couldn't handle the tension. We told Dr Karenin, and others. We had to, or the police arriving to find three men fighting over the dead body might think it a bit odd.'

'You've just abandoned what I've told you? All you knew?'

'We can prove none of it. Jason has never been a resident at Vernon Day's place, though he visits there. In fact, we found him there. And what did Vernon Day say? Nothing. He denies he ever spoke to you about any complaint. When we ask why you were there he just smiled. If you are not careful he may make allegations against you; calling in, he says you were. We've already got the number of your car, kerb-crawling that evening, from an observant police constable.'

'And the child?'

'We had to get him a solicitor before we spoke to him. And what did the solicitor tell him? Say nothing.'

Abbott lifted his hands up, palms open. He said, 'Do you see now what this insistence on rights for people suspected of crime can do? With Burns gone, we can do nothing.'

Abbott smiled. He didn't want to let this happen. Scott was probably right, otherwise why should he say it? But Abbott was a realist. He had even attended the party for Fulton, and slapped his back along with the others. There was no way any case against Fulton would work, especially when what the police knew about Burns came out in front of a jury. A jury would just say good riddance.

'That's one in the eye, or rather the throat, for the crack trade,' someone at the party had said, making a sick joke. Everyone had laughed. It meant Billy Burns had taken two of his own out and then gone himself. Yes, good riddance.

Alleycat was going to be much easier to handle, and she

332

would soon be back buffing people's nails, since she had had the good sense to go and talk to the police. But even she did not mention the twins.

Abbott went on, 'No doubt you, as defence counsel, would argue that safeguards ought to remain. But now you see what happens. People don't answer questions and some other people just don't get justice. It's usually the victim in our experience who gets the short end of the stick, but this time the victim is in jail.'

'You mean you'll do nothing?'

'We can do nothing, Mr Scott, sir.'

Scott had noticed that when Abbott called him 'sir', he meant something quite different.

Deep down Jimmy Reilly wouldn't believe it either. 'Not Billy. He was a good sort. If he did this to me, why should he come and give evidence?'

'Because he didn't want you actually convicted, Mr Reilly. He only wanted to be able to tell his backers that you had been dealt with. He probably liked you.'

'He did. We got on together. I enjoyed his Tommy Cooper.'

Scott didn't understand what he meant by Tommy Cooper; it must be rhyming slang or something. He tried a few rhymes as he walked away from Belmarsh Prison but nothing would come. Blooper? Stupor? It didn't work.

He looked at the time. He had an hour to get to chambers. His clerk had insisted he be there for a conference. 'It's a good one, sir, and you haven't worked for ten days. They just want to meet you, a beauty contest, no brief yet.'

He wasn't sure he wanted to do it, even if it was a good one, but then he had to earn a living, even if the thought of being involved in courts again made him feel dizzy.

An hour was enough, he was going against the traffic, and at half past six he would be able to park in the

Temple – always assuming he could persuade the people on the gate to let him through.

Scott tried to work out how he was going to get back into life. Routine was the way to do it. Replace the important things with routine. Make everything efficient, then let it all fall into place and give up thinking.

He had met Andrew once, in a hurry in the Temple, and he had told Scott breathlessly how he was off to a Bar Council meeting, to propose a phrasing amendment to Article 67b of the consolidated regulations. His eyes were with bright with it; wasn't that a good enough purpose in life? No, it wasn't.

There was no purpose adequate to the grinding frustration this job involved.

Scott met one or two people as he went into chambers. Tony said, 'Have you been away?' He didn't reply, indifferent, not that Tony noticed. Again Scott realised what he had diagnosed over the last few days of waiting. He was becoming depressed. He had switched from the intensity of helping Jimmy to complete failure; to having to tell Mary Reilly what had happened.

He had been depressed before, many years ago, and he knew depression begins to show in the way matters start to get out of control. Things at the edge fray. People are repelled, friends get pushed away, and you stop looking after yourself. You can't prevent it, save by keeping busy, getting a routine – but then, always you think, why bother?

'You're in the first room. Your conference hasn't arrived yet,' young Richard said.

Scott waited.

He didn't even have a set of papers to read to pass the time. Instead he read a stray edition of *Bar News*. He noticed that people were pleased to announce that other people had joined their chambers. It was happening everywhere. Then the phone rang. 'They're not coming, sir. Been a problem with the client. They said they'll reschedule. Come on down.'

He went downstairs. Maryanne was in the clerk's room. 'I'm meeting Grace,' she said.

He said, 'What are you doing in a criminal set of chambers?'

'I just had to pop in to give something to Terry,' she said. Terry looked pleased, with a bottle wrapped up on the table in front of him.

'How do you know our Terry?'

'No matter,' said Maryanne, 'but I'm meeting Grace tonight at El Vino for a drink. Last time I saw her, she said she hadn't seen you since all that stuff in her clinic. Why don't you drop in as well?'

'I don't know. Things got a bit overdramatic and I thought, I thought . . . I didn't think she would want to be reminded of it all, especially the way I behaved.'

Scott had taken the easy way out and hadn't rung. To be more accurate, he didn't see the point. Grace must have been shocked at what he had done, and with what Abbott had told her.

'Don't be silly. I rather think she likes you,' Maryanne said. 'And I'm not sure it would be particularly good form now to refuse to come to see her, given I just told you something she said to me in private.'

She had got him in some sort of good-manners armlock. He could only refuse by giving solid offence. He said, 'Well, if you put it that way, Maryanne.'

'In an hour?' said Maryanne.

El Vino is a different sort of place now the journalists have gone, rather quieter, serving food, but still ruinously expensive. Scott sat at the table on the left in the box compartment. He ordered a Velvin.

335

He rehearsed how he might apologise for his behaviour, but he also thought you can't apologise for a fault of character. Then he saw a movement by the partition and there was Grace.

The same 'hello' face, the same grin. Something inside him lurched slightly.

'Can I sit down?' she said.

He got up. 'Of course,' and pulled a chair out.

They looked at each other, then he said, 'How are you?'

'Working as normal.'

'Busy?'

'Yes. Once we got over the shock of it all.'

'I was going to ring you,' Scott said.

'But you didn't.'

'No.'

'Why not?'

'I don't know. I didn't want to start it up again, or intrude, I suppose.' He opened his mouth to explain but couldn't get anything out. There was no explanation.

She watched him and when she saw he was going to say nothing, she said, 'Why did you think it would be an intrusion?'

'Well, you're right there. Perhaps intrusion is the wrong word.'

'Maybe it's all words.'

He didn't know what to say to that.

She said, 'How are you, Jeremy?' It was a proper question.

'OK. I'm still very angry at what happened, but it'll be all right.' He made a good strong effort to be bright.

'How is Jennet?' he said.

'She's well. And she feels good, because we tell her that if she hadn't given Fulton my phone number, he wouldn't have come along that evening at all. She was upset, of course, off work for a week, but that policeman, Reynolds, helped her.'

336

Some wine arrived.

'They're an item now. They'll be married soon, my guess.'

'Really? Has she said so?'

'No, but it doesn't need saying. It'll happen. He's a little more decisive than you are. At least in these matters.'

'Have you come here to register a complaint?'

'Yes.' She looked up. 'Where else would I go to do it?'

They both laughed and then they both spoke at the same time.

'He's—' she said.

'He's got more going for him than I thought,' Scott said.

'That's what I was going to say,' said Grace. 'I think I misjudged him.'

It was good to hear her voice, though she seemed different. She said, 'You were prejudiced against him, and, to be honest, so was I. You know what he told me? He told me when he went into child work he heard me lecture and it fired him up from the start. Amazing.' She laughed. 'But then he took the shine off it by saying that he had learned more from Jennet than from any lectures he'd been given.'

She toyed with her glass. Scott did not want to say anything to break the moment. He had nearly let all this slip away.

She looked up and said, 'I must admit I was suspicious of his motives, but then I'm a bit suspicious of all men.' For a short moment she allowed herself to seem vulnerable, showing a little of herself, then she said, 'In a professional capacity, of course.'

Scott saw a way of explaining himself. 'I had good reason to be suspicious of him. That's what all the fighting was about.'

'Why?'

'I was against him in that case. The guy who was

wrongly convicted of assaulting a child. I told you a little about it. I made the mistake of getting involved.'

Scott said wrongly convicted, because he believed it, and saying it out loud was always a relief.

'That's what you meant at the time, when you shouted at Fulton? I never really understood all that.'

They were talking about it now.

'Yes.'

'All I know is I don't believe what that Abbott man told me about you, about how you had lost control. I didn't when he said it and I told him so.'

'Oh.'

'Is that what you've been upset about?'

'How do you know I've been upset?'

'Depressed,' she said. 'I can see it a mile off. Depression is real, you know, it isn't some sort of self indulgence.'

He said, 'You're right, but it feels as though my occupation's gone. Something I thought had value is just rubbish. What else should I feel?'

At last she took the risk, the one she had waited a long time to take. She put her hand on his. He looked at it. She said, 'I'm sorry I laughed at your work. I can imagine it must be very . . .' She stopped, then she said, 'You know, I don't think this sort of work is very good for someone like you. It hangs too heavy on you, you feel too much. I was wrong when I said you think too much; thinking is what you do, to escape the pain of feeling.'

She looked at him. She seemed to have got it right. She said, 'Tell me about that case.'

Where she was touching him his hand became warm, hot even; the feeling travelled up his arm. With it came a sense of lightness, renewal. He saw the top of her head as she looked down at the table, obviously she didn't want him to see her eyes, but he could. They were full. Tiredness was flowing out of him, through her, soaking away.

338

They both sat quietly, then he told her Jimmy Reilly's story.

He said, 'Now I know Reynolds had nothing to do with it, he was just doing his job, but I despised him for it and the way he was doing it. Quite wrongly. He was just doing it the way he thought was right. But with Burns gone, there's nothing that can be done to correct it. The others are saying nothing and the child won't answer questions. And all along it was Burns who set Reilly up; but what you know is not always what you can prove.'

Grace remembered.

'What did you say the name of the child was?'

'Jason Lee.'

'Ten-year-old, in care?'

'Yes, about that age.'

'Is his mother called Tina?' Grace thought back to what Tina Lee had said to her.

Scott said, 'I've no idea about his mother. That's the really frustrating bit. We're not allowed to know anything about his family or his circumstances, I only know he was in care.' Then realising what she had said, he asked, 'Why? Do you know him?'

'Does he live near the Cummin Estate?'

'He was from near the Cummin, yes. I saw an address once, Tinwood House, or something.'

'And you are trying to show that the child made up an allegation of sexual abuse?'

'Yes.'

Grace thought about it. It had to be the same family. There was no doubt about it, that was the address. Jason was in care at flat number 9, Tinwood House. Tina Lee said her son Jason had done something exactly like this before, accusing his mother's new man of assaulting him; had done it so he could go and live with his father. And what's more, later he had admitted doing it. The child was

339

very disturbed; now she could remember the interview in which he admitted lying.

'Do it once, and you'll do it again'; she knew how lawyers thought. No conviction based on Jason's word could survive this information.

Then she decided. Life's too short, and for the first time she broke a confidence; although even then, she did it with such care that really no one could have complained.

'I know about him. Why don't you get his lawyers . . . though, of course, that's you, isn't it? Why don't you get hold of the papers I have on him and his family? Get the court to ask to have a look at them, that's how it works, isn't it? I can give them to the court for them to look at.'

'Yes,' he said, 'pretty good. How do you know that?'

She didn't say, instead she went on, 'I won't argue when the court asks. I'll just send them the papers, with the bits that matter highlighted.'

'Can I ask you what it is?'

'No, you better not. But don't worry, in this case the information will certainly free your Mr Reilly. If we had been asked for it before, it would certainly have acquitted him.'

'Why?'

'Jason Lee has done this before.'

Scott sat amazed.

She said, 'Enough of that. We'd better change the subject, before I get struck off the register. We don't tell anybody, even policemen, about our patients.'

She smoothed her skirt down and looked round. 'So where are we going?'

'Going?' said Scott.

Then he regained his balance.

Of course. Maryanne was nowhere in sight, and anyway the idea of Maryanne in El Vino was ridiculous. And the

340

bottle for the clerk, and the cancelled conference. Why hadn't he realised? This had been arranged.

'Going?' he said. 'Well, I thought . . .'

He produced his list of restaurants. All the places you could say were *u zivot* – *full of life*.